Fairest of Heart

Books by Karen Witemeyer

A Tailor-Made Bride
Head in the Clouds
To Win Her Heart
Short-Straw Bride
Stealing the Preacher
Full Steam Ahead
A Worthy Pursuit
No Other Will Do
Heart on the Line
More Than Meets the Eye
More Than Words Can Say

Hanger's Horsemen

At Love's Command
The Heart's Charge
In Honor's Defense

Texas Ever After

Fairest of Heart

Novellas

A Cowboy Unmatched from *A Match Made in Texas: A Novella Collection*

Love on the Mend: A Full Steam Ahead Novella from *With All My Heart Romance Collection*

The Husband Maneuver: A Worthy Pursuit Novella from *With This Ring? A Novella Collection of Proposals Gone Awry*

Worth the Wait: A Ladies of Harper's Station *Novella*

The Love Knot: A Ladies of Harper's Station *Novella* from *Hearts Entwined: A Historical Romance Novella Collection*

Gift of the Heart from *Christmas Heirloom Novella Collection*

More Than a Pretty Face from *Serving Up Love: A Four-in-One Harvey House Brides Collection*

An Archer Family Christmas from *An Old-Fashioned Texas Christmas*

Inn for a Surprise from *The Kissing Tree: Four Novellas Rooted in Timeless Love*

A Texas Christmas Carol from *Under the Texas Mistletoe*

TEXAS EVER AFTER

FAIREST of HEART

KAREN WITEMEYER

BETHANY HOUSE

a division of Baker Publishing Group

Minneapolis, Minnesota

Published by Bethany House Publishers
Minneapolis, Minnesota
www.bethanyhouse.com

Bethany House Publishers is a division of
Baker Publishing Group, Grand Rapids, Michigan

Printed in the United States of America

Library of Congress Cataloging-in-Publication Data
Names: Witemeyer, Karen, author.
Title: Fairest of heart / Karen Witemeyer.
Description: Minneapolis, Minnesota : Bethany House, a division of Baker Publishing Group, [2023] | Series: Texas ever after
Identifiers: LCCN 2022055234 | ISBN 9780764241802 (casebound) | ISBN 9780764240416 (paperback) | ISBN 9781493442119 (ebook)
Subjects: LCGFT: Western fiction. | Romance fiction. | Novels.
Classification: LCC PS3623.I864 F35 2023 | DDC 813/.6—dc23/eng/20221220
LC record available at https://lccn.loc.gov/2022055234

Scripture quotations are from the King James Version of the Bible.

This is a work of historical reconstruction; the appearances of certain historical figures are therefore inevitable. All other characters, however, are products of the author's imagination, and any resemblance to actual persons, living or dead, is coincidental.

Cover design by James Hall
Cover model photography by Joanna Czogala / Trevillion Images

Published in association with Books & Such Literary Management, www.booksandsuch.com.

Baker Publishing Group publications use paper produced from sustainable forestry practices and post-consumer waste whenever possible.

23 24 25 26 27 28 29 7 6 5 4 3 2 1

To Wyatt and McKenna.
Your fairy-tale romance has been a joy to witness.
May the Lord bless you with a love so true that it can withstand any obstacle and keep you smiling as you walk hand in hand through your happily ever after.

In the world ye shall have tribulation:
but be of good cheer;
I have overcome the world.

John 16:33

Prologue

Chicago, Illinois
Spring 1892

Keep your eyes down and head bowed," Edith instructed. "Do nothing to draw attention. A woman like Narcissa LaBelle lives for the spotlight, so you must make yourself dim in comparison. I won't be able to help you once her troupe leaves town."

Penelope Snow bit her lip and nodded, doing her best to stave off the tears misting her eyes as she smoothed the brown calico apron she wore over a shapeless, mud-colored dress. She and Edith had selected her wardrobe with care—opting for functional, drab pieces that would hide the figure that had caused so much trouble in her last position.

You're going on an adventure, Pen. A chance to see new places. Meet new people. Don't dwell on what you're leaving behind. The Lord has provided a fresh start. Make the most of it.

"Ah, my lamb." Edith clutched Penelope to her breast in an unexpected embrace. "I'm going to miss you so."

The cook from Wyndham's School for Girls rarely showed emotion and seemed to regret her outburst a heartbeat after it happened. Stiffening, she set Penelope away from her with a sniff and paced to the window of Madame LaBelle's sitting room, where they'd been asked to wait.

Penelope followed and placed her hand on the elderly woman's shoulder. "I'll miss you, too. Miss Wyndham might have taught me grammar, literature, and history, but the lessons I learned at your knee are the ones I carry in my heart."

Edith reached across her chest to cover Penelope's hand with gnarled fingers. Knuckles swollen and arthritic from years of hard work. Skin rough and calloused. Yet those same hands had cradled Penelope as a baby, lifting her from the basket a stranger had abandoned on the school's back stoop in the middle of a winter storm. Those hands had taught her to knead bread and sew a fine stitch. They'd folded over hers while she learned to pray to a God who loved all his children, no matter how humble their beginnings.

The sitting room door opened, and Penelope jerked her hand away from Edith's shoulder. She turned to face whoever entered, ducking her chin as she'd been coached. The maid who had shown them into the small parlor upon their arrival now held the door wide as a striking woman swept inside.

Penelope stole a quick glance at the woman who would be her employer and had to lock her jaw to keep from gaping like a fish. Madame LaBelle was the most beautiful woman Penelope had ever seen. So elegant and sophisticated. She moved with such grace, her skirt didn't even rustle. And what a skirt it was! Bright red silk patterned with delicate black flowers that danced like blooms in a breeze, silhouetted against a sunset. Black lace fanned out along the hem with matching lace accents hugging the actress's waist to emphasize her hourglass figure. The squared-off neckline dipped lower than the current high-necked style, setting her apart as a woman of boldness and confidence. Her presence demanded attention.

"Ah! Here you are, my dears." Madame LaBelle's face lit up

as if she'd been searching for them for hours. "Let's get down to business, shall we?"

Her arm moved in an artful flourish as she gestured for Penelope and Edith to precede her into the seating area located in front of the small hearth.

"Have a seat on the settee," she invited as she alit on the longer, pale green sofa. "You'll have to excuse my ragged appearance." She lifted a hand to her perfectly coifed chestnut locks. "I've been packing all day. It's quite fatiguing." She smiled at Penelope. "Which is why I'm so grateful to have you joining our merry band of travelers."

Madame LaBelle arched one brow as she examined Penelope from head to toe. Her smile flattened into something much more assessing and calculated. Too late to hide now. Though the idea of this glamorous woman with her rich olive skin, sculpted cheekbones, and worldly air finding anything the least bit threatening in Penelope's appearance was laughable. Like comparing a queen to a milkmaid.

Although, if the papers were correct, Madame LaBelle's last-minute decision to leave Chicago and join a troupe touring the West stemmed from a review in the *Tribune* that dared to suggest she had grown too old to play a convincing ingenue on stage. Penelope imagined such harsh criticism could make even the most beautiful woman insecure. Her heart stirred. How difficult it must be to have others constantly scrutinizing and picking apart one's appearance and talent.

"Your appearance is far from ragged, Madame." Honest admiration colored Penelope's tone. "You're the most compelling woman I've ever seen."

Madame LaBelle stopped her perusal of Penelope and blinked, a hint of vulnerability visible in her brown eyes for half a second before her polished poise slipped back into place.

"Well, aren't you a delightful girl?" A new smile blossomed

across the actress's face, one wide enough to show off her straight, white teeth, but not so wide as to draw lines around her eyes. The expression emphasized the small beauty mark at the bottom edge of her left cheekbone. "How old are you, child?"

"Nineteen, ma'am. I'll be twenty next month," Penelope answered, bowing her head in a show of submission.

A servant didn't volunteer her opinions or converse with her betters like an equal. Madame LaBelle might forgive her forwardness in offering a well-intentioned compliment, but from this point forward, Penelope intended to demonstrate that she knew her place.

Answer directly. Speak only when spoken to. Display deference and decorum at all times.

"When Miss Wyndham recommended you, she assured me you were literate and wrote with a fine hand. Is that an accurate assessment?"

"Yes, ma'am."

Edith leaned forward and pulled a folded sheet of paper from her purse. "I brought a sample of her penmanship, Madame." She held out an essay Penelope had written before she'd left Wyndham to take a position in the Carlisle household. "She graduated with top marks."

"Excellent." Madame LaBelle gave a cursory glance to the essay, then handed it back to Edith, obviously not caring about the content, only the appearance of the handwriting. "I'll need someone to oversee my correspondence in addition to tending to more mundane duties." She returned her attention to Penelope. "Sometimes I have difficulty falling asleep. I'll likely ask you to read to me on those occasions. If I were to ask you to fetch me a book of poetry to sooth my restless spirit, which would you select?"

It was a test. Penelope's pulse reacted instantly. She searched her mind for the poems she had learned in school, trying to guess what a famous actress might prefer. But she knew nothing of Madame LaBelle's tastes. Before the silence could stretch too long, she mentally clasped the one piece of verse that had always spoken to her heart, a tale of love between ordinary people. A man's adoration and a woman's dedication. A love lasting from first blush through old age.

"Tennyson," Penelope said. "I find his rhythms soothing, and his idyllic scenes conjure peaceful images."

Madame LaBelle leaned forward, her gaze challenging, expectant. "Such as?"

Penelope gripped her hands together tightly in her lap, closed her eyes, and recited a few of her favorite lines from *The Miller's Daughter*.

> "With farther lookings on. The kiss,
> The woven arms, seem but to be
> Weak symbols of the settled bliss,
> The comfort, I have found in thee."

Madame LaBelle leaned back, a gleam of satisfaction shining in her dark eyes. "Ah, so you're a romantic."

"Sentimental, perhaps," Penelope conceded. "I find that men in the real world rarely live up to poetical expectations." Hence the need to clobber Gerard Carlisle over the head with a silver tea tray last week, forcing her to leave his mother's employ without a reference.

Madame LaBelle laughed, the sound throaty and jaded. "I like you, Penelope. If you're as good at removing stains and pressing dresses as you are at reciting sappy poetry, you will suit my purposes admirably."

Penelope lifted her chin to look her new employer in the eye. "I'll work hard for you, ma'am. You'll have no cause to question my dedication."

"That's good." Madame LaBelle rose gracefully from the sofa, an intensity firing in her eyes that dispelled all comradery from the room.

A frisson scurried down Penelope's spine as she pushed to her feet.

"I demand unswerving loyalty from my employees, Miss Snow. Serve me well, and you will be rewarded. Betray me, and you'll find yourself tossed out on your ear. Are you willing to accept my terms?"

Penelope swallowed. Miss Wyndham had made it clear when Penelope left the school this morning that she would not be welcomed back. Scandal tainted her after the incident with the Carlisles, and scandal would destroy a school that relied on a pristine reputation to recruit students.

Edith had called this position with Narcissa LaBelle an answer to prayer, arising at just the right time to meet Penelope's greatest need.

A sea parting to open a way for her to escape her troubles would have been preferred, but it seemed her miracle was more in line with the caravan that arrived at just the right time to spare Joseph's life when his brothers sought to kill him. Slavery hadn't been much of an improvement of his lot, but Joseph made a life for himself through hard work and integrity. He earned his master's respect, and in the end, God led him to a life of blessing. She could do the same. She *would* do the same.

Fighting off a shiver of trepidation, Penelope steeled her nerves and straightened her spine.

"I accept."

1

Bosque County, Texas
Six months later

"Come out with your hands up!" Titus Kingsley sighted down the barrel of his Winchester repeater from his protected position behind a dilapidated wagon.

It had taken three days to track the Buchanan brothers to this homestead outside Walnut Springs after they robbed the bank in Meridian. Captain Bill McDonald had assigned Titus the case along with two other Texas Rangers from Company B. It was his first time to ride lead, and he aimed to bring his quarry to justice. At twenty-seven, he lacked the experience of the more seasoned officers, but he'd been the one to piece together the connection between the Buchanans and the railroad machine shops in Walnut Springs, so Captain Bill had given him free rein to follow his hunch and chase the bank robbers to ground.

"You're surrounded by Rangers, Buchanan."

Carson was covering the rear, and Hoffman stood ready, tucked behind the side of the barn about forty yards west of the ramshackle house where the brothers were holed up.

Titus lifted his head just enough to throw his voice across

the yard. "You ain't gonna win a shootout. Better to surrender peacefully."

The loud clink of breaking glass drew Titus's attention to the window left of the door. A pistol barrel poked through the opening, knocking away the jagged shards of the rectangular windowpane a second before the gun fired.

Titus ducked behind the wagon bed. He'd suspected the Buchanans weren't terribly bright, but opening fire on a group of trained Rangers confirmed it.

Hoffman's rifle cracked off a three-shot volley from the barn, drawing their attention and giving Titus the chance to find a better angle. Dropping to his knees, he crawled under the wagon and slithered down to the hitching end, where he'd have a clear line of sight to the window.

A second weapon broke through the glass. Higher and to the left. Revolvers. Deadly, but they lacked range. Hoffman should be fine if he held his position at the barn. Carson was the one Titus worried about. The kid was wet behind the ears. Good marksman, but he tended to rely on his gun more than his brain. Which was why Titus assigned him the rear guard. Carson would keep the Buchanans from escaping, if it came to that, but Titus intended to keep the brothers occupied and take them down before they made the attempt.

Titus flattened onto his belly and dragged his Winchester in front of him. Raising up on his elbows, he tucked the rifle stock into his right shoulder and used his left hand to support the barrel. He slowed his breathing. Sighted his target. And fired.

One of the Buchanans cried out. The second revolver disappeared from the window. The first continued firing, but the shots flew wild. Titus sighted the second man, aiming for his shoulder. If he would just stand a little taller or move slightly to the left . . .

A shot rang out. Muted. Distant. From behind the house. Was Carson trying to breach on his own? Foolish kid was gonna get himself killed.

"Hoffman! Cover me!"

Titus drew his rifle to his chest and rolled out into the open. As soon as he cleared the edge of the wagon, he sprang into a crouch, ready to fire at the fugitive behind the window, but Hoffman had a steady percussion of shots working. His repeater echoed loudly as he moved away from the barn with a slow, even stride. He'd have to reload soon. The '73 Winchester favored by the Rangers held fifteen cartridges. More than the six-shooters the Buchanan brothers sported, but Hoffman was probably down to his last few rounds.

Staying low, Titus ran for the house. When he reached the door, he brought his bootheel up and smashed it near the lock, splintering the wood and sending the door crashing into the house.

"On the floor!" His barked order bounced off the walls like cannon fire. It didn't matter that he couldn't see the brothers yet, they knew he was in the house. He'd use that to his advantage. Assert control. Demand compliance. Instill fear. "Guns down. Hands up. Now!"

At least one brother was still in the front room. Titus couldn't be sure of the second without visual confirmation. The second Buchanan could have retreated deeper into the house after taking Titus's bullet to the shoulder.

A heavy bang announced a breach from the rear. Carson. So he'd held his position as instructed. Good. But if Carson hadn't been advancing on the house, what had he been shooting at?

No time to ponder. Had to press the advantage.

Flattening his back against the wall by the open doorway that led into the front room, Titus inched toward the opening, then snapped a quick peek into the room before dodging back to safety. The view was a blur, but he'd located two men. One hunkered at the base of the window, shoving bullets into his revolver's cylinder with shaky hands. The other huddled in a corner, whimpering.

"Gun down, Buchanan," Titus ordered as he spun into the room, rifle first, "or I give you a souvenir to match the one your brother's got in his shoulder."

The half-loaded revolver fell to the floor. The younger Buchanan raised his hands above his head.

"I got the big one." Carson's voice echoed low behind Titus.

Titus nodded, glad to have another Ranger in the room to watch his back. He focused his attention on the thief in front of him. "On the floor. Face down."

Percy Buchanan complied, his movements slow, his chin tucked toward his chest in submission. Titus moved deeper into the room and kicked the revolver out of Percy's reach. Circling a chair, he approached the prone suspect, then knelt over him, pressing one knee into Percy's back. After glancing to the far wall to ensure Carson had big brother Ted contained, Titus set his rifle down and pulled out the leather strap he used for binding prisoners. He pulled back one wrist at a time and secured Percy's hands behind his back.

"You good in there, Kingsley?" Hoffman called from outside the window.

"Yep. Got both suspects in custody. Check the perimeter, then bring the horses round."

"Will do."

Titus pulled Percy to his feet and dragged him toward his brother. "How's his shoulder, Carson?"

The other Ranger shrugged. "He'll live."

Titus bit back a sigh. Carson's callous attitude grated. Just because they hunted criminals didn't mean they couldn't extend a little common decency. Rangering made a man hard, but if that hardness calcified his soul, he'd be no better than the thieves and murderers he hunted.

"I've got bandages in my saddlebag. Take him out front and dress the wound. We'll get him back to Walnut Springs and see if there's a doctor there to patch him up."

"Walnut Springs ain't got no doctor," Ted ground out between moans as Carson jerked him to his feet.

"Maybe you shoulda thought of that before you opened fire on a company of Texas Rangers." Carson crooked the man's good arm behind his back and herded him toward the hall. The pair drew up short, however, when Hoffman braced himself in the doorway. He glared at Carson, then turned his head to meet Titus's gaze.

"Found this stuffed in the pie safe." He held up a bulging gunnysack.

Percy's muttered curse confirmed the contents. The money from the First National robbery in Meridian. But that didn't explain the scowl on Hoffman's face or Carson's agitation.

"Found somethin' else out back," Hoffman continued. "Somethin' you should see."

Titus's gut clenched. That shot he'd heard from behind the house. Someone had taken a hit. Titus released Percy and immediately strode for the doorway, trusting Hoffman to take charge of the prisoner.

"It's just a mangy dog," Carson blurted as Titus stepped around him. "Nothin' to get all worked up about."

Titus jerked to a halt. "You shot a dog?"

"He came out from behind the woodpile, growlin' at me. What was I supposed to do? Just let him attack?"

"The critter's still breathin'," Hoffman said, his tone thick with disapproval. "Wasn't sure if I should put him down. Thought you oughta take a look first."

Ever since Titus had brought a mutt to headquarters and nursed him back to health after finding him half-starved during a scouting mission, the Rangers of Company B treated Titus like some kind of animal expert. Seeking his opinion on everything from horse ailments to cat conniptions. One fella even asked for advice on fowl feed after getting a letter from his mother bemoaning the fact that her favorite laying hen had stopped producing. Titus really didn't know more than the average rancher or farmer, but he'd always had an affinity for God's creatures, and they seemed to sense that about him, finding peace in his presence, just as he did in theirs. And now one of those creatures might be dying thanks to a situation he'd orchestrated.

Titus rushed through the house and out the back door. He spotted the fallen dog immediately, its black fur dark against the dusty brown earth. Not wanting to frighten him, Titus slowed his step and circled around to the front, so the animal could see him coming. Its ribcage rose and fell in ragged, shallow pants.

"Easy, boy." Titus held out his palm as he approached.

The dog tried to lift his head, but barely managed to elevate his snout. His glossy black eyes radiated pain and confusion, tearing a hole in Titus's heart.

He crouched beside the dog and gently stroked a floppy ear. Light brown fur marked the nose, chest, and belly, reminding Titus of a black-and-tan coonhound, though he was likely a mixed breed.

"It's all right, boy. I'm here to help." He ran his hand over the dog's neck and down its side. A soft whine sounded when his hand skimmed over the dog's left front leg. Moving carefully, Titus slipped his hand around to the dog's underside and felt the warm wetness of blood.

Titus didn't know much about canine anatomy, but he figured he could treat him like he would a human and at least give the dog a chance to pull through. He rolled the dog onto his back to expose his belly, then Titus pulled a handkerchief from his trouser pocket and pressed it against the hole where Carson's bullet had entered.

Movement flashed above him, and Titus discovered a red bandanna dangling above his head, Hoffman on the other end.

"Here."

Titus accepted it with a nod, then glanced over at Percy Buchanan, who stood scowling at Hoffman's side. "What's your dog's name?"

"Ain't our dog. Just some stray Ted's been feedin' since we came here."

Titus turned back to his patient. "No one looking after you, huh, boy? Well, that's about to change. You got me now. I'll see to it you get patched up. You just gotta hang in there for a bit."

He twirled the bandanna into a rope, placed it over the handkerchief, then wrapped it up and over the dog's back and tied it off.

"Easy now," he coaxed as he scooped the dog into his arms and pushed to his feet.

The small pool of blood that remained behind didn't bode well for the dog's chances, but his chances would be zero if Titus didn't try.

"Where you gonna take him?" Hoffman slung the confiscated gunnysack over his shoulder and reached out a hand to pat the dog on the head. "Ain't no doc in Walnut Springs, and I doubt he'll make it much farther."

"I know a place. 'Bout ten miles north of here." He leveled his gaze at Hoffman. "I'll need you to take charge of the Buchanans for me, though. Get them to the sheriff in Meridian."

"Consider it done. I'll keep an eye on Carson, too. Make sure Ted gets to a doctor."

"Thanks." Titus strode toward his horse. "Tell Captain Bill I'll report to headquarters in a day or two. He can dock my pay for the missed time if needed."

Hoffman ambled along at his side, dragging Percy with him. "If docking is needed, it'll come from Carson's pay, not yours," the Ranger grumbled.

As they approached the horses, Carson looked up from where he'd been digging around in Titus's saddlebag for bandages. He scowled at the load Titus carried.

"You oughta just put the thing out of its misery and leave it be. We're commissioned to uphold the law and protect the citizens of this state from theft and violence. Animals ain't our jurisdiction."

Titus leveled a glare at him. "I think the good Lord might disagree. I seem to recall him giving man dominion over the beasts at creation. That puts them under our protection. And I aim to protect this one as best as I am able." The last pup Titus had rescued was living out his days on the Kingsley family farm, chasing rabbits and coons to his heart's content. This one deserved the same chance, but it was gonna take more than food and a bath to set this fella to rights. "Step aside, Carson. I got a man to see about a dog."

Hoffman held out his arms. "I'll hold him while you mount."

In a matter of minutes, Titus was settled in the saddle with his patient draped across his lap.

"Hang in there, boy." Titus wrapped an arm around the dog's body as he nudged his mount into a slow canter. "Doc will fix you up."

If they got to the Diamond D in time.

2

After six months of traveling with Madame LaBelle, Penelope had learned to make the most of the rare occasions when she was granted an hour or two of freedom. And today she'd been given an entire afternoon. She could barely believe her good fortune, especially on such a fine day. The sun shining overhead. A gentle breeze cooling her as she walked. The only thing missing was a cozy reading tree to sit beneath as she escaped reality for a few hours. Thankfully, she'd spotted one a few moments ago that would suit her perfectly. All she had to do was surmount one tiny obstacle.

Well, *tiny* might have been a misnomer. The embankment had seemed small enough from a distance, but now that she stood at its base and craned her neck back to see the top, it proved quite imposing. Not to worry, though. She was young. Nimble. Relatively intelligent. She'd find a way to overcome.

The sling bag carrying her worn copy of *Oliver Twist* banged against Penelope's thigh as she began her ascent. Loose dirt made it difficult to gain purchase on the ravine wall, but after a handful of failed attempts, she sought out protruding tree roots and clumps of vegetation for hand- and footholds and started making progress.

The first six feet proved easy enough. Sure, her nose was

pressed into a dirt wall, and a family of ants circled her wrist in search of a way inside her sleeve, but all in all, she'd made admirable progress. She would be reading beneath her tree in no time.

"Almost there, Oliver." She tipped her head backward to judge the remaining distance. "About three more feet. Hang in there."

Talking to books now, Pen?

She shook her head and chuckled softly. One made friends where one could, she supposed. Madame LaBelle demanded such constant attention that Penelope had little opportunity to interact with the other troupe staff. Even during performances, her mistress insisted Penelope be on hand to assist with costume changes as well as keeping her throat atomizer ready in the wings. So when Narcissa took ill with a megrim this afternoon and closed herself up in her tent demanding to be left alone until supper, Penelope grabbed freedom with both hands and didn't look back.

Until now. Yet seeing the camp in the distance only strengthened her resolve. This was her chance to be her own woman. Set her own agenda and absorb a peace only nature could supply. Returning her attention to the climb, Penelope bent her right knee and planted her toe in a crevice that looked somewhat stable. Then she took aim at a thin tree shoot near the ridgeline and lunged for it. Her right hand fisted around the slender stem at the same moment her foothold gave way. She squealed and scrambled for purchase. Thankful for scrawny saplings with deep root systems, Penelope dangled for a heart-stopping moment before catching the toe of her shoe against a sliver of rock.

No time to catch her breath, however, for the dirt around her anchor shifted, dusting her face. Gritting her teeth, she pushed off the rock, lunged upward, and grabbed wildly at the grass atop the embankment. A tuft in each hand, she steadied herself and clambered the rest of the way over the rim. Penelope rested on her hands and knees, catching her breath and enjoying the feel of solid, *flat* earth beneath her. She whispered a quick but heartfelt thank you to the One who'd kept her from falling, then, with victory surging through her veins, she jumped to her feet and celebrated her triumph with an arms-spread pirouette.

A horse's high-pitched cry pierced her whirling haze. A pair of black hooves pawed the air not four feet from her face. She gasped and squeezed her eyes tightly closed but fought the instinct to dart away. More flailing on her part would only agitate the horse further. Besides, she didn't want to risk tumbling down the ravine she'd fought so hard to scale.

"Steady, Rex. Steady." The deep voice echoed with such calm authority that Penelope's pounding heart slowed in response.

The thud of hooves hitting the earth told her the voice had worked its magic on the horse as well, encouraging Penelope to open her eyes.

"Are you all right, miss?"

She had to look up quite far to find the face attached to the voice. Shaded by a hat as black as his horse, the rider's features were obscured, but she could make out a chiseled jaw, a straight nose, and a thick mustache that framed a mouth pulled tight in concern. Or perhaps disapproval. He couldn't be too pleased to have his ride interrupted by a woman popping out of the ground and twirling about like some kind of deranged prairie dog.

"I'm sorry for startling your horse." Keeping her movements slow and measured so as not to repeat her offense, she approached the cowboy. "I should have paid closer attention to my surroundings. I didn't realize I was so near a . . . road."

The word dissolved on her tongue as she noted the field of untamed prairie grass spreading in all directions. Not even a game trail in evidence. She shrugged, and her lips curved in a self-deprecating smile. "Well, road or not, I was clearly in the wrong, and I apologize."

Embarrassment at her mistake tugged her gaze downward, where it snagged on the dark form draped across the cowboy's lap. Her breath caught, and her eyes grew moist. "Oh no."

She moved nearer, drawn by a dog's limp form. "Is he . . . ?" She couldn't finish the sentence, aching for the poor creature.

A small whine echoed in answer, and a weight lifted from Penelope's heart. Thank heaven! She stroked the dog's head, trying to impart some small measure of comfort. That's when she noticed the bandage tied beneath his front leg.

"What happened to him?" Slowly, she raised her attention from the injured dog to the man who cared enough to carry him upon his horse.

The cowboy's expression proved hard to read. His mouth and jaw were set in hard lines, but his eyes . . . She glanced down.

Don't be foolish, Pen. This man doesn't need you. He's a complete stranger. One you'll never see again.

Yet that truth didn't stop the twinge of recognition from vibrating across her chest. God had blessed her with a compassionate nature. Too compassionate sometimes, leaving her open to the machinations of people like Gerard Carlisle, who had no qualms about taking advantage of a young woman's naïveté and tender heart. Nevertheless, she couldn't ignore people or animals who were alone or in pain. Perhaps because she herself had been unwanted and discarded, she recognized loneliness and heartbreak in others. And this man, with all his strength and capability, had been hurt. Deeply.

By the time she found the courage to study his face again,

he had turned his eyes away from her, lifting his head to gaze upon the land before him. A muscle in his jaw ticked, and his horse sidestepped as if sensing his rider's impatience.

"Dog took a bullet in a shootout with a pair of bank robbers. I'm trying to get him to a retired doctor I know who lives out this way. So if you're not hurt, I need to be on my way."

A shootout? Bank robbers? Good heavens. Who was this man?

It didn't matter. Such a wild tale was bound to be fiction. Nevertheless, the dog's injury was genuine and needed to be tended.

"Of course." Penelope withdrew her hand and stepped back. "I'm perfectly fit. Please go. Get him the help he needs."

The man nodded and nudged his horse forward.

"I'll say a prayer for him," Penelope called as the horse's gait expanded into a canter. Beneath her breath, she murmured a second promise. "I'll say one for you, too."

Don't look back. Your concern is the dog, not the girl.

Yet it required physical effort to keep from twisting in the saddle and staring over his shoulder. Would she still be there? Or would she have disappeared back into whatever fairyland she had come from?

Where *had* she come from? Titus frowned. There were no towns nearby. Very few ranches or farms this far out from Glen Rose. She'd had no horse or mule. Her apron had been streaked with dirt, and bits of grass and debris had clung to her dress and hair as if she'd rolled down a hill or been tossed from a moving wagon. Could she be the victim of foul play, left alone in the middle of nowhere to make her way to the nearest homestead or town? Should he turn back? Ask her if she needed help?

Titus clenched his jaw. Should've thought of that before he rode off. The dog's situation might be critical, but a person's well-being—especially a female person's—outweighed that of an animal.

There'd been no indication she was in any distress, though. In fact, she'd seemed almost celebratory. Spinning in circles. Smiling with a purity so rare it had momentarily stolen his wits. If Rex had reared a second time, Titus likely would have slid straight off the horse's rump and landed on his backside in the dust.

Which made no sense. He was immune to pretty faces. After what happened to his brother, Tate, he despised beautiful women. And, no doubt about it, the mystery girl had been beautiful. Shiny black hair gathered loosely atop her head and tied with a red ribbon. A few loose strands curled around her oval face. Her complexion had been too pale for a woman used to working outdoors, yet the pink blooming in her cheeks radiated vitality. This wasn't an indolent, pampered woman afraid to let the sun mar her porcelain complexion with freckles. She was a fair-skinned pixie alive in her element. A kindhearted pixie moved to tears by a dying dog's plight.

Who was she?

He'd likely never know, despite the fact that the detective in him was already cataloging clues. Serviceable boots and a plain, shapeless dress. Not a woman of means. A servant in a wealthy household, perhaps? One who didn't work outdoors overmuch? She spoke well. As if she'd been educated. So maybe not a servant. A poor relation? Or maybe she only dressed that way when she decided to ramble across the countryside and spook unsuspecting horses.

She obviously possessed an adventurous spirit, judging by the dirt and debris on her person. The small cloth bag she carried didn't bulge, so she couldn't be on a long journey. Her people must be nearby. Whoever her people were.

Forget her, he ordered himself as he spotted the road that would take him to the Diamond D Ranch.

Rangers hunted criminals, not mysterious pixies. So unless her name showed up in the black book headquarters handed down, he had no business giving her a second thought.

Narcissa LaBelle pried the ruby free of its setting and held it between thumb and forefinger. Extending her arm, she moved the gem into the path of a sunbeam that had found its way into her tent.

"Hello, beauty."

Light danced through the facets, sparking an eruption of fire inside the small stone.

"That's right. Glitter for Mama."

A purr rumbled in Narcissa's throat as she beheld her latest acquisition. She'd not expected to meet up with a man of means in the tiny, depressingly named town of Eulogy, Texas. But the moment she'd laid eyes on Mr. Hubert Hathaway, she'd recognized his worth. The ring on his hand. The pin on his lapel. The lustful gleam in his eye. He'd been perfect.

Narcissa placed the gem atop a square of black velvet spread upon her dressing table, then turned her attention to the silver stick pen now void of its focal point. She opened a slender drawer to her right, pulled out a handkerchief, and slid the pin inside the folds. Cecil would see to the silver for her. Melt it down. Transform it. Give it a new role to play—that of nugget. Gold. Silver. She had quite a collection. Gifts from admirers who knew of her fascination with the big strikes. That was the story she'd tell should anyone discover the sack in the bottom of her locked chest.

The California Gold Rush in the '40s and '50s, the Comstock Lode in Nevada in the '60s and '70s, and the silver boom in Leadville, Colorado, in the '80s. Such transformative events. A man could change his fortune in the blink of an eye. All he needed was ingenuity, intelligence, and the willingness to take risks.

Narcissa possessed all three.

Lifting her chin, she gazed at herself in the large vanity mirror propped atop her portable dressing table. She stretched her neck and twisted her face first to the left, then to the right. Was that a new line around her mouth? She relaxed her smile into a seductive pout. Better. The line disappeared. Mostly.

Narcissa continued her inspection, her gaze snagging on a gray sprig above her temple. No! Were there others? She leaned close to the mirror and examined her hairline, her fingers shaking. What if there were some in the back that she couldn't see? She couldn't afford to be marked by age. Not yet. Narcissa fumbled for her tweezers. Latching on near the hair's root, she snatched the vile offender from her scalp and tossed it onto the ground where it belonged.

Shaken by the encounter, she breathed deeply and calmed the demon inside who taunted her with visions of old crones possessing bent backs and warts on their noses. She smoothed the skin over her cheekbones with her fingertips, then added a touch of color from the rouge pot to brighten them further.

"There, you see? Nothing to worry about. You're as beautiful as ever."

Narcissa lowered her eyelids in a sultry stare and swiveled on her cushioned stool to view herself from the left, the side with the beauty mark men found so intriguing. Plumping her lips in a provocative moue, she kissed the air, then ran a hand down the length of her neck, pleased by the swanlike elegance. Tugging down the neckline of her bodice slightly, she eyed the abundant curves swelling above the snug fabric. Still her best feature.

No one in this wilderness could rival her. There might be pretty, fresh-faced girls in the vicinity, but none of them knew how to wield their looks like a weapon. How to invest their assets and create a return that would allow them to leave this dusty place behind.

Like any good miner, Narcissa knew where to dig. How to plan. To scout out investors who would provide the funds she required. Funds that would take her to Europe, where she would play the most important role of her career. American heiress. A widow, perhaps. Wealthy. Refined. All of society would be her stage. Men would flock to her. Desire her. But her heart would beat for only one. Her true love. An elderly nobleman or a ridiculously rich merchant. A gentleman in want of a wife, a grand beauty to impress his associates and grace his home. His very large, very opulent home. A place for her to live happily ever after.

Narcissa stroked the edge of the mirror as if it were a pet.

Oh yes. She had plans. And thanks to her latest *investor*, she was one step closer to achieving them.

Picking up the spare corset that lay draped across her lap, she moved it into the light to better see the small opening she'd pulled threads from earlier. She fit her little finger into the opening, a narrow pocket designed to hold a piece of boning. But this corset used more lucrative support. Narcissa lifted the small ruby from the saucer and slid it inside the corset seam. Working it down the length of the pocket with her fingers, she smiled when it came to rest against the other stones already inside. At this rate, she'd have the boning channel filled before they left Texas.

She ran her finger over the small bumps hiding beneath the white cotton coutil fabric and licked her lips. "It's the little things that make life worth living."

3

Titus's pulse kicked up when he finally rode beneath the wooden crossbeam that served as the entrance gate for the Diamond D Ranch. The coonhound draped across his lap had grown alarmingly still over the last mile of their ride, and Titus worried they might be too late.

The farmhouse at the center of the yard looked the same as ever, two stories of white clapboard that needed a new coat of paint. A covered porch wrapped around the south and east sides with a line of gingerbread trim on the overhang that seemed far too feminine for a house occupied by a gang of overaged drovers. Seven that he knew of, though that number could have changed since his last visit. Doc collected geriatric cowhands the way a Ranger collected guns. There was always room for one more. Including the scowling fella slowly pushing up out of one of the many rocking chairs scattered around the front porch.

"Well, look what the cat drug in. The high and mighty Ranger Kingsley." The old grump couldn't quite hide his wince as he put weight on his right leg and limped over to the railing. "'Bout time ya showed yer face around here, whelp." He cleared his throat and shot a wad of spittle over the railing.

"Good to see you, too, Jeb." Titus tipped his hat to his elder like his mama had taught him. The retired bronc buster might dish out more sour than a barrel of pickle brine, but he was loyal to the men at the Diamond D, and that earned him Titus's respect. "Doc around? I got a patient for him."

Jeb raised a skeptical brow. "Where?"

As gently as he could manage, Titus hefted the listless dog up onto his right shoulder, then dismounted, using his left hand on the saddle horn to balance his descent.

Jeb's eyes widened, and his face lost all trace of hostility. "Doc!" He hollered over his shoulder as he worked his way down the porch railing toward the steps. "Better come quick. And bring yer bag!"

A snuffled snort echoed from around the corner, punctuated by the thud of boots hitting the porch floor.

"We under attack?" A heavyset man rounded the corner brandishing a broom like a club, his suspenders stretching over the long johns he wore in lieu of a shirt.

"Go back to sleep, ya old fool," Jeb groused. "Ain't no one attackin' anything."

Angus lowered the broom, a yawn overtaking him. Once it passed, he scratched a spot on his chest and moseyed forward. "What's all the hollerin' about, then?"

"Kid brought us a half-dead dog."

Titus adjusted his hold on the patient as he moved toward the house, cradling the dog in both arms.

"Looks like he might be *all* dead," Angus muttered.

Jeb swatted the big man's arm. "Bite yer tongue. Doc'll set him right. You'll see."

"Doc knows his business, shore 'nough, but he ain't the Almighty." Angus jerked his chin toward Titus. "That critter looks like he's gonna need more than Doc can give."

"Well, he's already got one person praying for him," Titus said as he climbed the porch steps, the young woman's promise ringing with church-bell clarity in his memory. "Maybe you can toss a few sticks of your own onto that fire."

Angus raised a brow, then shrugged and pulled the floppy hat from his head and clutched it to his chest. "Lord, we beseech you on behalf of this here critter. So woebegone and bedraggled—"

"Not out loud, you old windbag." Jeb swatted him again, earning a scowl from the much larger Angus.

"I'm gonna bag *you* if you don't quit thumpin' my arm."

A third graybeard wandered out of the nearby garden and approached the railing, a cautious smile on his face. "Fellas, no need to get testy, now."

Jeb and Angus turned on him and growled in unison. "Butt out, Ike."

The thin man with the twinkling eyes chuckled. "See? I knew the two of you could come to an agreement."

By the time Titus laid the dog down on the porch, his head had started to pound from all the chatter swimming around him. "Doc?" he called into the house from his crouched position. "You comin'?"

"Sweet salamanders! No need to shout the house down." The voice filtered through the open windows a heartbeat before the front door pulled open. "I heard ya the first . . . Titus?"

Doc was the only old-timer at the Diamond D who didn't wear a beard. Just a mustache and a pair of spectacles, when he could remember where he'd last laid them. The man's eyes rounded to match his glasses as he threw the door wide.

"Where are you hurt, boy?" He dropped his doctor's bag and hunkered next to Titus, grabbing hold of his shoulder. "Blade or bullet?" His eyes scoured Titus for evidence of injury.

"Bullet. But not me, Grandpa." Titus swiveled and laid a light hand on the dog's ribcage, relieved to feel it still rising and falling. "This is your patient."

Doc leaned backward and straightened his glasses on his nose. "A dog?" He shook his head, not in a refusing to help sort of way, but as a warning against Titus getting his hopes up. "Canine anatomy is very different from that of humans."

Titus met his grandfather's gaze, silently pleading with him the same way he had when he'd been eight and found a bird with a broken wing. "He took some friendly fire during a standoff with a pair of bank robbers in Walnut Springs. I feel responsible for him."

Doc looked Titus straight in the eye. "I know you, son. There's no way you shot this dog. Even by accident."

Because Enoch Kingsley had known him since the day he was born. The *minute* he was born, actually, having been the doctor who delivered him.

"Yeah, well, I know you, too," Titus countered. "And there's no way you'll let this fella die just because he's hairier than your usual clientele."

"Not without a fight." Doc's features tightened as he grabbed hold of his medical kit and dragged it close.

This was a man Titus loved and respected. A healer with the heart of a Ranger. One who'd never willingly surrender a battle, even if it broke him in the process.

A memory flashed of Doc bending over Tate four years ago, pounding the young man's chest again and again in a futile attempt to restart his grandson's heart. Titus's father had been the one who'd eventually pulled him away. The one who'd tearfully voiced the words no one in the family wanted to hear. *"He's gone, Dad."* Doc had crumpled beside Tate's bed, buried his head against the mattress, and repeatedly rasped, *"I'm sorry,"* until his voice grew too clogged with tears to speak.

He'd taken down his shingle the next day and retired his medical practice.

"We're going to need to clean this wound," Doc said, yanking

Titus back into the present. "Angus, put the kettle on, then dip out a basinful of water from the stove reservoir and bring it to me along with soap and towels."

All grogginess vanished from the big man's face as he nodded and hurried into the house.

"Jeb, I'm going to need you to hold the dog's head. If he wakes, he might fight, so beware of those teeth."

"I know what to do," Jeb groused, but an unmistakable gleam entered his eyes, one Titus imagined harkened back to the days when the old cowhand was one of the most sought-after bronco busters in the state.

"Titus, keep his lower half still and his belly exposed so I have room to work."

Titus moved into position and took a gentle yet firm hold on the dog's hips. "Got it."

"Good." Doc extracted a pair of surgical scissors from his bag and snipped away the bandage. "Now let's see what we're dealing with."

"I'm dealing with amateurs!"

Madame LaBelle's screech brought Penelope running out of the small tent designated for female staff. She'd been coated with dirt and dust after her excursion and had needed a wash and change before checking in with her mistress. Snatching the white mobcap off her cot, she fit it to her head as she scurried to her mistress's private quarters. She ducked under the flap and nearly got hit in the face with a flying hairbrush. A quick dodge spared her forehead, but the troupe's costume designer hadn't fared as well. A red welt bloomed on her cheek. Had Narcissa struck the seamstress? Usually she simply yelled and threw things while in one of her rages, but the angry mark on Mildred's cheek indicated things had escalated. Probably due to the half-empty decanter of wine on Narcissa's bedside table.

"You incompetent, idiotic—"

"Madame?" Penelope hurried inside and drew her mistress's attention away from the cowering Mildred. "May I be of assistance?"

Over the last six months, Penelope had learned how to manage her employer's moods. Anticipating needs and fulfilling them before being asked was key. Unfortunately, she didn't know what the current need entailed, and she doubted a footbath with Epsom salts would help this particular situation.

"Penelope, look what she's done to me!" Madame LaBelle flung herself sideways to give Penelope the full view of the dress she was to wear to the ball given in her honor at Kerr's Hall in Granbury tomorrow evening.

The troupe intended to set out at first light and arrive in Granbury midday for the start of a two-week engagement. But judging by the dramatics of their lead actress, part of the plan had gone awry.

Madame LaBelle's fingers spread wide as she gestured to herself with great flourish. "She was supposed to make me look voluptuous, not *vulgar*." She turned to face the oversized mirror attached to her dressing table. "I look like a scarlet woman." Yet she still preened as she beheld her reflection, twisting slightly to view herself at the most flattering angle.

"We'll have it altered to your specifications before tomorrow night, Madame." Penelope made the vow without the slightest hint that anything other than success would be the outcome. "I'll assist Mildred myself."

Narcissa eyed her in the mirror for a long moment before coming to a decision. "Very well. But I'm holding you personally responsible, Miss Snow. If the dress fails to please me, I'm taking the cost of the gown out of your wages." Her gaze dared Penelope to back down.

Penelope lifted her chin. "I'll see that you aren't disappointed, ma'am."

"I better not be." She turned away from the mirror and held out her arms. "Now get me out of this travesty. I need fresh air."

Penelope scurried forward and began undoing buttons on the ball gown constructed of deep purple silk and black lace that surely cost more than the entirety of all her earnings to date. Once she had the dress removed, she handed it to Mildred, then helped her mistress into an ensemble more fitting for a walk by the river. Neither she nor Mildred said a word until their mistress was a good ten yards from the tent.

Penelope dropped the tent flap back into place, then turned, ready to offer Mildred whatever help she needed, but the older woman's downcast face stilled her tongue.

"You shouldn't have done that." Mildred shook her head. "What she asks is impossible."

Penelope stepped closer. "I've experience wielding a needle. Surely between the two of us—"

"You don't understand!" Mildred grabbed the bodice in both hands and waved it under Penelope's nose. "I've altered this neckline three times. Square to scoop. It didn't lay right. Then I added darts, but it pinched under her arms. Then I lowered it to make the most of her *assets*, and now she accuses me of making her look like a strumpet. The only way to ensure a perfect fit is to tailor it to her while she has it on, but she refuses. She says she's already wasted too much time with pointless fittings."

"Do you have a dressmaker's dummy? Can we work with just her measurements?"

"There wasn't room to pack such a large item. I had to leave it and my Singer machine behind in Chicago. I didn't think we would need them since all of the costumes were already made. I was just supposed to take care of mending and the occasional alteration. It's hopeless."

Penelope looked around the tent, seeking inspiration. Surely there was a way to make this work. They didn't have a dummy but maybe . . . "We can use a stand-in."

"What?"

Penelope grinned. "I stand in for Madame during rehearsals sometimes when she doesn't feel up to practicing. I can do the same thing with the dress."

"That's a nice thought, but you don't have the same . . . assets." Mildred eyed Penelope's shapeless dress. "You don't even have a waist. It'd never w—"

Mildred's voice faded as Penelope drew the fabric of her dress tight from behind and allowed her true figure to show.

"Oh . . ." Mildred's whisper heated Penelope's cheeks. She circled Penelope, her dressmaker's eye taking in her natural hourglass shape and bountiful bosom. "This just might work. You'll need a proper corset, though. Something of Madame's so that we can match the shape."

Penelope hurried to her mistress's trunk and dug through the pile of colorful undergarments. So flamboyant, just like their owner. Penelope couldn't bear to wear any of those. The dress itself was scandalous enough, but to don an undergarment specifically designed to entice men felt . . . sinful. Didn't Madame have an old corset? Something simple and ordinary? Penelope caught a glimpse of plain white cotton at the very bottom of the trunk and pounced.

Pulling it out, she darted a daring look at Mildred. "We'll have to hurry."

Mildred grinned. "I'll tie down the tent flap. You get out of those rags and into that ball gown."

4

Loosen the neckline of your camisole and tuck the cotton down the front of the corset." Mildred eyed Penelope's bosoms as she studied the bodice's construction.

"Can't you just work around it?" Penelope asked. "I'm afraid if I undo the ribbon, I'll spill straight out of the dress."

How did Madame wear gowns like this and still radiate confidence? It was like walking along the edge of a cliff where, at any moment, a false step would send one plunging into shame and scandal. Gracious. An expensive ball gown should make her feel elegant and sophisticated, but all Penelope felt was naked. And Mildred wanted her to expose *more* skin?

"That's exactly what I need to happen," Mildred said as she armed herself with straight pins.

"What?" Penelope's arms crisscrossed over her chest to dam up the spillway.

Mildred waved her arms away impatiently. "Be grateful I let you keep the corset cover on. Madame never wears one. She's afraid a wrinkle in the undergarment will ruin the effect of her gown. And she's probably right. The tight bodices currently in fashion require precise tailoring."

Tired of waiting for Penelope to get up the nerve to comply, the seamstress took matters into her own hands. She untied the ribbon herself, yanked on the gathered fabric until it loosened, then tucked the excess into crevices that made Penelope cringe.

"No time for shyness, young lady. I need to see exactly where to position the décolletage, and to do that without being 'vulgar,' I need to see how much volume I'm expected to contain."

Biting her lip, Penelope lifted her gaze to the tent's canvas ceiling and did her best to ignore the indelicate poking and prodding going on below her neck. It didn't help that the corset pinched in odd places. She'd gotten used to wearing simple supports built for practicality of movement. The over-the-shoulder straps she preferred kept her annoying bounty contained. Madame LaBelle's corset, on the other hand, seemed designed for one purpose—to thrust as many curves out the top as possible. Thank heaven, no one besides Mildred was around to witness her exposure.

Imagine her mortification if that handsome cowboy with the intense eyes happened upon her in such a state! Mercy. She'd likely combust into a pile of ash on the spot. Then his big horse would get a tickle in his nose, sneeze, and blow her sooty remains all over creation. Penelope pressed her lips together to keep a giggle from escaping. She was such a goose. And her mystery cowboy was . . . not. He'd been stoic and serious during their encounter. Though that might have been due to the serious nature of his errand. His poor dog. Barely clinging to life.

Watch over them, Lord. Dog and man.

Penelope wasn't usually one to daydream about men—she'd been doing her best to avoid their notice for the last six months, after all—but something about the cowboy she'd met today kept calling her back. She'd barely read two chapters of

Oliver Twist, so distracted was she by questions that insisted on popping up in her mind.

Had he really been part of a shootout with bank robbers? Did that make him a lawman of some sort or maybe part of a posse who had been temporarily deputized? Or was he one of the thieves? No, he'd been too chivalrous to be a criminal. Besides, he didn't strike her as lacking intelligence. Only a dimwit would bring up a crime he committed in casual conversation, and this man exuded authority and competence. The way he'd calmed his horse and controlled his own seat all while protecting the injured dog he carried—impressive. She was no expert in horsemanship, but if she'd been the one in the saddle when that horse reared, she would have ended up sprawled on the ground with a mouthful of dirt.

Something sharp jabbed the flesh under her left arm. "Ow!"

"Sorry," Mildred mumbled around a mouthful of pins. "I'm almost done."

Penelope glanced sideways toward the tent entrance, suddenly thankful for the painful prick that had brought her attention back to the present. Mooning over a man dulled a girl's senses, and she couldn't afford to be distracted. Keeping Narcissa LaBelle happy required continual adjustment and recalibration since the target remained in constant motion. The flamboyant nature that made Madame such a riveting actress on the stage created quite a challenge for those serving her behind the scenes, as Mildred had experienced firsthand this afternoon.

"Last pin," the seamstress announced at the same moment a masculine voice boomed on the other side of the tent wall.

"Cover yourself, Narci. I'm coming in." The ties on the door flap pulled loose. "You've avoided nailing down the program long enough. We'll be in Granbury tomorrow, and we need a finalized schedule to give to the printer."

Penelope froze. *No, no, no.* Her eyes met Mildred's. "Cover" was all she managed to whisper before the flap opened and the troupe manager strolled in.

Mildred grabbed Penelope's dress from the chair in front of the dressing table. The corset beneath it slipped to the floor. The seamstress turned back to Penelope, but it was too late. Alfred Billings's gaze had already found Penelope, roosting on her like a hen settling in for the night. Penelope crossed her arms over her chest and dropped her chin, staring a hole in the ground as heat engulfed her face.

"Madame isn't here, Mr. Billings." Mildred, bless her, stepped between Penelope and the manager, but her short figure didn't block much of Penelope's display since Penelope was standing on a crate to keep the hem of the ball gown off the ground. "Perhaps you can return later?"

Penelope swiveled to show him her back, but the dressing table mirror made it impossible to hide. A gentleman would leave. But Alfred Billings had never been one to let scruples interfere with business.

"Shame on you, Miss Snow." Instead of retreating, the man advanced. "Hiding all of these curves beneath those shapeless servant dresses of yours."

Penelope made a grab for the tan dress Mildred held out to her, but Mr. Billings intercepted it and flung it into a far corner.

He clicked his tongue. "You've hidden long enough, Miss Snow." He clasped her wrist and tugged her arm down. "This is marvelous! A figure to rival Narci's combined with youth and delicate beauty . . . you'll make the perfect understudy. You already fit the costumes, and with that face, no one will care if your acting is unpolished. Can you sing?"

On stage? In front of people? Penelope shook her head and pulled against his hold. "Please, Mr. Billings, I have no interest in acting. Let me go. I need to get back to work." And into her own clothes.

"Work? Fetching and carrying for Madame LaBelle? I think not. You need to start training immediately. I've heard you run lines with Narci. You've a quick mind. With a little practice, you could fill her shoes when the occasion warrants. I can teach you how to internalize character and provoke emotion. You might not have her command of the stage, but that will come in time. Once you get a taste of the applause, your confidence will grow. Even the great Madame LaBelle started somewhere. You can be just as successful. Maybe more so. She might be a siren, but audiences love a sweetheart." He grinned and rubbed his hands together. "I'd worried about what would become of the troupe once Narci retired, but now I know. You, Miss Snow, are going to make us all rich."

"No!" Pulse racing, she jerked her arm away from his grasp. She had to flee. Hide. Escape. She jumped off the crate, rounded the dressing table, and ducked behind the nearest large object—the dressing table mirror. "I want nothing to do with the stage."

All those men staring at her? *Ogling* her? Making her the very thing she'd vowed never to be—a body to lust after with no mind, heart, or soul.

"Penny, dear, don't be so dramatic." Madame LaBelle strolled into the tent. "Freddie is paying you a compliment."

The knots of anxiety pulling tight in Penelope's belly calcified into stone. How long had her mistress been standing at the door? How much had she heard? As she approached Mr. Billings and set a hand on his shoulder, she looked the picture of grace and serenity. But the woman was a first-rate actress, and Penelope didn't trust the sheep's clothing she'd donned. Not when a wolfish gleam hardened her eyes when her gaze slid over Penelope.

Mr. Billings's smile tightened as he turned to greet his headliner. "Narci, you naughty girl, keeping Miss Snow's marketable attributes hidden all this time."

Narcissa's manicured fingers walked down Mr. Billings's arm as her lips plumped in a semipout. "Only because I knew you'd rush your fences and spook her, precisely as you've done. Our little Penny might have been blessed with a figure to draw a standing-room-only crowd, but she possesses a shy nature. She must be wooed gently, Freddie. Something I've been working on for the last six months."

Madame circled the troupe manager to clear a path to Penelope, her movements poised and sleek like a panther stalking her prey. "I recognized her potential immediately, of course. Knew she would make the perfect protégé if I could just cure her of that pesky timidity. Why else would I encourage her to stand in for me during rehearsals and run lines with the other actors?"

Because you scorn the rest of the cast and have no patience for their missteps, Penelope thought. Surely Mr. Billings was not so naïve as to think Madame's absence from rehearsals had anything to do with nudging a fledgling starlet into the limelight.

Narcissa reached the side of the dressing table, her mouth twitching slightly as her gaze raked over Penelope's profile. Then in a swirl of muslin skirt, she spun to face Mr. Billings. "Leave us, Freddie. I must undo the damage you've done and calm our dear Penny."

The way she kept calling her "dear Penny" couldn't possibly bode well. She'd never been anything but Penelope, Miss Snow, or *you there* for the entirety of her time in Madame LaBelle's employ. An explosion threatened, and Penelope feared the eruption would entail more than a flying hairbrush.

"After Penny and I have had our chat, I'll come find you in the dining tent to discuss the flyers."

Penelope's heart faltered. *Flyers*. Madame had heard everything.

Mr. Billings waved a hand in surrender and bowed out of the tent. Madame then turned her attention to the seamstress. "Mildred?" Her voice flowed like sticky sweet syrup. "Have you finished marking the needed alterations on my gown?"

Mildred's hands trembled slightly as she collected her sewing box. "Yes, ma'am."

"Excellent. Then help Penny out of the dress and take it away. I expect it to be completed tonight."

"Yes, ma'am."

Mildred scurried to do as Narcissa bid, coming around to Penelope's back and undoing the buttons. As exposed as Penelope had felt in front of Mr. Billings, her vulnerability only worsened as the purple silk was stripped from her body under her mistress's pointed attention. Mildred met her gaze only briefly as Penelope gathered her thin petticoat in front of her and stepped out of the skirt. The sympathy in the older woman's eyes offered little comfort.

Every small rustle of silk echoed like a trumpet blast in the too-silent tent. When Madame crossed to collect Penelope's dress from where it lay crumpled in the corner, each padding footstep vibrated through Penelope with the force of a slamming door.

"Oh, Mildred?"

Arms full of fabric, the seamstress halted by the exit and glanced over her shoulder. "Yes, Madame?"

"Send Cecil to me, will you?"

Mildred didn't waste time on words. She nodded and hurried from the tent. The moment the flap dropped back into place, Madame LaBelle dropped the character she'd been playing. Her eyes narrowed to slits, and her mouth contorted into a snarl that would be at home on a rabid wolf.

"How dare you." The guttural words were barely audible over the pounding of Penelope's heart. "I give you work, take you under my wing, and you repay me by making a fool of me?"

Penelope shook her head. "No, ma'am. I would nev—"

"Silence!" Narcissa stalked forward. "Little schemer. You had me fooled, but no more. I'll not be usurped or upstaged. You think yourself so clever, don't you? Hiding your attributes until the perfect moment presented itself. And I handed it to you on a silver platter. Leaving you with my dress so you could *accidentally* get caught by Freddie."

"No! That's not what I—"

"Your looks might be enough to get a man to do your bidding, but it won't save you from me. I've sharpened my claws on more experienced schemers than you. I'll shred you to ribbons."

Penelope's eyes burned with tears. "I want nothing to do with the stage, I promise. I was only trying to help Mildred get the proper measurements for your gown so you would look your best tomorrow."

"Oh, I'll look my best. Don't you worry." Narcissa smiled as she reached the front of the dressing table, opened a drawer, and pulled out a small pair of scissors. "It's you who will dress in disgrace, all of your secrets exposed."

Holding up Penelope's dress, Narcissa set the scissors to the neckline and sliced the garment straight down the center. She set shears to fabric again, this time a couple of inches from the bottom hem. After cutting a small notch, she grabbed both sides of the cloth and yanked. The sound of rending fabric slashed Penelope's composure. A chill swept over her skin, and she trembled as the tears she'd held at bay finally spilled down her cheeks.

"Narcissa?" Cecil Hunt lifted the flap and stepped into the tent. "Mildred said you needed my help."

"Ah yes, I do." A wicked smile gleamed. "Miss Snow has betrayed my trust. I want you to dispose of her for me."

Dispose of her? Penelope's heart thudded. Her breathing shallowed. Her eyes darted around the tent, seeking an escape. Mr. Hunt's bulk blocked the exit. The stagehand was built like an ox and possessed a similar level of intelligence, yet his loyalty to Narcissa was ironclad. Completely besotted, he would do whatever she bid. Even now, his face tightened in displeasure as he marched toward Penelope.

Releasing the dressing table mirror, Penelope sprinted toward the back of the tent, diving to the ground and thrusting her head and arms beneath the heavy canvas. She wriggled as fast as she could, but Hunt proved too fast. His weight landed on top of her legs, and he quickly reeled her in. She kicked and flailed, but to no avail. In a matter of minutes, he had her hands bound behind her back with the cloth strip Madame had torn from her dress. He shoved his handkerchief in her mouth to keep her from crying out, then secured her to the support pole at the center of the tent.

"I knew I could count on you, Cecil." Madame sauntered up behind him and nibbled on his earlobe. "Strong work from a strong man." Her hands roamed down his arms, then up over his chest.

His eyes slid closed as he leaned into her caress.

Distraught and horribly embarrassed, Penelope looked away from his face only to discover that Narcissa was looking at *her*, not lost in a romantic moment with her lover. Triumph radiated from the actress as she displayed her power for Penelope's benefit.

"Take her away while everyone is busy at dinner," she murmured into Hunt's ear. "Find a secluded area. No roads, no houses, no one around to come to her rescue. Tie her to a tree and leave her there to face her fate. I want her exposed. To the elements. To shame. To hungry, wild animals. Then return to me and receive your reward."

Mr. Hunt's eyes opened, yet he immediately ducked his gaze to avoid looking at Penelope. Twisting to face Narcissa, he dipped his chin. "I'll see it done."

5

How had a good deed gone so terribly wrong?

Bound, gagged, and wearing nothing but her underclothes, Penelope bounced face down across Cecil Hunt's lap as he rode away from camp. Twilight dimmed the sky, concealing her abduction. She screamed for help, but the gag muffled her cries and choked her breath. She tried to writhe her way off the horse but couldn't break free of Mr. Hunt's grip. Blood rushed to her head. The saddle horn bruised her hip. Tears clogged her throat and nose, making it hard to breathe. Mr. Hunt had wrapped a dark brown blanket around her to camouflage the white of her petticoat and camisole. The fabric trapped her. Stole her sight. Drained her hope.

Penelope's body slackened. She couldn't escape. Not yet, anyway. Better to save her strength in case a better opportunity presented itself. Though at the moment, Penelope found it hard to believe any such chance would materialize. How could it when her opponent was so big and so determined to fulfill his duty?

As the horse slowed to navigate the thickening vegetation, the memory of another rider flashed through her mind. One who'd carried a passenger across his lap as well, though his intention had been to heal, not destroy. The thought of the stoic cowboy—a possible lawman, no less—restored a bit of her hope. He was out here somewhere.

He'd been concerned for her welfare when they'd met mere hours ago. Ready to lend aid. Surely, he'd assist her escape should he cross her path. *Lord, cross his path with mine. Please.*

As Penelope watched the darkening ground pass under the horse's hooves, she clung to the image of that rugged cowboy, building him up in her mind. He was no mere deputy. Not even a town marshal or county sheriff. He was a Texas Ranger, one of the men of legend she'd heard about since entering the state. Men who would stop at nothing to see justice done. Driven. Fierce. The best of the best. He would come for her.

It didn't matter that he had no reason to be out on the trail after dark. Nor did it matter that Mr. Hunt might be taking her in a completely different direction than the cowboy had traveled. Her Ranger would come. She had to believe that. Otherwise she'd be crushed by despair.

Yet the night grew darker, and no one came.

Mr. Hunt finally drew his mount to a halt and dumped her off his lap. She fell to the ground, her legs collapsing under her, her head thumping the earth. The blanket slipped down her body, exposing her face and shoulders. Cool night air slapped against her skin, but it also jarred her mind.

Run!

Arms bound behind her back, she struggled to get her legs beneath her. Hunt's saddle creaked. Penelope lurched upward.

Run!

Her half-numb legs did their best to obey her command, but they'd barely carried her three steps before a thick arm snagged her from behind.

"Not so fast."

Her heel connected with the inside of his thigh. He grunted, but his grip held firm. As if she were a calf he'd roped, he tossed her on the ground and pressed a knee into her lower back. She arched her back, her muffled cries filling the night air.

"Hold still," he groused. "I ain't gonna kill you. I'm not even gonna hurt you, unless your squirmin' puts you in the way of my knife."

Knife? Penelope stilled.

"That's better."

Something tugged at the fabric binding her wrists, then all at once, the tie snapped. Her arms fell to her sides, and her shoulders throbbed in relief. She grabbed for the gag and yanked it down over her chin.

"Please, Mr. Hunt. This is a mistake. I was only trying to help Mildred with her alterations so Madame's dress would fit properly. I want nothing to do with the stage. Madame misunderstood."

"Don't matter," he said as he drew her to her feet. "I have my instructions."

"But this is wrong. Don't you see?"

Apparently not, for he wrapped a length of rope around her midsection, dragged her over to an oak tree, and secured her against the trunk, trapping her arms inside the multiple coils.

"Please." Her voice cracked. "You can't leave me defenseless like this. I'll die."

He ducked his head. From a twinge of conscience? Penelope's chest ached with hope.

"You don't have to take me back," she bargained. "You can leave me out here in the middle of nowhere, just don't tether me to the tree. I'll stay away from Granbury. From the troupe. Madame will be rid of me just as she wishes, but you won't have a young girl's blood on your hands. She'll never know."

He stepped back but didn't walk away. His chin slowly lifted, and his eyes met hers.

"Please, Mr. Hunt. I know you're not a cruel man. You're

just trying to make the woman you love happy. But sometimes Madame says things when she's in a temper that she regrets later."

His gaze softened just a tad. Uncertainty drew lines in his forehead.

"If I die out here," Penelope pressed, "Madame's soul will carry the same stain of guilt as yours. But you can protect her from that. All you have to do is untie me. Then my survival will rest on my own shoulders. *Please.*"

He hesitated for a long moment, then shook his head. "I can't. She'll ask me about you, and she'll know if I lie."

Penelope closed her eyes and slumped against the tree, the rough bark scratching her exposed shoulder blades. So this was it. She was to die alone in the middle of nowhere. Horrifying options flashed through her mind. Starvation. Wolves. A random lightning strike.

Lord, if I get a vote, I'll take the lightning.

Something hard pushed up into her right palm. Penelope's eyes flew open. Mr. Hunt said nothing, but he held his knife in place until her fingers wrapped firmly around the hilt. His eyes met hers for a moment, an apology written in their depths. Then before she could fully process what had happened, he strode to his horse and rode off into the night.

"Thank you," she whispered in his wake. How odd to feel gratitude toward the man who had abducted her and left her tied to a tree. Yet his smidgeon of pity might just save her life.

No, the knife is in my hand because of you, Lord. You softened Hunt's heart at the last hour. You are the one who deserves my gratitude.

Now she just had to find a way to use what she'd been given. With the uncomfortable angle of her hand and her paranoia about dropping the blade, progress was painfully slow. The night air continued growing cooler, numbing her fingers and besetting her with shivers that made it increasingly difficult to grip the knife. Praying for stamina, she kept scratching at the rope despite the ache in her arms and the chattering of her teeth.

Her sawing slowed as energy drained from her body. Too . . . cold. Too . . . tired. Too . . . discouraged.

"Don't g-give up." The words were no more than a rasp, but hearing them aloud pushed the darkness back enough for her to catch a breath.

"This isn't the f-first time y-you've been ab-bandoned." Her strokes strengthened along with her voice. "G-God saved you that s-snowy night when y-your mother abandoned you on the s-school's doorstep. You d-didn't freeze t-to death then. He w-won't let you f-freeze n-now."

Another rope fiber frayed. Her sawing became more forceful, her voice louder.

"He s-sent Edith to r-rescue you as a b-babe. Tonight, he g-gave you a knife. Use it!"

With a loud grunt, she scraped the blade downward, pressing as hard as she could. The rope popped. The knife fell. She bent forward, straining after the lost tool, but gravity proved too efficient. The blade clunked against the ground, hilt-first, barely an inch from her stockinged feet.

Penelope banged her skull against the tree, then forced herself to take three deep breaths. The knife was gone, but the rope was severed. She could shimmy out of this. She just had to create enough strain on the rope to loosen the coils and create slack.

She slid up and down, her movements so minuscule at first that it felt as if nothing were happening. Her head scraped against the trunk, her hair catching in the bark and yanking at her scalp. Gradually, her range of motion increased. She twisted in every direction possible. Over and over. The skin along her shoulder blades rubbed raw. Her hair fell across her face in a ratted mess, and acorns poked the undersides of her feet. But the rope was loosening. She could feel it!

Turning sideways the few inches she could, she stretched the rope against her left side, then slid her right arm upward. It moved! Shrugging her right shoulder nearly to her ear, she pulled again, but her elbow caught in the rope. She raised up on tiptoes. Not enough. She planted her left sole against the base of the tree and pushed with her leg to lever herself another inch outward. She wriggled her elbow back and forth. The rope stretched. Her elbow emerged and extricated the rest of her arm.

Tears streamed down Penelope's face. Tears of relief. Of exhaustion. Of gratitude.

But she wasn't free yet.

Feeling her way along the coils, she searched for the cut end, found it, and jerked it outward. Other coils had been wrapped atop it, so it didn't give way easily. But it *did* move. One beautiful inch at a time. She tugged and twisted, twisted and tugged, until, finally, the rope slackened enough for her to push the coils over her hips. With the widest barrier out of the way, gravity did the rest and carried the rope to the ground.

Penelope staggered away from the tree, wrapping her arms around herself to ward off the air's chill and keep the trembling at bay. Her attention was drawn heavenward, where a three-quarter moon shone in the inky sky. Light in the darkness.

"Thank you," she whispered.

A handful of stars winked back at her. She wasn't alone. She had a Father who would never leave her or forsake her. Yet even as the comforting truth embraced her heart, a cloud stole across the sky and blocked the moon's light. Wind blew through the trees, creating a moaning sound that quickened Penelope's pulse.

An owl screeched. A twig snapped. She spun to look behind her. Nothing but shadows. Creepy shadows. Ominous shadows.

The knife!

Penelope dropped to her hands and knees and felt around the base of the tree. There. Beneath the rope. She clasped the hilt and drew the weapon close to her body, her breaths coming in heavy pants.

Get ahold of yourself, Pen. You tromped across this very countryside mere hours ago. You're fine.

The howl of a coyote shredded her logic to bits. She took off running. Three strides into her flight, her feet tangled in something lying on the ground, and Penelope sprawled face first in the dirt. She scrambled to rise, but the snakelike creature wrapped itself around her ankles.

"Get off!" She kicked herself free and had started to run again when the fog of panic finally cleared from her brain.

She halted. Turned. Took a tentative step back the way she had come.

The cloud obscuring the moon passed by and gentle light filtered down over the scene. A blanket. That's what her feet had tangled in. Brown wool. The blanket Mr. Hunt had used to conceal her. He'd left it behind.

You goose.

Fear had stolen her sanity, but no more. Penelope slid the knife blade beneath the ties of her petticoat, securing it above her left hip. Then she set her jaw and stepped forward.

"'Yea, though I walk through the valley of the shadow of death, I will fear no evil.'" Reaching the blanket, she bent down to retrieve it, gave it a firm snap to knock off the worst of the dirt and leaves, then wrapped it around her shoulders like a cloak. "'For thou art with me; thy rod and thy staff they comfort me.'"

"Thou art with me."

No more running blindly through the dark. Or jumping at every strange sound. She'd wait for morning, then seek help.

Bedding down beneath the very tree that had held her captive moments before, Penelope piled up the rope to use as a pillow, then curled into a ball beneath her blanket. But sleep eluded her most of the night. Cold chilled her bones. Hunger clawed her belly. And despite her best intentions, worry pecked at her mind.

What if there were no homesteads within walking distance?

What if she couldn't find water?

What if she stepped on a rattlesnake?

As soon as she batted one fretful thought away, a new one rose to take its place. Not knowing what else to do, she began to rock, imagining herself as a child in Edith's arms, sitting by the warm cookstove in the school's kitchen. Edith's slightly off-key voice that sang hymns in place of lullabies. Taking inspiration from the memory, Penelope filled her mind with the lyrics of one of her favorite hymns.

> *"Guide me, O Thou great Jehovah,*
> *Pilgrim through this barren land;*
> *I am weak, but Thou are mighty,*
> *Hold me with Thy pow'rful hand . . ."*

Each repeated stanza placed a brick in the wall that took her fearful thoughts captive. She hummed and rocked and prayed the words of the song until her mind finally began to drift, and exhaustion forced peace upon her battered spirit.

6

Titus had forgotten how good it felt to sleep in a bed that wasn't attached to a saloon. Doc's spare room might smell like liniment and old socks, but it was blessedly void of the ruckus spawned by piano music, dancing girls, and drunken cowboys that could plague a fellow into the wee hours of the morning. Not to mention that he didn't have to worry about what kind of unsavory activities might have occurred in the bed before he took occupancy. Saloon accommodations and thin bedrolls spread on hard ground didn't exactly position a man for a good night's rest. He felt downright spoiled this morning as he headed to the kitchen for coffee without a single neck crick or sore muscle to work back into place.

A bald man with impressive chin whiskers stood at the cookstove flipping bacon in an iron skillet. Grease sizzled and popped, and the salty aroma set Titus's mouth to watering.

"That smells mighty good, Coy." Titus grinned and leaned a shoulder against the kitchen doorway. "You tryin' to fatten me up before I leave?"

The man's face reddened, the color stretching upward to turn his bald pate pink. "It ain't nuthin' fancy. Threw a few strips in the pan when I heard you movin' around." He shrugged as if such thoughtfulness were an everyday occurrence. "Got some leftover flapjacks in the warmin' oven if ya want 'em."

"Everyone else eat already?" Titus glanced out the window positioned over the sink. The sun hung within spitting distance of the horizon, so he wasn't *that* late, but men who'd been working as cowhands all their lives didn't know how to stay in bed past sunrise.

They probably considered him a slugabed for not rising until seven. Normally, he'd agree with that assessment, but he'd been up till after midnight assisting Doc with the surgery on the gunshot dog. Still, he felt like a loafer when fellas in their sixties and seventies beat him out of bed.

"Doc's not been down yet. He ain't used to them late hours. I held back a few hot cakes for him, too."

Titus wouldn't have expected anything else. The men at the Diamond D revered Doc. Not only because he was the eldest among them at seventy-six, but because most of them would've been dead by now without him.

Doc had created a family when he'd opened the Diamond D to retired cowhands, and there wasn't one man among them who wouldn't give up his right arm if Doc needed it. Most had no family of their own. They'd spent their days workin' cows for whichever brand had need of their skills, living like nomads all over the West. No wives. No children. No home. And when age stole their ability to work, they found themselves with no purpose and no place.

Jeb had been the first. Doc took him in as a favor to a medical colleague who'd been concerned that his patient had nowhere to recuperate from his career-ending injury. No one wanted to put up with his famously sour disposition for an extended period. Jeb had broken an ankle so severely the physician expected him never to walk again. Doc had different ideas. It took nearly a year and more patience than Job to put up with Jeb's cantankerous demeanor, but Doc got him walking again.

Rowdy had been much the same. A kick to the head by an unruly stallion had nearly ended his life. When he came to the Diamond D, he'd been unable to do more than sit in a chair and stare into space. Now he could dress and feed himself and go on long, rambling walks around the ranch. He didn't talk much, and he'd taken up some peculiar habits, but he was self-sufficient.

After that, word spread, and retired drovers started showing up at Grandpa's door. Doc didn't allow drinkin', cussin', or tobacco chawin' at the Diamond D, and he made it clear that every resident would be required to attend Sunday morning Bible study in the parlor. The unpopular rules kept the place from being overrun, but they'd also served to bring a few wild old cowboys back into the Lord's fold. Coy among them.

One wouldn't guess it by the fella's shy, kindhearted demeanor, but he'd run with an outlaw gang for most of his youth before moving on to more honest ranch work when the rest of his cohorts either died or were carted off to prison. Titus had supposed the man was just shy around him because of his work with the Rangers, but Doc claimed Coy acted bashful around everyone. Almost as if he wanted so badly to hide the shameful deeds of his past that he hid part of himself along with them.

Pushing away from the doorjamb, Titus entered the kitchen and crossed over to the corner near the stove. Hunkering down, he ran a hand lightly over the black fur of the dog curled up on a pallet of old quilts.

"How's our patient this morning?"

Coy set the skillet aside and took a mug down from the nearby cabinet. "Still breathin'. I got him to lap up a little water an hour ago, but he's just been sleepin' the rest of the time. I suppose that's what he needs after all he's been through."

Titus stroked the dog's head, careful not to disturb his slumber. "Doc said if he made it through the night, he'd have a decent chance at recovering. I'm glad he cleared the first hurdle."

"Most men wouldn't have done what you did, Titus. Cartin' that critter miles outta the way instead of just puttin' him out of his misery. Speaks well of ya." Coy poured coffee into the mug and extended it to Titus like a medal of commendation.

Titus straightened and accepted the mug, though he found accepting the praise more difficult. He'd just carried the dog here. Doc had done all the saving.

Coy nodded toward the table, and Titus took the hint. He pulled out a chair and sat down. A few seconds later, a plate filled with four pieces of bacon and three flapjacks plopped down in front of him.

"Butter's in the crock, and there's honey in the jar behind it."

Titus set his coffee down and reached for the jar. Little bits of honeycomb floated in the golden-brown goo. "From Ike's bees?"

"Yup. Them little stingers give me the willies, but they sure make good honey."

The bees had been a new addition last spring when Ike had run across a displaced swarm in a tree behind his garden. The hive had been new the last time Titus had visited. Hard to believe he'd been gone long enough for them to get established and create enough honey to be harvested. But then, he hadn't been to the Diamond D in months. His work with the Rangers had kept him too busy. He probably wouldn't have stopped by this time if it hadn't been for the dog.

Titus frowned as he set the honey jar down and chomped on a strip of bacon. He'd gone too long between visits. His grandfather wasn't going to be around forever. And frankly, Titus worried about the old coot. He'd withdrawn from Titus's parents after what happened to Tate. His pa had placed no blame, but Doc heaped it upon himself. He'd up and left Fairfield a month after he'd closed his practice, seeking a change of scenery, a place unstained by memories of Tate. He bought the Diamond D and, as far as Titus knew, had never returned to Fairfield. Pa received the occasional letter from him, but his correspondence centered on the exploits of his cohorts and provided precious few clues about how he himself fared.

After Titus joined the Rangers and started traveling around the state, his pa had urged him to drop in on Doc every now and again, trusting that Doc wouldn't have the heart to turn away his grandson. He hadn't, of course. In fact, Titus was pretty sure he'd seen tears in the old man's eyes the first time Titus stopped by for a visit. He'd urged Titus to come back often, so Titus arranged to be in the area at least once every few months. Until recently. There'd been talk about possible promotions being awarded in his company, so he'd been loath to spend any time away. Even now, he itched to get back to headquarters. But maybe he'd stay an extra day. Get a real visit in before letting duty call him away.

He'd just reached for the butter crock and a spreading knife when the back door shoved open and Dusty, a former mule skinner and current Diamond D wrangler, lurched inside. "Is Doc up yet? Something's agitatin' Rowdy. He's all worked up, but none of us can understand what he's tryin' to say."

Titus pushed back his chair. "Maybe I can help. We can wake Doc if needed, but I'd like to let him sleep if possible. Last night wore him out."

"All right." Dusty's face suddenly crinkled. He grabbed for the handkerchief he always kept at the ready and covered his nose right as a sneeze exploded. "Come on, then." He gestured for Titus to follow him as he tucked the handkerchief back into his trouser pocket.

The poor guy suffered from hay fever nearly year-round, but that didn't stop him from working with the animals he loved. He just made a point to keep a half-dozen hankies on his person at all times.

Titus grabbed his hat from the line of hooks by the back door and trailed after the barrel-chested man.

Coy dogged his heels. "It's odd for Rowdy to be back this early. Usually his morning rambles last until noon or later. He musta run across somethin' that spooked him."

The scraggly-looking fellow certainly looked spooked. He'd drawn a crowd over by the paddock. His arms gesticulated in wild, jerky motions. His hat hung down his back, the slackened chin cord anchored against his windpipe. White hair stood out at crazy angles. Sweat beaded his brow. His chest heaved as if he'd been running.

"Was it a coyote?" Angus mimicked some of Rowdy's motions as if trying to distinguish a shape. "A feral hog?"

"This ain't charades, numbskull." Jeb batted Angus's hands down.

Angus glared at him. "I don't hear you spoutin' any wisdom. At least I'm tryin' to guess what he's sayin'."

"And aggrivatin' him in the process. Can't you see how red his face is gettin'?"

Titus picked up his pace. Rowdy really was looking frazzled, and typically, the more upset the man became, the more difficulty he had communicating. Thankfully, Ike stepped in and steered the two quarreling drovers a few steps backward toward the paddock fence, giving Rowdy a little space.

As if deciding it wasn't worth his time to stick with the three fellas he had found, Rowdy slashed his arm in frustration and turned toward the house. His gaze locked on Titus, and his eyes widened with renewed urgency. He started running, and Titus jogged forward to meet him halfway.

Rowdy grabbed hold of his arm. "Er. Ep er."

The grunts made no sense, but the intent was clear. There was a problem. Something that needed to be addressed quickly.

Titus gripped Rowdy's elbow, trying to calm him. To assure him that he would assist. Whatever the need. "Is there a threat heading toward the ranch?"

Rowdy growled and shook his head.

If no threat was imminent, that left only one other cause for urgency. "Does someone need help?"

The small man's eyes lit. He nodded and started tugging Titus away from the paddock.

"Wait." Titus resisted the man's pull, then had to bite his tongue when Rowdy leveled a stare at him that clearly indicated his worth was lessening with each second that ticked past without him moving. Titus held out a conciliatory palm. "Let me fetch my guns."

Rowdy shook his head, smacked his own empty hips, then told Titus with a look to quit being a sissy and start moving, for heaven's sake.

"All right. Lead on."

Rowdy headed off to the east at a fast clip. Titus followed. As did the other five men who'd witnessed the entire spectacle. Not knowing what they'd find or where it would be kept, the men remained wide-eyed and quiet for the first ten minutes. Then it was the exertion of keeping up with Rowdy that hushed them for the next twenty. By the time Rowdy wound his way into an oak grove and finally slowed down, Angus and Coy were wheezing, Jeb was leaning hard on a walking stick he picked up along the way, and Ike and Dusty, though better off than their companions, were still looking a little red in the face.

After assuring himself that none of his grandfather's friends were about to keel over, Titus turned back to Rowdy and scanned the area in the direction he pointed.

"Erl," Rowdy said in a low rumble. "Ep er."

It took a moment for Titus to decipher that something other than a mound of brown dirt lay beneath the tree Rowdy indicated. He crept closer.

Suddenly the mound moved. The men behind him sucked in a collective breath as a slender, pale arm poked out of the cocoon. Then a foot. A small foot. Wearing ladies' stockings. But it was the face that captivated Titus and beckoned him closer. A face that seemed familiar even though reposed in sleep.

The young woman from yesterday. The wood nymph who'd appeared out of nowhere, twirling and smiling. But this woman looked nothing like the one he'd met. Her dark hair hung in a matted nest of twigs and leaves. Scratches marred the skin of her face and hands. Hands that led to bare arms with nothing but a blanket to cover them.

What had happened to her? Had she been attacked after he left her? Titus's jaw clenched. He should have escorted her back to her people. Maybe he could have prevented . . .

"Is she sleepin' on a rope?"

"Poor thing."

"What's she doin' out here?"

"And where are her clothes? You figure she's one of them saloon gals?"

"What would a saloon gal be doing way out here?"

"I dunno. Maybe she got lost."

"Your mind's what got lost."

Titus turned around and shushed the whisperers who'd crept in behind him. The last thing this young woman needed was to wake up to the sight of seven strange men hovering over her. He was about to suggest the others retreat to their original position when Dusty let out a sneeze loud enough to rival a gunshot.

The girl jolted awake and yanked a wicked-looking hunting knife out from under her blanket.

7

Stay back!" Penelope waved Hunt's knife in front of her as if it had the power to stave off . . . five . . . no, six . . . good heavens . . . *seven* men.

She raised the blade in front of her face, noticed the sharpened side was aimed the wrong direction, and quickly twisted it around.

Maybe they didn't notice.

"Ya probably want to fold yer thumb over yer fingers like a fist. It'll give ya more control."

So much for them not noticing.

A heavyset man elbowed the thinner fellow who'd offered the advice. "Shut up, Jeb," he said in a stage whisper. "You'll scare her."

"I'm helpin' by tellin' her how to hold her knife. The way she's got it now she'll prob'ly drop the thing before it can do any damage."

Well, if he was willing to teach, she was willing to learn. Penelope corrected her grip on the knife and slowly rose to her feet. The blanket started to slip off her shoulders. Her heart pounded. She dropped the knife in order to grab the edges of the blanket and draw them closed beneath her chin. None of the men lunged at her. They kept their distance, waiting patiently for her to bend down and reclaim her knife before anyone said anything.

"We're not going to hurt you."

She jerked her gaze to the left, toward the only beardless man of the group. It was *him*.

He took one slow step closer, separating himself from the others. "We met yesterday. Do you remember me?"

Remember him? She'd been clinging to the hope of him for the last twelve hours.

His dark brown eyes latched onto hers. Calm. Steady. Kind. "I had the dog."

"I remember."

He took another step, hands outstretched. She glanced at his hip. No gun—that she could see. He might have one stuck in his waistband. Or a knife in his boot. A man who participated in shootouts wouldn't run around unarmed, would he?

She pressed her back against the tree and shifted her knife to point at his chest. "That's close enough."

He stopped. "I'm a Texas Ranger, ma'am. Company B, Frontier Battalion. Name's Titus Kingsley. The fellas with me are hands from the Diamond D Ranch, about a couple miles west of here. Rowdy found you," he said, turning to point at a short, thin man wearing a misbuttoned shirt. "He fetched the rest of us. We just want to help you."

He really *was* a Ranger?

Penelope fought the urge to relax her guard. If Madame LaBelle had taught her one thing, it was that people were not always what they seemed.

She lifted her chin. "Where's your badge?"

He wore a blue shirt and suspenders with brown trousers, but no star, tin or otherwise, glistened in the early morning light.

Mr. Kingsley's eyes lit with respect, as if he viewed her suspicions as a sign of intelligence, not paranoia. A nice change.

Most men of her acquaintance grew testy when a woman didn't automatically accept their word as law.

"The state doesn't give us badges." He straightened his posture and slowly lowered his hands. "Some Rangers opt to make their own, but I haven't seen the need."

"How am I to know you're telling me the truth, then?"

He might have a handsome visage and a friendly air about him, but a woman surrounded by seven men had few advantages, and she intended to hold on to the one she had for as long as possible.

"I carry papers." His right hand moved toward his waist. "A Warrant of Authority and Descriptive List. I'll show you, if you want." His hand hovered above his trouser pocket as his eyes asked for permission.

Penelope nodded.

He extracted a sheet of paper folded into a square and held it out to her. Keeping the knife secured in her right hand, she reached out with her left. The moment her fingers closed on the edge of the paper, she realized exactly how little control she actually wielded. Mr. Kingsley stood at least half a foot taller than her medium height. His shoulders were broad, his chest and arms well-muscled. And his movements were so smooth and self-assured that she had no doubt he could disarm her in a heartbeat should he make the attempt. But he didn't. He handed over his credentials and stepped back, giving her space to examine them without feeling trapped.

It took some finagling to unfold the paper while keeping half an eye on the scraggly bunch who watched her with rapt fascination. Thankfully, there was no leering among the group, despite her lack of proper attire. Just heavy curiosity with a bit of pity thrown in. She still didn't enjoy being the focal point of so much scrutiny, though. Even if the fear she felt for her safety was beginning to subside.

Once she managed to get the paper open, she scanned the contents to verify the Ranger's story. The preprinted form contained pertinent information scribed by hand into lined blanks.

WARRANT OF AUTHORITY AND DESCRIPTIVE LIST

The bearer is a member of Company B Frontier Battalion.
Name: Titus Kingsley
Rank: Private
Age: 23 years Height: 5 ft 11½ inches
Color of hair: Brown Color of Complexion: Light
Where born Fairfield, Texas Occupation: Rancher
Enlisted when October 15, 1888 Enlisted where Austin, TX
Enlisted by Sam McMurray

This Descriptive List, for identification, will be kept in possession of the Ranger to whom it refers and will be exhibited as a warrant of his authority as such, when called upon, and must be surrendered to his company commander when discharged.

The description certainly fit the man before her, but it hardly did him justice. Nowhere on the paper did it mention his competent demeanor, his kind eyes, or his soothing voice. It didn't even mention his thick mustache or the small cleft in his chin. It did grant him a Ranger's authority, however. An authority she no longer had reason to doubt.

Penelope refolded the paper and held it out to him. Only twenty-three when he'd enlisted four years ago. What would compel such a young man to enlist in the Frontier Battalion? Most men of that age were busy working the family farm, settling down with a young wife, or sowing wild oats. And wouldn't an elite peacekeeping force like the Rangers be difficult to join? They must've sensed a powerful potential in Mr. Kingsley to award him a place in their ranks.

As he reclaimed the credentials, his gaze met hers. Her breath caught. Powerful potential, indeed. One that caused her pulse to flutter.

For heaven's sake, Pen. Just because he's protective and in possession of enough honor not to take advantage of a woman in less than favorable circumstances doesn't mean there's potential in the air. Certainly not of the romantic variety.

Nevertheless, she lowered her knife and slipped it inside the blanket and into the petticoat strap where she'd secured it before. If Mr. Kingsley and his merry band of elderly cowboys intended her harm, it would have befallen her by now.

"Are you injured?" The Ranger's gaze traveled over her form as if searching for the answer himself.

All at once, she was hit by the realization of what she must look like to him. Completely unkempt. Covered in dirt and leaves. A rat's nest for hair. Wrapped in a mud-brown blanket that undoubtedly carried streaks of actual mud. Had she truly considered potential for a romantic connection blooming between them? Potential for her delivery to the closest asylum was more likely.

Swallowing a sigh, she shook her head. "Just some scrapes and bruises. Nothing that won't heal."

His jaw tightened. "Who did this to you?"

Penelope's stomach squeezed. She'd promised Mr. Hunt to disappear. To never bother the troupe again. And that's what she wanted. To make a fresh start somewhere and leave all thought of Narcissa LaBelle behind. Surely, she could find a job somewhere. A maid at a hotel or maybe a clerk in a shop. A lack of references would matter less out here than it did in Chicago. Of course, she had no money. Or clothes. Or even shoes.

"It doesn't matter," she finally answered. "I can't go back. Is there a church nearby? Someplace where I might acquire some cast-off clothing?"

"Closest church is in Glen Rose," one of the older gentlemen offered. "But that's at least five miles from here."

"And I don't 'spect they keep clothes for womenfolk hangin' in the pantry." A grim-looking fellow leaning on a walking stick offered that disheartening piece of information. "Leastwise, I never seen any."

Penelope wasn't ready to give up, though. God had seen her through the darkest night of her life. He'd see her through the realities of the day, as well. "Perhaps the minister's wife would be willing to loan—"

"Preacher's a young whippersnapper who ain't caught himself a filly yet," one of the heavier men reported. "I doubt he'll be of much help."

A debate arose among the grizzled gallery about preachers and poor boxes and what might be available where until Mr. Kingsley let out a sharp whistle. The men fell quiet.

"We can worry about finding clothes for her later."

Mr. Kingsley slipped his arm through one suspender strap and left the elastic to fall to his waist. What was he doing?

"She's been out here all night. She's shivering, and she's got no shoes."

He'd noticed her shivering?

"Angus, you and Coy look for a pair of strong branches. We'll use her blanket to rig a litter to carry her back to the ranch."

She was *not* giving up her blanket and leaving herself exposed in front of seven strange men. "I'm perfectly capable of walking." Good heavens, all that covered her was a petticoat, a camisole, and Narcissa's horrible corset that exposed more than it hid.

Mr. Kingsley turned to face her as he slid his second arm free of the suspenders. He arched a brow at her. "If we were in the middle of a manicured lawn or had access to a hard-packed path, I'd agree with you. But the terrain out here is filled with rocks, thorns, and rattlesnakes. You won't make it twenty yards before your feet are cut and bleeding. Unless you want to climb on my back, a litter is the best plan."

Heat scalded her cheeks at the thought of him carrying her in such an exposing fashion. "But I can't . . ." She stepped closer to him and dropped her voice to a whisper. "Please, I have to keep this blanket. I'm not . . . properly dressed."

His gaze softened in sympathy. "I know," he whispered back. "That's why I'm making a trade."

"A trade?"

He took off his hat, turned it upside down, and set it on the ground, brim-side up. Then he unbuttoned the top few buttons on his shirt, yanked the tails from the waistband of his trousers, and tugged the garment over his head.

Thankfully he wore a beige undershirt, but she still dropped her eyes. With as much as she hated men staring upon her person, she'd not be a woman who imposed her attention on a man. Especially one trying to lend her aid.

"Here," he said, handing her his shirt. "You can use the tree as a screen. None of us will bother you." His eyes met hers, honor glowing in their depths. "You have my word."

She believed him.

Penelope reached between the edges of the blanket to accept his gift. "Thank you."

This would be much more practical than trying to keep a blanket wrapped around her, but she still wasn't enamored by the prospect of stretching out on a litter carried by men she didn't know. Surrendering all control. Having them towering over her. Surely there was another way.

Mr. Kingsley finagled his suspenders back onto his shoulders and had just bent to retrieve his hat when an idea leapt to her mind.

"What if we make bandages from the blanket?" she blurted.

He straightened, his brow furrowing. "Are you bleeding?" He craned his neck to examine her from another angle. "I thought you said you weren't seriously injured."

"I'm not. But bandages aren't only used to slow bleeding. They are also used to protect wounds from encountering further harm. We could fold a thick pad to serve as a sole of sorts, then wrap strips around my feet to hold it in place. It wouldn't hold up for a long distance, but surely it would suffice for thirty or forty minutes."

He rubbed a hand over his face, obviously not too keen on giving up his original plan, but then he shrugged. "They're your feet, I suppose. If you'd rather walk around on bandages, that's your prerogative. Just watch where you step. It's easy to spot cacti, but greenbrier thorns will sneak up on you. A few strips of wool won't keep them from gouging your instep."

"I'll be careful. I promise."

He fit his hat to his head, the brim coming down to shade his eyes. Was he angry with her? No. He probably just wanted to make it clear that he wasn't responsible for any harm that might befall her should she make her way on foot.

"Come on, fellas. Let's give the lady some privacy." Like a sheepdog herding two-legged woolly creatures, Mr. Kingsley spread his arms wide and ushered his aged companions away from the tree.

Doing her best to avoid stepping on acorns and twigs, she picked her way around the tree to a low-hanging branch. After taking a quick peek to ensure no male eyes were aimed her direction, she unwrapped her blanket and hung it up on the branch as if it were a clothesline. The cool morning air brought chill bumps out on her arms and urged her to hurry. She tended to some pressing private business, then slipped the Ranger's shirt over her head.

Warmth immediately engulfed her. His warmth. She wrapped her arms around herself and held on for a long minute, giving the heat a chance to penetrate her skin. Strange how slipping on his shirt not only made her feel warm but safe.

8

"What do you think happened to her?" Ike asked the question in a hushed tone as the group moseyed over to the outlying stand of trees.

Titus braced a hand on the nearest tree trunk and leaned his weight against it. "Can't know for sure unless she tells me."

It bothered him that she hadn't. Did embarrassment keep her silent? Misplaced loyalty to the perpetrator? Or was she involved in something larger, something she felt compelled to hide from a man of the law?

Or maybe she was just a scared young woman who'd survived a terrible ordeal and didn't feel like talking to a gaggle of strange men. Couldn't really blame her for that.

"Best I can figure, someone dragged her out here and tied her to that tree," Dusty said as he reached for a handkerchief and raised it to his nose to catch the coming sneeze.

Titus couldn't argue with the obvious, so he nodded, but he kept the rest of his thoughts to himself. Who would do such a thing to a young woman? And why had they brought her out here in nothing but her underclothes? Her eyes didn't have the soul-shattered look he'd encountered in women who'd suffered defilement, so it was unlikely she'd been violated, thank God. Yet that made her situation all the more curious. And disturbing.

"I found some hoofprints." Jeb hobbled up to where Coy, Angus, Ike, and Titus had gathered. "You gonna track down the varmint that done this?" He flicked the end of his walking stick against the outer edge of Titus's boot.

Titus straightened away from the tree. "Not today. Right now, my duty is to the girl. We'll get her back to the Diamond D, let Doc tend to those cuts and scrapes she mentioned, then get her a warm bath and some clean clothes. Can't do much else at the moment. Without a description of her attacker, I have no way of identifying him." He scratched his chin. "Unless there's something distinctive in those markings you found."

Jeb scowled. "Nope. Just a direction." He raised his walking stick and pointed the end southeast. "That way."

Made sense. When Titus had run into her yesterday, it had been south of here. She'd been so lively and joyful when they'd crossed paths. What had happened to cause such a drastic turn in her circumstances?

"The snake that done this oughta be horsewhipped. You don't treat womenfolk this way. I don't care what they done. And this one don't look like she'd hurt a fly. Even with that man-sized knife she's got tucked away."

Man-sized knife. Jeb might be a grumpy old goat, but his observation skills were on point. The knife the girl had brandished had been too large and unwieldy for a woman. Add to that she clearly had no experience with such weaponry, and the only logical conclusion was that it belonged to someone else. Her attacker? But if she'd had his knife, why hadn't she used it to fend him off? Had she really been tied up, or was this some elaborate ruse?

Titus mentally rolled his eyes. His cynicism was getting

out of hand. What could she possibly have to gain from pretending to be tied up in the middle of nowhere? There was no one to blackmail or extort. If Rowdy hadn't wandered this direction—a happenstance impossible to predict since the fellow's strolls were notoriously erratic—no one would have even found her. Still, the knife was a clue. The rope had been sliced by someone. He'd seen the sheared edges. Titus would have to try to take a closer look at the knife later, see if he could learn anything about the man who'd owned it.

Finding the scoundrel who'd lashed this young woman to a tree and left her to die would be basically impossible without her cooperation, but a good Ranger gathered all available clues. Even ones with no immediate significance. Criminals rarely committed only one crime, so even if he couldn't tie the man to this assault, he might be able to tie him to other misdeeds if the evidence came together in the right way at the right time.

"What's Rowdy doin'?" Jeb jerked his chin toward a bent-over figure a couple of trees away.

Ike glanced behind him, then smiled. "Adding to his collection, I suppose."

Apparently, delivering help to the girl he'd found had ended Rowdy's interest in the matter. Ignoring the others, he ambled around the base of the trees, kicking at items until he found something that intrigued him. He'd stoop for a closer look, then hunker down if he liked what he saw. He tossed most of the debris aside, but every once in a while, a shiny rock or a particularly well-rounded acorn would catch his attention. He'd stuff the treasure in his pocket, then continue his search. Titus had no idea what made one rock a treasure and another trash, but the system made sense to Rowdy. He'd been known to walk off with buttons, pocket watches, pen nibs, and coins. He even absconded with a glass lens from Doc's spectacles one time. The shinier the object, the more likely it was to be collected. The rest of the men had taken to keeping their valuables close at hand, for once Rowdy "collected" something, it was never seen again.

"Uh, Titus?" Angus jabbed his chin in the direction of the girl's tree.

Titus pivoted slowly.

All coherent thought fled his brain save one unmistakable observation—his shirt had never looked that good when *he* was the one wearing it. The collar loosely circled her neck while the tail hung well past her waist, leaving the white ruffles of her petticoat to billow out in a bell shape from above her knees down to her ankles. The sleeves hung past her fingertips yet she looked far from childlike. The places where the fabric pulled snug made it impossible to mistake her for anything other than a woman.

Do something besides stare at her, you dolt.

Seeing the blanket draped over her right arm, Titus hurried forward to collect it from her.

"Thank you for the shirt," she said softly as she handed over her previous covering. A rosy glow touched her cheeks as her dark lashes lowered. When they lifted and allowed her eyes to meet his, something shifted in Titus's chest. Something he very much feared was his immunity to beautiful women unmooring and floating away.

"Glad to help."

What was wrong with him? She was covered in dirt and leaves, for Pete's sake. Not exactly the belle of the ball. Yet a man would have to be blind not to see the inherent loveliness beneath the grimy debris. Titus was the opposite of blind. The Rangers had trained him to observe everything, making it impossible to miss the way the fabric of his shirt tugged tightly across her chest and hips. Or the fact that she'd removed all the pins from her hair. The black tresses were still a mess, but instead of sitting lopsided atop her head like a nest built by a drunken mockingbird, her hair fell over her shoulders in an untamed cascade.

Her stomach let out a growl that broke him out of his trance. She pressed a hand to her belly as the pink in her cheeks deepened to apple red.

Titus grinned. "We better get you some breakfast."

She laughed, and her gray eyes danced, reminding him of the carefree girl he'd met yesterday. "I'll try not to eat you out of house and home."

"The Diamond D feeds a crew of seven every day. You could eat for a month and not put a dent in their stores."

"I don't plan to impose on you that long, I promise."

A pang of disappointment ricocheted inside his chest at her vow. Which was ridiculous. It wasn't like he was going to be around the Diamond D after today anyway. Her staying or leaving had no bearing on him.

"As soon as I find employment, I'll be out of your hair."

"It's not my hair that matters," Titus said, his voice a little sharper than it should have been. "I'm riding back to Ranger headquarters today. My grandfather, Enoch Kingsley, runs the Diamond D. Everyone calls him Doc on account of his being a retired physician. He'll be your host." He tipped his head toward the graybeards behind him. "Him and the rest of the geezer gang."

Her shoulders drooped slightly. "Oh."

"They're good men. Godly men. Every one of 'em. They have more than their fair share of quirks and oddities, but you'll be safe with them. Once you've recovered, they'll take you wherever you need to go."

He'd make sure of it. Leave some money for her. Enough to buy her a dress and a train ticket if she had family somewhere to return to.

Her stomach rumbled again, his cue to quit jawin' and get back to work. Lifting the blanket between them, he fingered his hat brim in a salute. "We'll get your strips torn and fit you with poor man's moccasins in a jiffy, ma'am."

Before those pale gray eyes of hers could mesmerize him further, Titus jogged back to where the others waited. Waited with smirks and knowing glances. Thankfully, none of them gave voice to any of their teasing thoughts—probably out of respect for the woman standing less than a stone's throw away—but more than one elbow knocked against his ribs as he handed them the edges of the blanket, then pulled out his knife.

Ignoring the silent ribbing and the heat crawling up the back of his neck, Titus began issuing orders. "Ike, why don't you and Dusty head on back to the ranch and let Doc know to expect company?"

"Sure thing, Titus."

Ike nodded, but instead of taking off down the path as expected, the affable fellow walked over to the woman, pulled off his hat, and held it over his heart as if he were pledging fealty to a medieval princess. Dusty traipsed behind his partner and followed his example.

"I just wanted to say how very sorry I am, miss, that you underwent such misfortune," Ike said. "And I want you to know that as long as you are at the Diamond D, I'll make it my personal duty to see that nothing so shameful happens to you again."

By gum. He *was* pledging fealty.

"That goes for me, too, ma'am." Dusty dipped his chin. "You ever need anything, you just call on old Dusty."

Before Titus knew what was happening, each of the other drovers marched forward and made similar promises. Even Rowdy stopped his acorn hunt long enough to touch the lady's shoulder. When she turned her gaze upon him, he crossed his right arm over his chest in a show of loyalty.

Besotted fools. They'd ribbed him for falling temporarily under her spell, but they were the smitten ones. Even Jeb managed to sound less surly than usual when he mumbled a few words to the girl.

Titus stood apart, determined not to soften. He'd do his duty, get the girl to safety, and see to her well-being, but he'd not follow in his brother's footsteps and let a pretty face and winsome figure steal his good sense.

Yet as the others made their vows, the girl was the one who softened. Tears welled in her eyes, making them shimmer like twin ponds bathed in summer moonlight.

"You all are so kind. I'm . . . overwhelmed." Her voice caught, and she wiped at her eyes. "Thank you." She stepped forward and touched the wrangler's arm. "Dusty." Then she turned to the thin man beside him. "And . . . ?"

"Ike, miss."

"Ike." She repeated the name in a way that gave the impression she was committing it to memory.

She made her rounds through all the drovers, thanking each man by name. Rowdy had wandered off, but she didn't let that stop her. She picked her way over to where he had squatted down to examine something near a tangle of exposed tree roots. She bent forward, bracing her hands on her knees.

"And Rowdy."

He paused long enough to look up at her.

"Thank *you* most of all. If it weren't for you, I'd still be alone in a strange place with no idea how to survive on my own." She bent closer to him and then did the oddest thing.

She kissed the top of Rowdy's head.

Rowdy. A man most people thought was crazier than a loon. She'd kissed him as if he were her knight in shining armor.

No one could fake that level of good-heartedness. Could they?

Rowdy's ears turned bright red, and he raised a hand to rub the spot her lips had touched before snatching his hat from where it dangled down his back and fit it back onto his head.

To make sure she didn't kiss him again? Or to keep the feeling of that kiss from escaping into the air?

Titus dug his heel into the ground. Keeping a kiss from escaping into the air? *Really, Kingsley? That's where your mind went?* He needed to turn this girl over to Doc and get out of range before she turned his brain to complete mush.

The gentle tinkle of her laughter over Rowdy's antics didn't help matters any, nor did the smile beaming across her face as she pivoted back to the main group.

She held out her petticoats as if they were a fine silk skirt and curtseyed to the old cowhands huddled around her. "I'm Penelope Snow, and I'm honored to make the acquaintance of such a fine group of gentlemen."

Titus stumbled back a step.

Her name was *Penelope*?

He gave his head a small shake, trying to dispel the eerie sense of destiny that name instilled. It was just coincidence. It didn't mean anything.

Nevertheless, the words his father spoke to him on the day he joined the Rangers rang loud in his memory.

"If you do this, son, it will change things. It's a noble calling to fight for justice, but it will make it harder to find a woman to share your life. A woman who will wait at home while you serve the law. A woman whose loyalty never wavers in your absence and whose spirit won't grow embittered when work calls you away again and again. A woman like Odysseus's Penelope. Faithful, clever, and brave. If you are to be a warrior, that is the type of wife you should seek. Find a Penelope, son, and never let her go."

9

Penelope had never felt more like a princess than she did in the moments leading up to their departure. Heaven knew she looked more like a scullery maid who'd taken a tumble down a mountainside than royalty, but that didn't seem to make a bit of difference to the cowboys catering to her every need.

Ike and Dusty set off at a trot to announce her impending arrival like heralds of old. Angus and Coy dragged over a log and steadied it as she sat down. Jeb folded blanket strips into thick pads while Titus finished tearing apart the final wrappings. And Rowdy . . . well, he provided entertainment as she tried to make sense of his actions. His search consumed him, yet the items that made it into his pocket didn't fit any particular pattern that she could discern. They didn't seem to generate much excitement on his end either until he found something at the base of the tree where she'd been tied amid the remains of the rope that had bound her. His eyes lit, and his gaze immediately shifted to her.

What had he found? An oversized acorn? A hollowed-out bird's egg? Whatever it was, it had him excited. She smiled at him, sharing the delight of his discovery even though she had no idea what it entailed. It pleased him, and that was enough to please her as well. He shoved his hand into his pocket, then pulled out enough other treasures to fill his palm. He pushed the items around with a finger, his brow knitted, until he pounced on the one he wanted. Clutching it in his opposite fist, he returned the rest of the bounty to his pocket, then marched up to her. He extended his left hand and peeled back his fingers to reveal a round gray rock crossed by a glittery band of quartz.

"For me?"

Rowdy nodded.

Moisture pooled in Penelope's eyes. Foolish, really. But she couldn't seem to stop the sentimental spillage. Outside of Edith's pragmatic affection, she'd never been treated with such kindness and acceptance as she had been by this ragtag bunch of cowboys. Miss Wyndham might have allowed her to be educated alongside the girls whose families paid for their education, but Penelope had never been allowed to forget that she lived on charity. While the other girls chatted and played, she scrubbed classroom floors and scoured kitchen pots. She took satisfaction in her work, whether at the Wyndham School for Girls or in Madame LaBelle's employ. But it wore on a person's soul not to have a place where her value lay in herself alone instead of in her work. A place rich in the love of family or friends, where dry reservoirs could be refilled and flagging spirits restored.

How dry her well must be if the gift of a rock brought her to tears.

"Thank you," she said, stretching her smile extra wide in an effort not to confuse the dear man with her watery eyes. "It's lovely."

"It's a rock."

Penelope twisted away from Rowdy to find Jeb and Titus standing in front of her, strips of blanket held in their hands. Jeb's look of consternation nearly made her chuckle aloud.

"It's not a rock," she countered, turning to wink at Rowdy. "It's a gift of friendship. A treasure."

Rowdy shot Jeb such a look of triumph that several muffled guffaws rumbled in the chests of the men around her. Before Jeb could grow too cross, Penelope opened her arms wide to encompass all the cowboys.

"Just like the gift of this bench and the fine new shoes you made for me."

The slashing line of Jeb's left brow arched upward in disbelief. "No wonder you took a shine to Rowdy's rock," he muttered under his breath as he passed his folded fabric over to Titus. "You're as crazy as he is." He turned his back with a wave of his hand and picked up his walking stick from where he'd left it resting against one of the nearby trees. "I'm gonna head back. Y'all don't need me slowin' you down once you get the gal's new shoes figured out." Shaking his head, he started muttering again. "New shoes, my eye. Strips of nonsense is what they are. I better tell Doc to get a footbath ready. Fool woman is gonna need it."

How could someone manage to be sour and sweet at the same time? Penelope pressed her lips together to keep from grinning. What a character. Jeb might put up a gruff front, but only a tender heart would think about preparing footbaths for foolish women.

She glanced up at Titus to see what the Ranger made of all the muttering. She expected to find eyes filled with exasperation or maybe amusement, but what she found instead was compassion as he tipped his head and shot a glance at Coy. The big man nodded and left his end of the log in order to saunter after the departing cowboy.

"Hold up, Jeb. I'll come with ya. I need to whip up some more flapjacks for our guest."

"Suit yerself." Jeb exhaled a heavy sigh as if he were being put out by having company, but he slowed down enough to let Coy catch up in a handful of steps.

"You think his leg is botherin' him?" Angus asked in a low voice.

Titus nodded. "He's leanin' pretty heavy on that walking stick."

Guilt squeezed Penelope's chest.

"He ain't used to walkin' on it this much." Angus pushed his hat high on his forehead as he watched Jeb and Coy amble out of the grove. "I'll ask Doc to make him a cold compress after we get the gal settled."

"Good idea." Titus turned his attention back to Penelope as he bent down on one knee in front of her. "Let's get you wrapped up, shall we?" He smiled, but it felt different from their earlier interaction. Not quite as warm. More . . . professional.

Penelope dropped her chin to her chest as she lifted her foot. "I hope he'll be all right. I would hate to be responsible for causing him pain."

"Shoot, you ain't responsible for his pain, Miss Penny." Angus sat beside her on the log, quaking her seat in the process. "A shattered ankle from bronc bustin' holds that honor."

Her leg wobbled in the air while the log settled, creating a challenge for Titus to catch it. Once his hand closed around her heel, he caught her eye. Laughter lit his gaze, sparking the warmth she'd been missing. She shared a smile with him as Angus continued his monologue.

"No one makes that stubborn cuss do anything he don't want to do. He tromped out here of his own free will, and he'll tromp back the same way. Can hardly blame him. This here's the most excitement we've seen at the Diamond D in ages. What with Titus showing up all unexpected-like yesterday and then you poppin' up this mornin'. There's a reason all of us traipsed out here to see what Rowdy found. We may be old, but we love an adventure. Gets the blood pumpin'. Reminds a man he's still got some livin' left to do."

As Angus chattered on, Titus got to work. His firm yet gentle touch had an odd effect on her pulse. His ministration felt intimate somehow, even if it was purely practical in nature. Which was silly because there was nothing the slightest bit romantic about a filthy, stinky foot that had been in the same ragged stockings for the last twenty-four hours. Titus confirmed that notion when he lifted her foot and frowned.

"Sorry," she murmured as she instinctively pulled her leg back. "You don't have to . . . I'm sure I can manage. . . ."

His grip tightened, refusing her retreat. "Your feet are already pretty battered. You sure you don't want me to carry you?"

"I'm sure." She set her jaw. Her short-lived flight last night might have left her soles bruised and scraped, but they'd get the job done. "I'm not some pampered princess, unable to withstand a little adversity, Mr. Kingsley. In fact, I'm fully capable of wrapping my own feet. So if you'll be so kind as to hand over the padding, I'll get to work."

She held out her palm.

He ignored it.

"Unprickle your pride, Miss Snow. I was just trying to keep you from suffering more harm than you already have." He jammed a pad against the bottom of her foot, folded the edges up over her toes and heel, then started wrapping. "If you want to walk, that's no skin off my nose."

In truth, he was doing a much better job than she could have managed on her own. She should be grateful, not . . . prickly.

"I'm sorry." The tension stiffening her spine released its grip. "I really do appreciate your help. I suppose I panicked a bit. The last time a man carried me, I ended up slung over a horse and tied to a tree."

Titus slowed his work and glanced up. "I hadn't thought of that."

The simple admission cleared the air between them as nothing else could. Penelope relaxed, and the Ranger turned back to his work, his touch slightly gentler than before. Angus, bless him, took it upon himself to fill the silence, and his idle chatter successfully swept away the last of the tension, leaving the atmosphere free of awkwardness by the time her shoeing was complete.

Titus offered her a hand up, then turned his attention toward the path they would take. "Follow behind me," he said as he headed out. "I'll scout the easiest terrain."

"If you need a hand at any point," Angus added, "just grab my arm. I'll keep it within reach."

"Thank you." The old man really was a dear.

And the younger one? Well, *dear* didn't seem the proper descriptor. Titus Kingsley possessed far too commanding a presence. Yet his thoughtfulness hinted at a tender heart. Even now, he brushed rocks and acorns out of her path with a sideways swipe of his boot.

She glanced behind, intending to urge Rowdy to join them, but the little man had disappeared.

"Don't worry," Angus said with a wave of his hand. "He'll show up when it's time to eat. Always does."

Trusting the man to know his friend's habits, Penelope set off in the Ranger's wake. Despite the dozen or more layers of padding buffering her feet, she still felt every bump and prod of the ground. Her bruises spread, and the wrappings shifted, but she soldiered on, determined to prove her hardiness.

Until a thorn jabbed between her toes.

She yelped and jerked her foot up so quickly she nearly

toppled. Angus steadied her, and Titus rushed back to her side. Holding on to Angus with one hand, she yanked the offending thorn free. The brown twig looked relatively innocuous. Save for the pairs of three-inch thorns shooting out in different directions along its length. Good heavens! If that had pierced her instep, it could have punctured her entire foot.

Titus took it from her. "Mesquite thorn. I missed it." Self-recrimination seeped from his voice in tight, angry drops. "Where did it get you?" He crouched down in front of her and reached for her foot.

She pulled it away from him, not wanting him to undo the wrappings. If there was any blood, it would be better to keep the bandages in place. "It just nicked my toes. I'm fine." She forced a smile even though her foot throbbed. "God was gracious. It passed between my first and second toes, doing very little damage. It could have been worse."

Titus stood and hurled the ugly barb into the brush with enough strength to fell any of the small trees around them. Scraggly, twisted little bush trees hiding nasty thorns.

"I'm carrying you." The Ranger pivoted toward her, his expression so dark, Penelope backed up a step and tightened her grip on Angus's arm. "Once we clear the mesquites, I'll set you back down." He pointed to a spot about fifty yards ahead where the land flattened into a grassland free of trees. "You have my word."

Penelope held his gaze for a long moment. Perhaps it was foolish to believe she could read honor in such dark, angry eyes, but she did, and her alarm faded. She'd been hurt on his watch. That's what spurred his high-handed demand. He wanted to protect her, not supplant his will over hers.

"All right. Just until we clear the thorn bushes."

He didn't give her time for second thoughts. One arm immediately wrapped around her back while the other caught her behind her knees. She barely had time to suck in a breath before he had her off the ground. She clutched his neck for balance and security, though within the first two steps she realized she had no chance of falling. His arms were far too strong. His chest too sturdy. His sense of duty far too pronounced. Exhaustion would take him to his knees before he let her tumble from his grasp.

Thankfully, exhaustion wasn't an issue. His long, powerful strides carried her away from the mesquites in a matter of minutes. And true to his word, he put her down as soon as the thorns were behind them, though his hands lingered at her waist to ensure her feet would indeed hold her upright.

"Thank you." She couldn't quite meet his eyes, not when he stood so close, his chest heaving slightly from his exertion, her hands feeling every breath as they slipped from around his neck.

"The, uh, ranch is just over that rise." He cleared his throat, then dropped his hands from around her waist and stepped away. "We'll be there soon."

He strode off without a backward glance, leaving Penelope's flustered heart throbbing as much as her sore foot when she moved to follow.

10

Titus scoured the ground in front of him for hazards as if he were an eagle scouting for prey. He couldn't afford another miss. That mesquite thorn could have impaled her foot if God's grace hadn't covered his failure.

The earth flattened as they neared the ranch, and the vegetation thinned. Titus refused to be lulled into inattention by the landscape's harmless façade. Snakes could slither out of the grass. Prairie dog holes could twist an ankle. Jagged rocks could—

"Ho, Titus!"

Dusty approached on horseback, leading Rex and a mount for Angus. Titus grinned, and the tightrope stretched across his shoulders finally found some slack. Leave it to a wrangler to problem solve with hooves instead of shoes.

"Thought you might wanna ride the rest of the way. Get the young lady off her feet."

"That I would, old man." Titus jogged forward and mounted Rex in one smooth motion.

Man, but it felt good to be in the saddle. Free to face the breeze and inhale the sky. Free to release his responsibility for Miss Snow's well-being. Sitting light in the saddle, he nudged

Rex into a trot and drew alongside the lady in his charge. He bent toward her and extended an arm. "Ma'am?"

She must have been starting to trust him at least a little, for she only hesitated a heartbeat or two before clasping his arm. Locking forearms with her, he solidified his hold, then pulled her up into his lap. The moment she pressed against him, all the distractions he'd so ruthlessly purged from his consciousness after carrying her out of the mesquite grove returned in a flood. Distractions he found nearly impossible to shove back in the bottle they'd escaped from now that the need for single-minded focus had become obsolete.

Memories of her arms wrapped around his neck. Her body nestled against his chest. Her narrow waist beneath his fingers.

Get it together, Kingsley. She's a job. Nothing more. Titus clenched his jaw as Miss Snow situated herself. He wrapped his arms around her—strictly for pragmatic purposes, couldn't have her slipping off the horse, after all—then nudged Rex into an easy lope that took them home in a matter of minutes. Angus and Dusty followed in his wake, though they turned off at the barn instead of following him to the back porch of the ranch house. Doc must've been keeping watch, for he swung the door open before Rex had fully halted.

"Bring her inside, Titus." Doc waved him forward as if worried his grandson might not be able to find the door. "I have tea steeping in the pot, and Coy's whipping up a new batch of flapjacks that should be ready in a few minutes."

Titus willed away the annoying instinct to keep Miss Snow in his arms and carry her across the threshold. The woman had made it clear she preferred to walk under her own power, and heaven knew it'd be unwise to revive all those disquieting sensations he'd experienced the last time he carried her. His equilibrium was out of kilter enough already.

So instead of prolonging his contact with her by dismounting together, he glued his rear to the saddle and lowered her to the ground with one arm. Doc rushed forward to meet her.

"Miss Snow? I'm Dr. Enoch Kingsley." He sketched a quick bow. "I understand you've endured a most trying ordeal." Taking her hand, he gently drew her toward the house. "I have a warm footbath with Epsom salts waiting for you along with soap and water for your hands and face. Ike is filling the tub upstairs, and Coy has extra kettles heating on the stove, so a full bath will be ready for you once you've eaten."

If the man flapped his gums any harder, he'd be in danger of taking flight. Titus ducked his head to hide his smile. It seemed none of the Diamond D men could resist stumbling over themselves to please her.

Miss Snow allowed Doc to lead her up the steps to the door, but she cast a wide-eyed glance over her shoulder as she went, searching out Titus's gaze and snatching something inside his chest in the process. His heart swelled at the notion of her seeking him out, looking to him for reassurance. As if she needed him. Trusted him. Preferred him.

Oh, for Pete's sake. She was surrounded by geriatric cowhands. Of course she would seek reassurance from the only man of the group *not* alive when the Alamo fell. It meant nothing.

He wouldn't let it mean anything. Titus gave her the nod she'd been seeking, then turned his attention to dismounting.

"Do you like your tea sweetened with honey?" Doc asked as he opened the door for her. "Ike has taken up beekeeping, and I've found that a cup of tea with honey does wonders for calming the nerves and fortifying the constitution."

Miss Snow finally smiled at him, and the effect was instantaneous. Doc's slightly stooped posture straightened, his ears reddened, and his normally intelligent eyes took on a decidedly bemused glaze behind his spectacles.

"Tea sounds heavenly, Dr. Kingsley. Thank you."

"Just call me Doc," he stammered as she moved past him into the kitchen.

Titus expected his grandfather to follow her inside, but the old man pivoted to face his grandson instead. "Come on in, boy. You hardly ate any breakfast yourself. Coy made enough for you, too."

"I'm going to tend to Rex first. I'll be in later." Hopefully, after Miss Snow was away from the table. The woman had an odd effect on his senses, and a Ranger couldn't afford to be anything other than clearheaded.

"Dusty will see to Rex," Doc countered. "I need you to do something for me."

"What?"

"Fetch a trunk from the attic. I kept a few of your grandma's things. Thought I'd hand them down to you one day if you ever had a little girl, but I think our guest has a more immediate need."

Titus's throat grew thick as he recalled the woman who always smelled of cookies and fresh-baked bread. Who'd sung hymns at full strength in church despite a dreadful lack of pitch.

"God told us to make a joyful noise, not a pretty song, Titus," she'd whispered to him one Sunday when she caught him cringing behind his hymnal. *"He hears the heart, not the voice. So make sure yours is in the right place."* He'd only been ten at the time, but he'd learned more about true worship in that one hushed conversation than he had in a dozen sermons. The woman had shaped him with love and wisdom. And if she were still alive, he had no doubt she'd take one look at Penelope Snow and give her the dress off her back.

"I'll take care of it."

"Thank you, son." Doc turned to walk through the door, then hesitated. "Bring it to my room," he said. "The poor girl will need rest after all she's been through, and that room is the quietest in the house."

Titus nodded, patted Rex on the neck, then made his way up the steps and into the house. He moved slowly, hoping to slip in unobserved. He had no doubt the Diamond D men would be tending to Miss Snow, but it wasn't their attention he hoped to dodge. It was hers. Something about those big gray eyes evoked a protective instinct in him that had proven difficult to ignore. That, combined with the residual guilt he felt over not seeing her home after their encounter yesterday, might tempt him to delay his departure. A happenstance he couldn't afford. Not if he hoped to earn the promotion to sergeant. He needed to demonstrate to Captain Bill that the Rangers came first. Besides, the men of Company B would never let him hear the end of it if they discovered a woman had kept him from his duty. Not after he'd gained a reputation for being immune to the charms of the fairer sex. The guys liked to joke that he was more likely to go soft over a dog than a woman. A claim he'd taken pride in. A claim that might no longer be true.

Especially when the woman in question was going soft over his dog.

Heedless of her own injuries, Penelope Snow knelt on the floor, head bent close to the dog, who, Titus was pleased to see, was awake and licking at the lady's face.

"Aren't you a good boy? So brave. So resilient." She rubbed his ears, then touched her forehead to his. "You're going to be fine. You'll see. Some time to heal. Some good food to fatten you up. Some people to love you. This little mishap won't hold you down. It might even be a blessing. The first day of a better life."

An odd tightness squeezed Titus's chest at her low, earnest voice, pitched solely at the dog, not intended to be heard by the others in the room.

Coy stood a few feet away ladling flapjack batter into a skillet. Doc clinked a spoon against the sides of a cup as he stirred honey into Miss Snow's tea. Neither seemed to be paying her any particular mind. But then Titus glanced at Jeb. The old bronc buster sat at the table nursing a cup of coffee. His gaze followed the girl, and his face softened with an empathy Titus hadn't thought the fellow capable of achieving.

Apparently even crusty hearts were susceptible to young women in dire circumstances trying to convince themselves that hope still existed. That good could come from bad, and that they weren't utterly alone in the world. For as much as her words had been murmured to encourage an injured coonhound, Titus couldn't help but recognize how well they fit her own situation.

It took impressive strength of character to face what she had and maintain an optimistic spirit. Heaven knew he'd not managed half so well after losing his brother. Anger had driven him. Anger at Tate for not seeing through Nora's deception. Anger at Nora and her scheming partner who'd left Tate to die after stealing his life savings at gunpoint. Anger at God for allowing it to happen. It had taken Titus three months to track his brother's killers and deliver them to the law. He'd thought finding justice would bring him peace, but it hadn't. What it *had* brought him was an open door to working with the Rangers, a position that offered him purpose and direction. Yet peace continued to elude him. Even after four years, when his anger had cooled and only a few dregs of bitterness lingered behind.

"Come, my dear," Doc said as he set Miss Snow's tea on the table and reached for her arm to help her up. "Let's get those wrappings off, shall we? I have a footbath all set up for you."

Miss Snow rose from the floor and smiled at Titus's grandfather. "Thank you. You're all so kind."

"I got some flapjacks ready." Coy plopped a plate on the table next to her tea along with a fork and knife.

Her stomach growled loud enough to echo in the rafters. Titus bit back a smile and slipped out of the kitchen. She was in good hands. Doc would tend her bruises and scrapes. Coy would fill her belly. The only other thing she needed was something decent to wear. His assignment.

It took a mere handful of minutes to fetch the trunk from the attic and cart it to Doc's room. Duty fulfilled, Titus headed downstairs but gave the kitchen a wide berth. No more delays. No more distractions. He was a Ranger, not a nursemaid. Doc and the others would take care of the girl.

He'd hoped to take a closer look at that knife of hers, but it hadn't made an appearance. Probably wouldn't. It was the only weapon she possessed in a strange place surrounded by strange men. If he were in her shoes, he'd keep the blade close at hand for a while, too.

Titus strode to his room, grabbed a spare shirt from his saddlebag, then packed his few belongings. He slipped his arms into the black vest that was as close to a uniform as the Texas Rangers were likely to get and looped a black string tie at his neck. He pulled a few greenbacks from his billfold and laid them on the dresser and placed a scribbled note on top. *For the girl.*

He dawdled in his room until conversation in the kitchen dwindled, indicating that breakfast had concluded. Lurking in the doorway of his room, Titus listened for an all-clear signal. Ike offered to take the kettles upstairs and warm the bathwater. Doc fussed at him about not splashing the nightgown he'd laid out for Miss Snow, then urged her to make use of the jar of salve he'd left on the cabinet top in the washroom. Footsteps on the stairs urged Titus to peek down the hall.

"You'll have the entire second floor to yourself today, Miss Snow," Doc assured her from the base of the stairs as she followed Ike to the second floor. "No one will disturb you. The bedroom at the end of the hall is mine. There's a trunk full of my late wife's things in there. Help yourself to anything you find. Then get some sleep. As much as you can. Doctor's orders."

Once Miss Snow was no longer visible, Titus stepped into the hall and met his grandfather when he turned away from the stairs. "I'm heading out."

Doc eyed him with an arched brow. "You're not going to say good-bye?"

Titus shrugged. "No time. I'm already late getting back to headquarters."

The old man's eyes glittered behind his spectacles. "We'll see she's taken care of."

"I know. Wouldn't leave her here otherwise."

Doc slapped Titus's shoulder. "Well, come see us again when you can. Check in on Lucky."

"Lucky?"

Doc grinned. "Your dog. Miss Snow was talking about how both she and the mutt were lucky to be looked after by kind-hearted strangers. Jeb overheard and decided to dub the critter Lucky. Said a dog staying under a man's roof needed a name."

Titus chuckled softly. "Can't argue with that. Sounds like you're gonna have another Diamond D resident if Lucky hangs around after he mends."

"He'll be welcome. As will Miss Snow." Doc's expression turned sentimental as his gaze traveled up the staircase. "She reminds me a bit of your grandma when we first met, with her dark hair and laughing eyes." His jaw tightened as he turned back to Titus. "The girl doesn't have any family. Least none she'd allow me to telegraph with her whereabouts. As far as I can tell, she's got no one lookin' out for her." Doc eyed Titus, the pain of experience gleaming in his eyes. "The world can be a dangerous place for a young woman on her own. I'm thinkin' we might need a family meeting to take a vote about lettin' her stay. Should she wish it."

Didn't take a fortune teller to predict how *that* vote would go. "Just promise me you'll be careful, Grandpa. All we really know about this girl is that she got herself tangled up in some kind of trouble. She might be involved with something nefarious that could put all of you in danger."

Doc squeezed his shoulder. "Your work with the Rangers has made you cynical, son."

"It's made me cautious. There's a difference."

"Either way, I think seven grown men with four centuries of combined life experience can handle one young lady, tangled in trouble or not. But should you feel the urge to stop by the ranch more regularly to check on us, I won't complain."

Doc gave him a wink and shuffled down to the parlor where he typically did his morning reading. He wasn't one to stand on the porch and wave good-bye. After losing Tate, he did his best to avoid farewells. Titus wasn't all that fond of them himself. In fact, he was happy to find the kitchen empty except for the dog when he stepped inside.

Coy had left him a couple of cold pancakes on a plate on the table. Titus picked up the top flapjack, folded it in half, then bit into it like a sandwich. As he chewed, he wandered over to the pallet by the stove and squatted down to rub the coonhound's black head. Lucky opened his eyes and whined slightly as if sensing Titus's imminent departure and lodging a protest.

"I'll be back," he said as he ruffled the dog's ears. "Then maybe you and I can go huntin' together. What do you think about that?"

Lucky struggled to stand until Titus urged him back down. "Easy, boy. There's plenty of time for huntin' later. Right now, you gotta focus on getting well. Hear me?"

Puppyish disappointment radiated from his dark eyes, but he didn't try to rise again.

Titus rubbed the dog's neck and head a final time. "Watch over them while I'm gone, all right?" He pushed to his feet. "I love these old goats."

Lucky's head bobbed as if in a nod, making Titus grin. He tore off a bit of his flapjack and fed it to the mutt before getting up. He stuffed the rest in his mouth, then grabbed the last flapjack from the plate and headed out.

He and Rex made good time, but it still took riding until nearly dusk to rendezvous with his battalion. After seeing to his horse, Titus headed to the officer's tent to make his report.

"Kingsley! Just the man I wanted to see." Captain Bill McDonald rose from his worktable and held out his hand.

Titus shook it, his chest expanding. Captain Bill didn't dole out handshakes on a regular basis.

"Good work on that robbery case. The folks of Meridian were mighty happy to see those Buchanan brothers behind bars." He leaned close. "Hoffman told me about the dog. He gonna pull through?"

"Looks like it. My grandfather's tendin' him."

Captain Bill nodded. "Good." He gestured for Titus to follow him over to his worktable and waved a hand over the papers spread across its surface. "I got another theft case for you. More complicated. Several small robberies scattered throughout the state, ones I suspect are connected."

Titus glanced at a list of names and cities, the last one being a Mr. Hubert Hathaway of Eulogy, Texas. A town not far from the Diamond D. "Money?"

"Jewelry. Men's jewelry. Stickpins, rings, watch fobs, cuff links, that sort of thing. Rather odd if you ask me. More money in women's jewels."

A second paper listed train schedules. A third itemized the

stolen items. A slender stack at the corner looked to be reports from town marshals. Probably included witness statements and investigator notes. "Sounds like an interesting case."

"It's yours."

Titus straightened and eyed his commanding officer. "Sir?"

"Solve this case, Kingsley, and I'll recommend you for sergeant."

"Thank you, sir." Heart thundering in his chest, Titus fought off the smile that begged for release and kept his tone modulated and controlled. "I won't let you down."

"Better not, son. There'll be a lot of eyes on you for this one. Several gents on the list have political ties to Austin. This could make your career. But it could also break it. Still want the job?"

Titus's mouth went dry, but he held his position. "Yes, sir."

Either God intended for him to be a Ranger, or he didn't. Seemed he was about to find out which path the good Lord had mapped out for him.

11

Penelope awoke with a start, jarred into wakefulness by a barb of dread insisting she had overslept. Madame LaBelle would not be happy if her morning tea was late. Penelope tossed off the covers and blinked into the dark as her feet hit the rug.

Rug? That wasn't right. Her spartan accommodations never included something as frivolous as a rug. She gripped the mattress edge as the happenings of the last day and a half splashed into her consciousness. This wasn't a hotel bed or her camp cot. She was in a ranch house, surrounded by kind old men. Men who'd rescued her. Fed her. Clothed her. Tended her wounds. Dear, sweet Doc had even given up his room to provide a quiet place for her to rest and recover. One she'd apparently needed more than she'd thought, for she'd obviously slept the entire day away along with at least half the night.

A swelling sense of gratitude pulled her from the bed and down onto her knees. Bowing until her forehead brushed the mattress, Penelope poured out her heart to the God who had kept her safe.

I've never felt such desperate fear or such abundant blessing. Lord, I am humbled by your goodness. I still don't fully understand why I was persecuted so harshly when I did nothing wrong, but

I can see now that you never abandoned me. Even in the darkest moments where I walked through the valley of the shadow of death, you were with me. You sent godly men with noble hearts to rescue me and surrounded me with compassion and chivalry. Thank you. May I honor your gift with a spirit of gratitude and compassion toward others, especially the men here at the Diamond D.

As she knelt there, eyes closed, heart meditating, a thought seeped into her mind. Could it be that her trial was necessary to bring her to a place of blessing? A place she never would have encountered had she remained on her previous path?

The notion instilled her with a measure of hope. She might have lost her job, her belongings, and even her clothes, but she wasn't destitute. Not when she had strength to work and the Lord to guide her. She'd been given a chance. A chance to make a fresh start. And start, she would. Even if dawn was still a couple of hours away.

Penelope pushed up from the floor, lit the bedside lamp, and surveyed the shadowy room around her. Time to return all the kindness she'd received from the Diamond D men. But first, she'd need something more substantial to wear than a cotton nightdress.

Praying there'd be a corset among the late Mrs. Kingsley's things, Penelope approached the trunk at the end of the bed, set the lamp on the floor beside her, then opened the lid. A Bible lay at the top of the packed items. The worn leather at the edges testified to its frequent use. Penelope ran her hand over the cover, thinking of her own small Bible left behind with her beloved copy of *Oliver Twist* and the photograph she and Edith had taken together before she left Chicago. The loss throbbed in her chest, but she'd not dwell on what had been taken from her. No, she'd focus on what she'd been given. A new path forward. One rich with blessings—some already known to her, others yet to be discovered. Penelope smiled as she lifted the Bible from the trunk and set it next to her on the floor. Doc had encouraged her to make use of whatever she found. Perhaps he'd allow her to borrow the Bible while she was here at the ranch so she could read a chapter or two before bed each night.

Penelope turned her attention back to the contents of the trunk and soon grew absorbed by the possibilities inside. Twenty minutes later, she had a dozen clothing items draped over the bed, including a selection of underclothes and stockings. Mrs. Kingsley must have been a few inches shorter than Penelope, for both skirts she tried on hit her above the ankle. The yellow one fit better around her waist, so Penelope selected that one to wear. The matching yellow bodice, however, was far too tight across the bust. All of the bodices and shirtwaists had the same problem.

Thankfully, the simple corset in Mrs. Kingsley's collection could be loosened enough to fit, though it didn't offer the same support as the over-the-shoulder style Penelope preferred. It was far more comfortable and modest than Madame LaBelle's monstrosity, so Penelope counted that as a blessing and thanked the Lord accordingly as she slipped it around her midsection and tightened the laces. Still, she'd need more than a camisole as covering. She checked the construction on the largest of the shirtwaists, but the seam allowance was too narrow. Letting it out wouldn't solve her problem.

Determined not to let discouragement gain the upper hand, Penelope scanned the room for inspiration and found it hanging on the edge of the washstand mirror—Titus's shirt. Memories of the man who'd given it to her sent warmth radiating through her neck and face. His tender touch as he'd wrapped her feet. His strong arms as he carried her away from the mesquite shrubs. The honor shining in his brown eyes as he offered his shirt in trade for her blanket. She'd thought to launder his shirt and return it to him, but it seemed she might need to make use of it a little longer.

Not that Mr. Kingsley would notice. The Ranger had left yesterday without a word to her. From the small bathroom window, she'd caught a glimpse of him riding out while Ike had heated her bathwater. His leaving left an ache in her chest, but he hadn't owed her any special consideration. He'd done his duty. More than his duty. Yet the intimacy they'd shared on the journey to the ranch had made it feel as if a friendship had been budding. At least to her.

She padded over to the washstand, took down his shirt, and ran her fingers over the dark blue cotton. *Bless him in his work, Lord, and protect him from harm.* What kind of business had called him away yesterday? Whatever he faced was bound to be dangerous. Chasing another gang of bank robbers, perhaps? Hunting outlaws? Stopping a range war? Titus certainly seemed capable of handling whatever trouble crossed his path, but a man who courted danger on a regular basis could do with an extra helping of divine defense. She'd add him to her evening prayer list.

Today, though, she let him rescue her again by making use of his shirt. It was far from feminine, but it was serviceable, and it fit. Sure, it hung practically to her knees, but that didn't matter. She'd just tuck the tails into her skirt and roll the sleeves above her elbows. She had no idea how long she'd be staying at the Diamond D, but while here, she intended to earn her keep. After washing, dressing, and pinning up her hair, she packed up the trunk, made the bed, and headed downstairs to get to work.

Not wanting to disturb anyone's slumber, Penelope decided to wait until after sunup to tackle the deep cleaning the house needed. For now, she'd focus on baking and mending. After stoking up the fire in the cookstove, she bloomed some yeast and mixed up a bowl of bread dough. It felt good to have her hands in dough again. Being raised by a cook, Penelope had learned to master a stove from a young age. Yet Edith had always encouraged her to use her education to move beyond the kitchen. Working as a lady's maid or a governess would carry more prestige and a better salary. Unfortunately in Penelope's case, those positions also came with scandal and false accusations, leaving her with neither prestige nor money. But that was a problem for another day. Today, she was counting her blessings, and being back in a kitchen with rich memories of Edith surrounding her was blessing indeed.

After setting the bread dough near the stove to rise, Penelope quietly took an inventory of the larder and cupboards. Finding a few inches of coffee left in the pot on the back of the stove, she decided to make Edith's famous coffee cake for breakfast. She found eggs, brown sugar, molasses, butter, baking soda, and flour, but cinnamon and cloves were harder to come by. A nutmeg seed rolled around in the spice box, so she grated a healthy dose into the molasses and coffee before adding the butter and eggs, followed by the dry ingredients. Unable to find any raisins or currants, she left the batter fruitless and poured it into a tubed cake pan.

The squeak of the oven door woke Lucky and brought him hobbling to her side.

"Look at you, up and about." Penelope hunkered next to the dog and petted his head. "At this rate, you'll be back to chasing squirrels in no time."

She let the dog out the back door to tend to his personal business. Not knowing if he might need help, she kept an eye on him but shivered in the predawn air. A tinge of gray light edged the horizon, announcing the sun's gradual approach, though she doubted any rooster would be crowing for at least another thirty minutes.

Lucky seemed to miss the warmth of the stove as much as

she did, for he hurried back as fast as his stiff, limping gait would allow. He took a few slurps from his water bowl, then laid down on his pallet.

"I don't suppose you know where the mending basket is, do you?"

The dog offered no insight, so Penelope carried her lamp over to the washroom to see if the basket was there. After Doc had unwrapped her feet yesterday, she'd peeled off her tattered stockings so he could examine the damage, especially the sore spot where the thorn had jabbed her toes. Jeb had wadded up her discarded stockings and muttered something about tossing them in the mending basket, though heaven knew no amount of darning could repair the shredded things. He hadn't gone far, so the basket should be nearby. She wished she'd paid more attention to where he'd gone, but her attention had been riveted on Doc's face as he examined her feet. Thankfully, he'd declared that stitches wouldn't be necessary, though he'd instructed her to keep the cuts clean and let him know at once if they worsened.

Keeping them clean would be a simple enough matter if she possessed proper footwear. Which she didn't. She'd found some woolen stockings in Mrs. Kingsley's trunk and had pulled them on, but there had been no shoes.

One problem at a time, Pen.

Shoes could wait. Right now, she was hunting the mending basket, and judging by the mound of clothes heaped in the corner just inside the washroom door, she'd found it. Her wadded stockings lay on the floor beside an overflowing market basket, probably because they weren't clean. She searched the shelf on the wall above the basket until she found a small box containing needles, thread, and a small jar of random buttons. Knowing she wouldn't have time to tackle the entire pile this morning, she grabbed an armful off the top and headed to the kitchen table. If the size of the pile was any indication, this was a chore no one at the Diamond D enjoyed. Which made it the perfect opportunity to show her appreciation. She was a little nervous regarding how Coy would feel about her commandeering his kitchen, but it looked like no one would mind her making free with the mending.

An hour later, four shirts sported new buttons and repaired seams, one set of trousers had a patched knee and a resewn pocket, and two pairs of socks had been darned. All items were folded and stacked on the spare chair sitting against the wall. Fresh coffee stood ready on the stove. Her cake was out and cooling, and her bread dough was rising nicely. As was the sun. Pink and orange painted the sky as she stared out the back window and sipped a cup of tea.

"You've been busy this mornin'."

Penelope spun around to find Doc shuffling into the kitchen, hair combed and glasses on, though it looked like he'd pulled on a pair of pants over his nightshirt.

"Did I wake you?"

"Nah." He waved off her concern. "The aches and pains of bein' an old man woke me. But the smell of somethin' sweet and tasty got me out of bed." He drew in a deep, appreciative sniff. "Is that cake I smell?"

Penelope grinned and pulled away the tea towel covering the cake she'd turned out a few minutes ago. "Coffee cake. Can I cut you a piece?"

"Mmm. Mmm. I can't remember the last time I had fresh-baked cake. Probably not since God called Mabel home." Nostalgia colored his voice. "My wife had a sweet tooth and always had cookies, cake, or a pie on hand just in case company came to call." He grinned at Penelope. "If getting up early gets me a piece of cake, I'll have to greet the dawn more often. You'll join me, won't you?"

"Of course."

Humming softly, Penelope cut two slices of cake and poured Doc a cup of hot coffee. She waited for him to take his place at the head of the table, then sat cattycorner to him. Her stomach knotted slightly as he tore off a bite with his fork and lifted it to his mouth, but the moment his eyes slid closed and a purr of satisfaction rumbled in his chest, her nerves vanished.

"Mercy, girl, but you can bake. This is delicious!"

She ducked her head, but modesty couldn't restrain the delighted smile that stretched her cheeks. "Thank you. The woman who raised me was a cook at a girls' school back in Chicago. Everything I know about baking, I learned from her."

Intelligence flickered in his eyes, and she had no doubt he was filing away the tidbits she'd revealed about her past, but he didn't press her for more details. "She taught you well, Miss Snow."

"Please, call me Penelope."

He nodded his head in her direction. "Penelope." He took another bite of coffee cake but slanted her a sideways glance. "Still wearing my grandson's shirt, I see."

Heat flared across her face. "None of the tops in your wife's trunk fit, I'm afraid."

He turned back to his cake and nodded, as if trying to put her back at ease by removing his attention. "I worried that might be the case." He swallowed a sip of coffee before finally catching her eye. "Do you sew? I can send one of the boys into town to fetch some fabric for you."

She shook her head. "I can't ask that of you. Maybe if you have some old flour sacks lying around, I can piece something from them. Maybe even alter one of your wife's pieces—if you don't mind, that is."

"'Course not. Mabel would want you to make use of them, so make whatever alterations you need. They're not doin' anyone any service stored away in that trunk." He pointed his fork at her as if he'd just remembered something. "Rowdy is going to clean up a pair of old boots for you to wear until we can get you some shoes. He's got the smallest feet. The boots might be a tad big, but if you stuff some newspaper into the toes, they should work. Ike's got a coat you can wear, too."

"I . . . don't know what to say." Penelope blinked at the moisture filming her eyes.

Doc looked at her over the rim of his wire spectacles. "We had a house meeting while you were sleeping yesterday, Penelope."

Her heart thumped an erratic beat at his serious tone, and she circled her hands around her mug of tea to keep them from shaking.

"We are all agreed that we will help you get back on your feet in whatever way you deem best. We can put you on a train back to Chicago if that is what you want. Or we can take you to Glen Rose and help you find a job. We'd even take you to the county sheriff in Granbury to press charges against the man who attacked you."

Panic seized her chest, and for a moment, she couldn't breathe. Not Granbury. Not with Madame LaBelle and her troupe in town.

Doc laid his hand over her forearm and squeezed slightly.

Had he sensed her fear? Her dread?

"But if you have nowhere in particular to go," he continued, his voice gentle and steady, "we would like you to consider staying here at the Diamond D."

Her chin lifted, and her brow pinched.

Doc favored her with a self-deprecating grin. "I know we're a bunch of old-timers without much to offer a young lady, but you'd be safe here. You'd have a roof over your head, food to eat, and seven overprotective grandfathers to make sure whatever trouble dragged you into those woods doesn't touch you again."

Penelope's vision blurred as she stared at Doc, overcome by the generosity of his offer. To have a place to hide until Narcissa left the area or, even better, until she left Texas altogether. A place that already felt more like home than any place she'd been outside of Edith's kitchen.

Titus's words flooded her mind. *"They're good men. Godly men. Every one of 'em."* She'd seen that truth play out over the last day. Had experienced nothing but kindness from their hands. Had never once felt like an object to be lusted after or a servant to be ordered about. Even now, respect rang through every word Doc uttered. Whatever choice she made, he'd see it carried out.

Her heart settled on a decision before her mind could fully sort through all her options.

"I'll stay." Peace settled over her as the words tripped off her tongue. "At least for a little while."

Perhaps long enough to see Titus again. To thank him, of course. And return his shirt. Not to pursue any kind of romantic connection. That would be foolish, and she was far too sensible to pine away for a man when there was work to do and life to live.

So why did her pulse flutter at the thought of his return?

12

Enoch Kingsley pulled his spectacles from his face and rubbed his tired eyes. He was getting too old for late-night bookkeeping. He needed quiet in order to think properly, though, and that only existed after the rest of the men retired to their beds.

Thankfully, the numbers added up cleanly tonight and reassured him that his decision to take in an impoverished girl without even a stitch of decent clothing to her name would bring no lasting hardship upon the Diamond D. The small income he earned from renting his old office space to the doctor who took over his practice would continue covering the cost of their supplies, even with eight to feed instead of seven. They only required a few staples, anyway. Flour, sugar, salt, cornmeal, coffee, and beans. Ike's garden kept them in vegetables. Coy managed the chickens and hogs. Angus enjoyed fishing—and napping—at the creek, and Jeb kept his shooting skills sharp by bringing in small game and the occasional deer. Even Rowdy brought back wild onions, berries, and dandelion greens when he ran across them while hiking.

A few head of cattle grazed in the upper pasture, too, thanks to Dusty's arrangement with the livery in Glen Rose. He rehabilitated horses for them, bringing one nag out to the ranch every three months on a rotating schedule. He gave them fresh grass, room to roam, and no wagons to pull or saddles to wear. The livery ended up with fresher, healthier mounts, and Dusty ended up with a new calf each spring.

No one paid rent at the Diamond D, but everyone contributed. However, in all his visions of a retirement ranch for aging cowhands, Enoch had never pictured a young woman taking up residence among them. A young woman in need of proper clothing and shoes.

Ike had already pulled him aside and offered a half-dozen pints of honey to trade at the mercantile. That combined with the money Titus left and funds Enoch planned to withdraw from his personal savings should cover the cost of fabric, thread, new stockings, and perhaps a set of hairpins. Penelope hadn't asked for anything, but she'd been working her fingers to the bone for the past week, scrubbing the place until it shone, taking over kitchen duties, and mending every tear and loose button in the mending closet. She deserved a treat.

A soft knock had Enoch reaching for his glasses. By the time he had them perched back on the bridge of his nose, the object of his thoughts had cracked the door open and stuck her head inside.

"Doc? I don't mean to disturb you, but I thought you might like some chamomile tea. May I bring it in?"

He closed the ledger and rose to his feet. "Of course, but you didn't have to go to all that trouble." He hurried to the door and held it wide so she could easily navigate through the portal with not only a cup of tea but a plate of cookies as well.

"It's no trouble." Her smile brightened the dim office more than the lamp on his desk.

He'd only known her for a week, but he'd already developed a huge soft spot for the girl. Besides his darling Mabel, he'd never met a more unselfish, giving woman. Penelope was always doing for others. Baking sweets, picking up after the men, even leaving Rowdy little treasures at the breakfast table every morning. There wasn't a man under this roof who hadn't been charmed. Jeb even groused less when she was around.

As she set the snack down, he found himself wishing he could do more for her. She'd lost so much. . . .

Her fingers hovered over the book at the top corner of his desk, the one he'd been planning to take upstairs. Since losing Mabel, he never went to bed without a book. Helped a man feel not quite so alone when he had the words of another to keep him company. Might Penelope feel the same?

"Have you read it?" Enoch asked. *The Count of Monte Cristo* was probably not regular reading material at girls' schools in Chicago, but one could never be certain. "It's quite a rousing tale."

As if his words had given her permission to explore, she allowed her fingers to alight upon the cover and trace the stamped title. "I haven't had the pleasure."

"Take it." The impulsive words left his mouth before he thought them through, but he didn't regret them. She needed a friend, and books made wonderful companions. "Perhaps we can discuss it after you finish."

Her face jerked up toward his, her eyes wide, her cheeks slightly pink. "Oh, I couldn't. Not when you were intending to read it."

He chuckled softly. "I've read it multiple times, Miss Snow. I can easily find another book to suit my needs. Although . . ." His gaze turned to the glassed-in bookcases that lined the back wall of his office. "There may be something else in my collection that would better fit your taste." He crossed to the nearest case, opened the cabinet door, and ran his hand along the spines. "I don't have any Austen or Brontë, I'm afraid, but you might enjoy *The Last of the Mohicans* or perhaps *Far from the Madding Crowd*." Those had a touch of romance in them. Women liked romantic stories, didn't they? "I've got some biographies as well, and a whole host of dull medical texts if you ever have trouble sleeping. You're welcome to borrow anything you like."

She inched up behind him, her footsteps light. Bending at the waist, she brought her eyes level with his cabinet shelves but kept her hands folded behind her back like a child trained not to touch.

"Do you happen to have a copy of *Oliver Twist*? I was in the midst of reading my copy when I was . . . released from my previous employment."

When she was carted off into the wild and left for dead. Enoch bristled. It was past time this child experienced compassion and comradery.

Enoch hunkered down to reach one of the lower shelves. "I'm afraid I don't have that particular work, but I have a couple others by Dickens." He fingered the top of a thick volume's spine and angled it outward. "Have you read *Great Expectations*? Some consider it his finest work."

Penelope inhaled an audible breath and straightened away from the bookshelf she'd been examining. "That story centers around an orphan, too, doesn't it? A boy named Pip?"

"That's right." Enoch pulled the book from the shelf and handed it to Penelope.

It took a moment for her to unlock her hands from behind her back, but she managed the feat and accepted the book from his hand. She stroked the cover with reverence, a smile blooming across her face.

"You're sure I can borrow this?" Her face tilted to meet his gaze, wonder dancing in her eyes.

Enoch chuckled. "I'm sure, lass."

"Thank you." She hugged the book to her chest. "I've always

had a fondness for stories about orphans making their way in the world. They give me hope that my own story will turn out well."

"With the kind heart and strong work ethic you possess," Enoch said, pushing the words through a sudden thickness in his throat, "I'm certain it will."

Lord, may it be so.

She smiled at him as if he'd bestowed a great gift when in truth he was the blessed one. Ever since losing Tate, he'd distanced himself from his family. Not because they blamed him for the loss, but because he felt undeserving of their forgiveness. Why had God made him a healer if he couldn't save the people who mattered most? First his wife. Then his grandson. Yet being around Penelope this past week and learning some of her history reminded him that family was a precious commodity that shouldn't be wasted.

This sweet child had been abandoned by her parents, raised in a school where she was treated more as a servant than a pupil, then thrown out into a world that abused and abandoned her again. A longing for connection and belonging radiated from her like heat from an oven. She hungered for the very things he'd thrown away.

Perhaps it was time to reach out to his son and attempt to mend a few fences. Maybe invite him and his wife to visit. Introduce them to Penelope. She was sure to charm them as thoroughly as she had the entire Diamond D. Including Titus.

Thoughts of his grandson had Enoch easing away from the cabinet. He reached for one of the cookies she'd brought and took a bite while he watched her flip through the opening pages of *Great Expectations.* The wheels in his mind spun as if they'd just been oiled.

The girl was a beauty, no question, but it was her heart that shone brightest. Exactly the attribute needed to penetrate

Titus's reserve. The boy didn't trust women, especially pretty ones. He had his reasons—valid ones—yet he'd taken his distrust to an unhealthy extreme. Even so, there had been something about Penelope that had breached his defenses. Titus hadn't left without saying good-bye to her because he was in a hurry to return to Ranger headquarters. No, he'd left to keep himself from getting entangled. As practiced as Enoch was with the avoidance technique, he easily recognized its deployment by another. Titus was attracted to Penelope, probably against his will, but the spark existed.

Maybe the Lord had led Penelope here for more than just protection. Enoch leaned a hip against the edge of the desk and took another bite of his cookie. He'd never been one to play matchmaker, but this seemed to be a night for turning over new leaves.

13

Titus had spent a fortnight traveling across Texas, interviewing the gentlemen on Captain Bill's list and hunting for patterns. All the men were wealthy, but beyond that, they didn't share much in common. Different ages. Different political parties. Some inherited their wealth, while others had manufactured their fortune themselves. Some were married. Others were single or widowed. Many had children, but not all.

Titus shoved his notes across the small desk and pushed to his feet. He needed to move. Change the scenery. *Something*. The walls seemed to be pushing in on him. Shrinking the hotel room. Trapping him. He strode over to the washstand and splashed some water on his face. The coolness helped. A little.

Big cities made Titus itch. Too many people. Not enough space. Austin was better than Houston, but even here he found it hard to relax. The fancy furnishings of this upscale room added to his discomfort. Chairs with spindly, untrustworthy legs. Rugs he avoided walking on for fear of tracking mud. A painting on the wall of a stern-faced woman whose judgmental gaze seemed to follow him around the room. He would have preferred a cot in a vacant jail cell. Men of Hathaway's standing, however, only conducted business at fine establishments.

Especially if they happened to own one. As proprietor of this particular hotel, Mr. Hathaway had insisted on putting Titus up last night to facilitate an early morning meeting. Hence Titus's lack of choice in accommodations.

He should have taken a walk after his breakfast tray arrived instead of going through his notes for the hundredth time, but it was too late to change tactics now. He was due to meet Hathaway in twenty minutes. Titus strode back to the desk, picked up the tablet, and flipped through his notes from the other interviews he'd conducted. Interviews with victims, lawmen, and any ancillary parties like servants or family members who hadn't already been questioned by the local law. As he scanned the contents, his eyes lit on words he'd underlined in his hunt for commonalities, threads, and oddities. He'd drawn a full box around Hathaway's name on the last page. His situation represented the biggest oddity yet.

Nothing notable linked the victims, meaning the thefts were crimes of opportunity, not targeted attacks. Therefore, the pattern lay with a thief who had been making his way across Texas in a methodical fashion. Houston, Brenham, Giddings, Austin, Cameron, Waco. All cities along railroad lines. All cities containing at least a handful of affluent citizens.

It made sense. The railroad offered a quick escape and a level of anonymity. One could blend in with other passengers, hide stolen property in luggage, and move easily between towns, thereby making it harder for lawmen to connect the crimes together into a single string.

The thief could work for the railroad or be a peddler or other frequent traveler. A theory Titus would subscribe to if the most recent theft had happened in Hillsboro or Cleburne. But it hadn't. It took place in Eulogy, a small town off the Brazos River. Nowhere near a railroad. It broke the pattern. Which meant they either had two thieves and the Eulogy case was unrelated to the others, or something beyond the railroad linked these crimes.

Titus doubted there were two crooks roaming Texas with a penchant for nabbing expensive male accessories. One such criminal had been strange enough to draw the attention of the Rangers. The chances of there being two were extremely slim. Unless the two were in cahoots. But even if that was the case, the thefts would still have to be connected. Therefore, there had to be a link between the crimes that Titus wasn't seeing. Something only Hubert Hathaway could reveal.

If Titus asked the right questions.

Ask. Seek. Knock.

When Titus had first joined the Rangers, those three words had become his motto. To find truth, he needed to ask questions and never make assumptions. Once he had his answers, he'd seek his target until the criminal was found. Then he'd knock down any obstacle that stood between him and enacting justice. The motto kept him objective and focused, and drove him to finish his task. Yet as those three words rose in his mind this morning, they didn't fire his determination as they usually did. No, they tugged him in a different direction. Toward the One who'd spoken them on a mountain centuries ago.

Titus slid into the desk chair and bowed his head as Christ's words filled his mind.

"Ask, and it shall be given you; seek, and ye shall find; knock, and it shall be opened unto you: For every one that asketh, receiveth; and he that seeketh findeth; and to him that knocketh it shall be opened."

"I seek truth, Lord," Titus whispered, "and ask you to help me find it. Give me the right questions to ask today. Questions that will open doors to knowledge. Give me eyes to see and ears to hear. Grant me wisdom and understanding and the courage to follow wherever the truth leads. May I be an instrument of justice in your hands."

A knock tapped on Titus's door. He opened his eyes, a smile tugging at his lips at the irony. It shouldn't surprise him, though. The Lord was famous for his uncanny timing. Titus rose from his seat and opened the door.

The desk clerk stood before him. "Mr. Kingsley?"

Titus nodded. "Yep."

"Mr. Hathaway is ready for you, sir."

Titus collected his black sack coat and slipped his arms into the sleeves. One didn't meet with the Hubert Hathaways of the world in shirtsleeves. He tucked his notepad into his coat pocket to nestle against the pencil already inside, then took his hat from the hook near the door and fit it to his head.

Stepping into the hall, he pulled the door closed behind him, then gestured to his escort. "Lead on."

The clerk led Titus downstairs, through the lobby, then wound to the back of the building before knocking on a large mahogany door.

"Enter."

The clerk unlatched the door and pushed it open to reveal an office the size of a small house, paneled in dark wood that had been oiled to a deep shine.

"Mr. Kingsley to see you, sir."

"Very good. Thank you, Peters."

Titus stepped into the room and strode up to the desk as if he weren't awed in the slightest by his surroundings. "Thank you for seeing me, Mr. Hathaway."

The hotel owner stood, came around the side of his desk, and extended his hand, a wide grin on his face. "I appreciate you coming, Ranger Kingsley."

The man's affable nature caught Titus by surprise. Actually, everything about Hubert Hathaway took him by surprise.

Short in stature, probably only two or three inches over five feet, Hathaway wore a royal blue suit with a thin plaid pattern woven through the fabric. As if he were some kind of blue sundae, he'd topped things off with a cherry red necktie. His wavy blond hair was parted slightly off-center and heavily pomaded, while his thick whiskers ran down his sideburns before draping over his upper lip like a garland on a railing. His bare chin reminded Titus a bit of a marionette puppet, yet it was his twinkling blue eyes that arrested Titus's attention.

Titus shook the man's hand, then removed his hat as Mr. Hathaway showed him to a chair.

"I'll take that for you," Hathaway said as he reached for Titus's hat.

"Thanks."

The man was certainly a good fit for the hospitality business. His friendly manner offered a vivid contrast from the other men Titus had interviewed. He'd dealt with impatience, arrogance, even outright hostility in his previous encounters. Mr. Hathaway's jovial nature was a pleasant surprise. Rather like the laughing young woman who'd popped out of the ground to spin circles in front of his horse a couple of weeks ago.

Titus slammed the door on that memory. Not the time.

Mr. Hathaway hung Titus's hat on the stand in the corner, then returned to his desk. Only, he didn't seat himself in the power position behind it. He placed his hands on the back of the chair next to Titus and scooted it a few feet away, turning it so it faced his guest, then sat down. Titus shifted his own chair around and met Hathaway's dancing gaze.

"When the sheriff notified me that my case was being turned over to the Rangers, I couldn't have been more pleased. No finer lawmen in the country." Hathaway slapped his chair arm. "So tell me, Kingsley. What can I do to help?"

Titus pulled his pencil and notebook from his pocket, then

flipped to the page containing the information gathered from the Eulogy town marshal. “I’d like to go over the events leading up to and immediately following the point that you realized your”—he checked the notes—“ruby stickpin disappeared.”

“Of course. I had traveled to Eulogy to visit my sister. Her husband owns a gristmill there. I like to visit a few times a year. Check in on Jenny and dote on my nieces and nephews. Their little house is too small for my liking, though, so my brother-in-law allows me to use his office at the mill. I purchased a large sofa that can double as a bed and installed it in the space. Lonnie gets a nice piece of furniture to impress his business associates, and I get private quarters whenever I’m in town.”

“You’re not married, correct?” Titus found it odd that such a lively and well-to-do fellow hadn’t been leg shackled by an enterprising woman.

“Me? Heavens, no.” Hathaway chuckled. “I can’t imagine tying myself to one woman. Jenny harps at me to settle down, but where’s the fun in that? I tell her I’ll settle down as soon as I find a lady interesting enough to hold my attention for more than a week or so. Until then, variety is the spice of life, eh?”

Hathaway gave him a man-to-man look that didn’t set well on Titus’s conscience. Keeping his expression blank, he jotted a note: *Ladies’ man.*

“When was the last time you recall seeing the jeweled pin?”

“Before attending the theater.”

Titus looked up from his notes. “There’s no theater in Eulogy.” The place barely had a post office. Population was probably only a hundred fifty.

“I know.” Hathaway chuckled. “Imagine my delight when I discovered there was a thespian troupe from Chicago passing through town offering a one-night-only comedic revue to be performed in the schoolhouse. A trial run for the show they planned to debut in Granbury.”

Something clicked in Titus's memory. Hadn't one of the other victims mentioned attending a play? Several of the men had had trouble pinpointing precisely when their items had gone missing, but each of the cities where the thefts occurred had opera houses or community centers large enough to support a theatrical performance. A tingling sensation climbed around in his chest. This could be the link he'd been missing. He'd have to wire the other lawmen, get them to confirm whether or not the other victims attended a similar performance.

"Jenny insisted on taking the children," Hathaway was saying, "and I indulged her. I think the entire town turned out. The show was quite good. On par with performances I've seen at the Scottish Rite here in Austin. The headlining actress, Madame LaBelle, was utterly captivating. I met her after the show, and she was kind enough to give me a tour backstage, where I stumbled across a second beauty.

"A shy little thing with big gray eyes. She clung to the shadows, but I managed to draw her out for a brief moment when Madame LaBelle excused herself to have a word with the manager. There was an innocence about the girl that drew me to her. So young and fresh-faced. Yet she had curves that would tempt a saint, a fact she tried to hide beneath a shapeless beige gown. Only a connoisseur of women like myself would have noticed."

Titus's pulse throbbed as visions of a fresh-faced girl with big gray eyes danced through his mind. A girl who'd worn a shapeless tan dress that might be considered beige. A girl who'd been in the vicinity of Eulogy the day he'd met her.

Titus cleared his throat. "Back to the pin."

"Ah, of course." Hathaway grinned, the expression slightly sheepish but not exactly repentant. "I discovered it missing the following morning."

"But you had it when you changed for bed that night?"

"Well, I cannot be completely certain." Hathaway shot another one of those man-to-man glances at Titus. "I took the lady to dinner and back to my quarters for a bottle of wine and a little . . . entertainment. Getting ready for bed that evening was a bit . . . shall we say . . . haphazard."

"Which lady?" Titus barely forced the words through his constricted throat. If this cad had touched Penelope . . .

Hathaway's blue eyes danced with mischief. "A gentleman never tells."

A gentleman never strangled an unarmed man with his bare hands, either, but Titus was seriously considering it.

Quit thinking about Penelope and focus on the facts of the case. Be objective.

"It's possible that the woman you were with is the one who stole your pin. I promise to keep the nature of your relationship private, but I really do need her name."

All joviality drained from Hathaway's gaze, leaving his eyes chips of blue ice. "Impossible. I will not sully a lady's reputation. Besides, it's more likely that one of the mill workers stumbled across my tiepin the next day while I was visiting Jenny and pocketed the trinket."

"The marshal interviewed all the mill employees and even searched their homes. Nothing was found."

Hathaway leaned forward. "Between you and me, I wasn't terribly impressed with Eulogy's marshal. He's a hardware-store manager. Did you know that? He's fit for breaking up the occasional brawl and keeping the Saturday night saloon crowd from getting too rowdy, but he's no professional investigator."

Titus had found the man capable and intelligent. He might lack investigative experience, but by all accounts, he'd made a thorough search.

"The reason the Rangers are looking into your case, Mr.

Hathaway, is because there has been a string of similar robberies throughout the state. We believe the same thief is responsible for all the missing pieces. Which means someone other than a Eulogy mill worker is to blame."

Hathaway frowned, obviously not liking the implication. But then, what man would want to believe he had been duped by a pretty face? Titus's brother had died because he couldn't admit he might have been wrong about the woman with whom he'd been keeping company.

"Perhaps you're right, Mr. Kingsley." Hathaway still didn't look convinced. "Or perhaps my case is completely unrelated."

Titus's gut said otherwise. The only way to settle the matter, however, was to recover the jewels. And thanks to Hubert Hathaway, Titus had a new lead to follow—one Madame LaBelle and her troupe of traveling actors.

14

"Another splendid performance, my dear." Ambrose Clayton steered Narcissa through the crowd who'd gathered at the saloon next door to Kerr's Hall to celebrate closing night. "Are you sure you won't consider extending your engagement? I don't think I could ever tire of watching you upon the stage."

Narcissa smiled at the man sporting a gorgeous pair of diamond-studded cuff links. "You might be able to tolerate seeing me night after night, but I'm sure the rest of Granbury is beyond weary of our little show."

"Nonsense! You held the entire audience spellbound."

She dipped her chin to hide the pleasure his words evoked. A lady must never appear proud if she wished to entice a powerful man. Humility and deference paid much larger dividends. "You're too kind."

"And you are too wonderful." Mr. Clayton patted her hand where it lay upon his arm, then pressed her fingers against his coat sleeve. Heat passed between them. Not only from his hand, but from the hungry look in his eyes.

Narcissa leaned into his side, angling her décolletage to best advantage as she discreetly blinked a sultry look up at him. His gaze dipped to her chest and lingered. Exactly as she'd designed. Ambrose Clayton and his diamonds would be hers for the taking this night.

"Madame LaBelle!" Henry Kerr, owner of the opera house, bounded their way.

Narcissa separated herself slightly from Ambrose and beamed a smile at her patron. Mr. Kerr had given a rather prudish speech to her troupe prior to their first performance, pontificating on his expectations that they exhibit high moral character while in his town. Apparently, the loose morals of some of his previously engaged thespians had caused the more puritanical of the townsfolk to look down upon Kerr and his opera house, going so far as to prohibit their young people from even walking on the south side of the square. Such hypocrisy only stoked the fire of rebellion in her soul, but she wasn't so foolish as to risk forfeiting a paying engagement. So she'd kept her flirtations to a minimum, using the past fortnight to narrow her field of admirers to the best possible gentleman to woo. With tickets sales in hand and her company leaving in the morning, the time had come to cast off her fetters. Yet, she'd play one final scene with Kerr. Remain in his good graces and ensure his positive opinion.

"Brava, Madame!" Kerr clapped silently as he sketched a small bow before her. "Your grand talent has elevated our humble town. What an honor to have you play our hall."

Narcissa dipped her chin in a well-practiced display of modesty. "The honor was mine, Mr. Kerr. Granbury might not be as large as Houston or Fort Worth, but your stage rivals any house I've played in. Those backdrops alone made me feel as if I were back at the Columbia in Chicago."

The new backdrops were Kerr's pride and joy, so she made sure to stroke the man's ego accordingly. Her efforts did not go unrewarded. The man's chest practically puffed before her eyes.

"I hope you'll consider coming back to our fair town in the future, Madame."

Not if she could help it. Still, she offered a smile that mixed a touch of fondness with starry-eyed hope. "One cannot say what the future will bring. If I am so blessed as to pass this way again, I will be sure to contact you, sir. Treading the boards of your stage has been an absolute delight."

Not wanting her escort to feel as if he were being ignored, Narcissa placed a hand to her throat and rumbled it lightly. "Please excuse us, Mr. Kerr. My throat is going dry. Mr. Clayton? I think I could do with a glass of sherry."

"Of course, my dear. Come with me."

The two men nodded to each other as Ambrose led her to the bar and ordered a sherry from the dark-haired man pouring drinks. The fellow carried himself differently than most barkeeps of her acquaintance. Setting her drink in front of her with a flourish, he orated in a clear voice that could have easily carried to the back of the room had he so desired. "'God hath given you one face, and you make yourselves another.'"

"Hamlet. I'm impressed." The fellow knew his Shakespeare. More than that, he delivered the line like a professional. Slipping into the character of Ophelia, she replied in kind.

> "I shall the effect of this good lesson keep
> As watchman to my heart. But, good my brother,
> Do not—as some ungracious pastors do—
> Show me the steep and thorny way to heaven,
> Whilst, like a puffed and reckless libertine,
> Himself the primrose path of dalliance treads,
> And recks not his own rede."

She'd always loved that line. Ophelia calling out the double standard society placed on women, expecting them to be all that is proper and moral while not holding men accountable for their misdeeds.

Ambrose brushed her arm. "Well played, my dear. Mr. St. Helen likes to quote the Bard on occasion. It's rare that anyone can answer in kind. Isn't that right, John?"

"Just so." The barkeep nodded, respect and a touch of challenge in his gaze, as if he wanted her to know that he saw beneath her façade but wouldn't cast judgment. "Your drink is on the house, Madame."

"Thank you." Something about the man unsettled her. Turning to remove him from her line of sight, she resolved to erase him from her mind just as easily. John St. Helen was not her target tonight. Her attention belonged on Ambrose Clayton. And that's where it would stay.

She slid her hand through Clayton's arm and leaned her face close to him. "You know," she murmured in a low, throaty voice, "as much as I love a good party, I was secretly hoping to spend some time alone with you this evening before I depart." She lowered her lashes and tilted her head with just the right blend of demure modesty and coquettish flirtation.

When he edged away from the bar toward a shadowy corner, she followed, satisfaction surging so strongly within her breast it became difficult to restrain her boldness. Overplaying her hand would gain her nothing, however. She took a sip of sherry, then tripped over an imaginary object on the floor. When he moved to steady her, she clutched his arms, taking care to turn and press herself against him. Not for long. She'd not have anyone call her vulgar. Just long enough to see desire flash in his eyes.

"I looked for you." She blinked up at him as she slid her hands slowly down the lapels of his coat to gently push away and recover her balance. "In the audience. Every time I took the stage." She peered at him as Juliet would gaze at Romeo.

"I couldn't believe you paid to attend each performance. You must truly appreciate the theatrical arts."

"It wasn't the show I came to see, my dear. It was you." His hand tightened on her arm as his voice growled the admission.

Her breath caught. "Oh, Ambrose."

His nostrils flared at her use of his given name. "My house is not far from here," he murmured. "We could be alone. Share a bottle of wine."

She glanced about the room to project an aura of uncertainty, then bit her lip and nodded. "We can't be seen leaving together, though. I must protect my reputation."

"Of course. I'll retrieve my carriage and meet you behind the theater."

Blood pumped through her veins at a staggering speed, fueled by nerves, anticipation, and intoxicating power. She hid the huntress behind a mask of new love's excitement and grinned at the middle-aged man with the soft middle as if he were Michelangelo's *David*. "I'll meet you in ten minutes."

She made her way through the partygoers, slowing only when necessary to accept a compliment or make an excuse for leaving early. Headaches were beautiful things. All one needed was a furrowed brow and a pained expression to achieve sympathetic acceptance.

Cecil Hunt met her at the door and helped her into her wrap. His deep frown made his disapproval clear. Placating men was so wearying.

"Thank you, Cecil. Wait the usual hour, then come fetch me."

He said nothing. Didn't even nod.

Narcissa raised a brow. He hadn't been himself since that dreadful Penelope left. Perhaps doing away with the chit had made him question his allegiance. She couldn't have that. He knew too much.

"These men mean nothing to me, Cecil." She stroked the length of his stiffened arm, then took hold of his hand. "It's an act, like any other performance. You are the only man who truly knows me. The one I trust with my secrets." She squeezed his fingers. "One day soon, we'll have enough to run away together, just like we planned. It will all be worth it in the end, my love. You'll see."

He still didn't meet her gaze. Hmm. Perhaps she'd been too neglectful of him the past two weeks. She'd have to make amends. Fan the flame of his ardor. Ensure he remained fully under her control. Now was not the time, however. She had other flames to fan.

Reaching into her handbag, she confirmed the presence of the bottle of laudanum she always packed for her romantic encounters. Mr. Ambrose Clayton wouldn't know what hit him. They'd share that wine he promised, she'd endure his overtures with an acting skill that would convince him he was the greatest lover she'd ever known, then he'd tumble into bed—unconscious. His lovely diamond cuff links would turn up missing the next morning, but his clothing would be strewn so wildly about the room that he'd easily imagine the studs rolling into a shadowy corner and turning up later. He'd savor her memory while she savored his diamonds. A fair trade.

Narcissa met her unsuspecting lover with all the breathy anticipation of a young woman being swept up in the excitement of her first tryst. Those Chicago critics who had dismissed her ability to play the ingenue would have eaten their words had they seen her performance with Ambrose Clayton. Absolutely magnificent. Never once did he believe her to be anything other than infatuated with him. Not even when his arms grew heavy and his knees weakened. She remained by his side, kissing his face and pandering his ego as if nothing were amiss until the laudanum did its job. Then, as if the curtain had come down, she pushed up from the bed, did up the buttons on her gaping bodice, and exited the scene. She did pause long enough to examine her appearance in the mirror above his bureau, holding up the cuff links to her ears and admiring their sparkle. She might have to remake them into earbobs. She deserved a few new baubles after all her efforts.

A low whistle echoed in the dark outside the window. Cecil had arrived. Narcissa gave the mirror one final glance to ensure all her buttons were done up properly and to appreciate the perfection of her figure from a couple of different angles. Then she returned to work and scribbled a note extolling the exquisite bliss of the night she and Ambrose supposedly shared and how she would never forget him. She left it on the vacant pillow for him to find, then misted a light layer of perfume over the sheets where she would have lain. He'd not remember her being there, but his pride and imagination would fill in the missing pieces.

Satisfied with the setting and props she'd arranged, Narcissa slipped out the back door and found her way to Cecil's buggy. He had her back to the hotel in minutes and escorted her to her room before leaving to return the rented carriage and team to the livery. Glad to have his melancholy face out of her room so she could fully enjoy her latest triumph, she took a seat at her dressing table and unlocked the carved wooden box that held her costume jewelry. She pulled up the false bottom and retrieved her set of jeweler's tools. She'd become quite adept at removing gems from their settings over the last few months, and Mr. Clayton's diamonds provided no great challenge. The stones were separated from the cuff links in less than ten minutes.

Now to hide them away with the others.

Narcissa crossed to where her trunk sat at the end of her bed. She lifted the lid, then peeled back the layers of underclothes piled on the left side until she reached the corsets. Satin and lace slipped over her fingers as she searched for cotton. She found wood instead. The bottom of her trunk.

Had she missed it?

Prying the stack of clothes away from the trunk's side, she peered into the hole, but no white cotton caught her eye amid the colorful satins. Heart pounding, she scooped out piles of clothes and dropped them on the rug next to her. She picked through each item, tossing them hither and yon, still not finding the item she sought.

This couldn't be happening. Months of work. Thousands of dollars. Gone!

She pushed to her feet and scurried over to the standing trunk by the wardrobe and tore through every dress hanging inside. Her white corset was nowhere to be found.

A soft knock tapped on her door, followed by Cecil's request to come in.

Narcissa threw the door wide. She yanked her accomplice into the room, then slammed the door behind him.

"Did you take it?" She grabbed Cecil by his coat lapels. "Did you steal from me?"

She tried to shake him but ended up shaking herself when his posture remained fixed. Hairpins already loosened from her evening with Ambrose fell free, leaving her hair to tumble down her shoulders.

"How could you do this? I trusted you!" Hot tears scored her cheeks. "You and your petty jealousies. If you don't give it back, you're dead to me. Do you understand? Dead!"

Large, strong hands encircled hers and pried her fingers from his coat. She fought his grip, but he held fast. His gaze scanned the room, then focused on her face, his eyes rather flat and sad. "What's missing, Narcissa?"

How dare he take that tone with her, as if she were a trial to be borne? He was the trial. Not her.

"My cotton corset. As if you didn't know." She spat the words at him. All he did was raise a brow. Infuriating man.

"I didn't take your corset, Narcissa. Or anything else." He heaved a sigh and released her wrists. "Haven't I proven my loyalty to you by now? Doing your bidding, abetting your crimes, abandoning innocent girls in the woods."

Innocent girls . . . All at once, a vision rose like a burning sun. Penelope in Narcissa's dress. Her abundant cleavage filling the bodice as if the dress had been made for her. But it hadn't been made for her. It had been made for Narcissa, and it would only fit properly when the correct support garments had been donned. Daring support garments. Garments foreign to a frumpy maid.

Narcissa spun. "The girl! She must've taken it from my trunk for the dress fitting." She launched herself at Cecil, grabbed his hand, and clutched it to her bosom. "You must fetch it back to me, Cecil. Our future depends on it."

"Maybe we should let it go before the law catches on. We don't need a pile of ill-gotten gains. I can take care of you myself."

They might not need them, but *she* did if she hoped to travel to Europe and pass herself off as a wealthy American widow in want of an aristocratic husband.

"Please, Cecil, you must do this for me. I'm sorry I accused you. I know you would never steal from me. I was in a panic and wasn't thinking straight. Please." She lifted his hand to her lips and kissed it, then turned her head and nestled her face against his knuckles like a kitten seeking to be petted. "It's such a little favor. Only a small ride out into the countryside. It's not too much to ask." She kissed his hand again, then looked up into his eyes with all the feigned affection she could muster. "If you love me, you'll do this for me."

He exhaled, and the tension left his arm. Sweet signs of capitulation.

"Thank you, my darling." She hid her triumphant smile in his chest as she snuggled into his embrace. "You're my hero."

15

After two days of wrangling telegraphs from half a dozen lawmen, Titus finally had enough corroboration from the other victims to merit questioning Madame LaBelle and her Chicago Theatrical Company. Five out of seven men on his list confirmed attending one of Madame LaBelle's performances. Three of those admitted to receiving a backstage tour. None of them admitted to any kind of romantic encounter with Madame LaBelle or any of the other actresses or staff. Not that Titus put too much stock in those reports. Hubert Hathaway's account had been more candid than most. Men of prestige tended to guard their reputations with great diligence. Especially the married ones. What happened behind closed doors stayed behind closed doors.

Good thing Rangers were adept at kicking doors down. Although, he'd have to limit himself to kicking down *back* doors. A Ranger fishing for a promotion couldn't afford to anger the wrong people.

Titus stepped onto the train platform in Weatherford, Texas, and immediately spotted a broadside plastered across the depot advertising the "spellbinding" Madame LaBelle at the Haynes Opera House on the square.

Kind of them to point him in the right direction. Titus slung his small knapsack over his shoulder, straightened his hat, and moseyed down Main Street toward the town square.

After tracking the troupe to Granbury, he'd taken the train from Austin, hoping to find them still in town. He'd missed them by two days. Thankfully, Henry Kerr, the opera house owner, had been aware of the next stop on their Western tour and directed Titus to Weatherford.

It felt good to stretch his legs after spending the better part of the day trapped in a railroad car. He contemplated dropping his bag off at the Commercial Hotel and renting a room since he was sure to be stuck here overnight, but if Madame LaBelle and her troupe were due to perform this evening, it'd be better to see them straightaway. The closer to show time it got, the less cooperative they were likely to be.

So he continued his march to the square. Nodded at the pair of men sitting outside the hardware shop playing checkers atop an old barrel, tipped his hat to an older lady exiting a dress shop, and chuckled at the antics of a group of boys running through the streets chasing a frantic chicken that must've escaped from a nearby coop. Titus crooked a grin. They reminded him of the chicken herding he and Tate had done as boys. Nothing honed a young man's reflexes like chasing chickens.

The Parker County Courthouse rose in front of him like a castle, its pale limestone edifice grand as it stretched three stories into the sky. Its central tower stretched even taller. A rounded recess seemed to indicate a clock would be installed in the tower at some point. Probably when the county managed to raise the funds. It really was a sight. Dome-capped roofs at each of the four corners sported red shingles, drawing attention upward. Thin, elongated windows expanded across the top two floors as if a heavenly hand had reached down and stretched the building from two stories into three.

Where had *that* fanciful thought come from?

Titus ducked his head and strode into the wide square. He needed to focus on business. Not on castle-esque buildings that reminded him of the whimsical Miss Snow.

Miss Snow. Titus grimaced as her far-too-lovely image rose in his mind. Innocent smile. Cheerful disposition. Courageous spirit. Or so he'd thought.

Had she been the woman keeping company with Hathaway and the other wealthy theater patrons? The one stealing their valuables? Or distracting them while a partner committed the actual crime? Had her sweet temperament and guileless aura been an act?

It hadn't felt like one. Everything about her had seemed genuine. But maybe he was just as susceptible to a woman's charms as his brother had been. Worse, since he'd been prideful enough to think himself immune.

Would Penelope steal from Doc and the others? The Diamond D hands didn't have much to tempt a thief, but whoever had been nabbing jewels across Texas specialized in poaching men over the age of forty. Maybe he should stop by the ranch after this interview. Make sure she hadn't taken advantage of anyone.

'Course, if she had, that would make it a lot easier to rid himself of the annoying feelings that plagued him whenever she crossed his mind. Which was far too often. He was twenty-seven, for heaven's sake. Too old and sensible to get wobbly over a woman.

"You lost, mister?" A boy around the age of nine stood in front him, head tipped to the side, forehead scrunched.

Apparently, Titus had been so deep in thought he'd stopped in the middle of the square. *Get your head on straight, Kingsley.*

"I'm looking for the Haynes Opera House." Better to be perceived as an out-of-place newcomer than a woolgathering sap. "Know where it is?"

"Sure!" The kid swiveled and pointed to the west side of the square. "Right there. Above the grocery."

Titus pulled a penny out of his pocket and flipped it toward the boy. "Thanks."

The kid's eyes widened, but his surprise didn't keep him from snatching the coin out of the air. "You're welcome!"

He clutched the coin tightly and took off, no doubt to hunt down his buddies and show off his prize.

Titus grinned, then sobered as he veered around the courthouse and stalked toward the opera house. He might not wear a physical badge, but he carried the weight of the Texas Ranger title and the duty it bestowed. He had a job to do. Even if it meant proving himself a fool for being beguiled by a pretty face.

A large sign stretched the length of the building with white letters that spelled out *China Hall Groceries*. Since Titus wasn't hunting potatoes and coffee, he bypassed the door and strode down Dallas Avenue, seeking an exterior staircase. He found one at the rear of the building. The door at the top opened when he tried the latch, and he slipped inside.

People bustled about in a swirl of chaos. Some in costume, some carting props, some in the rafters rigging ropes with sandbags. He must have found the backstage entrance. Titus wound his way through the throng, taking inventory of each person he spied, glad they were too busy to notice his presence. Until a harried woman carrying a dress with more fabric than the theater curtain nearly ran him down.

"Sorry. I . . ." Her mouth closed, and the corners dipped in a frown. "You're not supposed to be back here. The show doesn't start for another couple hours."

Titus touched the brim of his hat and dipped his chin. "I'm not here for the show, miss. I'm here to talk to the manager. Official Ranger business."

"As in Texas Ranger?"

He nodded. "Yes, ma'am."

Her gaze darted around the stage area, then she surprised him by jerking her head in the direction of an unoccupied corner. She scurried away, leaving him to follow.

"I want to report a missing person," she whispered when he caught up to her. "Penelope Snow. She's around twenty years old, dark hair, pale complexion. She was Madame's personal maid. She disappeared over two weeks ago. No one knows what happened to her."

Titus almost flinched at hearing her name. The confirmation that Miss Snow was indeed part of the theater troupe soured his stomach. Until this moment, he hadn't realized he'd been searching for another woman meeting her description among the company, hoping she wasn't the girl Hathaway had mentioned. That it was all a coincidence. But the small bit of wiggle room he'd managed to preserve vanished at the mention of her name.

Penelope *was* the girl Hubert Hathaway described. Meaning, she was one of two likely suspects for the position of Hathaway's paramour. A paramour who was either a thief or a thief's accomplice.

Shoving down his disappointment with ruthless efficiency, Titus sharpened his attention on the woman before him. "Did she have any enemies that you know of, or anyone who would wish her harm?"

Someone who would tie her to a tree and leave her in the middle of nowhere. Perhaps a disgruntled accomplice?

Tears suddenly flooded the woman's eyes. "It's my fault. She was just trying to help me. But Madame got so angry. I—"

"Mildred!"

The woman jumped as if the snapping voice had been a gunshot. Her lashes dropped over her eyes and her lips pressed together so tightly white lines appeared.

"Where have you been?" Another woman approached, Titus surmised by the tapping of shoes and swishing of petticoats. "I asked for that dress twenty minutes ago. I need it for the second . . . act."

Titus pivoted to greet the newcomer and had to fight to keep his jaw hinged in place. It was as if Cleopatra, Helen of Troy, and Bathsheba had been melted down and poured into a new vessel to create the woman before him. Power. Beauty. Temptation. Her dress fit her like a second skin, showing off every curve, of which there were many. All in the right places. He forced his gaze to her face, then quickly veered from the beauty mark determined to draw his attention to plump lips that pouted just enough to put kissing into a man's mind.

"Can I help you, Mr. . . . ?" Her voice took on a husky tone, and he didn't miss the way she adjusted her posture into just the right position to show off her figure to its best advantage.

Titus hardened his heart. "Ranger Titus Kingsley of the Frontier Battalion, ma'am."

He watched her carefully as he revealed his title. She was good. Only a blink and a slight change in her breathing gave away her surprise.

"Are you Madame LaBelle?" Of course she was. Everything about her commanded attention.

She smiled, her lips lifting slightly higher on the left, as if pointing to that beauty mark. "I am. Can I help you with something, Ranger Kingsley?"

"I'd like to ask you a few questions, if I may."

Her hand fluttered at her breast, but his gaze didn't follow. He knew this type of beauty. Seductive. Manipulative. Selfish. The same variety Nora had possessed. The kind that got Tate killed. Titus's pulse slowed. His control clicked into place. She could pose, flaunt, and flirt all she wanted. He'd not be distracted. Not anymore. The shock of her had worn off.

As if she sensed the change in him, she lowered her arm and touched Mildred's shoulder. "Please take the costume to my dressing room and inform Mr. Billings we have a guest."

"Yes, Madame." Mildred scurried away, sparing Titus a quick, pleading glance.

Pleading for what? His help? His silence?

"Why don't we head to the front of the house?" Madame LaBelle gestured toward a door to his right. "That way the troupe can complete their preparations without distraction, and we can speak in private."

He nodded, held the door open, and allowed her to go through ahead of him, not surprised when she passed close enough for her skirt to brush his leg. The woman was a skilled seductress. Nothing like Penelope.

Unless Penelope was even more clever. Able to project innocence the way Madame LaBelle projected allure. The notion rubbed against his grain, but he had to consider it. He couldn't afford to be suckered. Better a cynic than a fool.

Titus followed the actress into the gallery, the electric lights making it easy to scan the seat rows for threats. Not that there were any in the vacant theater, but Titus checked anyway. Danger could emerge from anywhere. Assumptions got a man killed.

"Now, Ranger Kingsley," Madame said as she turned to face him, "how can I be of assistance?"

Her smile had lost its seductive edge, taking on a polite veneer. He preferred this version, but the fact that she had recognized his preference and adjusted to match kept him on edge. The woman was a chameleon. Which would make discerning the truth a challenge.

"Do you know a Hubert Hathaway?"

She blinked, and her smile flattened. "Yes." She drew out the word as if not quite certain. "I believe so. I seem to recall a man by that name coming backstage after one of my shows." Her gaze tilted up. "Was it Waco? Or maybe Cameron?" She shrugged. "I've performed in so many places it's hard to keep track."

"It was in Eulogy."

"Eulogy! Of course." Her charm thickened. "Sweet little town by the river. I remember now."

Titus didn't return her smile. "He had a costly stickpin go missing sometime after attending your performance."

"How dreadful." Madame shook her head. "You don't think one of my troupe members had anything to do with . . . You *do.*" A fierce look crossed her face. "I can assure you that this troupe is comprised of hardworking, honest people. If anyone had found such a valuable piece of jewelry, they would have turned it in. I'm sure of it." A small frown puckered her brow. "I can see you are less than convinced. If you like, I can ask our manager, Alfred Billings, to do a search." She turned toward the stage and waved her hand. "Freddie, darling," she trilled. "Come here, please."

Billings handed something over to one of the stagehands, then made his way down the aisle.

"Before he joins us, Madame, I need to ask a personal question. Did you spend the night in the company of Hubert Hathaway after your performance in Eulogy?"

A quiet gasp echoed in the air around them. "How dare you insinuate such a thing, Mr. Kingsley. Ranger or not, you have no right to smear a lady's reputation. Just because I am an actress does *not* mean that I am a woman of loose morals."

Heat crept up the back of his neck, but he held his ground. "Please answer the question, miss."

"Of course I did not spend the night with him." She drew herself up, indignant. "Did he say otherwise? If he did, I'll be bringing charges against him for defamation."

"He claimed to have spent the evening with a woman from this company, but he did not mention anyone by name. He did mention the woman was exceptionally beautiful, though, and you seem to fit that description."

She raised a brow. "While I'm flattered you find me attractive, I think it prudent to mention that many of the women in our company fit that description." Her attention shifted to the manager, who had just reached them. "Isn't that right, Alfred? We have several beautiful women in this troupe."

Billings shot her an odd look but readily agreed. "That's right. Sarah and Peony, our other actresses, are quite lovely girls." His face brightened. "Oh, and then there was Miss Snow. I hadn't noticed her until a couple weeks ago. In a proper dress, that girl could bring down the house. I wanted her to train as Narci's understudy, but she balked at the idea. Ran off that night, as I recall."

"Ran off?"

"Yes, the ungrateful tart." Madame LaBelle shot a peeved look at Billings before catching herself and smoothing her features as she turned back to Titus. "She was my personal maid. Ran off without a word and left me completely in a lurch. It's been a trial trying to replace her."

Madame drew in a breath, then stopped. Her eyes lit as if she just remembered something.

"I hired her in Chicago at the start of my tour. I felt sorry for the poor dear." She leaned closer to Titus and lowered her voice. "She was escaping a scandal from what I understood. Something between her and the eldest son of a wealthy family where she worked." She lowered her lashes in a way that made her insinuation clear. "Carlisle was the name, in case you want to look into that. She couldn't get work in town, and I needed someone willing to leave for an extended period, so I took her on. Perhaps that was my mistake." She raised her chin. “If you’re looking for someone with a penchant for getting tangled up in trouble with wealthy men, Penelope Snow is the one you should find.”

Doubts pummeled Titus’s gut. Scandal? Wealthy men? Had she really duped him so thoroughly?

“I’ll be sure to look into Miss Snow,” he said, his voice tight. “In fact, when Mr. Billings and I conduct our search, we’ll start with any belongings Miss Snow might have left behind.”

Perhaps he’d find a clue to what had really happened to her. She hadn’t simply run away as Madame claimed. She’d been abducted and tied to a tree. He needed to determine whether that circumstance was a result of her own criminal actions or the actions of another.

“Excellent notion, Mr. Kingsley.”

A shiver of revulsion snaked down his neck when she winked at him. Madame LaBelle was self-absorbed and conniving, but was she a thief? Hard to tell. He’d search her quarters with extra thoroughness.

“If I can be of any assistance,” she practically purred, “do let me know.” Madame LaBelle stretched her neck and smiled like a pampered feline as she sauntered away, not a shade of worry in her dark eyes.

Titus clenched his jaw, wishing he had a dog around to watch his back.

16

Let go of that rope, you mangy mutt!" Jeb's cantankerous tone carried across the yard to where Penelope was taking clean sheets down from the line. "It ain't a toy."

Pausing in her work, Penelope twisted toward the barn to find Jeb and Lucky engaged in a tug-of-war battle in front of the corral.

"Never shoulda helped Doc save your ungrateful hide." Jeb's frown held enough vinegar to pickle a bushel of cucumbers. "Drop it!"

Lucky wagged his head, his jaw clamped tight.

Oh dear.

Penelope quickly replaced the clothespins on the flapping sheet she'd been taking down, then hurried to intercept the rope duel. "Lucky," she called in a singsong voice. "Come here, boy."

The coonhound's ears lifted, and his head turned, but he didn't release his prize. She rejoiced at seeing the dog so full of energy, but she didn't want him to jeopardize his position here by aggravating one of the Diamond D hands. She and Lucky shared a kinship—two down-on-their-luck creatures with nowhere to go. They needed to find a niche, a purpose. Something of value to contribute. Something other than trouble.

"Stupid dog," Jeb muttered under his breath, his ears reddening as Penelope joined them.

Was he embarrassed? Perhaps it wasn't impatience and frustration that brought on his fit of temper, but chagrin over his inability to win this battle of wills.

"Maybe if you drop your end, he'll think the game is over," she suggested.

"And maybe if I drop my end, he'll run off with the entire coil, and I'll have to hike all over creation to get it back."

Penelope shrugged. "If that happens, I'll fetch it for you. Only fair since it was my suggestion."

She thought removing the risk would ease Jeb's resistance, but his frown only intensified. "As if I'd let a lady fetch and carry for me."

Her heart pinched. She hadn't meant to hurt his pride.

"Forget it." He released his grip on the coil and stomped off toward the house.

Penelope sighed as she hunkered down beside a triumphant Lucky, who wagged his prize back and forth in celebration.

She leveled a stern look at the exuberant hound and pointed to the ground. "Drop it, please."

Lucky cocked his head and let out a small whine.

"That isn't yours."

Hanging his head, he opened his jaws and let the rope fall to the ground.

She smiled. "Good boy." She hugged his neck and petted him with great affection, digging her fingers into his fur and rubbing all his favorite spots.

Hugs and pats had never really been a part of Penelope's youth. She'd known Edith cared for her, but her guardian's affection had been shown through her cooking, not through kisses and handholding and other physical displays. Penelope had never realized how sterile her life had been until she took on the duty of tending to Lucky. He accepted her affection as if he'd been starved for kindness, lapping up as much as she could give. And she gave as if she'd been storing it up her entire life, just waiting for a willing receptacle. Two hungry souls seeking to love and be loved in return.

"You must behave better than this," she scolded gently as she rubbed his ears. "We need these men to like us."

As much as Doc and the others had made her feel welcome, she couldn't quite escape the nagging fear that she could be asked to leave at any time.

"We need to show them that we are assets, not liabilities." She laid her face against his neck. "We've given them two extra mouths to feed, you know."

Doc had surprised her earlier this week with an entire basketful of items he'd purchased on his last trip to town. An apron for her kitchen work, a box of hairpins, stockings, shoes—new ones, even though she'd insisted on secondhand when he'd asked her for her size. He'd told her not to worry about the cost. Said that Titus had left enough money to cover the cost of the shoes, and the others had chipped in for the rest. Such kind souls. It warmed her heart every time she placed a pin in her hair or tied the apron strings around her waist. The little flips her stomach turned each time she looked at her feet were another matter. She really needed to stop reacting like a silly schoolgirl. Titus was a good man who saw a need and addressed it. Nothing more. Reading any personal meaning into the gift would be foolish.

Then there'd been the fabric. A pretty, navy calico sprinkled with tiny yellow flowers. She'd tried to refuse it. After all, she'd made over one of his wife's bodices last week and didn't need a new dress. But maybe Doc was embarrassed by her patchwork fashion. *Peterson's Magazine* would certainly not be inviting her to model her ensemble for their summer issue, but she rather enjoyed the cheerful mix of colors. The deep blue bodice sported puffed sleeves that she was able to take in for the snugger fit currently in style, though she did leave a nice pouf at the shoulder to match some of the fashions she'd seen in Madame's magazines. The remake had required the addition of filler material beneath the arms to expand the bustline, and on a whim, she'd opted for red. The bold color was mostly hidden by her arms, but those crimson panels gave her an excuse to wear the red ribbon she'd found in Mabel's trunk. It reminded her of the one she lost in the woods the night of her abduction, and wearing it kindled gratitude for the chance she'd been given to restart her life.

Doc ignored her protests about the new fabric, of course, and insisted she make herself a dress. One that fit properly. And when she'd vowed to clean the house from top to bottom to try to cover such an expense, he'd waved her offer aside.

"You don't have to earn your place here, Penelope," he'd said. "This is your home now. You're one of us, and we take care of our own."

She didn't quite know what to do with such grace. Accepting it from her Lord made sense, because everyone had fallen short of God's glory and needed Christ's redemption. One's background or status made no difference to a God who did not show favoritism. But accepting grace in human form where status made all the difference? That was a new experience. One she didn't quite trust. She wanted to believe Doc. Her heart craved a home and a family with a soul-deep hunger. Yet she'd been taught that the best way to avoid disappointment in life was to work hard and expect little. So how was she to handle such a bountiful gift?

Lucky licked her face, erasing her thoughts and eliciting a giggle. Maybe the dog had the right idea. Enjoy the blessings the Lord provided in the moment and take each new day as it came.

"'This is the day which the Lord hath made,'" she quoted

softly as she rose to her feet. "'We will rejoice and be glad in it.' Won't we, Lucky?"

The hound wagged his tail in an enthusiastic manner, and her smile widened.

"But we'll also use our day to be a blessing to others." She picked up the coil of rope Jeb had left behind, avoiding the more slobbery sections, then pointed a finger at Lucky. "I expect you to apologize." He cocked his head, his ears crinkling. "Don't pretend not to know what I mean. You're going to help me return this rope, and I expect you to look contrite while doing so."

Lucky sat on his haunches and looked up at her expectantly. Mouth open, tongue lolling. Nothing the least bit repentant in his demeanor. Oh well. At least he was no longer chewing on Jeb's rope.

Penelope patted her leg. "Come on, then. Time to make amends."

Lucky yipped and ran a circle around her feet, nearly tripping her as she strolled toward the porch. When she reached the house, she pitched her voice low so as not to wake Angus, who snored peacefully in his favorite rocker, feet propped up on the railing and arms folded over his belly. Jeb's arms were folded as well, though she wouldn't classify his posture as *peaceful. Perturbed* seemed a better fit.

"Here's your rope, Jeb." Penelope handed it through the rail slats and set the coil next to Jeb's chair. "Lucky is very sorry for the trouble he caused."

Jeb grunted. "Uh-huh. The mutt looks real broke up about it."

Penelope glanced the dog's way and found Lucky chasing his tail. She bit back a sigh. "Well, *I'm* sorry that he misbehaved. I'll try to teach him some—"

"Miss Penny! Come quick!"

She spun at Ike's call, her heart fluttering in alarm until she caught a glimpse of the smile beaming across the man's face as he ran up to the house.

Angus snorted, his snore cutting off as his boots hit the porch floor. "What's goin' on?"

Ike ignored him, his attention locked on Penelope. He took her hand and urged her forward. His eyes sparkled with secrets, piquing her curiosity.

"You have to see them. Hurry. They won't linger for long."

His smile was contagious, drawing a matching grin from her. "What won't linger?"

He gave her arm a tug. "You'll see."

A laugh bubbled through her as she trotted after him. Past the laundry. Past his garden. What could he possibly . . . ?

Oh my.

Penelope's hand slid from Ike's as he drew to a halt. She continued forward, unable to stop herself from walking into the magic.

Ike murmured something about a fall migration, but Penelope's mind couldn't focus on mundane explanations. Not while inside a field of fairies.

Hundreds of monarch butterflies flitted like autumn leaves swirling on the wind. They danced above her, around her, everywhere she looked. She turned in a slow circle, arms outstretched, too awestruck to do more than smile. Then one landed on her skirt. Penelope stilled. Another alit on her hand. She tried to absorb the miracle by slowly bending her arm to bring the golden creature closer. It took to the air, but hovered near, flying so close to her face that its wings kissed her cheek.

Her breath caught, and her smile widened. Kissed by a butterfly. Could a moment ever be more perfect?

He couldn't have arrived at a worse moment.

Titus gritted his teeth as he dismounted from Rex and slowly stalked the group of men hovering at the edge of the garden.

He hardened his heart, refusing to succumb to the enchantment holding the Diamond D men enthralled. Miss Snow might look the picture of innocence, but he'd not be taken in. Insects were drawn to beauty, not character. So the fact that they danced around her, alighting in her hair and on her shoulders, meant nothing. Neither did her soft, delighted laughter. It might ring with childlike purity, but it wasn't real.

The telegram he'd received this morning from Captain Bill's contact in Chicago burned through the fabric of his shirt pocket to brand his chest with its truth. Penelope Snow had been dismissed from the Carlisle household after attempting to entice the son of the house, Mr. Gerard Carlisle, into a compromising liaison. Mrs. Carlisle believed the conniving maid intended either to trap her son into marriage or to use the resulting scandal as blackmail fodder to get her hands on a portion of the Carlisle fortune.

Doc and the others had no fortune to speak of, but that didn't mean Miss Snow didn't have a reason for staying here. The Diamond D Ranch was the perfect hideout for someone trying to escape the law's notice. Off the beaten path. Secluded. Although, why she would choose to stay when she knew a Texas Ranger had ties to the place didn't quite add up, but she didn't know he'd been assigned to her case. She probably thought she'd enchanted him as thoroughly as she had Doc and the others. That cockiness would be her downfall. His instincts might have steered him wrong initially, but he was on his guard now.

She could dance with butterflies all she liked. That wouldn't stop him from clipping her wings if that's what it took to see justice done.

"Miss Snow?" His words escaped his tight throat in a raspy growl. "I need a word."

Angus and Jeb stepped aside to the left and Ike and Doc stepped aside to the right, all four of them sporting bemused expressions that fed his indignation. How dare this woman take advantage of these good-hearted men?

The woman in question twirled to face him. Her eyes lit as she recognized him, and her already bright smile somehow increased its gleam.

A momentary doubt pinched his gut, but he shoved it down. He would not be one of her gaggle of conquests.

"Titus! Isn't it amazing?" She lifted her arms, and the butterflies swirling around her followed her movement. "It's like a fairy story."

"And you'd know all about fairy stories, wouldn't you?"

Her smile dimmed at his sharp tone, and her arms lowered to her sides. A crinkle formed between her brows as if she were trying to puzzle out his meaning.

Well, he'd be glad to clear it up for her. He stormed forward and grasped her wrist, sending the butterflies fluttering away in fright.

"You like weaving fiction, don't you? Manipulating men. Stealing their belongings, their good names."

She made no move to tug free of his hold, but the hurt in her eyes nearly had him letting go. He steeled himself against the pity rising inside him and tightened his grip.

"Titus Kingsley!" Doc stormed up beside him. "Unhand that young woman this instant."

He shook his head. "I'll do no such thing, Grandpa. She's a suspect in a robbery case. Not the innocent young woman you believe her to be."

Doc's face glowed red, and his glasses started to fog as he settled into place at Penelope's side. "I don't care if she's wanted for murder. You will treat her with kindness and respect, or you will leave my property."

Angus, Jeb, and Ike followed Doc's example and positioned themselves around Penelope, arms crossed and glowers dark. An angry bark sounded behind Titus, and he glanced over his shoulder to see Lucky running toward their little gathering with teeth bared, Dusty and Coy hot on his heels.

For Pete's sake. Had they all lost their minds?

He released Penelope's wrist, turned on his heels to pace a couple of steps away in a desperate bid to control his temper, then spun back to face the very men he was trying to protect. "She's not who you think she is." He grabbed the telegram from his pocket and shoved it at Doc. "She's a schemer and a seducer. I have evidence of her perfidy from the Carlisles of Chicago and a string of thefts that follow the route she traveled since her arrival in Texas. I'm taking her to headquarters for questioning."

Doc glanced at the telegram, but his chin only jutted more stubbornly. "And *I* have evidence of her sweet nature, honorable character, and giving spirit. You won't be taking her anywhere without something more concrete than this scrap of hearsay." He stepped up to Titus and crammed the telegram back into his pocket, the disappointment in his eyes cutting Titus to the quick.

"You don't understand—" Titus began.

"So now you think I'm feebleminded?"

"Of course not. It's just that she's pulled the wool over your eyes."

"So I'm a fool."

"That's not what I . . ." Titus groaned.

"Stop." Miss Snow squeezed between Jeb and Angus and laid a hand on Doc's shoulder. "Please." The old man seemed to melt at her touch. Even the dog ceased his growling when her skirt brushed his side. Then she lifted her eyes and met Titus's gaze. "I'll answer any questions you have. Here or at Ranger headquarters. Whichever you prefer."

Her gray eyes shimmered with heartbreak, making him feel like one of those mean-spirited kids who tore wings from butterflies. But he wasn't. He was a man of the law. Charged with bringing criminals to justice. And he'd do his duty regardless of how much his chest ached at the sight of her vulnerability.

17

Tiny glass shards pricked Penelope's heart, the shallow cuts coalescing into a hurt big enough to threaten tears as Titus ushered her into the house. She blinked the moisture away, not wanting Doc or the others to worry. It was her own fault, after all. She'd known better than to dream of fairy tales. Dreams got girls like her into trouble. Yet she'd not been able to resist the lure of imagining a fine man like Titus Kingsley turning a courting eye in her direction. A man who rode hours out of his way to save a dog's life. One who treated old men with dignity and bought shoes for destitute women he barely knew. A man capable and kind and strong enough to carry her through a mesquite grove without breaking a sweat. A man she'd foolishly imagined returning to the Diamond D someday to claim her as his own.

Well, he had. Only the claim he aimed to stake involved a jail cell instead of her heart. While she'd been daydreaming about him riding to her rescue, he'd been uncovering her darkest secrets. He thought her a villain, and she had no evidence to disprove his theory. All she had was the truth, but without corroboration, it would just be her word against that of the Carlisles. Those odds hadn't worked in her favor back in Chicago, and she doubted they'd do much better in Texas.

Give him ears to hear, Lord. She swallowed hard. *And help me to trust you to hold my future secure.*

God's protection didn't always mean immediate rescue, however. Joseph had been an innocent man, yet he'd been sold into slavery, thrown in jail, and left to rot for years before God's deliverance arrived.

She bit her lip and added a silent addendum to her divine petition. *I'd really prefer not to rot in jail if that's an option.*

"Use the parlor," Doc groused when Titus tried to steer her to the kitchen.

"Fine." He turned into the front room, then stutter stepped before escorting her to the small settee in front of the hearth.

Had he noticed the changes she'd made to the room? The parlor had been buried under three inches of dust the last time he'd been here. It had taken her a full day of scrubbing, polishing, and rug beating to make it habitable. Then she'd collected little items from each of the Diamond D gentlemen to make it feel more like home. A seed catalog and farmer's almanac on the side table for Ike. A glass jar to hold Rowdy's treasures on the corner of the mantle. One of Dusty's whittled horses on the opposite side. A photograph of Doc and his late wife in the place of honor in the center.

Over the last week, the men had taken to gathering in here in the evenings. They'd tell stories about the old days while she mended torn sleeves and replaced lost buttons by lamplight. How she'd miss those stories.

Doc settled on the settee cushion next to her and patted her hand. "Don't you worry, Miss Penny. I won't let him railroad you." He shot a scowl at his grandson.

Titus's hands flew upward in disgust. "For Pete's sake, Doc. When have you ever known me to railroad anyone? You're acting as if I'm part of the Spanish Inquisition."

Doc jutted out his chin. "That's because you charged in here spouting accusations as if they were facts. I intend to ensure she gets a fair hearing."

"This isn't court, Grandpa. It's just an interview." Titus sighed as he sank into the padded chair across from the settee. He hung his head a bit as he pulled his hat off.

"Maybe so, but I'd hate for those preconceived notions of yours to skew these proceedings."

Hurt flashed in Titus's eyes before he shuttered it away behind a mask of impatience, a hurt Penelope recognized all too well. It cut deeply when the people who were supposed to be on your side lined up against you. Coworkers, employers, friends. How much worse to feel as if family were turning against you? As much as she adored Doc for standing up for her, she couldn't be responsible for putting these two honorable men at odds.

"I trust him," she said softly. She even willed a small smile and a nod when Titus glanced her way. Unable to hold his gaze, she swiveled toward Doc and squeezed his hand. "You do too," she said. "Don't deny it. Just last night you were talking about how the Rangers would be fools not to grant him a promotion. 'No one can match his courage and integrity.' Isn't that what you said?"

Doc grunted. "I did."

"Then there you have it. I'll answer his questions, and all will be well. You'll see." She doubted her forced cheerfulness fooled anyone, but she had to believe things would work out. Faith was all she had.

Titus had no idea what to make of the woman sitting before him. He'd convinced himself over the last twenty-four hours that he'd be able to see through her charade now that he knew the truth about her past. But as she pushed her trembling bottom lip into a brave little smile, his confidence wavered. Nothing about her felt the least bit jaded or artificial.

The apron she wore sported pockets that bulged with clothespins, attesting to the fact that she'd been hanging laundry before taking a break to dance with butterflies. In his experience, women used to bending men to their will didn't engage in menial labor. Nor did they stop someone from defending them just to save another person's feelings. Which was exactly what she'd done. It could all be a master manipulation, but looking at the scared young woman before him, he found that theory harder and harder to credit. No one was that good. Even Madame LaBelle had slipped once or twice during his interview, letting him see flashes of the woman behind the actress.

His gut told him Narcissa LaBelle was a more likely suspect, but a search of her room had turned up none of the missing jewelry nor any concrete ties to the men on his list. He'd found nothing tying Penelope to the jewelry, either. Just a pitifully small pile of belongings consisting of a well-worn copy of *Oliver Twist*, a Bible, and a photograph and handful of letters from someone named Edith Johnson. Nevertheless, the Carlisle testimony established a pattern he couldn't ignore, one that fit the elements of his theft case far too well. He'd had no choice but to move Penelope Snow to the top of his suspect list.

"Tell me, Miss Snow," Titus said as pulled out his notebook and turned to the page where he'd written the names of the men who'd lost valuables. He handed the notebook to her. "Are you acquainted with any of these gentlemen?"

Her fingers shook as she took the tablet, but her eyes dutifully darted over each line. "No. At least I don't think so."

"You're not sure?"

"I . . ."

Doc raised a hand, causing Penelope to blink and shrink

back. "Just a moment, my dear." He turned his face toward the front window and cupped his hands around his mouth. "Jeb?"

"Yeah?" The response filtered through the window loud and clear.

"Take the others down to the barn for a spell, would ya? I'll come fetch you when we're done here."

Shuffles and grunts echoed from the porch. "You heard the man," Jeb groused. "Get a move on."

Penelope's fair complexion turned scarlet. Suddenly Titus was glad Penelope had an advocate who was more concerned with protecting her than getting answers.

He met his grandpa's eye. "Good idea."

Doc shrugged. "They care about her. Only natural for them to want to know what's goin' on."

Penelope swallowed hard as she lifted her chin. "I care about them, too. About all of you." She peered into Doc's weathered face, her face earnest. "No matter what happens with this interview, I want you to know that I appreciate everything you've done for me. You've all been so kind and welcoming. I promise that I won't let my past shame tarnish your good names."

Titus's ears pricked at her near admission. But before he could form a question, Doc responded, his voice thick with emotion.

"We all got things in our pasts we're not proud of, Penny. No need to throw around wild promises before we even get out of the starting block. Let's just take it one step at a time, all right?"

She pressed her lips together and nodded. Then she turned her wide gray eyes on Titus. "You may continue."

He cleared his throat, glancing down to his notepad to escape the haunted look in her eyes. "You said you didn't recognize any of these names, but each of these men attended a performance by the Chicago Theatrical Company. A company you worked for, correct?"

She nodded. "Yes, I worked as Madame LaBelle's personal maid, but I had no interaction with any of the patrons."

"Not even the ones who were granted backstage privileges?" Titus watched her carefully for any sign of scrambling, but her expression remained open and sincere.

"The men who get invited backstage are always wealthy patrons who Mr. Billings and Madame believe can be wooed into donating to the arts. My only interactions with them included taking their hats and gloves and fetching them a glass of wine. I was never introduced."

Which made sense for a servant. Yet Titus couldn't forget the way Hubert Hathaway had described her. It could be a way to catch her in a lie. . . .

"Did any of these patrons ever try to engage you in conversation?"

Doc arched a brow at the question, but Titus ignored him, more concerned with the touch of pink creeping back into Penelope's cheeks.

"Only one that I recall. Madame had been called away by some business with Mr. Billings, leaving the gentleman to explore on his own. He came across me in the wings as I was returning Madame's costumes to the rack. Servants are typically invisible to wealthy types, so I was quite startled when he struck up a conversation. I acknowledged him but did my best to discourage any further discourse. Madame has strict rules against fraternizing with patrons, and I knew better than to break one of her rules. Besides, the way he looked at me made me uncomfortable. I made up an excuse about needing to check on a missing bonnet and left him to his own devices."

Her accounting fit with Hathaway's story. Still, he didn't have proof the man she described was actually Hathaway. To build a case, he'd need something more definitive. "Do you remember what this man looked like?" Anyone who met Hubert Hathaway would be hard-pressed not to remember him.

Sure enough, Penelope nodded. "I remember his head just being visible over the clothes rack, so he must not have been very tall, but the way he carried himself made him seem larger. He had sandy hair and thick sideburns. Oh, and he wore the oddest suit I'd ever seen—dark purple with a bright yellow waistcoat."

Definitely Hubert Hathaway. Now Titus had proof Penelope had interactions with one of the victims.

"Do you recall a jeweled stickpin the man wore?"

She shook her head. "No. Sorry. I was trying to discourage his attention, so I looked at him as little as possible."

Plausible. Although, it made for a convenient excuse as well.

"Is the stickpin one of the items that was stolen?"

Titus looked at her sharply.

She shrugged. "You accused me rather loudly of being a suspect in a robbery case. Something must've been stolen."

He obviously needed to take more care with his words.

"I didn't take it," she volunteered.

He had little reason to take her at her word, yet his gut told him she spoke the truth. Captain Bill required more evidence than his gut, though. So Titus pressed on.

"Tell me about Gerard Carlisle."

Her gaze dropped to her lap. "He was the son of my employer back in Chicago."

Titus's throat constricted around his next question, but he pressed the words through. "Were you romantically involved with him?"

"No!" Her head lifted, and fire lit her eyes.

Her vehemence took him aback.

"I'm sure Mrs. Carlisle painted me as a woman of loose

morals, but it's not true. I was seventeen when I started working for the Carlisles. I knew nothing of men, having grown up at a girls' school. Edith warned me to avoid being caught alone with one. She said many wealthy men considered it sport to dally with female staff. I heeded her advice and kept my distance from Mrs. Carlisle's husband and any gentlemen guests they entertained. The strategy worked for the first year, but when their son returned from traveling abroad, everything changed. Despite my efforts to avoid interacting with him, Mr. Gerard took notice of me right away."

Of course he did. A man would have to be blind not to.

"He would seek me out when his mother was not at home. Try to engage me in conversation. I mentioned it to the housekeeper, and Mrs. Franklin agreed to shift me to other assignments. Apparently, he had a philandering reputation among the staff, though none would ever breathe a word of it in the mistress's hearing out of fear of being dismissed." She fell quiet for a moment. "Even though we took precautions, I still felt him watching me. One day I was passing the library, and I heard a kitten mewling. The mistress did not tolerate animals in the house, so however it had come to be there, I knew I had to get it outside before the mistress found out. The poor little thing couldn't have been more than a week old. Which should have raised my suspicions, but in the moment, I was too worried about the tiny creature to think it might be bait."

Titus's gut tightened painfully. He fought to keep his cynicism in place. This could all be a sob story designed to elicit sympathy, after all. That pill was becoming harder and harder to swallow, though. Wealthy men taking advantage of young women were far too common.

Penelope curled her hands in her lap, one over the other, almost as if she were trying the shelter the tiny beast even now. "When I hurried to the crying kitten's aid, Mr. Gerard locked the library door. He tried to woo me with flattery at first, but when I tried to flee, he abandoned all pretense of manners." Her chin dropped to her chest, and her arms wrapped around themselves as if she'd suddenly grown cold. "He grabbed hold of me," she recounted, her voice quiet and flat. "Pressed his mouth hard against mine. I struggled. Begged him to let me go. He laughed. Dragged me toward the sofa. I flailed and knocked over a tea service, making a dreadful racket. The crash startled him, allowing me to jerk one of my arms free. I grabbed the heavy tea tray off the floor and bashed him over the head." She straightened a bit and took a breath to collect herself. "I reported the incident straightaway to the housekeeper, but there was little she could do. Mrs. Carlisle dismissed me that very day without pay or reference. I was ruined."

Unable to sit still, Titus pushed to his feet and paced over to the window. His hands balled into fists as he struggled to keep his anger in check.

"I'm so sorry that happened to you, Penny," Doc soothed. "Carlisle should have been the one ruined after such vile behavior."

"After Edith got me the job with Madame LaBelle, I did my best to avoid notice," she said, a lost element to her voice that only fueled Titus's ire. "I kept to myself and spoke as little as possible. Wore baggy dresses and drab colors. I didn't socialize with the troupe members and only interacted with them when my duties required it."

He recalled the dress she wore the first time he'd seen her. It was exactly as she described—shapeless and the color of dirt. Not part of a costume worn to influence a passing Ranger of her innocence, for no one, including him, had known he would pass that way. Yet his chance witness served to validate her story.

The second time he'd met her, she'd worn almost nothing.

Stripped and left in the woods to fend for herself. Such callous neglect could have ended in Penelope's death if Rowdy hadn't found her. Even if there had been evidence to support the theory that she'd been double-crossed by an accomplice, she'd still been a victim. A victim more in need of his protection than the Hubert Hathaways of the world.

Titus stared out the window as truth sank into his soul. He'd been wrong. Utterly and completely wrong. Penelope Snow was no seductive thief who manipulated men with her feminine wiles. She was a young woman with a kind heart whose beauty had been used against her—including by him. But no more.

Her mind would be of more use to him now, anyway.

Penelope possessed insight that would prove valuable to his case. She'd lived with the troupe for months. Understood their workings, their relationships. Understood Madame LaBelle herself. Perhaps even her habits when it came to entertaining men. He'd not jump to conclusions again and assume the actress's beauty equaled guilt, but *someone* in the Chicago Theatrical Company was the thief he sought, and Penelope Snow offered the best chance to figure out who.

If she would forgive him.

18

Penelope nibbled on her bottom lip and stared at Titus Kingsley's back. What was he thinking? He looked so tense. His hands balled into fists as he stared out the window. Would he drag her off to Ranger headquarters? Or would he just cart her straight to jail? She'd have to write to Edith. Her only ally. Perhaps she could convince Mrs. Franklin to send in a written statement attesting to Penelope's character and Gerard Carlisle's lack thereof. The housekeeper's testimony wouldn't prove she wasn't a thief, but it might help convince a judge that she wasn't a—what had Titus called her?—a schemer and seducer.

She could still hear those words. His voice echoed in her head, making her chest ache. No one cared to be portrayed in unflattering terms, but having the depiction come from someone she admired drove the knife even deeper. Doc's support helped, but it didn't eliminate the soreness in her spirit.

What was going to become of her? How was she going to—

Titus pivoted to face her, and the movement chopped off her thoughts as effectively as a butcher's cleaver. "I owe you an apology, Miss Snow."

Penelope's mind seemed to freeze in place, sluggish to process what he was saying.

He blew out a breath, then strode away from the window and retook his seat across from her. He leaned forward and braced his forearms on his thighs. Craning his neck, he peered up into her face, regret softening his dark brown eyes.

"I wronged you, Miss Snow, and I'm deeply sorry."

Her pulse pounded, and her breath caught. "Are you saying you . . . believe me?"

He dipped his chin in affirmation, and Penelope's spine buckled in relief. Her arms quivered, and her fingers twitched as a flood of emotions overwhelmed her senses. She turned to smile at Doc, only to find him looking at his grandson with an *It's about time* expression. His annoyance heightened her joy, bringing a small laugh gurgling from her throat as she twisted back to Titus. She tugged her hand away from Doc, then clasped the Ranger's hand between both of hers.

"Thank you, Titus. I . . . I don't know what to say."

"Say you'll forgive me?" His gaze penetrated her giddiness to touch her heart and stir her compassion. True remorse etched his face. And when shame bowed his head and hid his eyes from her, she instinctively tightened her hold on his hand.

"I should never have accused you in such a public manner," he said. "I swooped in here determined to protect Doc and the others from a deceitful woman, but even if you had been up to something nefarious, you posed no imminent threat to anyone when I arrived. You were standing in a field of butterflies, for Pete's sake. I should have pulled you aside and questioned you privately."

"I forgive you."

How could she not? He believed her. In the face of no concrete proof, he believed her. Not only that, but he'd humbled himself and offered the most beautiful, sincere apology she'd ever received.

Slowly, his head lifted, and his eyes met hers. "Thank you."

Something passed between them in that moment. She couldn't define it or even truly identify it. Yet she felt it just the same. Something raw and vulnerable. Delicate yet powerful. Something that carried the promise of a second chance. For both of them.

His eyes widened slightly as if he felt it, too, then he gave his head a little wag before he leaned back in his chair, pulling his hands from her hold. "Doc was right when he mentioned preconceived notions. I tend to expect the worst when it comes to beautiful women. I've seen good men turn their backs on family and honor because of the manipulations of an attractive woman with a selfish agenda. Some even lost their lives." His voice thickened before he cleared his throat and continued. "So when I learned of your questionable history with the Carlisles, I let that overshadow everything I had personally observed of your character. I think a part of me wanted to believe you were guilty because that would mean I was right to categorize all beautiful women as deceitful and untrustworthy. But you don't fit that mold, Miss Snow, and it was wrong of me to assume you did simply because you are fair of face and form."

He thought her fair? How could that be? She wore cobbled-together clothing that no one would consider fashionable, covered by a dusty work apron. She'd shoved her feet into Rowdy's clunky boots so she wouldn't ruin her new shoes with outdoor chores. Her hair was windblown, and her hands probably smelled like dog slobber.

Ever since her encounter with Gerard Carlisle, she'd feared drawing a man's notice. But when Titus looked at her, she didn't want to hide. In fact, a vain little part of her wished she had finished her new dress so he could see her in something that might actually flatter her a little.

Penelope tucked a stray strand of hair behind her ear even

as she reminded herself that God valued the beauty of a person's heart, not the packaging it was wrapped in.

"I know it's presumptuous of me," Titus began, his tone more tentative than she'd ever heard it, "but I'd like to ask for your assistance."

Penelope couldn't imagine what help she could possibly offer a Texas Ranger, but she nodded anyway. "Of course. What can I do?"

He smiled, and his entire face changed. He looked younger. Less . . . burdened.

"Just like that, huh?" He shook his head as if he couldn't quite believe her capitulation.

Penelope shrugged. "'As we have therefore opportunity, let us do good unto all men, especially unto them who are of the household of faith.' You serve a just cause, Mr. Kingsley. I'm not sure how I can help, but I'm willing to try."

Of course she could quote Scripture at the drop of a hat. He'd seen the small Bible among her possessions. The leather worn. The pages crinkled. Ribbon scraps marking a dozen or more passages.

His cynicism was under siege, and he wasn't sure how much longer he could withstand her barrage. Her forgiveness given without hesitation. Her willingness to help him despite the fact that he'd treated her abominably. The way she touched his hand and offered comfort when he was the one who'd wronged her.

He'd never met someone with such generosity of spirit. And to find it packaged inside the most beautiful young woman he'd ever seen left him untethered and adrift.

At least he still had his job to give him stability.

"There has been a string of thefts lately that seem to follow the route taken by the Chicago Theatrical Company. I have reason to believe that a member of the company is responsible for these thefts. As a former member of the troupe, I'm hoping you can share some insight to help me narrow down my pool of suspects."

Penelope frowned slightly. "I didn't interact with many members of the company. Madame LaBelle is a rather . . . demanding employer. She expected me to stay nearby at all times in case she needed something. I didn't mingle much."

Titus struggled with how much to reveal about the case. Telling her that Madame LaBelle was his chief suspect could tempt her to skew her testimony to implicate her former employer, either in retribution for the woman's onerous treatment or to ensure he continued to believe in Penelope's innocence. Neither scenario seemed likely given Penelope's guileless nature, but he couldn't toss out his Ranger training because a potential witness seemed overly wholesome.

"You might know more than you think," he said, opting to keep at least a few cards close to the vest. "For example, when Mr. Billings and Madame LaBelle selected patrons to invite backstage, did they woo these patrons outside the theater as well?"

Penelope leaned back against the settee's cushion, a thoughtful look puckering her brow. "In cities where we offered multiple performances, there was usually a party to celebrate closing night. Madame always took extra care with her appearance for those events. She once had me redo her hair three times before she was satisfied, insisting that everything had to be perfect if she hoped to secure the patron's support."

"So she took the lead with these special guests?"

"Yes. Mr. Billings manages the company, but Madame handles all the wealthy clients personally."

Making her the most likely suspect. Titus stretched his legs out in front of him as he took a minute to cogitate. Not only did Madame have access to men of wealth and prestige, but she bestowed personalized attention on them, giving her opportunity. Especially if that personalized attention took them away from prying eyes.

Titus straightened. "Did Madame LaBelle ever entertain these patrons privately?"

Doc stiffened and shot him a frown. "I hardly think that type of question is appropriate, Titus."

"It might not be appropriate, but it's plenty pertinent." Titus hesitated before turning back to Penelope, allowing some of the awkwardness to fade before encouraging her to continue. "I realize this is an indelicate question, but I wouldn't ask if it didn't have bearing on the case."

Penelope bent her head and started picking at her apron pockets. "I never attended any of those parties, so I really can't say. . . ."

She knew something. Or suspected something. Why else would she leave that sentence hanging?

Titus couldn't let it go. "When Madame was entertaining the patrons at the theater, how did she act toward them? Businesslike? Flirtatious?"

Penelope's head jerked upward at the second descriptor. Flirtatious, then.

"You have to understand," she said. "Madame makes her living off the persona she presents to the world. On stage as well as off. She might act the coquette around the wealthy men she hopes to impress, but I think that is because she believes her beauty is the only thing that gives her value. It's sad, really. She constantly examines herself in the mirror and picks out every flaw and imperfection, no matter how tiny. She is one of the most striking women I've ever seen, yet she is also one of the most unhappy people I've ever known."

The contrast of how Penelope described her mistress and Madame LaBelle's description of her maid could not have been starker. Penelope defended her former employer with unmerited loyalty and compassion, while Madame LaBelle painted her maid as an ungrateful tart. It held a rather unflattering mirror in front of his own soul, for Titus doubted he could have spoken as kindly about someone who had wronged him.

"Forgive me for asking," Titus continued, "but did you ever notice a night, perhaps when one of these parties was going on, that Madame did not return to her room?"

Penelope shook her head. "There were nights when she returned late, but she always returned well before dawn. All the cast members returned late after one of those parties."

"Did she usually return with the other cast members or alone?"

"Alone. Well . . ." She hesitated. "Not alone, exactly. She usually returned with Mr. Hunt."

Titus leaned forward. "Mr. Hunt?"

She evaded his gaze as pink returned to her cheeks. "Cecil Hunt. He's one of the stagehands. He runs errands for her."

"Is that all he does for her?" With the way she was blushing, Titus would bet the man was far more than an errand boy.

"I don't know the precise nature of their relationship, but they are very . . . close."

Now they were getting somewhere. If Hunt and Madame were partners, that could explain why he didn't find any of the missing items in Madame's room. Although, he didn't recall meeting a man named Cecil Hunt when he visited the troupe.

"Does Mr. Hunt run personal errands for Madame?"

She nodded but didn't give any further answer. The way she dipped her chin snagged Titus's attention, however. He remembered that look. She'd looked the same way when he'd asked her about Gerard Carlisle.

Titus's gut tightened. "Penelope, did Hunt hurt you?"

When she finally lifted her face, tears shimmered in her wide eyes. "He helped me in the end, so don't rush off to arrest him, all right? He was only carrying out Madame's orders. She gets in these rages sometimes . . . it was partially my fault . . . I was trying to help Mildred . . . I thought if I wore the dress, Mildred would be able to get the alterations corrected, but Madame saw it as an act of betrayal . . . sh-she went a little crazy . . ."

Titus struggled to make sense of the disjointed story. All he knew for sure was that Hunt had done something worthy of an arrest. To Penelope. Something Madame LaBelle had ordered.

Shoving aside his own rising tension, Titus reached out and clasped Penelope's hand, seeking to comfort her the way she had him. She stilled at his touch, and her gaze finally melded with his.

"What did Hunt do to you?"

She inhaled a shaky breath, and he felt a tremor course down her arm.

"He's the one who tied me to the tree."

19

By the time she finished telling Titus the story of how she came to be cast out of Madame's troupe, Penelope felt as if she'd been stripped bare again. Exposed, not to the elements this time, but to the scrutiny of a man whose opinion mattered more to her than it probably should. Doc, bless his heart, must have sensed her ragged state, for he shooed her off into the kitchen, telling Titus in no uncertain terms that any further questioning could wait until after supper.

He was such a dear. They all were, really. Even Jeb with his grouching. A small smile touched her lips as she took out a mixing bowl from the cupboard and measured out flour, sugar, cornmeal, soda, and salt. She'd never had grandparents growing up, but the Lord had blessed her with seven grandfathers to watch over her when she'd been at her most vulnerable. Seven grandfathers and one Texas Ranger.

A disturbing tickle ran through her midsection at the thought of Titus watching over her. Good heavens. She really needed to stop thinking of the man as some kind of romantic hero. He was a man doing a job. That's all. He needed her for information, nothing else. He held her in no particular esteem. Why, he would've arrested her without a single qualm had she been guilty of a crime . . . which made him a man of integrity. She sighed. Another reason to admire him. Was there no escape?

Swallowing a small growl of frustration, she added milk and eggs to the dry mixture and whipped a wooden spoon through the batter. She stirred until her arm grew tired, diligently searching the bowl for any dry bits of meal and flour as if they were grains of gunpowder that would ignite if she didn't thoroughly dampen them.

Get your mind where it belongs, Pen. On cooking.

The admonition might have worked had the Ranger inducing her ticklish thoughts not walked through the back door right after she'd scraped the last of her batter into a cast-iron skillet.

"Mr. Kingsley!" She startled at his unexpected appearance, the spoon in her hand wiggling wildly enough to splatter a blob of yellow batter onto the front of her apron.

So much for looking her best the next time she saw him. Oh well. Maybe that little dose of reality would keep her mind in check.

Titus pulled his hat off, then rubbed a hand over his head as if to fluff up the wavy hair that had been flattened by his Stetson. Her pulse jumped at the idea that he might be wanting to make himself more attractive for her benefit, but she squelched the unhelpful notion. His head probably just itched.

"I, uh, brought you something." He held out a sling bag she hadn't noticed him carrying. An olive-green one she thought never to see again.

She dropped her spoon into the empty bowl and took a tentative step toward him. "Is that . . . ?

"It's not everything. Mildred said your dresses had already been cut up for rags, but she had pulled together the rest of your belongings and slipped them to me after Mr. Billings and I finished searching the personal quarters of all the troupe members. I made some excuse about how they might offer some insight that would help me track you down, and Billings encouraged me to take them." Titus moved a step closer, his movement drawing her to meet him by the edge of the table. "There's not much here," he said with a shrug, "but maybe having a few belongings restored to you will provide some comfort."

Penelope reached for the bag, her heart pounding in her chest. When he placed it in her hand, her legs wobbled, and she had to grip the back of one of the kitchen chairs to steady herself. It was heavy. Praise God, it was heavy. Her books. They had to be inside.

She slipped into the chair and gently laid the bag on the tabletop in front of her. As she peeled back the cloth flap, she stretched the opening wide and peered inside. One by one, she extracted each treasure, the joy of discovery so keen, she found herself constantly blinking away tears.

Her Bible. She clutched the holy book to her chest and kissed the top of the leather spine. *Thank you, Lord. If the rest of the bag were empty this would be enough.* But the rest of the bag wasn't empty. It held an abundance of riches. The photograph she and Edith had taken together in front of Miss Wyndham's school and the small packet of letters the dear woman had written. Her hairbrush and pins. And Oliver! A whisper-soft chuckle escaped her as she extracted her battered copy of *Oliver Twist.* Such a faithful companion. "'My dear child,'" she quoted under her breath, stroking the cover, "'you need not be afraid of my deserting you, unless you give me cause.'" Or unless she was abducted again. But she couldn't imagine such a thing happening under the watchful eye of so many Diamond D men.

She set the book aside, then smoothed the bag against the table, surprised when her fingers rubbed against a lump at the bottom. Not knowing what it could be, she reached in and clasped the rolled-up item. Stiff ribs met her fingers. Boning? She peeked inside, a grin stretching across her face. *Mildred, you angel!* She'd packed Penelope's corset.

Beaming, she jumped to her feet and just barely stopped herself from throwing her arms around the Ranger's neck.

"Oh, Titus! I never expected . . ." She wrapped her arms around herself and bounced on her toes. "What a precious gift."

Light touched his eyes, and his mouth turned up just a bit at one corner. It softened him. Made him seem more man than Ranger. A man who, in that moment, seemed to care more about *her* than about what information she could provide to his investigation.

Penelope released her hold on her midsection and touched his arm, needing somehow to convey the depth of difference he had just made in her life. "Thank you."

A frisson of energy radiated up Titus's arm from the place where her fingertips brushed against his bicep to course through his chest, causing his heart to start thumping at an abnormal rate. What was happening to him? He was supposed to be immune to beautiful women.

As she smiled up at him, the truth dawned. It wasn't her beauty that stirred his blood and threw his pulse into chaos. It was her spirit. Her humility and joy. The delight she found in items that carried no real monetary value. The gratitude that glistened in her eyes without a hint of entitlement to dim the shine. The way she returned to calling him Titus in her excitement, bypassing the formality he'd tried to establish between them—a formality that no longer held any appeal.

That's where the danger lay. Not in the delicate perfection

of her face or the shapeliness of her figure. It was her exuberant heart he found so hard to resist. It called to him. Tempted him to consider that the solitary life he'd planned for himself might not be the only road open to him.

Uncomfortable with the direction of his thoughts and the disturbing effect of her touch, Titus nodded in response to her appreciation, then eased back toward the door. "Glad to be of service."

When her hand fell away, he told himself it was relief he felt, not loss, but the lie was too flimsy to bear scrutiny. Which was why he sent a prayer of thanks heavenward when Coy pushed through the back door, his big hands shoved through the handles of a laundry basket.

"Took down the rest of the sheets for ya," Coy said, his face reddening when he met Penelope's gaze. Ducking away from her attention, he glanced at Titus as he shimmied between him and Penelope. His expression was not nearly as friendly or eager to please when aimed in Titus's direction. "Ike and I will get 'em folded and put away before supper," Coy promised her as he strode toward the parlor, "so don't give 'em another thought."

"Thank you!" Penelope beamed a smile at the man's back, as if he might feel the warmth through his spine even if he was too bashful to experience it firsthand. "I'd completely forgotten about the clothesline."

Ike came through the door next and picked up the conversation where Coy had left off. "Jeb and Angus volunteered for dish duty, too, so you'll have the entire evening to yourself, Miss Penny." He patted her shoulder as he walked by, his usual grin in place. Until he glanced in Titus's direction. His mouth flattened into a line that seemed almost . . . threatening. "You've had a trying day, my dear. It's only right that you enjoy some peace and quiet after supper."

Titus read the man's meaning loud and clear. No more interrogation. No more digging up of painful memories. No more causing Penelope any kind of discomfort whatsoever. Titus had done enough damage for one day.

He dipped his chin at Ike, signaling his agreement. He still had plenty of questions to ask and insight to gather, but that could wait until tomorrow. Ike was right. He'd run her through the wringer this afternoon. She deserved a break.

"I don't mind doing the dishes, Ike. Really."

Ike cut off her protest with a shake of his head. "Not tonight. We've got it covered."

Titus couldn't imagine how much arm-twisting Ike had done to get Jeb to volunteer for dish duty. Then again, with the way all of the Diamond D hands doted on Penelope, Jeb might have been the one leading the charge.

After Ike cleared the kitchen doorway, Penelope busied herself with repacking her belongings into the cloth bag. "I suppose I better put these away and get back to cooking supper. Thank you again, Mr. Kingsley, for bringing them to me."

"Titus," he grumbled, feeling oddly out of sorts at her reverting back to calling him Mr. Kingsley when she had no problems calling Ike by his given name.

Her movements slowed and a small vee formed between her brows. "What was that?"

"The name's Titus." He probably sounded like an idiot, his voice all gruff and grouchy, but he had no liking for being the only *mister* in a house full of men who were more than twice his age.

She dipped her chin, but not in time to hide the smile that had started to blossom. The teasing light in her eyes should have made him feel more like an idiot, yet somehow, it enhanced the intimacy of the moment, as if they shared a jest.

"Titus."

Yep. He definitely liked the sound of that better. Especially when she said it all quiet and shy, looking up at him through those thick, dark lashes.

Pink dusted her cheeks a second before she pivoted back to her bag, breaking the connection that had stretched between them. "I'll just put these in my room and get back to—Oh!"

"What?" Titus craned his neck from side to side, his hand hovering over his holster as he searched the room for whatever had startled her.

"I just realized that my room is actually your room." She clutched her bag to her chest, her free hand fluttering about in the air like a bird that couldn't decide where to land. "Let me clear out my things. It won't take long. I changed the sheets this morning before the washing, so the linens are clean." She darted around the table, heading for the hall. "It won't take but a minute. I can sleep on the settee in the parlor. It's no trouble."

"Penelope, stop." The sound of her name on his tongue startled him almost as much as it did her. Or maybe him coming up behind her and capturing her arm had done the startling.

He released her immediately, not wanting to dredge up recollections of the insensitive lawman he'd been earlier in the day.

"I'm bunking in the barn," he hurried to explain. He tipped his head toward the wall that separated the guest room from the kitchen. "This is your home, and that's *your* room. There'll be no sleeping in the parlor."

Something strange came over her face when he said the word *home*. It only lasted for a moment, but it held such longing, he almost had to look away.

"In fact, I should probably head out there now," he said. "See if Dusty has any preference over where I set up camp." And escape this woman before he did something crazy like pull her into his arms and promise her a home of her own . . . with him.

Jumpin' Jehoshaphat. What was wrong with him? He barely knew her.

Clapping his hat on his head, he murmured a gruff, "See you at supper," then hightailed it out of the house.

Dusty directed him to an empty stall near the rear of the barn, his demeanor about as warm as a blue norther. Seemed Titus would not be winning any popularity contests with the Diamond D hands today. At least Lucky seemed to have forgiven him. 'Course that might be because Titus had bribed him with a piece of jerky from his saddlebag when the hound had started sniffing his way through Titus's gear.

"You gonna be all right out here?" Doc appeared at the stall's opening and leaned against the wall.

Titus finished laying out his bedroll, then pushed to his feet. "I've stayed in worse. Probably warmer out here than in the house anyway, with all those cold shoulders aimed my way."

Doc chuckled. "They'll get over it soon enough. I told them you realized your mistake and apologized. Most of them are just cartin' around a bunch of pent-up frustration over the ill treatment that sweet girl has suffered and their inability to do anything about it. Makes us a little cranky."

"Me too," Titus admitted.

He wanted to hang Gerard Carlisle and Narcissa LaBelle upside down by their toenails and let them pick at each other until the buzzards took over. But Carlisle was outside his jurisdiction and Madame LaBelle was the lead suspect in his robbery case. As much as he wanted to arrest her for attempted murder, he feared the charges wouldn't stick. Yes, he could testify to finding Penelope stripped and left for dead in the woods, but Madame had an entire troupe of witnesses who could attest to her being with the company that evening. He might be able to convince Mildred to testify to Madame's state of mind, but the seamstress hadn't heard the woman's threats against Penelope or her orders to Hunt. With Narcissa LaBelle's power and influence, they would need more than Penelope's word to get a conviction. Especially if this Hunt fellow was as in love with the actress as Penelope seemed to think. He'd probably take the fall for his lover. That was *if* Titus could find him.

The man was guilty as sin, having been the one to carry out Madame's orders, but Penelope had pleaded with Titus not to arrest him since he'd shown her kindness by leaving his knife to aid her escape. The spineless coward had done pitifully little to Titus's way of thinking. He'd be happy to let Hunt rot in jail, but that would mean the true villain would go free. And that stuck in Titus's craw. His best chance to take Madame LaBelle down was to prove her guilty of robbery. With hard evidence and multiple men testifying against her—men who were upstanding citizens with their own power and influence—she'd not be able to talk her way out of a conviction.

"Penelope's an orphan, you know." Doc dropped that little nugget into the stalled conversation, drawing Titus's attention. "Found on the back steps of a girls' school by the cook."

"That a fact?" Titus moseyed over to join his grandfather at the edge of the stall. Instinct told him the old man wasn't just telling him this to whet his appetite for supper.

"From what I gather, the woman who raised her was a God-fearing woman who was kind in her own way but not particularly nurturing. I've never heard Penny refer to her as *mother*. Only Edith."

The woman in the picture Titus had found.

"Penny was raised on the school's charity." Doc eyed him over the top of his spectacles. "Educated but never really accepted. Without a wealthy parent to sponsor her learning, she earned her education by cooking and cleaning, even as a child. When I went to town and bought her a new pair of shoes and a few yards of fabric, she cleaned the entire house the next day. Her way of trying to earn the gift she'd been given." Doc narrowed his gaze. "The girl couldn't accept a gift freely given without trying to pay for it with the sweat of her brow. Had you asked me, I could have told you that there's no way she's your thief."

Titus raised a brow. "Feel better now that you've got that *I told you so* out of your system?"

Doc sniffed. "As a matter of fact I do." He pushed away from the support beam, then waved a hand in Titus's direction. "You young folks like to think you got this world all figured out. It's the duty of us old-timers to remind you, you ain't always as smart as you think you are."

Titus chuckled as he tipped his hat to his grandfather. "Lesson learned."

Doc clapped Titus's arm and nodded at him, pride lighting his eyes. "Good. Then come on up to the house. You won't want to miss Penny's corn bread. It's about as close to heaven as a man can get this side of the grave."

The tension that had hovered between the two men all afternoon lifted as they strolled up to the house. Titus still faced a handful of frosty glares from the other Diamond D men, but by the time dinner had finished, most of them had warmed back up. Partially due to Doc's example, but mostly due to Penelope's friendly manner toward Titus. Her ready smile and cheerful demeanor brightened everyone's mood.

Which was why the atmosphere of the house mellowed when she closed herself in her room to work on a dress she was sewing. She'd taken the vibrancy with her. Over the course of the evening, the men retired one by one until Titus decided he should say his good-nights as well and head out to the barn.

It was too early to sleep, though, so he lit a lantern and went over his case notes, incorporating the new information he'd gleaned from Penelope. After an hour, his neck ached and his eyes burned, and he still had no definitive plan for trapping his thief.

Lucky nudged his hand. Titus took the hint and rubbed the hound's head. "Ready to turn in, fella?"

The dog whined, then suddenly stiffened. A quiet growl rumbled in his throat a heartbeat before he shot out of the stall. His barks stabbed holes into the night's silence.

Titus jumped to his feet, grabbed the lantern in one hand and his revolver in the other, then gave chase. By the time he made it out of the barn, Lucky had already reached the house and was barking furiously at a shadowy figure.

A shadowy figure in the process of climbing out of Penelope's bedroom window.

20

You! Stop!" Titus shouted the demand as he sprinted toward the house, but the prowler raced away in the opposite direction.

Lucky barked but didn't attack as the man ran past. With distance and darkness working against him, Titus could make out pitifully few details. About all he could tell was that the housebreaker was a male of average height with a bulky build, dressed in dark clothing.

And fast. He was actually pulling away.

"Stop!" Titus called again. "I'll shoot!"

His quarry paid him no heed, just ran without once looking over his shoulder. Titus raised his pistol and fired into the air, hoping to scare him into stopping. The scoundrel ducked but kept moving toward the trees behind the house.

If the man had returned fire, Titus could have targeted him, but he never reached for a weapon. Just kept running. Probably hoped Titus was too honorable to shoot him in the back. Which he was. Confound it.

Titus continued to give chase and started to gain ground until the man mounted a horse that had been waiting behind the tree line. The sound of retreating hooves drummed defeat against Titus's chest as he reached the trees. He swiveled the lantern left and right but saw nothing. The man was gone.

Titus growled, and his grip on the lantern tightened until his fingernails dug into his palm. His breath heaved as he stared into the night, helpless to pursue. He tried to console himself with the knowledge that even if Rex had been ready to ride, it was likely that the prowler still would have slipped away. A man in dark clothing on a dark horse racing through a wooded area at night would be nearly impossible to track. Titus would return after sunrise and follow what trail remained, but he didn't hold out much hope that he'd find his quarry. As soon as the tracks merged with the traffic on a main road or disappeared in a creek bed, the trail would go cold.

Unless Penelope had recognized the intruder.

Penelope!

Had the wretch hurt her?

Titus spun and dashed back to the house, his heart pumping with new purpose. Light shone from a couple of the upstairs windows, and the front door opened right as Titus reached the porch.

"Kingsley? That you?"

Light from Titus's lantern danced off Coy's bald head. The man hoisted his sagging britches up with one hand and wielded a cast-iron skillet with the other.

"Yep." Titus didn't slow. He took the steps two at a time and pushed his way into the house, only to find himself swimming upstream against a current of old men in various states of undress. Exposed long johns, drooping suspenders, disheveled gray hair pointing every which way. And every last one of them hindering his progress.

Questions peppered him from all sides.

"What's goin' on?"

"You the one shootin'?"

"Was it a coyote?"

"The horses all right?"

He took no time to answer, just shouldered his way through the throng. "Let me pass. I need to get to Penelope."

The Red Sea could not have parted more dramatically. Men glued backsides to walls as they made a path for him. He handed off his lantern to a yawning Angus, who stood next to her door, then Titus holstered his revolver and knocked.

"Penelope? It's Titus. Are you all right?"

Whispers filled the hall, but Titus focused his attention on picking up sounds coming from the other side of the door. There were precious few.

His gut tightened. "Penelope?"

He didn't want to barge in on her, but if she didn't answer him soon, that's exactly what he'd do.

She could be in there bleeding.

Or thinking up a lie to cover up a late-night meeting with her partner in crime.

Titus's fist tightened as the cynical thought jabbed his brain. He clenched his jaw and forced the thought from his mind. Penelope was *not* in cahoots with anyone. She was an innocent young woman caught up in an unfortunate situation. He would *not* let his distrustful nature keep him from seeing the truth again. She didn't deserve his suspicions. She deserved his help.

Clenching his jaw, he knocked again. "I'm coming in."

He unfurled his fingers and reached for the handle, but the knob turned before he could grab it.

Hinges creaked quietly as the door opened inward. Penelope stood on the other side in a white cotton nightgown that seemed to be swallowing her whole. Her slightly glazed eyes blinked at him as if trying to make sense of her surroundings, and her hands trembled where she clutched a knitted throw around her shoulders like a shawl.

"Titus?"

Thank God she wasn't hurt. But she looked so lost. Shaken. Her voice was a broken whisper. It took an act of will not to wrap his arms around her. He ached to smooth her hair and rub her back until her tremors subsided.

Then a thought occurred to him. One that turned his gut rock hard. "Did he . . ." He couldn't say it.

She shook her head and clutched the throw more tightly around her shoulders. "I-I didn't even know he was here until Lucky's barking woke me. He was g-going through my dresser." She nodded toward the wall where the small bureau stood, the top drawer askew, stockings and white undergarments haphazardly hanging over the edges.

Penelope stepped backward, granting Titus permission to enter and investigate. But when she lifted the back of her hand to wipe a tear from the edge of her eye, walking past her became impossible. He cupped her arm and rubbed his hand up and down over the blanket cocoon she'd wrapped herself in.

"He's gone, Penelope. You're safe."

She bit her lip and nodded, but he could still feel her quivering.

Hang propriety.

"Come here," he groused as he tugged her gently toward him.

As if she'd been waiting for an invitation, she fell against him and pressed her face to his chest. He closed his arms around her and leaned his cheek against the top of her head.

"It's all right," he soothed, one hand reaching up to support the back of her head as he held her tightly against him. "It's over. You're safe."

"And you're gonna stay that way." Jeb pushed his way into the room and crossed to the still-open window. He pulled the sash down until it smashed against the sill. "Dusty and I will rig up a block so you can open the window enough to let in a breeze while keepin' out anything taller than a couple inches. We'll make sure no one sneaks in here again."

Titus bit back a groan as, one after another, the graybeard brigade made themselves known. Not that he'd forgotten they were there exactly. He'd just been . . . well . . . absorbed. Penelope felt better in his arms than he'd expected. And not just in a physical sense. In truth, he'd been so focused on banishing her fear and restoring her equilibrium he hadn't given much thought to how well she fit against him until Jeb came in and she pulled away from his hold. Even now, he kept a hand at her back and stroked his thumb up and down, compelled to offer comfort somehow.

Coy shrugged into his suspenders and nodded to Titus from the doorway. "I'll put some tea on. My ma used to say that nothing calms a woman's nerves better than a cup of tea."

"I'll fetch an extra blanket," Ike offered, as if Penelope's trembling was due to a draft instead of a break-in.

Her face had felt cold, though, when her cheek pressed against his chest, so maybe the idea had some merit.

Doc scurried in next. He commandeered Penelope, wrapping an arm around her and leading her to edge of the bed. "Come sit down while Titus has a look around. I'll stay with you."

Titus clenched his jaw and reined in a scowl. What if he wasn't ready to take that look around just yet? What if investigating wasn't the most important thing to him at the moment? Penelope allowed Doc to usher her away, but once she took her seat, her gaze sought out Titus. Was she wishing he were the one sitting at her side? Did she prefer his company to that of his grandfather? Or was she simply eager to see if he could learn anything about her unwanted visitor?

It didn't really matter. He was the lawman in the group. It was his job to investigate. Others could offer comfort.

Still, he held her gaze for a moment, not wanting to abandon her to his grandfather just yet. But when Doc patted her hand and drew her attention away, Titus knew it was time to get to work.

Telling himself he was a fool to be jealous of a man nearing his eighth decade, Titus pivoted toward the dresser and started making mental notes. The intruder had been looking for something. But what? And why did he think to find it in a drawer of women's unmentionables?

Was he some kind of deviant who found pleasure in invading a woman's privacy and touching her intimate clothing? He'd run across a fellow or two with strange proclivities during his time as a Ranger, but that explanation didn't sit right. Those types frequented towns where women were plentiful and easier to access. The Diamond D was isolated and, until recently, inhabited only by men. The folks in Glen Rose might have heard about a female boarder at the ranch after Doc bought shoes and dress makings, but why would a fellow traipse all the way out here when there was lower hanging fruit in town?

A more likely scenario was that this was a targeted search. By someone who thought Penelope a jewel thief? Perhaps someone from the troupe had overheard his conversation with Madame LaBelle and come to the same false conclusion he had. But how would they have known where to find her?

Unless . . .

He spun around and headed back to the bed, nearly stumbling over Rowdy, who was on all fours by the side of the dresser where some of Penelope's clothing had fallen. Probably chasing after a dropped hairpin or some other object reflecting the lamplight. Catching himself before he tripped over

Rowdy's bare feet, Titus sidestepped, then moved to stand in front of Penelope.

"Could it have been Cecil Hunt?"

It would fit. He was the only one who would know where to look for Penelope since he'd been the one to drag her out here in the first place. But why would he think she had the jewels? She'd been stripped down to her underclothes when he'd carried her out into the woods, for Pete's sake.

"I-I don't know." Her brow crinkled. "I didn't see his face." She glanced at the window, where Jeb was fiddling with the latch. "He must have been startled by the barking, too. I remember hearing footsteps in the room when I woke. And breathing."

That lost look returned to her eyes, twisting something in Titus's chest. He dropped onto the bed beside her and took her hand, not caring that there really wasn't room for him with Doc on the other side. The wooden footboard jabbed him in the hip, but he ignored it.

"Look at me, Pen."

It took a moment, but the glaze of fear gradually cleared enough for her to focus on his face.

"He's gone. He can't hurt you."

She nodded, accepting his words, but he knew it would take time for her to feel safe.

He rubbed his thumb over the back of her hand. "Is there anything you remember about the man? His height? His clothing? Did you hear his voice?"

"No." She shook her head and dipped her chin as if ashamed. "When I realized someone was in my room, I froze. I thought if I pretended to be asleep, he would leave me alone." Her chin lifted and lamplight gleamed off the moisture collecting in her eyes. "I squeezed my eyelids shut like a scared little girl and prayed for him to go away. By the time I found the courage to open my eyes, all I saw was his back as he climbed out the window." She shook her head. "I should have done more, Titus. I'm sorry. I was a coward."

He tightened his grip on her hand. "You were no such thing." The words emerged sharper than he intended, but he was angry.

No one should have their security stripped from them like this. Made to feel vulnerable and exposed in their own home. And the fact that his questions had added to her distress only heightened his ire.

"It was clever of you to feign sleep," he said, willing her to believe him. "Criminals are unpredictable when trapped. There's no telling what he might have done if he'd felt threatened. You did the right thing."

"I just wish I could help more." She blinked away the moisture from her eyes and straightened her posture. "Maybe I can figure out what he was looking for." She tugged her hand free of Titus's hold and stood, her mouth tightening with determination.

"It can wait, Penny," Doc said as he and Titus rose to flank her on either side. "You don't have to do this now."

"Yes, I do." She stared at those dresser drawers like a gunman stared at an opponent from twenty paces.

Titus had no doubt who would emerge victorious. Even so, he stayed close as she worked, wanting to be on hand if she needed him.

It took several minutes for her to take inventory since she folded and tidied everything as she went. Restoring order. Controlling her environment. Erasing the evidence that another had gone through her things.

The top drawer on the right side of the dresser lay open, but there were no clothes inside. Curious. He opened it all the way and felt around inside. Penelope's face swiveled his direction. "I didn't keep anything in . . . oh." She looked up at him. "The knife. The one Mr. Hunt gave me. I put it in there."

Titus frowned. "Well, it's gone now."

"That doesn't necessarily mean the intruder was Mr. Hunt. Anyone could have found the knife and deemed it worth keeping."

Why did she want to believe Hunt innocent? Did she think she owed him her loyalty because he didn't kill her outright?

"It's more likely he broke in to retrieve it and make sure nothing could tie him to the attack on you." Which was a shame, because Titus had been hoping to use that knife as evidence against him. He'd planned to ask her about it in the morning. Too late now.

Titus set aside his goals as a lawman when Penelope deflated at his statement. Shoot. It probably hurt less to believe a stranger broke in than to admit someone she knew had violated her space in such a frightening way.

Needing to bolster her somehow, he placed a hand on her arm and offered what encouragement he could. "You're right, though. We don't know for sure that it was Hunt. Better keep going with the inventory to make sure nothing else is missing."

Her posture straightened, and some of the tightness around his heart eased. She nodded her agreement and turned back to her tidying.

Rowdy collected the few things that had fallen near the door and handed them to Penny, his face beet red. As soon as she took them, he shoved his hands in his pockets and scurried out the door.

Her own cheeks pink, Penelope turned her attention to the drawer that held her most intimate apparel. Lines formed across her forehead as she set the drawer to rights.

Titus stepped closer and looked over her shoulder. "Is something else missing?"

She frowned. "My corset."

Her *corset*? Titus leaned back and shared a look with Doc. His grandfather looked as baffled as Titus felt.

Why on earth would Cecil Hunt, or any man, break into a house and steal a lady's corset?

21

"The Lord gave, and the Lord hath taken away," Penelope thought as she fastened Grandma Kingsley's corset around curves it hadn't been designed to contain. *"Blessed be the name of the Lord."*

She *was* blessed. Despite last night's unsettling adventure, she was unharmed. The Diamond D men that she'd grown so fond of were unharmed. Titus was unharmed. Yes, she was blessed. But also . . . disappointed. She'd been so surprised and delighted to find the corset she'd brought from Chicago among the things Titus had retrieved for her. To have something of her own again. Something made for her body shape and size. A corset that didn't pinch or jab. One that supported in all the right places and instilled confidence in its ability to keep everything where it belonged no matter her activity level. She'd been looking forward to donning it far more than was rational.

Penelope shook her head at herself, then exhaled a quiet chuckle. What kind of pitiful creature grew melancholy over underclothes? Mrs. Kingsley's corset worked just fine. Penelope had loosened and reconfigured the laces several times over the last three weeks and had found a fit that accommodated her inconvenient bounty well enough. It was far more practical than the scanty contraption she'd inadvertently inherited from Madame LaBelle. She'd thought about stuffing that one in the cookstove's firebox to rid herself of the memories tied to it, but she'd not been able to bring herself to do something so destructive.

Setting aside the corset problem to ponder another day, Penelope finished dressing and rolled her hair into a simple chignon. She'd gathered wool long enough. Breakfast wouldn't start itself.

Or maybe it would. The smell of freshly brewed coffee wafted over her when she stepped from her room into the hall. She hurried down the few feet of corridor that separated her room from the kitchen, expecting to find Coy at the stove. The dear man probably thought to give her a break from her morning chores after all that had happened last night. But truth be told, she wanted to be busy. Too busy to think about a stranger being in her room. Too busy to wonder if he would return.

"Coy, you didn't have to—" The rest of the words died on her tongue when Titus looked up at her from the table, cup raised halfway to his mouth.

The cup reversed course and headed back down to the table. "Mornin', Penelope."

He dipped his chin in her direction, and the welcome in his gaze caused her heart to do a little twirl in her chest.

Mercy. The man looked far too good first thing in the morning.

"Morning." She willed her feet to restart, though the nearer they brought her to him, the more she recognized signs of a restless night etched into his face. Dark smudges beneath his eyes. The slight slump to his posture. The weariness lining his brow. She placed a hand on his forearm. "You didn't sleep, did you?"

He shrugged as if his lack of rest didn't matter, but it did. To her. "I snagged a few winks. Just wanted to grab some coffee and a cold biscuit before heading out."

Her chest squeezed. "You're leaving?"

The small wag of his head brought more relief than she had a right to feel. True, she felt safer when he was near. But she knew herself well enough to admit that her reluctance for him to leave stemmed from something far more personal than simple safety.

Titus fiddled with the handle on his mug. "I'm gonna see if our visitor last night left a trail. I doubt I'll be able to follow him far, but if I can at least determine which direction he headed, that might give me ammunition to fire at Hunt when I catch up with him."

Penelope moved to the stove and poured herself a small cup of coffee. She preferred tea, but talking about what happened last night brought a chill to her insides and left her craving warmth.

"You really believe Mr. Hunt did this?" She stirred a spoonful of sugar into her coffee, the clink of the spoon echoing loudly in the quiet kitchen.

Titus turned in his chair to face her. "I do. This wasn't a random robbery. Thieves don't typically break into houses and make off with ladies' undergarments."

In all the daydreams she'd woven about her and Titus sharing intimate conversations, never once did they entail discussing corset burglary. Oh well. Her life had veered away from ordinary long ago.

Locking away her missish sensibilities, Penelope joined Titus at the table, determined to handle the conversation with practical resolve.

"If it was Mr. Hunt, he was likely here at Madame's bidding."

Titus nodded, then raised a brow and pinned her with a look. "Why would Narcissa LaBelle want your corset?"

"I have no idea. Certainly not to wear." Penelope dropped her gaze to her coffee cup. Conversing about corsets was one thing. Looking him in the eye while doing so was quite another. "Madame's taste is far more . . . stylish."

"That's putting it kindly."

Penelope glanced up to find him looking at her in a way that was hard to read. All she knew for sure was that she didn't need the coffee to warm her insides anymore.

"I prefer substance over style in a woman," he said, his voice a tad rough, "and after meeting Narcissa LaBelle, I got the impression her substance is rather lacking."

And his impression of *her*? Penelope hid the ill-timed thought behind her cup as she lifted the coffee to her mouth and took a small sip. As much as she was dying to know the answer, she refused to be one of those flirtatious sorts who batted their lashes and probed for compliments. A woman of substance would be more concerned about solving a crime than padding her ego.

"You're a rare man, Titus Kingsley," she said instead. And he was. Few men made the effort to look past Narcissa's beauty to assess her character. Most didn't care. Her physical perfection was all they wanted. Titus was different. But then, she'd sensed that about him from the beginning. Hence the daydreams.

"I don't know about that." He wagged his head a bit and did some hiding of his own behind a raised coffee cup. "I just got a disliking for manipulative women is all."

Her cup came down. "Were you hurt by one?"

She didn't like the image that sprang to mind. Titus with a beautiful woman on his arm. Laughing with her. Sharing his hopes and dreams. His love.

But what she disliked even more was the idea of such a woman causing him pain. It brought an answering ache to her own chest, leading her to reach out and touch his arm in sympathy.

He blew out a breath and leaned back in his chair. His arm stretched away from her touch, but before she could snatch her hand back in embarrassment for overstepping, he captured it in his and rubbed his thumb over her knuckles in a simple yet terribly sweet caress. Her insides didn't just warm, they melted.

"Yeah, I was hurt by one," he admitted. "But not the way you think."

He gave her hand a small squeeze, then let her go as his gaze drifted down to the table between them. She expected him to withdraw his words, too, but they trickled out, slowly at first, like dripping water evolving into a steady stream.

"Her name was Nora. She had shiny blond hair, blue eyes, rosy cheeks, and a figure that had every man in town turning his head. It wasn't just her looks, though. She was magnetic. Always having fun and making sure those around her did, too. Vibrant, funny, and just a tad bit dangerous. A combination Tate couldn't resist."

"Tate?"

"My brother." Titus's mouth tightened, as if it physically hurt to speak of him. "He was eighteen months older than me, but we were so close growing up, people often mistook us for twins." Titus shook his head. "The older we grew, the more competitive we became, though never to the point of disloyalty. He should have known I would never betray him, but he let Nora's whispers infect his mind.

"Looking back, I can see the signs of a long con at work. Building trust. Sharing secrets. Pulling him away from his family. Our mother invited Nora to the house several times, but she always had an excuse not to come. She convinced Tate that I made her uncomfortable. Said I looked at her improperly.

Lustfully. She'd be more comfortable meeting with him alone. She fed Tate's jealousy with lies about me until the two of us nearly came to blows."

Penelope ached at the raw pain in Titus's voice. To be vilified unjustly was bad enough, but to have his own brother believe the lies must have been torture.

"Nora flirted with all the men in town, but she seemed particularly focused on Tate, almost like she had targeted him. It didn't make sense until I recalled the newspaper article that had been published about him the week before she arrived. About the prize shorthorn bull Tate had raised from a calf and sold at market for a county record of $500. Troubadour had placed first at the county fair that year, and a buyer from Kansas had offered top dollar. Tate planned to purchase his own acreage with the money and set up a cattle breeding business with one of Troubadour's progeny, but Nora got her hooks in him before he had the chance."

Anger flashed in Titus's eyes, and the hand that had held hers so sweetly a moment ago curled into a fist. "A stranger named George Middleton showed up in town two months after Nora, claiming she was his fiancée. Said she'd run away from him, and he'd come to fetch her back. Nora begged Tate to save her from the unwanted marriage. Told him Middleton was controlling and abusive. Tate would've done anything for Nora at this point, so he confronted Middleton. Told him he was marrying Nora himself. Middleton threatened to sue her for breach of contract. He'd provided her with a new wardrobe and jewelry as an engagement gift and demanded repayment. She, of course, didn't have any jewelry. She'd sold it to make her escape.

"I doubted the story. Too convenient. I knew Tate wouldn't listen to me, so I shared my concerns with my folks, but Tate was so in love with Nora, he wouldn't listen to anyone. Not even our mother. Middleton quoted a thousand-dollar price tag. Tate offered him six hundred fifty, every last penny he had in the bank. Middleton agreed."

Titus's head bowed. "I tried to stop him. Told him to wait until a suit was filed and a judgment pronounced before he handed over his life's savings. But Tate was swayed by Nora's pleas and driven to be her hero.

"I'm not sure what happened the night he went to meet Middleton for the payoff. Perhaps something I said finally sank in, and he started asking questions. All I know is that Middleton put a bullet in him and took his money. Doc tried to save him, but Tate had lost too much blood by the time I found him. He died that night. The same night Nora disappeared."

"Oh, Titus." The words emerged from Penelope's throat in a broken whisper. "I'm so sorry."

Her heart broke for him. For Tate. For their parents. And Doc.

"I made it my mission to track them down. To bring them to justice for what they'd done to Tate. To our family. It took three months to find them. In a different town, using different names. I turned them over to a group of Texas Rangers led by Sam McMurray. Captain McMurray heard my story and recruited me to join the Frontier Battalion. Convinced me I could make a difference. Could spare other families the pain we'd faced."

Titus raised his head and poured himself into her eyes. "I won't let her win, Penelope. If Narcissa LaBelle is behind these thefts, I'll bring her to justice. I swear it. She won't hurt you or anyone else ever again."

His need to make things right thickened the air. But there was something else emanating from him. Something protective and personal. A promise that seemed unrelated to the missing jewels.

"There has to be a reason she would send Hunt to retrieve your corset." The warm tone of his voice hardened into a tenacious resolve. "She must have known somehow that it was in the bag Mildred gave me. Or asked about it after I left." His brow crinkled. "Although . . . Hunt was gone when I visited the troupe. For him to get here so soon after me, he would have had to return sometime that evening, then board one of the first trains out of Weatherford yesterday morning, like I did. But how would he have known where to find you? I took measures to ensure no one followed me." Titus drew lines over the tabletop with his finger, as if tracing a map. "I suppose he could have returned to the tree where he left you and started searching from there. Still, the chances of him stumbling across the Diamond D and spotting you before I dragged you inside for questioning are incredibly slim."

Penelope followed the path of his logic, then stumbled onto her own bit of insight. "What if he took the wrong corset?"

Titus jerked his face toward hers.

Penelope continued, slowly working through her thoughts. "It does seem unlikely that Mr. Hunt could find me so quickly. It makes me wonder if he was out here already. From *before* you visited the troupe." Her pulse quickened as the pieces started coming together. "That would explain why he was gone when you questioned the company."

She scooted to the edge of her chair, excitement building. Titus responded in kind. The distance between them shrank to mere inches.

"I wasn't wearing *my* corset that night. I had to borrow one of hers in order for the dress to fit properly." She bent closer to Titus, her heart racing at full gallop. "I found a plain one at the bottom of her trunk. One I'd never seen her wear. What if that was the corset she sent Mr. Hunt to fetch?"

Titus's eyes lit, and he jumped to his feet. "Show it to me."

Penelope launched off her chair and started down the hall. Being on the cusp of discovery dissolved her earlier embarrassment. It was just a piece of cotton in a drawer, after all. Perfectly harmless.

Maybe too harmless.

"I'm not sure what we'll find," she admitted, her theory losing a bit of shine as her mind continued working the puzzle. "Corsets don't have much fabric."

But maybe there was a tiny map showing the way to the illicit stash squirreled away in a hidden pocket somewhere. Or a key to a locked treasure chest tucked beneath a seam.

Or maybe she read too many adventure nov—

"Oh!" Penelope pulled up short as Rowdy barreled out of her room, nearly colliding with her in his rush.

"Rowdy?" Titus clasped her arms to steady her from behind. "What the devil . . . ?"

Feeling his grip tighten on her arms and sensing he was about to chase after the poor man, who was probably already mortified, Penelope covered Titus's hand with hers and twisted to face him. "It's all right, Titus. Let him go. Sometimes he comes into my room when I'm not there and leaves me gifts on my dresser. After last night, he probably thought to soothe me with a sweet little gesture."

She tugged him toward her doorway and peered inside. "See?" Relieved to indeed find something new on her dresser top, Penelope urged Titus closer. "A handful of buttons. Aren't they pretty?" She touched the collection with her finger, spreading them out to see them better. "A shiny brass button, a couple blue ones, oh, and a silver one embossed with a flower. That one looks like an antique."

"I don't like the idea of him coming into your room uninvited." Titus stood in the doorway, one foot still in the hall, his narrowed gaze aimed at the front door that had just slammed closed.

"He doesn't mean any harm," Penelope said, pulling on his arm until he finally relented and joined her at the dresser. "Rowdy communicates in his own way. I'm still learning the nuances, but he's never given me any reason to feel uncomfortable."

Titus let the matter drop, but the scowl on his face didn't abate.

"Here it is!" Penelope added an extra helping of cheerfulness to her voice as she pulled out Madame's corset and set it on the dresser top. She ran her hands over the fabric, pressing her fingertips along each seam in search of any lump or abnormality. "I might have to take it apart seam by seam before I figure out its secrets, but I can work on that while you trail Mr. H—"

"What is it?" Titus bent his head close to hers.

"One of the seams is ripped. Near one of the boning channels." She ran a finger over the ragged tear. There should be a stiff piece of boning there, but it was flat. She bit her lip. "I don't remember this channel being empty before. All the stays had been in place. The fabric must have snagged on something when it was being tossed about last night." She glanced at the floor around the dresser, then hunkered down and peered beneath. "I don't see a lost stay, though. Do you think . . . ?" She stood and turned to look at him. "Could something have been secreted in there? Like the missing jewels? Did Hunt find them after all?"

Titus took the corset from her and examined the tear. "If he had, he wouldn't have taken the wrong corset back with him."

An odd look crossed his face. "Last night," Titus murmured the words beneath his breath, not really talking to her. He moved toward the door, looking around as if recreating a scene from memory. "He was over here." Titus dropped to his knees. He ran his fingers along the crevice between the floorboard and wall. Then felt under the dresser. Then around the dresser's rear leg.

"Got it." He pulled back his arm and held up his hand. A small red stone glimmered between his thumb and forefinger. "I don't think Hunt got the jewels last night. I think Rowdy did."

Oh dear.

22

Titus heaved a sigh as he directed Rex toward the Glen Rose post office. What was he going to do about Rowdy? The sneaky little rascal had given him the slip. Most likely with a pocketful of stolen jewels.

Did he even understand the value of what he'd taken? Or in his mind, did buttons serve as an equal trade? It was hard to tell with Rowdy. The fellow wasn't exactly playing with a full deck. Then again, the wily old-timer had outmaneuvered a trained Texas Ranger, so it might be best not to make too many assumptions regarding Rowdy's intellect. The cowpuncher might have a few dents in his noggin, but he also had about forty years of experience on Titus. Right now, experience was winning.

It didn't help his mood any that Titus had been unable to track Hunt down either. As he'd expected, the trail had run cold once his tracks merged with the traffic on the main road. Years' worth of hoofprints and wagon ruts made it impossible to pick out one specific rider. At least he'd been able to determine that Hunt had been heading north. It wasn't much, but it aligned with his theory about him rendezvousing with Narcissa.

Titus hated feeling ineffective. It stole his confidence and stirred his ire. Especially when people he cared about were in the line of fire. He'd gotten very little sleep last night. Partially because he kept watch for a couple of hours to make sure the intruder didn't return, but most of his insomnia could be blamed on an unquiet mind. Sure, he'd plotted and planned the best way to catch Narcissa and Hunt with the evidence needed to convict them. And, yes, he'd expended a good deal of mental energy trying to unravel the whole corset conundrum. But what had crawled under his skin the most was the vision of Penelope moving around in a shocked daze after Hunt had broken into her room. She'd done her best to put on a brave face, but he'd felt her trembling when he'd held her against him. Seen the lost, vulnerable look in her eyes. It had haunted him. Angered him. Hardened him.

Had she not suffered enough at their hands?

He was losing his detachment. His objectivity. And all because of a pair of gray eyes, a pure heart, and a smile that twisted his insides into knots every time she aimed it his direction.

Having reached the post office, Titus dismounted and looped Rex's reins around the hitching rail. He patted the black gelding's neck and murmured a few distracted words of praise. A quiet urge drew his attention away from his horse and onto his saddlebag. Titus hesitated for only a moment before lifting the flap and reaching inside. His hand closed around the spine of a small, thick book. He drew it out, then dropped it into his jacket pocket. It seemed the Lord wanted to talk to him. He'd better oblige. As soon as he sent his report.

It didn't take long to send the telegram, seeing as how he was the only customer in the post office this late in the afternoon. He wired Ranger headquarters with an update on his investigation—minus the bit about Rowdy—then headed outside to wait for a reply.

An unoccupied bench invited him to take a load off, so Titus plopped onto the seat, wishing he could take the load off his mind as well as his feet. *That's what you're for*, he thought as drew his Bible from his pocket and thumbed it open.

He fanned the pages to Proverbs, then started scanning Solomon's words of wisdom, figuring that's what he needed before heading back to the ranch to confront Rowdy. He started at the beginning of the book and slowly turned pages until he spotted a note made in the margin near the top of chapter three. A note written in his mother's hand. He smiled. His parents had given him this Bible when he joined the Rangers, admonishing him not to be so consumed with seeking justice that he neglected to seek the Lord.

He remembered opening the book during his first night at headquarters. How he'd propped a lantern next to his bedroll in his tent and reached for the ribbon marker. A marker that had been inserted near the end of the book, not in the middle as he would've expected with a new Bible. He'd tugged on the ribbon and opened to the book of Third John. Verse four had been underlined, and his mother had written in the margin, *I'm praying for you*. When he read the verse, he swore he heard her voice whisper to his heart. *"I have no greater joy than to hear that my children walk in truth."* Walk in the truth. Not the world's truth but God's truth. The truth personified in Christ. A truth that balanced justice with grace.

Focusing again on Proverbs, Titus drank in his mother's guidance. *Follow this path*, she'd written. Then she'd underlined the first twelve verses. He read over the words, the tension in his neck loosening at the reminder that God would direct his paths if he would trust him. The warning not to be wise in his own eyes brought a rueful reminder of how he'd misjudged Penelope and urged him to hold on to patience in his dealings with Rowdy. But it was verse three that kept drawing his attention again and again.

"Let not mercy and truth forsake thee: bind them about thy neck; write them upon the table of thine heart."

For the first time, the order of the words struck him. *Mercy* preceded *truth*. Did that make it more important? That couldn't be right. Nothing was more important than the truth. It was the only absolute a man could hold on to. It was what drove Titus as an agent of the law. Truth and justice. The two couldn't be separated. Yet truth could be mishandled. The Pharisees had wielded it like a weapon to maintain their position of power. Satan himself used God's truth by quoting Scripture when tempting Jesus in the desert. Could it be that truth without mercy was like knowledge without love?

Titus spotted another note in the margin. Not a personal note but a reference: Psalm 25:10. He flipped to Psalms. *"All the paths of the Lord are mercy and truth. . . ."* Another reference. Psalm 85:10. He turned. *"Mercy and truth are met together; righteousness and peace have kissed each other."* His mother tied one verse to another like clues on a treasure map. The next, Psalm 89:14, *"Justice and judgment are the habitation of thy throne; mercy and truth shall go before thy face."* Then back to Proverbs. Proverbs 14:22, *"Do they not err that devise evil? But mercy and truth shall be to them that devise good."* The clues ended with Proverbs 16:6, *"By mercy and truth iniquity is purged: and by the fear of the Lord men depart from evil."*

Mercy and truth. Always together. Mercy always leading the way.

How am I supposed to be merciful and *be an agent of justice, Lord? Am I supposed to let Narcissa LaBelle and Cecil Hunt run free to continue their thieving ways? Wrongdoers must be punished, or evil will abound. Even you sent your people into exile when they broke your laws.*

The reference in the margin completed the circle, urging him to return once again to Proverbs chapter three. But this time, instead of focusing on the third verse, Titus's eyes drifted down to the last verse his mother had underlined. Verse twelve. *"For whom the Lord loveth he correcteth; even as a father the son in whom he delighteth."*

Mercy did not negate correction. In fact, mercy often demanded correction. God sent his people into exile in order to bring them back into relationship with him instead of letting them fall further into idolatry and wickedness. Because he loved them.

Perhaps mercy accompanied truth when a lawman viewed those he hunted as God's creation first and criminals second. When justice served the people of Texas instead of a personal vendetta. When preserving the innocent took precedence over prosecuting the guilty.

His mother must have sensed how close to the edge he'd walked while tracking Nora. How the line between justice and retribution had started to blur. He thought he'd matured since then, that he had a better handle on his emotions, but the more he came to care for Penelope, the more the old desires for retribution knocked on his door when he thought of how she'd suffered.

Titus shook his head as he pressed his hand over the open Bible. Tate would be jabbing him with an *I told you so* if he'd been here. How many times had Titus warned his brother against falling for a girl he barely knew? And he'd been right. At least when it came to Nora. But now he was falling for a girl himself. And after being acquainted with her for an even shorter time. Tate must be kicking back by those pearly gates feeling mighty smug as he watched Titus eat his words.

"Penelope's nothing like Nora," Titus murmured, only to

have an image rise to mind of Tate guffawing at his need to justify himself to his dead brother.

A chuckle rose in his own throat as he closed the Bible's cover. It felt good to picture Tate laughing and bustin' Titus's chops just like he had when they'd been growing up.

"I miss you, brother."

Tate had always been eager to give everyone the benefit of the doubt. To extend second and third chances. He'd favored mercy where Titus had leaned hard into truth. Yes, his brother had been led astray by his soft heart, but Titus had closed himself off with a hard one. He might be the one still breathing, but was he actually living?

The post office door opened, and Titus glanced up to see the clerk step through with a telegram in his hand.

"I have that reply you were waiting on, sir."

Titus rose and accepted the telegram. "Thanks." He slipped the young man a coin, then tromped down the steps to the street to read his captain's response in private.

ANOTHER THEFT REPORTED. AMBROSE CLAYTON. GRANBURY. DIAMOND CUFF LINKS. MATCHES YOUR THEORY AND TROUPE TIMELINE. PURSUE LEADS. MAKE ARREST AND MAKE SERGEANT.

Another theft? Titus scowled at the paper, frustration rising until he realized the significance of the timing and location. His chest expanded as the last dregs of doubt drained away. His heart had recognized Penelope's innocence, but now his head had inconvertible proof. Penelope had never traveled to Granbury. Madame LaBelle had expelled her from the troupe before arriving in town, which meant Penelope could no longer be considered a viable suspect. By anyone. Not when seven men of good character could provide her with alibis and testify as to her whereabouts on the date in question.

"I told you she was nothing like Nora," he murmured beneath his breath as a smile stretched his face.

The oddest sensation came over Titus when he unhitched Rex and swung into the saddle. It was as if his big brother's approval shone down from heaven and warmed his back. It was probably just the sun slipping out from behind a cloud, but he didn't check the sky to confirm. He preferred attributing the warmth to Tate wishing him well, so he kicked logic out the back door and went with his gut.

Mercy and truth. Isn't that what his mama and the good Lord had been reminding him of this afternoon? The truth was that Tate was gone. Yet by God's mercy, the love they'd shared remained. Honoring his brother's memory by bringing the wicked to justice served him well, but perhaps it was time to consider that life was about more than work, no matter how noble. Life was about love. Love for God, love for family, love for . . .

A vision of Penelope arrested his thoughts. He tried to shoo it away. He wasn't ready to think of her in conjunction with the idea of love. Yet her image refused to be scattered. Her hand on his arm as she offered comfort and compassion. Her blushing cheeks as their discussion turned to corsets. Her ethereal beauty as she danced with butterflies.

Titus tucked his Bible back into his saddlebag, then mounted Rex and urged him into a canter as they left Glen Rose behind. He told himself he needed to make good time to get back to the ranch before dark, but the anticipation building in his chest had little to do with the setting sun.

When he finally reached the Diamond D, he spotted Penelope right away, sitting on the back porch. Waiting for him?

Titus grinned at the thought until she jumped up and ran

toward him. Not like a woman eager to greet her man, but like a woman who had trouble dogging her heels.

He swept the yard with his gaze. Too quiet. Lucky wasn't barking. No sign of the men. His gut turned to stone.

"Titus! Thank heaven you're here." Penelope's gray eyes brimmed with worry.

He dismounted in a heartbeat and reached for her before he even recognized his intent. "What's wrong?"

She pressed a hand to his chest as she peered up into his face. "Rowdy's missing."

23

Penelope had never considered herself to be a hand-wringing type of woman. One who fretted helplessly while waiting for the men around her to solve her problems. She hadn't had that luxury since there'd never been any men around to offer. Necessity had taught her to be a *roll up her sleeves and get to work* kind of woman. Yet for the last hour and a half, she'd been doing more fretting and praying than working, and her nerves had about reached their limit. So when Titus slid off his horse and reached for her, she didn't hesitate to lean into his sturdy strength.

"What happened?" His arm came around her waist like warm scaffolding. Secure. Steady. Supportive.

"No one knows. He didn't come home for lunch, but the men weren't too concerned. They told me Rowdy sometimes gets distracted and misses the midday meal, but he never misses supper. Today he did." Penelope's fingers fisted in Titus's shirt. "What if he ran away because of what happened this morning?" Unable to meet Titus's gaze, she turned her attention to the darkening horizon, to the ranchland that hid Rowdy from them. "I should have gone after him. Assured him I wasn't angry. Encouraged him to talk to us."

"I doubt he woulda listened." Titus's hand stroked the small of her back, his touch loosening a few of the knots she'd tied herself into since the others left. "A guilty conscience builds up a mighty strong hankering for escape in a man."

"But what if he's out there hurt somewhere? He hasn't eaten a thing all day. You know how confused he can get. What if he's gotten lost?"

Titus covered her hand with his and pressed her fingers flat against his chest. "Easy, Pen. Rowdy knows this land better than any of us. He's not lost. Probably not hungry, either. Wouldn't surprise me if he spent the afternoon fishing and is sitting in a shelter somewhere with a fire, water, and panful of fried bass. He knows how to take care of himself and live off the land."

"But he needs to come home. To the people who love him." Rowdy might very well be camping out with fried fish and a warm fire, but that didn't mean he wasn't hurting. "Something is keeping him away, Titus. It might be an injury, a bout of confusion, or even a guilty conscience. The reason doesn't matter. What matters is that he shouldn't be alone. He should be with family so we can support and encourage him."

Titus pulled back slightly, his gaze penetrating her in a way that made her feel exposed. "That's the first time I've heard you count yourself as part of the Diamond D family."

Had she? She ducked her face away from the path of his eyes. "I-I didn't mean to presume."

"Don't you dare take it back." The roughness in his voice startled her. She peeked up. The fierceness in his face made her breath catch. He crooked a finger and placed it beneath her chin to keep her from hiding from him. "You *are* a part of the Diamond D family. Have been since the day you decided to stay. Doc and the others love you like a daughter and would protect you with their dying breath. You aren't some stray they decided to take in. You're family, Penelope. I'm just glad you're finally starting to feel the same way about them."

"Starting to?" Penelope swallowed against the emotion thickening in her throat. "I *adore* these men. They are the grandfathers I wished for when I was a little girl. I just . . . I suppose I've been holding a piece of myself back because I know how much it hurts to wish for a family and be disappointed. I lived on the charity of others most of my life, and I've felt the difference between being tolerated and being wanted. I'm living on charity again here, and I . . . I guess I was afraid of being merely tolerated."

She lowered her lashes to hide her eyes from him.

His hand moved around her chin to cup the side of her face, his fingers slipping into the hair at her nape. "Penelope."

She held her eyes closed, not wanting to see his pity. Not wanting to reveal her tears.

"Pen. Look at me. Please." His voice permeated her like the heat from a freshly stoked hearth on a cold winter morning.

Slowly, her lashes lifted. His eyes. Lord have mercy. She'd never seen such sweet intensity. Such fierce tenderness. Her pulse throbbed in her veins.

"You, my dear Penelope, could not be more wanted."

Pleasure shot through her at his words. Pleasure and longing. She knew he referred to Doc and the others, but the way he looked at her made her think there might be just a tad bit of himself included in that statement.

"It doesn't take blood ties to make a family, especially not at the Diamond D. There's not a drop of matching blood between my grandpa, Jeb, Angus, and the rest, but I doubt you could find natural brothers any closer than those seven." He rubbed his thumb along her cheek. "And now there are eight in the Diamond D family." A crooked grin tugged at the corner of his mouth. "Eight and a half, if you count Lucky."

Her skin tingled where he stroked her face. "We definitely need to count Lucky."

Good heavens. What had happened to her voice? It sounded so . . . breathy. Which was strange since she seemed to be having trouble filling her lungs. Her chest felt too tight as her heart ricocheted against its walls.

Was he looking at her mouth? His lids had lowered a bit, so it was hard to tell, but every instinct she possessed confirmed the theory. Was he thinking about kissing her? Merciful stars. She'd dreamed of her first kiss. Of magic and fairy tales. But something told her that Titus's kiss wouldn't be the slightest bit ethereal. It would be solid and firm and . . . earth-shattering. A craving built inside her. A hunger. Her chin lifted ever so slightly in invitation.

Heat flared in his gaze. His head dipped closer. Then at the last moment, his neck twisted, and his lips pressed against her forehead.

Penelope's eyes slid closed as she savored the sweet touch. It might not be the kiss of her dreams, but it soaked into her like a promise. Hinting of a future that might someday entwine her life with his.

Her heart slowed its ferocious pounding as the tender kiss soothed the frenzy, leaving a pool of warmth in its place.

Titus's lips lifted from her brow, but he hovered near her hairline for a moment before raising his head and sliding his hand away from her cheek. Slowly, Penelope opened her eyes. Regret warred with lingering desire in his gaze, spawning a need within her to smooth things for him. She'd not pester him with questions or try to hold on to a moment that needed to pass. Instead, she offered a smile. Not one marked with giddiness or embarrassment, but one that revealed her heart. She held his gaze for a charged moment, then patted the place on his chest where her hand lay and stepped out of his embrace. Time to refocus on the matter at hand.

"I have some supper in the warming oven for you," she said

as she turned back toward the house. "Come eat. Then we can join the search for Rowdy."

Titus fell into step beside her after swatting Rex on the rump and sending him toward the water trough by the corral. "It'll be full dark soon," he said, the huskier-than-usual timbre of his voice having an odd effect on her pulse. "Better for you to stay here. Keep the coffee going for Doc and the others as they start stragglin' in."

Penelope stopped in her tracks and spun to face him. "I'm not going to sit in the house doing nothing while Rowdy is out there somewhere, alone and possibly hurt. The only reason I'm not out there looking for him right now is because someone needed to stay behind to explain things to you."

Well, that wasn't precisely true. They could've left a note. But Doc hadn't wanted her out there, either, and he'd asked her to wait for Titus as a stalling maneuver. Since he'd asked and not demanded, she'd given in to his wishes, wanting to please him. She'd not give in to Titus so easily, though. Not when she knew what kind of mental torture awaited her if she stayed behind again. She needed to *do* something, and heating coffee wasn't enough.

Titus recognized the stubborn tilt of her chin and the determination firing her gray eyes like lightning inside a storm cloud. Man, but she was beautiful when her passionate nature exerted itself. Of course, she'd been beautiful when she'd shyly tipped her face up to his out in the yard, too. His gut tightened at the memory. He'd nearly kissed her. *Really* kissed her. The desire to clutch her tightly against him, slant his mouth over hers, and kiss her deep and long had been nearly impossible to resist. Even now, he wasn't quite sure how he'd diverted at the last minute to place a tame little buss on her brow instead.

Though even that innocent gesture had been a sweet torture he'd be reliving for many nights to come. The softness of her skin, the clean scent of her hair, her quiet sigh as she leaned her body into him. His pulse had yet to recover.

He'd never felt an attraction so strong. And not just because she was the most beautiful woman he'd ever seen. No, it was because she needed him. Trusted him. Wanted him. Although, looking at her now, her wanting had more to do with him giving in to her wishes than him giving her kisses. An unfortunate turn, seeing as how he didn't intend to allow her to put herself in danger.

"I know you want to help Rowdy," he began, choosing his words with care, "but you're not an experienced rider." He actually had no idea of her horsemanship skills but figured an orphaned girl growing up in a big city wouldn't have had many opportunities to ride. "I'll be able to cover more ground on my own."

"But Rowdy never rides. He always ventures out on foot."

"He ventures *far* on foot," Titus countered. "Several miles, I'd wager, since no one at the Diamond D seems to know exactly where he goes."

Her lower lip wobbled, and his gut reacted with a few wobbles of its own. Softening his resolve. Urging him to give in to make her happy. But he couldn't. Everything he'd told her was true. She *would* slow him down. Distract him from his purpose.

"Please, Titus." She stepped closer to him, and his heart thumped in response. "I need to do something to help. Sitting here alone, contributing nothing, is torture."

"I know." He reached for her hand and laced his fingers through hers. "I felt that same helplessness watching Tate slip further and further away from the family. I know how it eats at a person. But you're one of the strongest people I've ever met,

Penelope. You've endured so much hardship, yet your soul remains guileless and optimistic. If anyone has the strength to hold on to hope in a dark situation, it's you."

Eyes glistening, she shook her head.

"Hey." He squeezed her hand. "Don't underestimate the power of hope. The hope of gaining justice for my brother kept me sane in those first months after losing him. I've heard stories among the Rangers about men who persevered through deprivation, injury, and torture solely on the hope of seeing their families again. Hope can draw a man home, Penelope. It can draw Rowdy home."

It could draw me home.

The thought snuck past his defenses and planted itself in his mind. Penelope waiting for him. Drawing him home with her love. Him aching to see her smile, to hold her in his arms after a long stint of Rangering. Her welcoming kiss erasing every ugly thing he'd seen since the last time he'd been home.

Whoa, partner. Better tighten those reins before things get out of hand.

Hard to do when she was standing so close, looking at him as if he was what she pinned her hopes on. He swallowed. He might have to dash her hopes about going with him now, but he'd do everything in his power not to disappoint her in the important things.

He cupped her cheek in his hand. "Tracking people down is what I do for a living, Pen. I'll bring him back to you. I promise."

She closed her eyes and leaned into his hand for a moment before bobbing her head in a shaky nod.

A dog's bark sounded outside, and Titus swiveled to peer through the kitchen window. "Maybe I won't have to bring him back."

"What?"

Still holding her hand, Titus led her over to the window for a better look. He tipped his head toward the shadowy figures in the distance led by a dog running toward the house.

"Pretty sure that's Lucky, and I'm guessing Rowdy's somewhere in that group of folks clearing the rise."

"Oh, Titus!" She clutched their entwined hands to her chest and beamed a smile at him. "You were right. Hope *did* bring him home. Hope and prayer and the efforts of valiant men." Her glance shifted from him to the ceiling. "Thank you, Lord."

Before he could get his hat off to join her impromptu prayer, she switched things up again by planting a kiss on his cheek. He barely had time to register the sweet feel of her lips on his scruffy face before she pulled away from him.

"Your plate's in the warming oven," she called over her shoulder as she dashed for the back door. "I've got to go."

"Hold up. I'll come with you."

There was no reining her in, though. She hitched up her skirts and ran past the corral. Titus followed at a more reasonable pace, enjoying the view. Lucky met her halfway, barking and jumping around like an excited pup. Penelope slowed long enough to pat his side and offer words of praise, then chased after the dog when he darted back the way he had come.

One would think Rowdy had been missing for a week instead of a day the way Penelope greeted him. She embraced him and wept and told him over and over how glad she was to have him home.

By the time Titus caught up to the group she was leading Rowdy by the hand back to the house, exclaiming over how hungry he must be and how she had food waiting in the warmer for him and lots of coffee on the stove.

It seemed Titus wasn't the only fella she kept food ready for.

She tugged Rowdy along at a rapid pace. The old hand

trailed after her looking bewildered and bewitched at the same time.

Titus grinned. He knew the feeling.

Dusty, Angus, and Ike broke away from the others to take the horses that had been plodding behind the group back to the barn. Coy and Jeb headed for the house, nodding to Titus as they passed. Doc drew to a halt at the edge of the corral. Titus joined him, bracing a boot on the bottom rail.

"She's something, isn't she?" Doc asked.

"Yep." The woman had so much love to give, it just poured out onto everyone around her. Which made it awful hard for a fella to do his job when that job entailed leaving. Like his did. Tomorrow.

"She told us about the gems and the likelihood that Rowdy took them to add to his collection." Doc finally pulled his gaze away from where Penelope was ushering Rowdy through the back door and turned to Titus. "We searched him when we found him out by the old caves. He doesn't have them, Titus. At least not on his person. If he did take them, they're either gone or hidden somewhere."

Titus craned his neck to look back over the rugged country stretching between the ranch and the hills where the caves lay. Mighty big haystack for a man on a needle hunt.

24

Titus bided his time. Ate supper. Drank some coffee. Watched Penelope fuss over Rowdy as if he were some kind of visiting dignitary instead of a confused old man with sticky fingers. Eventually the crowd began to thin. The emotional stress and physical exertion brought on by the evening's search had left its mark. After Angus nodded off for the third time and started snoring at the kitchen table, Jeb jabbed an elbow into his side.

"Come on, old man. Better to rattle the rafters upstairs where there ain't glassware to shatter from all them vibrations."

Angus snorted awake, though his eyelids still drooped heavily. "Who you callin' old? I'm eight months younger'n you, ya grump."

Jeb scooted back his chair and hefted Angus to his feet. "Yeah, well, at least I can keep my eyes open longer'n five minutes after the sun goes down."

"Doc says sleep is good for a man," Angus grumbled as Jeb steered him out to the hall.

"Says the same thing 'bout exercise, but I don't see you puttin' *that* one into practice." A grunt followed Jeb's retort. "Keep movin', old man. I ain't draggin' your sorry hide all the way up these stairs."

"Quit callin' me old."

"Quit walkin' like a thirty-year-old plow horse on his way to the glue factory."

The walls and floorboards absorbed the rest of the verbal sparring as the pair progressed to the second story. The other hands shuffled around the kitchen, making their own preparations to retire, showing no signs that they'd heard the comical exchange. Probably too used to Angus and Jeb's bickering to notice. Then again, it was equally likely they hadn't actually heard anything after Jeb and Angus left the kitchen. Their senses weren't exactly the keenest. Penelope, on the other hand, looked as if she were holding in a chuckle. Her eyes danced with humor. Titus caught her gaze from across the table and let his own amusement show over the rim of his coffee cup. The smile that blossomed across her face in response would have rivaled the finest Texas sunset. Left him feeling a mite awestruck.

"Night, son," Doc said as he moseyed past, laying a hand on Titus's shoulder.

When Titus glanced up to wish his grandpa a good night, the gleam in the older man's eye brought a flush of heat to the back of Titus's neck. It seemed his grandpa had his own source of entertainment. One that had nothing to do with a pair of cantankerous cowboys and everything to do with his grandson flirtin' with the pretty gal at the other end of the table.

"Night, Doc." Annoyance colored his tone, making the farewell sound more like he was shooing a cat from underfoot. Which, of course, made his grandpa's knowing look gleam even brighter.

Interfering rascal.

Rowdy rose from the table, drawing Titus's attention and orienting his mind back on work. The small man kept his head down and tried to hide among the others as they trickled out of the kitchen, but Titus wasn't ready to let him heigh-ho off to bed just yet.

"Hold up there a minute, Rowdy."

Rowdy slowed, but he didn't meet Titus's gaze. In fact, the fellow looked like he might bolt at any moment. Grabbing the man's arm was bound to escalate the tension, but Titus wasn't sure how else to detain him.

Before Titus could rise from his seat, however, Penelope came to his rescue. Setting down the pair of coffee mugs she had hooked over her index finger, she hurried over to Rowdy's side and slid her hand through his elbow.

"Come sit by me," she urged, that sweet smile of hers working its magic.

Helpless to resist, Rowdy let her guide him back to the table. They sat opposite Titus, Penelope keeping a friendly hand on Rowdy's arm.

Titus was about to start his questioning when Penelope gave him a tiny shake of her head, then leaned in close to Rowdy. "Thank you for the beautiful buttons you left on my dresser this morning."

Rowdy's ears reddened slightly.

"You have a gift for finding pretty things," she continued. "In fact, I'm hoping you found some others last night when you came to my room. I think the lady I used to work for sewed some fancy baubles inside her corset. Such a strange thing to do, don't you think? I never would have thought to look for them there. In fact, I didn't even realize I had them with me until Titus found one on the floor this morning."

Her light, unthreatening tone reeled Rowdy in, drawing his attention from the tabletop to her face. The way she praised his cleverness and invited him to help her find what was lost was a cunning backdoor tactic. Only it wasn't a tactic. Not with Penelope. Yes, she hoped to elicit information from Rowdy, but that wasn't her main goal. Above all, she wanted to protect his feelings and ensure he didn't run off again.

The irritation Titus had initially felt when she waved him off vanished. He preferred brusque and to-the-point questioning, a fact Penelope knew all too well. Yet intimidation and interrogation wouldn't work with Rowdy. Titus had recognized that truth and planned to be gentle, but gentle didn't come naturally to him. Not like it did to Penelope. No, in this case, he'd be better off buttoning his lip and letting her take the lead. For now.

"Did you find any shiny rocks when you were in my room, Rowdy?"

The man shrugged.

Had he forgotten already? Or was he trying to skirt the truth?

"It's all right if you did," Penelope assured him. "In fact, it would really help if you knew where they were." She leaned closer and lowered her voice to a volume reserved for secrets. "Titus has been on a treasure hunt, you see." She tipped her head toward Titus, and Rowdy's gaze flickered over to him before settling again on Penelope. "A hunt for *stolen* treasure. We need to find those jewels so we can return them to their rightful owners." She paused, then finally asked the question Titus had been waiting for. "Do you know where those pretty rocks are, Rowdy?"

For a long moment the old man didn't move. Finally, he lifted a gnarled hand and rubbed it over his head. His gaze dropped to the table once again, but his chin dipped in a nod.

Yes! Now they were getting somewhere.

Titus leaned across the table. "Where are they?" He took pains to keep his voice as bland as possible, but Rowdy still recoiled.

Penelope frowned at Titus, which stirred his ire. He hadn't

attacked the man, for Pete's sake. He'd just asked a simple question. In a perfectly reasonable tone, too.

"Look, Rowdy," Titus tried again. "You're not in any trouble. I just need the stones so I can return them to their owners, all right? Can you tell me where they are?"

Rowdy's face scrunched in concentration like it did whenever he tried to speak. His mouth opened, worked a bit, then finally spit out a word.

"M-Mine."

Titus bit his tongue to keep his frustration in check. After all their patient cajoling, this is how he wanted to play things?

"No, Rowdy, they aren't yours. They were stolen, and they need to be returned." An idea sparked. The fellow liked to trade, right? Titus dug in his pocket and pulled out a half-dozen coins. Some of them were shinier than others, but this was a man who considered buttons a fair trade for rubies. "I'll give you these. We can swap. All right?"

He set the coins in front of Rowdy, but the old man shook his head and pushed the money back toward Titus.

"Keep . . . Mine."

"But they're not yours." Titus lurched to his feet. "You have to give them back."

Rowdy shot to his feet as well, his gaze hardening. "I . . . no . . ." He jabbed a finger toward the back door. "G-get . . ."

Was he telling Titus to leave?

"Mine."

If he said *mine* one more time, Titus's head was gonna explode.

He rounded the table, his finger aiming for Rowdy's chest, but it ended up jabbed against Penelope's shoulder instead when she whirled between them.

"You know what? It's been a long day. I'm exhausted. I bet we all are. Why don't we get a good night's rest and talk in the morning?" She shot a censoring look at Titus, then wrapped an arm around Rowdy and steered him toward the hall. "I'm so glad to have you home. I'm going to make you a big breakfast tomorrow. A tall stack of flapjacks with strawberry jam, bacon, and eggs. How does that sound?"

Titus scowled. It sounded like a reward for bad behavior. He stalked over to the sink and dumped out the remains of his coffee. They didn't have time to tiptoe around. Rowdy might be a little confused, but he was a grown man. He shouldn't be given permission to act like a petulant child just because he didn't feel like sharing. And he blamed sure shouldn't have the fatted calf killed for him just because the others dragged his stubborn carcass home.

A quiet footfall alerted him that he was no longer alone. He turned. "You shouldn't've interfered."

Penelope crossed her arms over her chest. "*You* shouldn't've interrupted. Things were progressing just fine until you forced your way into the conversation, demanding to know where the stones were."

He reached behind his back and gripped the counter behind him. "That's my job, in case you've forgotten. To find the stones."

Her arms unfolded and circled in the air. "Of course I haven't forgotten. But you can't treat Rowdy like one of your suspects."

"So I should treat him like a child instead? Patting his head and buying his cooperation with sweets? You're too soft on him."

"And you're in too much of a hurry. He obviously felt guilty about taking the gems. If you had just given me a little more time, he would have told us what he did with them."

Titus pushed away from the counter. "Are you sure? Because he didn't seem too forthcoming to me. Seemed pretty adamant about keeping the rocks for himself."

Fire flashed in her eyes. "You don't know that."

"How many times does the man have to say 'mine' before you'll admit that he's being uncooperative?" He paced closer, determined to seal his point, but the more the distance between them shrank, the more distracted he became by the effects of her passionate defense. Roses in her cheeks. Animated movements. The way her chest heaved slightly as if she were doing physical battle.

"You know how flustered he gets with his words." She advanced, closing the distance even further, her eyes sparking fire. "You can't just demand answers from him like you would a criminal. He needs patience and kindness."

Penelope Snow in her natural state—sweet and unassuming—was like a meadow of wildflowers. Beautiful and delicate. A site a man could appreciate. One that tempted the setting up of a permanent camp. But Penelope Snow in the midst of a passionate display? That was like encountering a towering waterfall, a vision so stunning, all a man could do was stare.

And apparently lose his mind. What had he been saying?

She sighed and dropped her arms to her sides. "I'll talk to him in the morning. Ask him to show me where they are. I'll ask Doc to help. We'll find the jewels, Titus. One way or another."

Ah yes. The jewels.

"Unfortunately, I don't have time to wait for Rowdy to decide to be cooperative." He rubbed a hand over his jaw. "I got a message from headquarters. Another theft happened in Granbury. I need to interview the victim and see if I can tie him to Madame LaBelle. Even if not, I have to go after the troupe. If Hunt has reported back, she'll be on her guard. Might even try to run. If I don't go after her now, I might not get another chance."

Penelope touched his arm. "You do what you need to do, Titus. I'll take care of things here."

Had he really thought he preferred the sizzle of her passion while they'd been sparring? Having her on his side, supporting and partnering him, stoked a slow burn in his belly that set those temporary fireworks to shame. This wasn't a flash that would burst brightly, then extinguish. This was a bed of deep red coals that, if tended properly, could keep a man warm the rest of his days.

The silence grew between them, along with an undeniable tug. Stepping backward, Titus broke free of her touch before he gave in to his desire to crush her to him and stoke those coals into flames. He'd not dishonor her, especially not under his grandfather's roof. Perhaps when this case was over, he'd come calling. Court her proper, and see where it led. But for now, he had a job to do, and he couldn't afford to be distracted from his purpose.

"I'll ride out at first light," he said. "It'd be best if you stayed close to the house while I'm gone. If you go out with Rowdy, take Jeb or Dusty with you. They're the best shots. I don't expect Hunt to come back, but it'd be best not to take any chances."

She nodded. "You be careful, too, Titus."

"I will."

But as he bid her goodnight, it wasn't the thieves and lawbreakers who worried him. It was the sweet-spirited woman with the soft heart and soul-aching smile standing in the doorway. Bullets he could dodge. Love, on the other hand, snuck up on a fellow when he wasn't looking, and he very much feared he'd already taken a lethal hit.

25

"This is the wrong one." Narcissa hurled the corset against the wall of her hotel room, then spun to face her incompetent associate. "What happened? Did you forget where you left the girl? Did you raid some farmhouse wife's boudoir in the hopes that I wouldn't notice the difference? Idiot!"

Her shout bounced off the rafters. She braced an arm against the wall and pinched the bridge of her nose between two fingers.

Breathe, Narcissa. Don't let Cecil's stupidity lead to your own.

Ever since that interfering Ranger came by two days ago and questioned everyone, curiosity was running rampant through the company. She couldn't afford someone happening by and overhearing her rant. She needed less suspicion aimed in her direction, not more.

Cecil stomped across the room and retrieved the imposter bodice. "This is Miss Snow's corset. I swear."

He shook it at her as if expecting it to change into the correct undergarment by the sheer force of his will. But he was no magician. Just a dull-witted clod who—

"I took it from the very room she was sleeping in."

Narcissa's thoughts froze. "What did you say?"

Cecil's eyes widened, and his mouth slammed shut.

Narcissa stalked him across the room. One slow, panther-like step after another until she backed him into a corner. "Did you say she was *sleeping* in a room?"

The corset slid from his grip as his Adam's apple bobbed in answer.

"She's not supposed to be sleeping in a snug little bed somewhere safe and sound," she murmured in a tight, low voice, rage simmering in her veins. "She's supposed to be rotting under a tree in the middle of nowhere—dead."

Cecil found his backbone and straightened away from the wall. "Yeah, well, she must've escaped. When I went back to the tree where I'd left her, she was gone." He lifted a finger and jabbed it toward her face. "And before you go insultin' me by assuming it were the wrong tree, I know it weren't 'cause the rope was still there. Cut and lying on the ground."

Narcissa narrowed her gaze and raised a brow until he retracted that insolent finger. "And how exactly did she cut herself free?"

"How should I know? I wasn't there. Maybe someone found her and sliced her bonds." He shrugged, but the shiftiness of his gaze left Narcissa less than convinced of his veracity. "Knowin' how much you wanted that cotton-pickin' corset, I spent a day and a half trackin' the gal to a ranch a couple miles away. The Diamond D. Run by a bunch of old men. I scoped out the place at the crack of dawn the next mornin', figured out which room was hers, then laid low until dark fell before breakin' in. Went through her drawers and grabbed the first corset I found. No reason to expect her to have more than one," Cecil grumbled.

Narcissa planted both hands on her hips and gave him her most withering glare.

"When you tracked her down to this ranch, was she still running around in her underclothes?"

"No, but—"

"Therefore, she obviously had access to women's clothing. Yet your tiny male brain couldn't extrapolate from there that she might also have access to additional undergarments? Really, Cecil. I thought better of you."

Instead of hanging his head as he usually did when she scolded him, he met her gaze straight on.

"Maybe next time *you* should be the one to retrieve the things you lose. Spend two days in the saddle under a scorching summer sun, scouring the countryside for a girl who doesn't want to be found. Then nearly get your leg taken off by a guard dog and get shot at by a gunman who was far too fast on his feet to be one of the old men who lives there." Cecil leaned across the sliver of space separating them, his face so close to hers, she could almost feel the rasp of his days-old beard against her cheek. "I could have been killed last night, Narcissa. But you don't care about that, do you?" His voice rumbled low in her ear. Hurt. Angry. "I'm not one of those sparkly rocks you put so much store in, after all. Just a faithful hound to kick in the ribs when I don't fetch properly."

He fit his hand to her throat and stroked the length of her neck. His touch was gentle. Controlled. But there was an air of menace she'd not sensed in him before. One that made her feel the tiniest bit . . . afraid.

Narcissa stiffened. The magnificent Madame LaBelle would not be cowed by a man. She was in charge in this relationship.

As if his touch excited her, Narcissa leaned into him and wrapped her arms around his neck. "Of course I care about you, Cecil. I need you."

She laid a trail of kisses along his jawline, then nibbled on his earlobe. His breath caught, and satisfaction surged through her.

She pressed her body against his and murmured in his ear.

"The only reason I got so upset was because we need those stones to start our life together." Pulling back slightly, she walked her fingers along the arm extending from his shoulder to her throat to a hand that was quickly relaxing its grip in order to slide lower. Narcissa smiled and gave his hand a little nudge in the right direction. "I'm tired of all this traveling." She puckered her lips in a sultry pout and watched his gaze zero in on her mouth. "Moving from one town to the next with no reprieve. It's exhausting."

Narcissa undid the button at the top of his shirt. Cecil inhaled. The power had shifted, just as she'd known it would. He was completely at her mercy, and that was the way it would stay.

"Aren't you tired of all these games, Cecil? Aren't you ready for the two of us to finally be together?"

A growl tore from his throat as he clasped her to him. "You know I am."

"Then we must get those jewels back," she said as she stretched her head backward and gave him room to kiss her neck. She added an extra dose of huskiness to her voice. "It's the only way we can start the new life we want."

Well, she'd start the new life *she* wanted. He'd have to adjust what he wanted a bit since she planned to leave him for Europe at the earliest opportunity. He could keep the gold and silver from the settings though. Payment for his work and motivation for him to keep her secrets after she left. Shared guilt was an excellent silencer.

"I'll go with you next time," she vowed. "You were right. I *should* take on more of the responsibility in reclaiming what we lost."

He pulled back and looked at her, disbelief shining in his eyes.

It was rare for her to admit that someone else might be

right about something. Not that she was *wrong*, of course. She wasn't. If Cecil had taken care of Miss Snow properly in the first place, they wouldn't be in this mess. He could have simply retrieved the corset from her corpse, and all would be well. But no. He'd left her where she could be found. Rescued. Now the industrious little hussy had wormed her way onto a ranch beneath the protection of not one but several men.

Thankfully, they were old men. Narcissa's specialty.

But what about the young one? The one who'd chased Cecil? She'd have to get more information on that, but now wasn't the time. She had to rid Cecil of his frustration and make him more pliable to her will first.

Clasping Cecil's hand, she led him toward the bed, laughing playfully as she tugged. "We obviously need to give you a lesson in ladies' corsets before we make another attempt to retrieve the one we seek." Narcissa turned her back toward him so he could unfasten the buttons running down her spine. She twisted her face over one shoulder and gave him a saucy look. "I suggest we start by studying the one I'm wearing. What do you say?"

His fingers tore through her buttons, providing all the answer she needed.

Half an hour later, Narcissa slipped out of bed, leaving Cecil to doze. She needed to think. To plan. Without wasting precious energy placating a prickly subordinate.

She crossed to her dressing table and slid into the silk wrapper waiting for her, not bothering with donning any of the undergarments that lay scattered about the floor. The maid could deal with those in the morning. Besides, she rather enjoyed the feel of the silk against her skin, reminding her of all the fine things she would enjoy as the wife of a nobleman. She knotted the robe's tie loosely around her waist, then sat upon a cushioned stool. Light from the streetlamp outside her room filtered through the lace curtains to provide a soft glow in the room, one that flattered her reflection, erasing lines and imperfections. Returning to her the beauty of her youth.

"You're a triumph, Narcissa," she whispered to her reflection, meeting her own gaze and willing the naïve girl in the mirror to believe it.

The girl who'd hungered to be more than a farmer's wife. She was special. Everyone said so. Her face so fair, her figure so comely. She'd been blessed by God. Well, she'd not waste her gift by pushing out babies and working from sunup to sundown until she withered on the vine like her mother. She deserved more than a life of hard work and scant luxuries.

Her mother had begged her not to go to the city. She warned of dangerous men who would use her for their own purposes, then discard her. But Narcissa went anyway. And never looked back. Partly out of shame when her first months in Chicago had proven her mother right. But mostly because she knew the future she wanted was out there, and she was willing to do whatever it took to attain it.

So she'd endured the pawing hands and leering grins when she got her first job singing in a dance hall. She'd watched how the girls who worked upstairs handled their clients and took notes. Beauty didn't open the right doors on its own. A woman had to be cunning in how she used it. Like any weapon, those who mastered its use positioned themselves for victory. No emotion or sentiment. Only calculation. In time, she learned to recognize the men who could be manipulated and those who couldn't and only gave herself to those who could give her something in return. Opportunity. Power.

"You're a triumph," she repeated, her eyes narrowing slightly. "And you *will* have the life you deserve."

Unfortunately, to do that, she'd need to convince Billings

to take the tour out of Texas now that the Rangers were involved. Not only had they managed to connect the thefts, they'd started sniffing around her troupe, putting her in a vulnerable position. Vulnerable was not acceptable. They'd have to divert. Go north to Denver after finishing in Texas as they'd planned. Just a bit earlier than originally scheduled. Their tentative booking with the Elitch Theatre was a couple of months away, but they'd bump up the engagement. Surely, a big-name talent from Chicago outweighed any two-bit vaudeville acts currently on the books. Billings possessed a knack for negotiating. He'd see to it.

After Denver, they'd head to San Francisco. Play a few houses there, then dissolve the troupe. She'd take a train to Galveston, catch a steamer to Europe, and all this unpleasantness would be behind her. She might not have quite as large a nest egg as she'd hoped, but she'd make do. She always did.

Drat those Rangers, though. None of the other states she'd passed through had given her any trouble. Local law handled each case individually, never suspecting the thefts were connected. Of course, all the other states she'd passed through had been significantly smaller, so even if a lawman or two started to piece things together, she was well out of their jurisdiction before they could act. Texas was too large, and she'd been operating inside its borders too long. A situation she would rectify as soon as she had her corset back. The real one. She scowled through the mirror at the garment crumpled against the wall where she'd thrown it earlier. Not that frumpy excuse for a . . .

Narcissa swiveled on her stool until her gaze landed on the white clump by the wall. She rose from her seat and sauntered over to the place where the undergarment lay. She picked it up. Sturdy. Well-worn. With shoulder straps one didn't usually see on such a piece. A health corset. One shaped for a narrow waist and large bust. One worn by a deceitful little maid who thought to hide her figure and make Narcissa look the fool. One that had been left behind by that maid until a certain Ranger took it, along with the rest of her belongings, in an effort to track her down. The fact that she had it in her possession when Cecil found her meant the Ranger had found her first. Found her but *hadn't* arrested her.

Narcissa strangled the corset in a quickly tightening fist. She would not be outperformed by an inexperienced child. If Miss Snow was no longer a suspect, Narcissa would have to provide the Rangers with a new one. Her gaze shifted to the man sleeping in her bed, and her grip on the corset relaxed. Two problems, one solution. A smile slowly stretched across her face.

Cecil had already shown himself a villain. Abducting poor maids and ransacking their rooms in the dead of night. Taking advantage of long-standing friendships with actresses who were too trusting.

She'd have to make sure he eluded the law long enough to help her retrieve the jewels, but after that . . . well, the mention of a certain black velvet sack filled with melted-down gold and silver pieces in the right ear should do the trick.

Narcissa dropped Penelope's corset and crossed back to the bed. Sliding beneath the covers, she smiled when Cecil reached for her in his sleep and tugged her close.

The heroic man was about to sacrifice his future for hers. He just didn't know it yet.

26

The three-hour ride to Granbury in the quiet of the early morning gave Titus plenty of time to think. Unfortunately, most of his thinking centered on recollections of the almost-kiss he'd shared with Penelope the previous evening. The woman was proving quite difficult to dislodge from his mind. Yet the closer he came to Granbury, the more his senses sharpened.

Sometime during the last two days, the investigation's purpose had shifted from seeking justice and an occupational promotion to ensuring Penelope's safety. Hunt had been in her bedroom, for Pete's sake. He could have strangled her or slit her throat while she slept, and Titus wouldn't have even known of the danger until it was too late. The thought iced his blood.

Thank you for protecting her, Lord. Help me do the same.

A part of him wanted to turn Rex around and head back to the ranch to watch over her himself. But a good Ranger didn't sit around waiting for trouble to knock on his door. He sought it where it lived and cut it down before it could wreak its havoc on law-abiding citizens.

The best way for him to protect Penelope was to find the proof necessary to arrest Narcissa LaBelle. He probably had enough evidence to charge Cecil Hunt for abducting Penelope, *if* she would testify against him. When she first recounted the kidnapping, she'd asked him not to prosecute Hunt, but maybe he could get her to change her mind after Hunt had broken into her room. If not, Titus could still pursue the housebreaking and corset theft. The evidence was circumstantial since Penelope had kept her eyes shut during the invasion, but if Titus could find a few corroborating details, he might have enough to take it before a judge. Only problem was that Hunt was just a puppet. One that could likely be replaced. Titus needed to take down the woman pulling the strings. A woman skilled at stretching the wool over men's eyes and keeping them blind to her intent.

When the town of Granbury came into view, Titus eased Rex out of his canter and back into the walking pace he'd alternated between every three miles or so for rest.

"You made great time, boy," Titus praised as he leaned forward to pat the horse's neck. "Just a few more minutes before a nice long drink and the best rubdown money can buy."

Titus recalled seeing a livery half a block from the jailhouse when he'd been here at the start of the week. He'd stop there first.

It was too early in the day for the livery to have collected its normal contingent of jawing old-timers, so Titus had the owner's full attention when he dismounted.

"Name's McGaughy," the man said by way of introduction. He held out a hand to Titus, but his gaze fastened on Rex. "What can I do for this fine beast?"

"Titus Kingsley." He gripped the man's hand. "Just rode in from Glen Rose. If you'll see Rex gets water, a rubdown, and a good brushing, I'd appreciate it. Fresh hay, too, after he's had a chance to recover. I'm glad to pay extra. I'd like to board him overnight, as well, if you have the space."

"For this beauty?" McGaughy grinned as he patted Rex's shoulder. "I got all the room he needs." He turned back to Titus. "I'll tend him myself, Mr. Kingsley."

"Thanks."

After giving Rex a final pat, Titus headed over to the jail-house and found Sheriff Morris nursing a cup of coffee.

"You carry yourself like a lawman." Morris eyed Titus from hat to boots before setting down his cup and rising to greet his company. He was a rangy fellow, probably in his late fifties, sporting a gray mustache that matched his stern eyebrows. His forehead was tall, and his gaze direct. "You here about Clayton?"

"Yep. Ranger Titus Kingsley." Titus pulled his credentials from inside his jacket and handed them to the sheriff.

Morris unfolded them, gave them a cursory glance, then handed the papers back. "'Fraid Ambrose ain't here. Left town yesterday to tend to some business down in Austin. I can show you the statement I collected from him, though."

Titus swallowed his disappointment. "That would be helpful. Thanks."

Morris strode to a cabinet and opened the top drawer. He retrieved a leather-bound logbook, thumbed through the pages until he found what he was looking for, then, using his thumb as a placeholder, twisted the slender volume around to face Titus, and handed it into his keeping.

The sparse entry barely filled half a page. It listed a pair of diamond cuff links as the missing items, their estimated value, and the date Mr. Clayton first discovered they were missing. A short narrative followed outlining the interviews with Clayton and his housekeeper. Titus weeded out only one helpful piece of information. The last time Clayton recalled seeing the cuff links was when he dressed for a night at the theater. Unfortunately, he hadn't realized they were missing until he began packing for his trip to Austin a few days ago and discovered they weren't in the padded box where he kept them.

Morris leaned a hip against his desk. "Kerr told me a Texas Ranger passed through a few days back, asking about that group of actors from Chicago. Figured the Rangers were more interested in catching crooks than catching a show, so I wired in the details of the theft just in case it turned out to be pertinent." He tipped his head toward Titus. "With you showin' up, I reckon it was the right call."

"Yes, sir." Titus closed the logbook and handed it back to Morris. "There's been a string of robberies over the last few months. All in towns where that troupe has performed. I'm hoping to catch up to them in Weatherford this afternoon, but I wanted to talk to Clayton first. See if he could testify against any member in particular." He met the older lawman's experienced gaze. "We've got a pile of circumstantial evidence pointing to the guilty parties but nothing solid enough to ensure a conviction."

"And now that they know you're sniffin' around, they're likely to keep their hand outta the cookie jar."

Titus nodded. "Or make a run for the state line."

Morris slapped his leg, then straightened away from the desk. "When the rifle's empty, best reach for the six-shooter. Ain't as accurate, but it'll do in a pinch." As if slapping his own leg hadn't been sufficient, the cagey sheriff slapped Titus's shoulder, too. "Come on. I'll take ya to see St. Helen." Morris grabbed his hat from a hook near the door, then headed out to the street.

The wiry sheriff with his bowlegged stride ambled south down Crockett Street, past McGaughy's livery on the left and the Hood County Courthouse on the right. He tipped his hat to a pair of ladies with shopping baskets hooked over their arms. The ladies nodded in return, though their attention diverted to Titus with uncomfortable speed.

"Who's your friend, Burl?" The older of the two ladies, most likely the mother of the younger one, adjusted her target from the general store to take aim at Titus. She dragged the blushing young woman with her down to the street and would have planted herself in the men's path if Morris hadn't suddenly lengthened his stride just enough to sidestep the ambush.

"Sorry, Geraldine. Ranger Kingsley and I are in the middle of an investigation. Introductions will have to wait."

"A Ranger, you say?" The woman was starting to run short on breath in her effort to match their quickening pace. "My Delphinia has always wanted to meet a real Texas Ranger. Haven't you, dear?"

"Mama, *please*." The poor girl's face turned tomato red as she tripped along beside her overzealous parent.

Taking pity on the young lady, Titus tugged on the brim of his hat, though he didn't slow his stride. "Nice to meet you, Miss Delphinia."

A smile touched her face and gratitude lit her eyes. "You too, Ranger Kingsley."

Titus nodded, then turned his attention back to business. Thankfully, business took them into a saloon at the corner, a place the ladies would not be likely to follow. Morris held the door open for Titus, strategically positioning himself to guard his back.

Titus grinned. He was really starting to like ol' Burl. They slipped inside, leaving the petticoat brigade to find alternative entertainment.

"We don't open till noon." A man stepped out of a side room that looked to be an office and meandered through the dim interior, weaving through tables that had chairs stacked on top of them.

"We ain't here for a drink, Gordon," Morris said as he moved away from the closed door. "We need to talk to St. Helen. He around?"

Gordon eyed the sheriff warily. "He in some kind of trouble?"

"Nope. Just want to ask him some questions about the night we had that big shindig for them playactors from Chicago."

"Ah." Gordon's face smoothed. "He's in the back washin' glasses. I'll fetch him."

Morris dipped his chin. "Appreciate it."

Once the owner disappeared, Morris walked up to the bar and ran his hands over the polished wood. Titus joined him.

"St. Helen ain't too fond of lawmen," the sheriff murmured. "Probably runnin' from something in his past. Long as he don't stir up trouble in the here and now, I'm good with lettin' sleepin' dogs lie." He swiveled his face to meet Titus's gaze. "Best to keep a light hand on the reins, though, if ya don't want him to balk."

Titus nodded. "Understood."

A minute later, a slender, dark-haired man walked through the doorway behind the counter and approached the sheriff with caution. His gaze darted nervously to Titus before settling on the man he knew.

"Sheriff." He dipped his chin respectfully toward Morris. "Mr. Gordon said you wanted to see me?" The man spoke with cultured tones. No dropped syllables or slang. Every word contained crisp edges and a full-bodied tone.

"Thanks for sparin' us a few minutes, John. This shouldn't take long." Morris gestured to Titus. "This here is Titus Kingsley. He's with the Rangers. He's working a case and needs to know what you saw the night all them actors closed up shop. You were servin' drinks that night, right?"

"Yes, sir."

Titus leaned an elbow on the bar and kept his stance as well as his tone casual. "Did you happen to see Ambrose Clayton that evening?"

"Yes, sir."

"Was he with anyone?"

A small smile slipped onto St. Helen's face, softening his sober mien. "The fair Ophelia."

Titus frowned. That wasn't the name he expected to hear. "Was she one of the actresses from the troupe?" He'd hoped to tie Narcissa to Clayton.

"Indeed. The leading lady." St. Helen's grin widened. "She will ever be Ophelia to me as she and I shared a few lines from *Hamlet* together, but the rest of the world knows her as Madame LaBelle."

That's more like it.

"Do you recall if Clayton and Madame LaBelle left the party together?"

St. Helen's grin turned rakish. "They made a point *not* to leave together. Though Madame conveniently developed a headache a few minutes after Mr. Clayton departed. If I were to guess, I'd say the two found a more private place to celebrate closing night. I overheard Madame issue an invitation for such a rendezvous, but the two moved off to a corner away from my hearing before the gentleman replied."

Titus's pulse thrummed. This was what he needed. It wasn't exactly hard proof, but it strengthened their circumstantial case and placed Madame LaBelle with one of the victims on the day the missing items were last seen.

"She wouldn't be the first actress to supplement her stage earnings by sharing private company with a wealthy patron," St. Helen said with a shrug. "Though I would never disparage the lady's reputation by testifying that such was the case in this instance. I did not bear witness to anything improper between them, so all I can say for certain is that Mr. Clayton and Madame LaBelle appeared to be enjoying each other's company a great deal while they were here."

Titus took his tablet from his pocket and made a few notes before looking back up at the bartender. "Did you happen to notice if Clayton was wearing any jewelry that evening? Tiepin? Cuff links? Lapel pin?"

St. Helen's affable manner withered. It seemed he had no qualms about gossip, but anything hinting at criminality was a different matter.

"I don't recall." His words emerged stiff and clipped. "There had to have been over fifty people here that night. I cannot be expected to remember what each individual did or didn't wear."

"Of course." Titus backed off his questioning, not wanting the fellow to feel as if they were accusing him of anything. They might need him to testify in the future, and the man would be easier to convince if they remained on good terms. "I appreciate your time, Mr. St. Helen. I'll be in touch if we need anything else."

The hunted look in the man's eyes faded. He manufactured a smile and offered Titus a nod. "You know where to find me."

True. He also knew where to find Narcissa LaBelle. In Weatherford. Time to quit cutting bait and reel in the big fish.

Titus bid St. Helen and Morris a good day and made his way to the train station. He purchased a ticket for an early afternoon departure, then paid a call on Ambrose Clayton's housekeeper and Henry Kerr, the owner of the opera house.

The tight-lipped housekeeper could not or would not confirm any late-night guest Mr. Clayton might have entertained on the evening of the Chicago Theatrical Company's final performance. She did confirm that she'd conducted a thorough search of the house for the missing cuff links, and they were not to be found. The woman was obviously loyal to her employer and protective of his reputation, but she did mention that anyone who would steal from such an upstanding gentleman was a Jezebel of the worst order. And since Jezebels only came in one gender, Titus was pretty sure the woman at least suspected a female was to blame. Another arrow pointing to Madame's guilt.

Kerr hadn't been much help. He'd sung Madame's praises, calling her the finest actress to ever grace a stage west of the Mississippi. He bragged that she'd brought in capacity crowds every night and lamented that he hadn't extended their booking for another week.

By the time Titus boarded the train, he was more than ready to leave Granbury behind, but he still wasn't certain how best to handle Narcissa LaBelle. Without the jewels, his best hope was to arrest Hunt for abduction and housebreaking and get him to turn on his partner.

But when he disembarked in Weatherford and made his way to the Haynes Opera House, he found the flyers advertising the show torn down.

No! They were supposed to be here another week.

Hurrying around back, he found wagons being loaded with trunks and set pieces. Thanking God that he hadn't missed them altogether, he let himself in through a backstage door and searched for a familiar face. A woman bent over a trunk overflowing with colorful dresses caught his eye, and he hurried over.

"Mildred?"

The seamstress spun around. Her eyes widened at the sight of him. "Mr. Kingsley? What are you doing here?"

"Looking for Cecil Hunt."

"He's not here. He and Madame had a falling-out. She demanded he leave the troupe, then fell into a weeping spell so violent it made her ill. She insisted Mr. Billings cancel our bookings for the next month. We're traveling to Denver and will meet her there once she recovers."

She was running. Slipping the noose. He had to tighten it before she escaped.

"Where is she?" Titus lifted his head and started searching all the faces visible backstage. But none of them belonged to the troupe's leading lady.

"I don't know." Mildred raised empty palms. "She left yesterday on the train. You should ask Mr. Billings."

"And Mr. Billings is . . . ?"

Mildred pointed. "In the office, tallying the receipts from the refunded ticket sales."

Titus turned to go, but Mildred grabbed hold of his arm.

"Did you find Penelope?" she asked, worry lining her face. "Is she all right?"

Urgency tempted him to brush her hand away and search out Billings before he lost the only lead left to him, but an image of Penelope rose in his mind, and he knew he couldn't treat her friend with such shabby impatience.

"I found her," he said. "She's alive and well and staying with some friends of mine."

Mildred closed her eyes, and for a split second, Titus thought she might faint. Then she murmured a quiet "Thank God," and squeezed his arm for a heartbeat before releasing him. "Maybe this will work out for the best. Give that sweet girl a chance to make a life for herself out of the shrew's shadow."

Titus patted the woman's arm. "You have a month. Maybe you can use the time to find a different path for yourself as well. I imagine there are lots of towns between here and Denver that could use a seamstress with your talents."

A light entered her dull eyes, and she stood a little straighter. "I'll think on it, Mr. Kingsley."

"Good. Now, if you'll excuse me?"

She shooed him away, and he didn't stop until he found Alfred Billings. Unfortunately, the stage manager wasn't in the mood to be helpful.

"This is not a good time, Kingsley."

Titus ignored the man's scowl and dropped a hand on top of the papers he was busy shuffling, forcing the man to look him in the eye.

"I need to know where Madame LaBelle went."

The man blew out a disgruntled breath. "You and me both. She just up and left in the middle of an engagement with no warning. Very unprofessional. She refused to tell me where she was going, just said she had to get away for a couple of weeks, get her mind right. Left me no choice but to refund ticket sales and cut payroll for a month. I'll be surprised if we even *have* a troupe by the time she returns."

"What about Hunt?"

Please, God. Give me something to work with. Some clue to follow.

"Don't know, don't care." Billings knocked Titus's hand away from his papers, then dug something out from the bottom of the pile. An envelope with Titus's name written across the front in a looping, decorative hand. "Here." He shoved the envelope at him, then reached inside his coat and extracted a small pouch. He handed that to Titus as well. "Narci left these for you. Said the note would explain everything."

Reeling slightly, Titus stepped from the office and out into the front of the house where he took a seat in a theater chair. He opened the pouch and found a handful of misshapen balls. Nuggets, really. Gold nuggets. Although, a few silver ones glittered in the collection as well. From the settings? He knew the jewels had been removed. He'd seen the ruby. They must have melted down the gold and silver settings after prying the jewels free. Smart way to keep them from being identified as the stolen pieces. Made them easier to sell, too. But why would Madame LaBelle leave this evidence behind and turn it over to him?

Titus opened the envelope and pulled out a sheet of ivory stationery, scented lightly with perfume. He wrinkled his nose at the artificial scent as he opened the letter.

Ranger Kingsley,

I could not get our meeting out of my head. Nor could I continue to ignore the growing suspicions I harbored about a man I once thought above reproach. You see, there was one set of belongings you didn't search in their entirety when you were here last. One of our stagehands, Cecil Hunt, was away when you visited. Cecil has developed a bit of a tendre for me, I'm embarrassed to say, and he has been acting more and more possessive of late. He dislikes me spending time with our male patrons, and I have caught him looking at them in a predatory manner. When he returned after your visit, I stole into his room and searched his saddlebags. I found this pouch and knew at once that he must be behind the thefts, taking valued items from the men I showed attention to and disfiguring those items with fire. His mind is unhinged. I fear for my safety. That's why I have sent him away and removed myself from the limelight for a time. I must fortify my nerves.

Below, you will find the address of the place I believe he will go. He has friends there who will take him in. I won't feel safe until you have him behind bars, Mr. Kingsley, so please hurry. Lock him up before he does something worse than take jewelry and melt it into scarred remains.

I will watch the papers for news of his arrest and will know when it is safe to emerge. May God bless you in your duty, my courageous Ranger. My life is in your hands.

Narcissa LaBelle

The woman thought to throw him off the scent by handing him a scapegoat. But what she didn't realize was that she'd also handed him the means to turn that goat against her. Once Titus showed Hunt this letter, there was no way he'd continue to protect his lover. Not if he had a shred of self-respect.

Titus memorized the Fort Worth address that she'd printed at the bottom of the stationery, then headed for the depot. He had another train to catch.

27

Penelope had intended to get up early enough to see Titus off and to keep Rowdy from escaping the house without her, but she'd failed on both counts. By the time she dragged herself out of bed, the sun had fully emerged, and Coy had breakfast nearly finished. The men tiptoed around the kitchen, speaking in whispers instead of their usual boisterous banter until Dusty let out one of his window-rattling sneezes.

"Achoo!"

"Now you done it," Jeb groused. "No one can sleep through that cannon fire."

Dusty unfurled a handkerchief and held it to his nose. "Sorry. It snuck up on me."

"Snuck up on you? How do you not feel a lit gunpowder fuse winding through your—"

"Good morning!" Penelope stepped into the room before Jeb set off an explosion of his own. "Sorry to be such a slugabed." She made her way to the cabinet and pulled down plates, trying to assuage her guilt by lending Coy a helping hand. "I meant to be up with the sun, but I didn't hear the rooster."

"That's 'cause Dusty shot him with his nose cannon." This from a snickering Angus.

Good-natured chuckles warmed the room. Even Dusty grinned.

"Next time you're hankering for a chicken dinner," he said, "just let me know. I got plenty of ammunition."

"Lord knows that's the truth." The heat in Jeb's gaze eased into a teasing light, and the tension drained from the room.

Coy turned from the stove to point a spatula in her direction. "You go sit down, Miss Penny. We'll take care of everything this morning. You been pamperin' us plenty. It's time we return the favor."

"That's right." Ike came up beside her and steered her toward the foot of the table. "The kettle's full. I'll set some tea to steeping for you."

"But—"

"No buts, young lady," Doc said as he rose from his place at the table to hold out her chair. "You've had an extremely trying few days. Persistent stress like this takes a toll on a body. Even one as young and healthy as yours. You need rest, my dear, and your body knows it. That's why you slept so hard this morning." He waited for her to move in front of the chair, then scooted it up to the table as she lowered herself to the seat. "The boys and I have decided that today will be a Penelope Snow holiday. You aren't to lift a finger."

"But the laundry needs to be ironed, the rugs need a beating, and I have a mound of mending waiting."

"All of that will keep," Doc insisted with a stern, fatherly look that warned her against protesting. "Today is a day of rest. Doctor's orders."

She glanced around the table. Five heads nodded their agreement to Doc's decree. Five. Not six. Her heart stuttered. "Where's Rowdy?"

Had he run off again? She'd promised to make him a big flapjack breakfast, then she'd slept right through her window of opportunity.

She turned to Doc and gripped his hand. "I need Rowdy to show me where the gems are. Titus is counting on me."

Coy set a heaping platter of flapjacks in the center of the table. "Don't you worry none about Rowdy, Miss Penny." He peeked sideways at her, then turned to stare at the tabletop the instant she met his gaze. "I saw him afore he left. He promised to be home for lunch. There'll be plenty of time to hunt them jewels this afternoon."

Ike retrieved the stack of plates Penelope had removed from the cabinet and began handing them out around the table. "I think it would be safer for her to stay at the house," he said. "That Hunt fellow could be out there somewhere, waiting for another chance to strike." He set a plate in front of Penelope, and his kind eyes met hers. "With Titus gone, I'd feel better if you stayed close to home where we can look after you." He turned to the rest of the men. "Half of us can go with Rowdy, half can stay here. Just in case trouble comes."

All the nodding heads chafed Penelope's hard-won independence. Did they not see the double standard? Rowdy was out there alone right now, and no one seemed anxious on his behalf.

"I gave Titus my word," she insisted. "It's because of me that this trouble is at your door, and while I welcome your offer of protection, I won't hide from what needs to be done. Rowdy's out there unprotected. If you think it safe enough for him to gallivant around, surely it can't be too dangerous for me to go out with an armed escort."

Doc dipped his chin and shot a look at her over the rim of his glasses. "Hunt has no reason to suspect that Rowdy knows anything about the jewels. You, on the other hand, are his prime target."

"Not me exactly. He wants the corset."

The corset. A thread of an idea began to weave through her mind.

"Well, he wants the jewels inside the corset," Doc corrected. "Jewels that are no longer there."

"But he doesn't know that." Excitement swelled in Penelope's breast as the wisp of an idea solidified into a viable plan. "I could repair the tear and sew small rocks and beads back into that boning channel. It would feel the same. Look the same." She glanced over at Jeb. "We could use the corset like one of your fishing lures. Hang it on the clothesline and leave it unattended. He could grab it and run without having to threaten any of us."

Doc scratched at his chin. "Does Titus need the corset as evidence?"

"I don't think so. He would have taken it with him if he thought it important. There's nothing to prove it's hers besides my testimony that I retrieved it from her trunk. Mildred could corroborate, I suppose, but Madame could easily claim that I stashed it in her trunk, since I had regular access to her luggage."

"Hmmpf."

Choosing to interpret that cryptic grunt as Doc conceding to her logic, Penelope discarded the notion that Titus might need the corset as evidence and returned to selling her scheme to the skeptics in the room. "Mr. Hunt really isn't a violent man by nature. He could have killed me the night he tied me to the tree, but he didn't. If we give him an easy way to get what he wants, he'll take it."

"Say he does," Doc countered. "What happens when he discovers he's been tricked? That LaBelle woman will know you have the jewels, and it won't matter if Hunt has a violent nature or not. You'll be her target, and if Hunt won't go after you, she'll find someone else who will."

He wasn't wrong, but to her way of thinking, it was a gamble worth taking. "It would buy us time," she argued. "Time for Titus to make an arrest, or at the very least to return to the Diamond D." Doc didn't look convinced. "What's the alternative?" she asked gently. "Keep me locked in the house until Titus gets those two behind bars?"

"I'm not averse to that plan," Doc grumbled.

Penelope laughed. "Well, *I* am."

Doc heaved a sigh, and Penelope held her breath, hoping capitulation would follow. Hunt might not be out there waiting for a chance to invade the Diamond D again, but if he was, she wanted to give him an excuse to leave peacefully. She couldn't bear for one of her new grandfathers to get caught in Hunt's crossfire if things escalated. Doc and the others might believe it their duty to safeguard her, but she had a protective duty, too. These men were her family, and while she might not possess the skills to take up arms in their defense, she possessed other talents. If she could shield them with a patched corset and her wits, then that's what she was going to do.

The righteousness of her cause swelled within her chest, straightening her posture and lifting her chin. Oddly enough, the change in her did not deflate Doc's demeanor. His own posture straightened, but not in challenge. No, there was a different light altogether dancing in his eyes, one accompanied by a small smile that arched Penelope's eyebrows.

"I'll make you a deal," Doc said. "I'll agree to your undergarment subterfuge if you promise to stay at the house this afternoon while half of us search out Rowdy's hiding place."

She hesitated, still wanting to be the one who retrieved the jewels from wherever Rowdy had hidden them, but protecting the Diamond D men was more important than impressing Titus with a handful of recovered gems.

"Agreed."

Doc's smile widened. "Good. We'll leave Jeb, Angus, and Ike here with you. Jeb needs to rest his leg after yesterday's exertion anyway."

"Leg's fine," Jeb groused. "I rode most of the way."

Doc shot him an exasperated look. "We need a rifleman to watch over Penny. You up for the task or not?"

Jeb's scowl darkened, but he threw his shoulders back like a soldier reporting for duty. "Of course I am."

"Good. Then quit your bellyaching. You, Angus, and Ike stay here with Penelope. I'll take Dusty and Coy with me to follow Rowdy. Any questions?"

"I got one."

Everyone turned to look at Angus.

"Can we eat now? These flapjacks are getting cold."

Chuckles eased the tension, and food soon circled the table. Once plates were filled, heads bowed, and Doc spoke a blessing over the food. Penelope added her own silent prayer of thanks for unconventional families and the love that bound them together.

Whatever happens, Lord. Keep them safe.

Coy insisted on doing the breakfast dishes, but Penelope coaxed him into letting her dry. She really did hate to sit idle, after all. Though, the holiday Doc and others had forced upon her did provide opportunity to perfect her decoy scheme. With no other demands on her time, she was free to scour the house for filling material. Madame would not be easy to fool. If this plan was to succeed, Penelope had to find objects with faceted edges to mimic the feel of cut gems. If she filled the channel with smooth, round items like beans or beads, Madame would recognize the difference at once. If Narcissa believed the corset's contents remained undisturbed, maybe she wouldn't immediately pop the seams to verify the presence of the stolen gems. Perhaps she'd stuff the corset back into her trunk and wait for things to blow over. It was a slim chance, but worth the effort.

It took nearly an hour of hunting through the kindling box, dust bin, and forgotten crevices beneath beds before Penelope was satisfied with her collection of pebbles, seeds, and bits of metal. She even claimed what looked to be a gold filling from Rowdy's jar on the mantel in the parlor. Using a wooden skewer, she pushed the items into the repaired boning channel one by one until half an inch remained at the top. Then she slip-stitched the top shut and inspected her handiwork by giving the corset a sharp tug on either side of the channel. The seam held.

Now for the most difficult part. Acting.

One would think that after spending months with a thespian troupe, Penelope would have picked up a thing or two about playing a convincing role. Yet when she dragged the galvanized tin washtub out to the yard and filled it with water and a few soap flakes, her heart beat with the force of a stampeding buffalo herd.

Act normal, Pen. It's laundry, not Shakespeare.

Nevertheless, the nerves persisted, making her hands wobbly and her breathing erratic. How did Madame and the others do this with such calm aplomb night after night with scores of people watching? Penelope's performance was likely for an audience of one or even none, but even so, her stomach swirled as if she were on a raft heading for a waterfall.

Breathing in through her nose and out through her mouth, she pulled her mind from her stomach and placed it back on her task. She dropped three pairs of men's drawers, two handkerchiefs, and a white shirtwaist she'd pulled from the late Mrs. Kingsley's trunk. The bodice had been too small for Penelope to wear, but it did a fine job of bulking up her laundry pile, ensuring the corset wouldn't hang on the line alone. Most of the items she'd pilfered were already clean, since she'd done laundry so recently, but she made a point to soak, scrub, and rinse each one just in case her performance did indeed have an audience.

Ladies didn't typically wash their corsets, depending on their chemises and corset covers to protect them from perspiration and soiling. Although, sometimes a lady would spot-clean an area with a small brush, then leave the undergarment hanging in the sun to freshen and dry. So that's what Penelope did, hoping her actions didn't look as suspicious as they felt.

Once she finished the small load of washing and hung the items out to dry, Penelope took the corset to a section of the line farthest from the house, opened it flat, and draped it over the thick twine. She didn't bother pinning it. With little to no wind, the boning would be heavy enough to keep it in place. Besides, the easier she made it to snatch, the more it would entice their thief.

She finished setting her stage by noon, exactly as she hoped. She hurried into the house to help Coy serve up the chili and corn bread he'd made for lunch. Rowdy returned as promised, and the rest of the Diamond D hands filtered into the kitchen as soon as Angus rang the dinner bell.

Penelope picked at her food, too unsettled to eat more than a few bites. Conversation rumbled around her, but she was too distracted to contribute. Her mind held only one thought steady—the corset on the line outside. Had Hunt seen it? Would he take the chance to seize it while all the men were busy in the house?

When Doc set out with Rowdy, Coy, and Dusty, she pleaded with them to take care. But as soon as they departed, she ran upstairs to Doc's corner room, the one with a window overlooking the side yard. She peered out, examined the clothesline, then sucked in a breath filled with equal parts excitement and dread.

The corset was gone.

28

The sound of rustling vegetation accompanied by the smell of male exertion drew Narcissa's attention away from the handheld mirror in which she'd been examining her carefully crafted appearance.

"I got it," Cecil declared in a low voice as he jogged into their camp, his chest heaving.

He really was a fine specimen. Too bad he didn't possess the wealth or intelligence to match those muscles.

"What 'it,' exactly?" She tucked the mirror into the bag sitting on the floorboard of the wagon, then turned to face her coconspirator. "You were supposed to scout the ranch and let me know when the time was right to make my entrance. Not risk discovery by swiping some random . . ." She waved vaguely toward a crumpled white item clutched in his right hand. "Whatever that is."

He flicked his wrist and unfurled the item like a herald's scroll. Her breath caught.

"What this is, Madame, is your missing corset. Recognize it?"

His insolent tone irked, but she let it slide in light of the more pressing development. Perhaps Cecil possessed half a brain after all.

Narcissa shuffled forward as fast as her ungainly costume

would allow and snatched the corset from his hand. She sought out the boning channel positioned beneath the place the wearer's left arm would fall and ran her fingertips down its length. They were there. The stones were there!

"How did you get this?" Champagne bubbles danced in her belly. Having the corset simplified everything. Success was all but guaranteed!

"It was hanging on the line with the rest of the laundry," Cecil said, his breathing still a touch ragged. "I snagged it when everyone went in for lunch."

"Hanging on the line?" Her victory champagne flattened, souring her stomach.

Prudish Penelope Snow hung her corset out on the line for all those ranch hands to gape at? Petticoats were one thing, but a corset? Narcissa found that hard to believe. Harder, even, than the idea that Penelope had actually washed the thing. Women didn't wash corsets. The undergarments could stretch and lose their shape. The metal supports could rust. To remove a stain, a lady might clean a localized spot, but she would dry the undergarment in her chamber, not leave it to flap about in the breeze for all of creation to see.

A small throbbing developed behind Narcissa's right eyebrow. She held the corset up to the sunlight and examined the seam. The stitches. So tiny and neat. Neater than Narcissa's passable skill should have produced.

"Give me your knife." Not taking her eyes from the stitches, Narcissa thrust out her palm.

When Cecil moved too slowly for her liking, she growled her displeasure, batted his hands out of her way, and pulled the blade from his belt on her own.

"Watch it!" Cecil dodged backward when the exaggerated arc of her arm brought the knife's tip a little higher than intended.

So what if she nicked his chin the tiniest bit? It was no worse than what he'd likely done to himself shaving. He'd get over it. She had much more important things to worry about. Like finding her jewels.

Narcissa wedged the tip of the knife inside a stitch at the top of the boning chamber, then sliced through the thread. She snipped the next. And the next. Until she could wiggle her finger inside the small hole. Hooking the first stone beneath her fingernail, she dragged it out. Her breath stilled as her finger twisted to reveal the stone. The ugly, gray, worthless stone. She flicked it into the dirt where it belonged, then reached for the next. Dragged it out. Cursed. Went back a third time.

Trash. Nothing but useless, miserable trash.

She jabbed the blade deep into the seam and yanked it upward. Pebbles, seeds, and a few tiny screws exploded like buckshot. A snarl rumbled in her throat as she shook every last counterfeit bauble from the corset.

Months of work—gone. Narcissa crumpled the corset in her fist and flung it to the ground. This was *not* how her story ended. Not after all the risks she'd taken. The sacrifices she'd made. Leaving Chicago to travel through rustic Western villages with their tiny stages and uncultured audiences. She'd camped in the wild, on dirt floors, for crying out loud. And for what? To let some little nobody steal her glory? No one upstaged Madame LaBelle. *She* was the one who'd performed offstage, fawning over old men with wrinkled skin and bad breath. *She'd* pampered their egos and stroked their vanity. *She'd* done the work, and *she* deserved the reward. That deceitful cow would *not* steal Narcissa's future.

Fire licked her insides, lighting a fuse that burned hot and fast. When the explosion came, Narcissa did nothing to temper it. A primal scream clawed out of her throat as her grip tightened on the hilt of Cecil's knife. She hurled the weapon with all her strength, the release sweet as it left her hand. The force of her throw stabbed the blade deep into the bark of a nearby tree. A tree that took on the face and form of Penelope Snow. Penelope Snow with a dagger embedded in her traitorous, thieving heart.

Narcissa smiled at the image. A wicked, delicious smile. "'The croaking raven doth bellow for revenge.'"

"What?" Cecil's confused gaze searched the treetops as if expecting to see an actual raven.

The simpleton. *Hamlet* was wasted on him. But it fed her soul. Fueled her with determination. Helped her get into character. For she had a role to play. Perhaps her most important role to date. The role that would allow her to reclaim her future. Her freedom.

"Fetch my shawl," Narcissa ordered as she adjusted the padding around her midsection, ensuring it lay precisely where it must to conceal her figure beneath the oversized black dress she'd procured from the costume trunk.

In a stroke of creative genius, she'd stuffed a small bag with cotton batting and sewn it to the outside of her chemise, behind her left shoulder. It gave her a rather convincing hump, the perfect detail for eliciting sympathy from a naïve girl with a soft heart. Soft for everyone except her former employer.

"You still mean to go through with this?" Cecil retrieved the tattered shawl from where she'd draped it over the side of the wagon, his expression grim.

"Of course I mean to go through with this. Why else would I be dressed like an overweight crow?" She gestured to the widow's weeds she'd donned, fighting the urge to roll her eyes. "We need those jewels. And since you are apparently incapable of recovering them, the duty falls to me." She marched over to where he stood near the wagon, turned, and presented her shoulders to him.

Thankfully, Cecil took the hint and helped her with the charcoal gray shawl. His hands smoothed the knitted yarn down her shoulders, then paused to squeeze her upper arms.

"I don't like you going in there alone. It's dangerous. Seven men, Narcissa. If even one fails to go along with your plan, you'll be vulnerable. And what if Miss Snow recognizes you?"

"She won't." Really, did the man have no faith in her acting abilities? His concern was sweet but completely misplaced.

"Forget about the jewels." Cecil's grip tightened on her arms. "We can still make a good life together. We have the gold. We can sell it and buy a pretty little piece of land somewhere. Just you and me."

A little hovel in the wilderness with only Cecil for company? No society. No luxuries. No audience to impress. Narcissa suppressed a shiver. What a dreadful thought.

Besides, they didn't have the gold. Not anymore. Neither did they have each other. Not after this afternoon's adventure.

She turned in his hold and raised a hand to his face. "Your concern is endearing, Cecil, but I'm a professional. I know what I'm doing. Now, help me into the wagon. I have cider to sell and a promise to keep."

She'd warned Penelope of the cost of betrayal, and the time had come for her to pay the price.

Narcissa situated herself on the driver's bench and arranged her skirts just so. She reached up to her bonnet and pulled down the heavy mourning veil that would guard her identity, then took up the reins. Confidence flowed through her, tempting her to straighten her spine like the regal queen she was, but she did not submit to the urge. Instead, she hunched her shoulders and bent her back, leaving Madame LaBelle behind and becoming Agatha Bower, the sweet, downtrodden widow who would destroy Penelope Snow once and for all.

Jeb took his guardianship duty seriously. He'd not left the porch for more than a handful of minutes since Doc and the others had left. With Angus in the midst of his after-lunch doze and Ike working in the garden, Penelope had taken it upon herself to keep Jeb company. Her new dress in her lap, she worked her needle through the fabric, hemming the skirt and praying her ploy would keep Mr. Hunt away from the ranch. The Diamond D men didn't deserve to be tangled up in her trouble.

Penelope set her needle aside and rubbed her palm on her apron. The day wasn't overly warm, but her nerves had her sweating, making it difficult to ply her needle effectively.

"Ya don't have to worry none." Jeb's gruff voice drew Penelope's gaze. He turned his attention from the road, his eyes speaking promises that caused her heart to squeeze. "I won't let Hunt hurt ya."

She forced a smile as she reached for his arm. "I know. It's not me I'm worried about."

Something tender softened Jeb's eyes for a heartbeat before he jerked his head away and resumed his vigil on the road. "We ain't worth your worry, Miss Penny. Just a bunch of old goats that done lived their lives already. If it's our time, it's our time. You, on the other hand, got your whole life yet to live. Gettin' married, havin' babies."

"Jeb!" She swatted his arm lightly, a chuckle covering her embarrassment. "I don't even have a suitor. You can't go marrying me off and giving me babies all in one breath."

His mouth twitched. She would have called it a smile on anyone else, but she knew Jeb would deny it.

"I seen the way Titus looks at you." He gave her a sideways glance. "If that boy ain't got marriage on his mind, I'll eat my hat."

Heat scalded her cheeks even as pleasure blossomed in her

chest. Was Jeb right? Did Titus really think of her in those terms? Heaven knew she'd thought about *him* in that way for quite some time. She'd not allowed herself to go so far as to imagine children, but—

Penelope straightened. "Did you hear that?"

Jeb fit his hands around the rifle in his lap. "What?"

"I'm not sure." She peered down the road, unable to see beyond the bend. "Harness, maybe?"

Just then, Ike came into view, scurrying up to the house as fast as his arthritic knees would allow. "We got company."

Jeb pushed to his feet, rifle clutched across his body. "Rider?"

Ike shook his head. "Wagon. Driven by a woman."

"Any sign of Hunt?" Jeb moved to the edge of the porch, his gaze locked on the road.

"Not that I could see, but you know my eyes aren't as sharp as they used to be."

Jeb spared a quick glance for Penelope. "Wake Angus. Then stay inside the house. We'll deal with this."

Penelope set aside her sewing and hurried inside. Finding Angus snoring on the sofa, she touched his shoulder. "Angus?"

He snorted and tried to brush her hand away.

She raised her voice. "Angus!"

He startled, saw her bending over him, and widened his eyes. "Trouble?"

"I don't know. Jeb's calling for you, though."

He ran a hand down his face and over his beard, then pushed up to a sitting position and reached for the gun belt hooked over the arm of the sofa. "On my way." He stood and fastened his belt around his hips. "Stay here, Miss Penny."

She nodded. She'd stay inside. For now. But the moment she was needed, she'd be out the door in a heartbeat. Petitioning the Lord to keep the men safe, she took up vigil at the window and opened it wide. She'd be keeping both her ears and her eyes peeled.

A weathered buckboard rolled into view, a figure in black at the reins. A widow, by the looks of her. Dressed head to toe in black with only a gray shawl to add a touch of hope to the mourning attire. She looked weary, hunched in her seat, her shoulders drooping, her veiled face downcast. The pair of nags pulling the wagon seemed as worn as their mistress, their heads low as they plodded forward.

"We ain't acceptin' visitors," Jeb announced. "Turn yer rig around and head on back the way ya came."

The woman jumped slightly, her face lifting as the reins fell from her hands. "Oh . . . Oh dear. Please. I mean no harm." Her high-pitched voice rasped slightly, as if it had been roughened by illness or old age. "Mrs. Williams from the mercantile in Glen Rose sent me. I have cider to sell, you see." She twisted slightly, one gloved hand trembling as she gestured to the crates in the back of her wagon. "Mrs. Williams told me the men at the Diamond D didn't get homemade goods very often. She thought you might enjoy some of my cider. It's only three dollars a jug. A fair price for the quality, especially since you get to keep the jug."

"We don't want no cider," Jeb groused. "You'll have to pedal your juice elsewhere."

"Hold up a minute, Jeb." Angus strode forward, thumbs hooked in his suspenders. "You heard the lady. Miz Williams sent her. Least we can do is sample her wares. It's been a coon's age since I had me some cider." He took a step closer to the buckboard. "It ain't hard cider, is it, ma'am? Doc don't abide no liquor on the ranch."

"As well he shouldn't. Liquor is the devil's brew if you ask me. It's what took my husband." Her voice cracked. "My Rupert was a good man. Attended church with me every Sunday until some liquored-up cowboy decided to celebrate his poker winnings with a few wild shots into the night air. One of them shots hit more than air. It hit my Rupert." She pulled a white handkerchief from her sleeve and slipped it beneath her veil to dab at her eyes.

Penelope's heart ached for the woman. What a horrible way to lose a husband. So sudden and senseless. Yet the same could happen to Titus. He made his living tracking criminals. Bullets were aimed at him on purpose. His end could be just as sudden. However, the fear of losing him didn't make her care any less. If anything, it made every moment she had with him more precious. Still, a shiver danced across her skin at the realization that she could be that widow one day.

The handkerchief reappeared and fluttered in front of the lady in black. "Forgive me. I'm not here to talk about Rupert, may God rest his soul." She cleared her throat and straightened her spine. Well, lifted her chin at least. The bend in her spine remained. "We were talking about cider. And mine is lovely. Here, come sample some. See for yourself."

She scooted to the edge of her seat and made to climb down. Angus hurried forward and offered a hand to steady her.

"Thank you, Mr. . . . ?"

"Angus, ma'am. Call me Angus."

"Angus." A smile sounded in her voice. "I'm Agatha Bower. Pleased to meet you." She turned to Jeb and Ike and waved them forward. "Please have a taste. There's no obligation to buy."

Ike grinned and strutted forward, but Jeb hesitated.

"Come on, Jeb," Ike urged. "A little refreshment won't hurt you."

Mrs. Bower started setting up a tasting station at the edge of the buckboard, opening a basket and pulling out several tin cups. "Is there anyone else around? Mrs. Williams told me there were seven of you."

"Just us and Penny," Angus said, already rubbing his hands in anticipation. "The rest are out on a . . . walk." He darted a wary look at Jeb, having realized his slip.

"Penny?" Mrs. Bower turned her head toward the house. "There's a lady at the Diamond D? Oh, I'd love to meet her and get her opinion on my recipe. No offense to you men, but ladies have much more discerning palates."

Jeb growled Angus's name and stalked forward, his limp pronounced. Ike moved to intervene, but Penelope knew it was too late. She needed to distract Jeb. Give him a new target.

"Jeb?" she called through the open window. "Has someone come to call?"

He halted and immediately shot a glare her direction. Good. Better her than Angus.

Penelope waved at the woman dressed in black. "I'll be right out."

Jeb met her at the base of the porch steps. "Get on back in the house. We don't know this woman."

Penelope patted his arm. "Well, we know she's not Cecil Hunt, so I doubt she poses any real danger. Besides, the Good Book teaches that true religion is to care for widows and orphans. We can't just send her away. Peddling cider is probably her only means of support."

"Fine," Jeb groused, "but no dawdlin'." He looked down the road as if expecting Hunt to stroll down the lane. "I don't like it."

By the time Jeb and Penelope reached the wagon, Ike and Angus had already finished off their cups of cider.

"You make a fine cider, Mrs. Bower. I'll be happy to purchase a jug," Ike said.

Angus wasn't about to be outdone. "Me too." He shoved his hand into his trouser pocket and pulled out a bunch of coins.

He dropped them onto the wagon bed and started counting out the price.

"Oh, aren't you gentlemen just the dearest?" Mrs. Bower tittered as she fetched a pair of jugs from her crate.

Penelope slowed her step. That flirtatious laugh. It seemed familiar. She looked harder at Mrs. Bower and listened to her voice, but nothing else about the woman struck a chord. Her high-pitched voice had a bit of a nasal quality to it, different from anyone of Penelope's acquaintance. And her poor posture and the unfortunate small hump on her back denoted a woman who'd led a hard life. A woman who deserved pity and kindness.

"There she is." Mrs. Bower clapped her hands together as she moved to greet Penelope. Her steps were slow and a bit uneven. "Miss Penny, is it? I'm Agatha Bower. What a pleasure to meet such a lovely young lady. Come, try some of my apple cider. Tell me what you think."

It was a bit disconcerting to carry on a conversation with a veil between them, but it would be rude to stare, so Penelope smiled and focused on the cider instead.

"I'd love to try some." She reached for the full cup that sat on the wagon bed, but Mrs. Bower brushed her hands away.

"No, no, dear. Not that one. That's for your scowling friend. I have a different one for you. A sweeter batch, to match your sweet face."

"Oh, I don't mind having the same as the menfolk," Penelope protested, not wanting Mrs. Bower to go to any special trouble.

"I insist." She handed Penelope the cup for Jeb. "Be a dear, would you, and give this to your friend while I pour yours?"

Penelope did as she was asked. Jeb's scowl darkened as she approached, but Penelope extended the cup to him anyway, then sidled up beside him and whispered in his ear. "The faster we taste her cider, the faster she'll leave."

Jeb grabbed the cup, downed the contents in one long chug, then thrust the cup back at her with a glare.

Pressing her lips together to keep a laugh from escaping, Penelope returned to the wagon.

"Here you are, dearie," Mrs. Bower said, holding out a cup. "Drink up. Let me know what you think."

"Thank you." She took a sip, expecting it to be sweet and fruity, but there was an odd, bitter taste mixed in. It took effort not to make a face. "There's a strange aftertaste. Did you add herbs to this batch?"

"Herbs? No. Keep drinking. It gets better, I promise. It's my most popular recipe."

Penelope took another sip out of politeness and would have stopped except Mrs. Bower took hold of the cup and tipped it up, forcing so much into her mouth that Penelope had to swallow to avoid choking.

"That's a good girl." Mrs. Bower suddenly grabbed the bun at the back of Penelope's head and yanked.

Penelope yelped and tried to knock the woman's arm away, but Mrs. Bower's grip was surprisingly strong for a woman of advanced years. Penelope's chin tipped toward the sky as her hair was pulled back, then a cup smashed against her mouth, and more of the horrid cider was poured down her throat.

Swatting at the old woman, Penelope sputtered and gagged. She tried to twist her face away, but Mrs. Bower tightened her grip. Shards of pain sliced across Penelope's scalp.

"Drink it all down, my sweet. Then I'll let you go."

Penelope's lungs seized. If she didn't get rid of the cider, she wouldn't be able to breathe. She focused on swallowing. Nothing else.

"Take your . . . hands . . . off . . ." Jeb's voice began to slur.

As soon as Penelope gulped down the last of the vile juice, Mrs. Bower shoved her away. Penelope crashed into the side of the wagon and fell to the ground. She wasn't the only one. Jeb had fallen to one knee, and his rifle was slipping from his hands. She pushed to her feet, intending to go to him, but Mrs. Bower latched on to her arm, holding her fast. She spun back toward the wagon and found Angus draped over the edge, slipping slowly to the ground. Ike, too, staggered and fell forward, hitting his head against the wagon bed.

"Ike!" Penelope struggled, alarmed at the dizziness that assailed her. "Let me go!" she demanded. "He's hurt."

"He'll be fine, Penelope. As long as you tell me what I need to know."

That voice. Lower. Huskier. She knew that haughty tone. If only she could swim through the thickening fog in her mind and grasp the answer that dangled just out of reach.

The widow straightened. Lifted her veil. And the truth stabbed into Penelope's heart.

Madame LaBelle.

29

Narcissa shook Penelope, needing her to focus before the laudanum rendered her senseless. "Where are my jewels?"

The sanctimonious tart dared wag her head. "Not . . . telling . . . you."

They'd see about that. "You don't have much time left, Penny. Not with all the poison I fed you. You'll be dead before that Ranger can find you." An occurrence that would have happened weeks ago were it not for Cecil's wilted spine. "I've dosed your friends, too. Not as severely. They'll simply sleep for a while. If you tell me where the jewels are, I'll ensure no additional harm befalls them. But if you don't . . . Well, it's quite easy to kill a man when he's unable to fight back. A pillow over the face. Steady pressure. They'll never wake up."

"You can't!" Penelope struggled against Narcissa's hold, her weak attempts to break free laughable.

"Oh, but I can. Shall I prove it?" She released Penelope and pulled off her shawl.

Penelope grabbed the side of the wagon to steady herself as Narcissa wadded up the knitted shawl and knelt beside the old cowboy who'd cracked his head on the buckboard. She pressed the clumped shawl against his mouth and nose and leaned her weight into it. His limbs twitched. A muffled wheeze escaped. She couldn't have scripted it any better.

"Please," Penelope sobbed as she slid down to the ground. "Stop. I'll . . . tell you."

"Excellent."

Narcissa straightened right as a gunshot cracked. She jumped at the boom, heart pounding. Had she been hit? Her hands wandered over her front, but she didn't find any holes. No blood. No pain. He missed!

Spying a holster on the man at her feet, she snatched his revolver and swiveled to face the cowboy with the gimpy leg and foul mood. He lay sprawled in the dirt where she'd left him, barely clinging to consciousness. Yet a curl of smoke wafted upward from the barrel of his fallen rifle. Somehow, he'd managed to get a shot off. Interfering idiot. Now she had even less time since the missing drovers would surely hear the warning and head back to the ranch.

After nudging the grumpy fellow with her foot to make sure he was out, Narcissa tossed the pistol away and stomped back over to Penelope. Bending over the crumpled girl, she grabbed hold of both her arms and shook her. "Tell me about the jewels. Now!"

"Only one left . . . ruby . . . in the coin purse . . . bottom . . . trunk." She slumped, her weight pulling Narcissa downward.

"Where are the others?" She released Penelope's arms and slapped her across the face, needing to stave off the drug's effects a little longer.

"Gone." The girl whimpered.

Weakling. Of all the worthless girls in the world, how did her future come to be tied to this one?

"Gone where?"

"Don't . . . know." Penelope braced her hands on the ground in front of her, trying to forestall collapse, but the slurring of her words made it clear the effort was futile. "Titus . . ."

Whatever else she intended to say was swallowed by the dirt when her face hit the ground.

Leaving her nemesis in the dust where she belonged, Narcissa hurried up the steps into the house. This day would not end in failure. If she couldn't reclaim all her jewels, she'd simply have to mine the Diamond D for whatever treasures it possessed.

She started with the first-floor bedroom, the one Cecil had told her belonged to Penelope. The girl had nothing of her own of any value, but the trunk at the end of the bed might. After flinging heaps of outdated clothing onto the floor, Narcissa uncovered the coin purse. She worked the clasp open and spread its jaws wide. There in the bottom was her ruby, just as Penelope had said. Narcissa took it out, held it to the light, and watched it shimmer for a heartbeat. Her chest relaxed ever so slightly as dreams resurrected and hope found new roots. She'd find her way to England yet.

But she needed more than a single gem. So after carefully tucking the ruby into the pocket in the lining of the coin purse, she dug through the rest of the trunk, tossing sentimental drivel aside in search of tangible rewards. A gold wedding band. Perfect. Into the coin purse. A lady's watch pin. An ivory cameo. A tortoiseshell hair comb. Into the purse.

At the base of the trunk, Narcissa found a wooden keepsake box. Her breath caught. Then whooshed out in disappointment when all she found was a stack of old letters and some toiletry items. She tossed the notes away but kept the silver-backed brush and mirror set. It might fetch a decent price. Tucking the box under her arm, she rose and made her way through the rest of the house.

The downstairs rooms didn't offer much of interest. Furniture was too large, books too heavy. She found an office with an enticing desk, but it only contained stationery and business ledgers. A doctor's bag in the corner caught her eye. Too bad it was monogrammed. It might have fetched a good price somewhere. There was one thing of value to her that every physician carried in his bag, however—laudanum. She pried open the bag, dug around, and came up with two bottles.

"I'll make excellent use of these, Doctor," she said with a grin. "I promise." She added the medication to the keepsake box, then headed upstairs.

Bachelor lodgings of itinerant cowhands had little to offer in the form of jewels, but simple men of a certain age tended to prefer their own hidey holes to banks when it came to storing funds. Overturning mattresses, digging through sock drawers, and lifting up loose floorboards netted her a handsome return. She didn't take the time to count it, but the coins and bills she found filled the keepsake box.

The freedom to take whatever she liked exhilarated her. She ran from room to room, adding to her plunder as if she were Anne Bonny or Mary Read, the daring female pirates who sailed with Calico Jack. No need for caution or discretion since no one could identify her. The men could only testify to a hunchbacked widow using a false name. And Penelope couldn't testify at all. Eternal sleep hampered one's ability to point fingers.

A vibrant yellow handkerchief dangling from a dresser drawer caught her fancy as she darted toward the door of the second upstairs bedroom. She grabbed the handkerchief and stuffed it into her pocket just because she could. Laughing, Narcissa danced down the hall to the room on the corner. A room with only one bed, unlike the previous two that had housed three apiece.

The master's room.

She set the keepsake box and coin purse on the edge of the dresser. If the Diamond D was going to boast any actual diamonds, surely they would be here. Yet the longer she mined the room, the more frustrated she became. No cash tucked under the mattress or in a drawer. Nothing of value in the desk in the corner. Just pens, paper, and old journals. A glassed-in bookcase flanked the desk. Narcissa pulled book after book from the shelves, fanned the pages, and found nothing. The infernal tomes contained nothing but words. Worthless! With a cry, she hurled the book in her hand against the wall, then swiped her arm across the desktop, scraping everything to the floor. Inkstand, framed photographs, papers, a pair of spectacles. The clatter made when the collection crashed against the wooden floorboards offered paltry satisfaction.

There had to be *something.*

She turned a circle, scouring the room for potential hiding places. Only the wardrobe had yet to be searched. Narcissa rushed over to the tall furnishing and flung open the doors. Just musty old-man clothes. Great. But wait. On the shelves to the left, among the shoes and grooming implements, sat a metal case. One bearing a lock. Her belly tightened.

"What are you hiding, you little pretty?" The whispered words fell from her lips as she collected the case and moved to the bed.

Once seated on the edge of the mattress, she pulled a pin from the knot of hair at her nape and wiggled it around inside the keyhole. Something clicked, and the lock sprang open. A little purr rumbled in her throat as she folded back the lid. Her gaze skimmed over the bankbook and checks to settle on two stacks of greenbacks, each tied with a piece of string.

That's more like it.

She stuffed a stack of bills into each pocket of her ugly black skirt, then continued rummaging through the lockbox. Legal papers, family photographs, a pair of letters tied with a lady's hair ribbon. Finally, she uncovered something of actual value—a pair of slender boxes that looked like they could have come from a jeweler. She didn't hold her breath for diamonds this time, rendering the discovery of two gold watches moderately satisfying. The pair were identical in size though slightly different in design. Not exactly a king's ransom, but they'd have to do.

A horse whickered outside. One of hers, she was pretty sure, but alarm bells rang in her head all the same. Narcissa slipped the watches into her pockets, then scurried for the door, grabbing the keepsake box and coin purse on her way. Time for the pirate queen to make her escape before the fleet arrived.

Urgency pounded in her chest as she raced down the stairs and into the sunlight. Scanning the horizon, she spotted movement in the distance. A dog barked. They were coming!

Narcissa threaded her way through the prone forms of Penelope and her three sleeping guards, then clambered into the wagon and released the brake. After sparing a moment to tug her veil back into place just in case she passed anyone on the road, she slapped the reins and set her team into motion. The pair of nags Cecil had rented for her moved with all the speed of a pair of drunk turtles. Fine for a widow lady peddling cider. Not so good for a pirate rowing for open water.

"Yah! Get up there!"

The barking grew louder. Closer. Narcissa snatched up a buggy whip from the wagon's floorboard and applied it with gusto to the backs of the sluggish team. The horses tossed their heads in protest, but they picked up their pace and ran in earnest. Finally.

The more distance Narcissa placed between herself and the Diamond D, the more her confidence grew. By the time she reached the hidden clearing where Cecil waited for her, triumph surged through her veins.

She'd done it! Now she just needed to dispose of her last loose end and her future would be assured.

Cecil met the wagon, taking charge of the horses and working to calm them as she set the brake. He frowned over their lathered state, but when she moved to disembark, he abandoned the animals to tend to her. He fit his hands to her waist and helped her down.

"Are you all right? I thought I heard a gunshot."

"You did." She pushed away from him and started peeling off her costume. "One of the hands got a shot off," she explained as she removed the hatpin securing the mourning bonnet to her hair. "We've got no time to waste." She turned her back to him. "Help me get this off."

His fingers fumbled with the buttons, but he managed to get the dress undone enough for her to drag it down her hips and step out of it. The padding came off next, followed by her lumpy chemise. Blessed coolness hit her skin, but she didn't take the time to enjoy it. Like a quick change between scenes, she had to strip away every last vestige of Agatha Bower and become Madame LaBelle once again.

Cecil produced a gunnysack and held it open while she stuffed the costume inside.

"I'll take it for you," he offered when she took the sack from him, but she shook her head.

"No, I'll keep it with me." Couldn't risk losing all the treasure she'd stuffed into the dress pockets. "You need to get to Fort Worth. I'll meet you there in a couple days. You have the address I gave you, right?"

He nodded.

"Good."

More than likely, Titus Kingsley had the address by now, too. She rather enjoyed the irony of having a lawman do her dirty work.

Narcissa bent down to open the second sack Cecil had brought over. She pulled out a brown split skirt along with an ivory blouse, cropped red jacket, and a pair of boots. No reason she couldn't look stylish while making her getaway. She'd be taking Cecil's mount south, while he traveled north to return the wagon and dispose of the cider.

Cecil offered a steadying hand as she stepped into her skirt. "Did you find the stones?" he asked.

She frowned at the reminder of her failure. "No. I think that little shrew gave them to Kingsley. I ransacked the house, though, and came up with enough cash to get us started in that new life you were talking about." She pouted her lips slightly. "You still want that, right?"

He snaked his arm around her waist and drew her tight against his chest. "You know I do."

"Good. Then meet me in Fort Worth, and we'll disappear together."

His grip tightened. "No more acting?"

She shook her head. "I'm weary of the stage, Cecil." She sagged into his strength as if she'd be lost without his support. "I'm ready to settle down. To belong to one man. To let that man take care of me for the rest of my days."

Heat flared in his eyes. He slanted his mouth over hers in a hard, possessive kiss. One meant to dominate. To celebrate. To stake a claim.

She played along, of course. Rising up to meet him. Clasping his shirt. Inflaming his passion. Making sure he'd do exactly as she bid.

As his kiss roughened and grew more desperate, her last loose end tied itself into a nice, tidy knot.

30

Enoch Kingsley had never been fond of dark, enclosed spaces, so when Rowdy led their little expedition back to the caves, he had volunteered to stay outside to keep watch. Rather cowardly of him, he knew, but he was willing to let his ego take the hit. It didn't require four men to retrieve a handful of gems.

"I appreciate you keepin' me company." Enoch patted Lucky's head as he leaned against the rock wall to the right of the cave entrance. "Wouldn't want you gettin' lost in there. It'd break Penny's heart to lose you."

Lucky whined softly and bumped his head into Enoch's leg.

"I know. It'd break all our hearts if anything happened to *her*. That's why we gotta clear up this mess with the jewels. Once Titus gets that thievin' actress and her huntsman behind bars, Penny will be safe. That's what mat—"

A faraway sound broke off his words. Sharp. Resonant. A gunshot?

Lucky jerked away from him and barked. The dog bounded a few strides toward home, turned an impatient gaze on Enoch, then barked again.

Penny!

Enoch lurched away from the hillside, his chest tightening.

He might not trust his own ancient ears to recognize gunfire from two miles away, but he trusted Lucky.

"Go home, boy. I'll fetch the others." Enoch waved the dog on. Lucky took off like a shot.

Without giving himself time to think, Enoch plunged into the cave, scurrying down the corridor as fast as his old bones would carry him.

"Dusty! Coy! Rowdy! There's trouble at the ranch." He cupped his hands around his mouth to amplify his shout, but his voice, like the rest of him, had been ravaged by time and didn't project like it had in his younger years. He coughed a bit and tried again. "Dusty! Coy!"

No reply echoed through the chambers.

Enoch moved deeper into the cave. The path veered sharply to the left, cutting him off from the light pooling at the entrance. The ceiling pressed down until he had to hunch over to fit in the space. The walls narrowed. Dimness became darkness with only blackness ahead of him.

God, give me strength.

Keeping one hand on the wall to his right to orient himself, Enoch crept forward, his breathing shallow, his pulse thready.

"Rowdy!" He tried again. "Coy! We gotta go!"

A sound echoed from deep within the bowels of the cave. Enoch closed his eyes, trying to decipher what he heard, but it was too muddled. Praying they could hear him better than he could hear them, Enoch leaned against the wall, cupped his hands around his mouth, and shouted with all the strength he could muster.

"PENNY'S . . . IN . . . TROUBLE!"

Enoch opened his eyes and steeled his spine. *Don't be an infant,* he chastised himself. He forced his feet to move. His head knocked against the lowering ceiling. He winced, rearranged his skewed hat, then bent his frame a little lower before marching on.

"'Yea, the darkness hideth not from thee; but the night shineth as the day.'" He quoted Psalm 139 under his breath as he put one foot in front of the other. "'The darkness and the light are both alike to thee.'"

God could see. God would lead. Enoch just had to follow in faith.

He felt his way deeper into the cave, praying with every step for God's guidance.

"Dusty? Coy?" He called his friends' names again and again. Then miracle of miracles, one answered.

"We're comin', Doc! Hold on."

Thank you, Lord.

A halo of light emerged from around a corner. Behind it were three familiar shadowy forms. Rowdy held the lantern aloft while Dusty and Coy squeezed through a window-sized opening about twenty feet ahead. The light nearly vanished when Coy crammed his more sizable girth through the dwarfish doorway. He pushed through, though, and Rowdy quickly followed, bringing the beautiful glow of light with him.

Dusty reached Enoch first. "What's wrong? We heard your shout but couldn't quite make out the words."

Enoch latched on to Dusty's arm and started tugging him back toward the cave entrance. "We've got to get back to the ranch. I heard a gunshot. Something's wrong."

"Come on," Dusty called over his shoulder. "The stones'll keep." He waved the others forward. Rowdy hurried to the front of the group, lighting the way as Dusty's bowlegged stride set a fast pace. Coy offered Enoch an arm as the two taller men struggled to keep up with their shorter comrades who didn't have to bend as they walked. Once outside, though, Enoch and Coy put their longer legs to work. While Rowdy stored his lantern for future use, the others started back. Ever since his accident, Rowdy preferred walking to riding, so they'd not brought the horses—a fact Enoch now regretted. He felt every one of his seventy-six years as they scrambled to get back to the ranch.

Rowdy caught up easily, then passed them, his daily excursions standing him in good stead. Enoch waved Dusty ahead, urging him to keep up with Rowdy if he could. He and Coy would bring up the rear.

Let them be alive.

Let them be alive.

Let them be alive.

His soul repeated the petition over and over, his gaze locked on the path in front of him. He couldn't spare the time to twist an ankle in a critter hole or trip over a root. His family was counting on him. He wouldn't let them down. Not this time.

Suddenly, Lucky was there, barking and running a circle around him and Coy, urging them to hurry. The coonhound sprinted a few feet away, then stopped and looked back, his eyes dark pools. That's when certainty settled in Enoch's heart. This wasn't a false alarm. Whatever had happened, it was bad.

He couldn't afford the luxury of being a worried friend any longer. He had to be a physician. *Only* a physician. Shut off the valve to his heart, and work solely with his head.

His mouth firmed. His chin lifted. His shoulders straightened. *I am your hands, Lord. Use me as you will.*

Despite his mental preparation, his knees still nearly buckled when he rounded the barn and caught his first glimpse of the front yard.

Bodies. Four unmoving bodies strewn across the yard as if it were a battlefield.

"God have mercy," Coy murmured beside him, his step

stumbling a bit before he dropped Enoch's arm and ran to where Jeb lay near the porch steps.

Dusty moved between Angus and Ike. Rowdy knelt beside Penelope, his ear pressed to her chest, as if trying to find a heartbeat.

Enoch set a course for Rowdy, his mind running through an invisible list.

"Coy, fetch my bag. Dusty, report."

"There ain't a mark on 'em," Dusty responded. "No blood. No wounds that I can see. I don't understand it."

"Are they breathing?"

"Yessir. It's like they just . . . fell asleep and forgot how to wake up."

Chloral hydrate? An opiate? Chloroform?

Something had rendered them unconscious. Enoch kicked a tin cup out of the way as he moved to Penelope's side, thinking only to remove the impediment, but then the significance of its existence clicked in his brain. He retrieved it and gave it a sniff. It smelled like apples, but there was a different sweetness present, too. A sickly-sweet smell reminiscent of opium.

Rowdy grabbed Enoch's arm, his grip painful and panicked. Enoch glanced his way only to have a razor of dread slash through the professional curtain he'd gathered around his heart. Tears flowed unchecked down Rowdy's weathered cheeks. His mouth worked over words that refused to come. Grief and guilt twisted his features.

No! God have mercy. I can't be too late again. Not again.

Enoch pressed his fingers to her wrist but found no pulse. He switched to her neck. He waited. Adjusted his placement. There. Was that . . . ? A second faint throb registered against his fingers. *Thank you, God!* She wasn't dead. But she teetered dangerously close to the edge. Her respiration was so depressed he couldn't detect her chest rising. When he placed his cheek directly above her mouth, however, the barest whisper of breath grazed his skin.

Coy arrived with the doctor's bag, but one look at Penelope's ashen face, and his hand started shaking. "Is she . . . ?"

"Not yet, but it's a near thing."

"What can I do?" Coy's voice quivered as he set the bag on the ground.

"Help Dusty get Jeb and the others into the house. Put them to bed and keep vigil. As long as they are breathing well, they should be fine. We'll just have to wait for the effects of whatever drug is in their system to abate. If any of them take a turn for the worse, though, come fetch me."

Coy nodded, but he didn't move away. His gaze remained locked on the girl they'd all adopted in their hearts.

"Rowdy and I will tend to Miss Penny," Enoch said gently, giving Coy a little nudge to get him moving. Then he glanced over at his companion to make sure he was up for the task. Rowdy set his chin and gave a firm nod.

Good. Rowdy was probably the strongest, physically, of all of the Diamond D men. He might be small, but he was tough as boot leather with muscles well-toned from constant exercise. Plus, he *needed* to be the one to help. He likely felt responsible for what had happened here. He wasn't. The villain who'd dosed the cider with poison was to blame. But self-recrimination was a brutal foe. One that held grace hostage and buried forgiveness. Enoch had battled that demon for years. Best to get out in front of it before it found a foothold.

"Prop her head up with your jacket, then open her mouth," Enoch instructed as he dug in his bag for his syrup of ipecac. "We need to rid her body of whatever poison has yet to be absorbed."

All the dangers of dosing an unconscious patient with ipecac flooded his mind, pulmonary aspiration being the deadliest. But if they did nothing, they'd lose her for sure.

Rowdy stripped out of his coat in a heartbeat, folded it, and placed it gently beneath Penny's head. Then he tugged her chin down and slid his thumbs between her teeth to hold the door of her mouth open.

Enoch positioned the medicine dropper above her lips, then looked to Rowdy. "I'm going to drizzle this on the back of her tongue. Once it's in, close her mouth and tilt her head back. It's going to make her vomit. As soon as she swallows, we'll need to turn her onto her side. When the vomiting begins, lift her head and shoulders from the ground. We have to make sure she doesn't breathe any of it back in. Understand?"

Rowdy nodded.

Enoch positioned the dropper, then paused.

Please, Lord. Expel the poison and spare her life. As you did for the daughter of Jairus, awaken this precious child from her deathly slumber.

Resolved, Enoch squeezed the bulb and released the ipecac. It didn't take long for the vomiting to start, though not even the violent retching woke Penny from her unnatural sleep.

An hour later, they had her laid out on her bed, her soiled clothing removed and replaced with a nightdress. He'd bathed her skin and freshened her mouth with a bit of tooth powder and a wet sponge. She looked so peaceful. Yet he feared she was slipping away.

Rowdy stood at the foot of the bed, hat in hand, head bowed in prayer when Dusty slipped into the room.

"The others are starting to stir, Doc."

Thank God.

He didn't want to leave Penny's side, afraid that if he did, she might stop breathing. But he wasn't the one keeping her alive. The Lord was. And right now, God was calling Enoch to serve other patients.

He rose, though he couldn't quite find the energy to straighten the hunch from his shoulders. Rowdy rounded the bed to take his vacated chair, ensuring the vigil would continue in his absence. His heart heavy and his steps slow, Enoch met Dusty at the doorway and clapped a hand on his shoulder.

"Better ride to Glen Rose and telegraph the Rangers. They'll know where to find Titus." He glanced down at Penelope, a new sorrow flooding his soul at the thought of the devastation about to tear through his grandson. "The boy will want to be here."

31

Hunting entailed ninety percent patience and ten percent marksmanship. Titus's father had drilled that truth into him and Tate when they'd been boys full of restless energy with a compulsion to wiggle. They'd frightened away game more times than Titus could count before they'd learned to master the art of watchful waiting. A skill essential for a Ranger on a manhunt.

Yet as Titus lurked in a shadowy Fort Worth alleyway across the street from the house where Cecil Hunt was supposed to take refuge, all those hard-earned lessons in patience eroded. Second thoughts plagued his mind, making it nearly impossible to sit still. What if this was a bigger ruse than he'd initially assumed? Deception was Narcissa LaBelle's lifeblood, but a betrayal of her partner to spare herself had seemed in keeping with her self-serving character. She'd cast blame before, convincing him that Penelope was a woman of low morals and therefore a viable theft suspect. It made sense that she'd serve up Hunt on a similar platter.

Watching for Hunt seemed a solid strategy. Find him. Show him the letter. Leverage Narcissa's betrayal. Get him to turn on her. However, for the last hour or two, Titus's skin had itched in a way that made him antsy. His gut had tangled into knots as if something were wrong. Like he should be somewhere else. Watching someone else.

He shifted his position, and his heel knocked softly against the pair of empty liquor bottles he'd salvaged from the trash bin behind the saloon three doors down. People tended to avoid conversing with drunks in alleyways. They averted their eyes. Hurried past. Scrubbed the image from their minds so they could focus on more pleasant things. A sad commentary on social reform, but a rather convenient practice for a lawman wanting to escape notice and questions. Titus had been sitting in the dirt with his back propped against the wall since dawn.

No sign of Hunt. Yet.

Titus had scouted the property last night after arriving in Fort Worth on the late train. A banker lived in the residence with his wife and two daughters. A woman wearing a plain gray dress arrived around seven this morning and let herself in with a key. Probably the housekeeper. The wealth of the family seemed more in keeping with a connection of Madame LaBelle than a simple man like Hunt, but it was still the best lead Titus had. He'd give it a day. If Hunt didn't show up by noon tomorrow, Titus would head back to—

Instinct shut off his wandering thoughts when a man in a dark suit turned down the rutted path that led to the banker's carriage house. Titus slid his hand beneath the horse blanket he'd draped over his lap to hide his gun belt and clasped the butt of his pistol. Slowly, he pushed to his feet, his gaze locked on the stranger ducking inside the carriage house door.

It could be a workman. The fellow didn't have the same build he remembered from when he'd chased Hunt, but it had been night then. Things sometimes looked different in daylight. Best to make sure.

Leaving the alley, Titus strolled across the street, then circled around to approach the carriage house from the rear. Unlike the barn-sized door at the front of the building that was large enough to accommodate the exit of a carriage and team, the door at the back was more ordinary in size and easier to crack open unnoticed. It took a moment for Titus's eyes to adjust to the dim interior, so he concentrated on sounds instead. Particularly, the quiet shuffling of shoe leather on floorboards somewhere to his left. He pivoted that direction.

His vision sharpened, allowing him to make out the lines of the black buggy and the legs of someone standing on the far side of the vehicle. Keeping his footfalls as silent as possible, Titus drew his weapon and edged his way through the tack room to stalk around the back of the buggy.

Settling his finger on the trigger, he darted around the buggy, gun first. A raised revolver in a steady hand greeted him. As did a face he knew well.

"Hoffman?" Titus lowered his weapon.

The weathered Ranger dropped his gun arm. "Figured that was you, but didn't want to call out just in case it weren't."

Titus holstered his gun but didn't relax. "Why are you here?"

"Captain Bill sent me to relieve you." The man's somber tone and penetrating gaze tightened the screws on the vise squeezing Titus's chest. "There was an attack at the Diamond D yesterday afternoon."

Titus tensed. "Casualties?"

Please, God, no.

"Not yet." Hoffman rested a hand atop Titus's shoulder and gave his collarbone a squeeze. "Telegram urged you to come home quick. Some gal named Penny is in dire straits."

Titus's knees nearly buckled.

He never should have left. He should have been there.

Guarding her. Protecting her. He'd only just found Penelope. He couldn't lose her. Not now. Not when his heart was finally learning how to beat again.

"Here." Hoffman shoved a sliver of paper into his hand. "There's a train leavin' in thirty minutes. Go take care of your girl."

Titus's fingers closed around the ticket. His legs managed to take on his weight, but his mind took longer to recover. "She's not my girl."

Not yet, anyway. Not in any formal capacity.

Hoffman released his grip and thumped him on the back. "Uh-huh."

Eyes brimming with compassion met Titus's gaze, spearing urgency through him like a javelin. This was no time to give up. To let defeat run unopposed. Penelope was under the care of the best doctor he knew and a God who could bring the dead to life. This battle wasn't over.

Energy surged through Titus, strengthening his muscles and straightening his spine. "I gotta go."

Hoffman smiled. "Yes, you do. But first, give me a rundown on this Hunt fellow."

Titus shared what he knew about Cecil, then handed over the sack of gold nuggets Narcissa had left behind along with her note.

"She's using him as a scapegoat," Titus explained. "Show him the letter when you take him into custody. Get him to turn on her."

Hoffman nodded as he tucked the bag and note into his jacket pocket. "If he won't talk to me, I'll let Captain Bill take a run at him. We'll get this she-wolf one way or another. Now get outta here. You got a train to catch."

Titus didn't argue. He ran all the way to the depot. This case, his promotion . . . none of it mattered anymore. All he cared about was getting to Penelope before she was lost to him forever.

Titus rode up to the Diamond D well after dark. Exhausted. Heartsore. And terrified of what he might find inside. Lucky roused himself from the porch to announce Titus's arrival with a morose bark that lacked conviction. Head hanging low, the hound padded over to him as he dismounted and rubbed his head against Titus's leg, seeking comfort. Titus crouched down and wrapped his arms around the dog, burying his face in his fur as he rubbed and patted his head and body.

Tears threatened, but Titus forced them back. Tears were a product of grief, and he'd not shed a single one as long as hope remained. He'd be strong for her. Believe for her. Pray with every drop of faith in his soul for her.

Giving Lucky a final pat, Titus rose and faced the house. A pall had fallen over the place, leaving the air oppressive and heavy despite the mild autumn weather. The weight of it bowed his head and stooped his shoulders.

Someone had left a lantern lit and hanging from a hook by the front door, but the dim light failed to dispel the gloom. Giving his horse an apologetic pat for not seeing to his needs immediately, Titus left Rex standing in the yard and strode for the porch, his legs feeling as if he were slogging through a river of mud.

The front door creaked open before he reached the top step. "Titus? That you?"

Titus faltered at the weak sound of his grandfather's voice. Doc looked so haggard and frail standing in the doorway. As if the smallest breeze would topple him.

"It's me, Grandpa." Titus finished his climb up the steps and met Doc at the door. He had to swallow twice before he could squeeze his question from where it had lodged in his throat. "Penelope?"

Doc gripped Titus's arm. "She still lives."

"Thank God." The largest knot in his stomach unwound. He wasn't too late.

Yet Doc's sober features forecasted storms, not sunshine. Doc's grip tightened above Titus's elbow. "Opium poisoning. It's depressed her system and sent her into an unnatural sleep. She . . . she might never wake up."

The words hit him square in the chest like the blow from a prizefighter's fist. "How . . . ?"

Doc's tortured gaze met his as a tear rolled down his weathered cheek. "I thought I was keeping her safe by insisting she stay at the ranch." Doc dropped his gaze to the ground, his head wagging back and forth in denial. "I took Dusty and Coy with me to search out Rowdy's hiding place, leaving Jeb, Ike, and Angus to watch over Penny. I never should have left. Maybe if I'd stayed, they wouldn't have drunk that widow woman's poison. I—"

"What widow woman?" Titus interrupted, his voice sharp.

Doc blinked at him from behind his spectacles. "When Jeb and the others woke, they told me of a widow in a heavy black veil who'd come by the ranch peddling cider. They all drank some. But the woman gave Penny a cupful from a different jug. Must've been a stronger concoction."

Narcissa. It had to be. She could have disguised her voice and appearance to keep Penelope from recognizing her. Easy enough for an accomplished actress.

"Jeb got off a warning shot," Doc continued, "and we set off for home right away, but the poison had been in Penny's system for at least thirty minutes. I did my best to purge it from her, but her respiration is so slowed, I fear . . ." He raised his eyes to meet Titus's again. "I'm so sorry, son. So very sorry."

Titus pulled his grandfather into an embrace. Doc's body shook as he wept.

"None of this is your fault," Titus said, his voice raw as he hugged his grandfather. "I shouldn't have left, either, but I did, and there's no guarantee that if either of us had stayed the situation would have turned out any differently. She's in God's hands, and we gotta trust him to do what's best. Even if that means . . ." He thumped the old man's back and straightened, fighting mightily to keep his own tears in check. "Even if that means we have to say good-bye."

God, please don't ask me to say good-bye again. Please!

Doing so just might kill him.

But he couldn't think about that now. It wasn't time to grieve. It was time to fight. To beat back despair and cling to hope.

"The end's not here yet, though." Titus cleared his throat to give his voice conviction. "The tide may still turn."

Doc sniffed, and his chin rose a notch. "You're right. Come." He stepped through the doorway into the house. "I'll take you to her."

Titus followed his grandfather, feeling a bit like he was walking into a church sanctuary instead of a ranch house. A flickering light in the parlor drew his attention as he passed, and what he saw when he peeked inside had him pulling his hat from his head.

All of the Diamond D men had gathered in the room. Some dozed in chairs, others knelt on arthritic knees, hands folded, heads bent.

"They're praying in shifts," Doc said softly. "It was Jeb's idea, if you can believe it. He was determined that they should pray without ceasing through the night, to see Penny through the darkness and into the light of day. They kept vigil all last night, and when she didn't wake decided to repeat the shifts tonight. Pretty sure it's the reason she's held on so long."

The sight humbled Titus and filled him with a level of peace he'd not felt in years. So much love and faith gathered in one place. No wonder it felt like a church. Surely the Lord was in their midst.

One of the drovers glanced up and met Titus's gaze. Dusty pushed up from the settee and made his way through the maze of men. "You just get in?"

Titus nodded.

"I'll see to Rex for ya."

"You don't need to—"

Dusty held up a hand to cut off Titus's protest. "You need to be with Penny. I'll tend to yer horse. I got the next shift, anyways. Might as well move around a bit to wake myself up."

"Thanks, Dusty."

The man shrugged, then pinned Titus with a look weighted with destiny. "That girl means the world to us, Kingsley, but it's you she needs. Go take care of our girl."

Titus nodded despite the fact that he felt completely ill-equipped for such an assignment. He had no medical skills or healing knowledge. But according to Doc, Penelope was beyond the reach of medical intervention anyhow. Could something else bring her back? He'd pray, of course. He'd been praying for the last twelve hours, but what else could he do?

Doc led the way into Penelope's bedroom. Titus held his breath, not realizing he did so until seeing her prompted the air to slowly leak from his lungs. She looked like an angel. So peaceful. Her black hair splayed over the white pillowcase. Her features in repose. Her long dark lashes feathered over pale cheeks. Cheeks missing the rosy tint of health. Lips that should be quirking upward in one of Penelope's ready smiles lay eerily flat and still. Hands unaccustomed to idleness were folded over her ribs, unmoving.

This was wrong. All wrong. She looked ready for the

undertaker. She shouldn't be laid out that way. She was still alive, doggone it.

Titus clasped one of her hands and tugged it away from her chest. He thought only to rearrange her position, to lay her arm by her side, but once her hand was in his, he couldn't let go. Heart throbbing, he lifted her hand to his lips and pressed a kiss into her limp palm.

"Talk to her, son." Doc patted his shoulder as Titus lowered himself into the chair by her bed. "Give her a reason to stay."

32

Talk to her? Titus blew out a quivery breath. He wasn't sure he could. Not without breaking down. But maybe being strong didn't matter as much as being present.

He turned in the chair to squarely face the bed, planting both feet flat on the floor as if preparing for a physical skirmish. He leaned forward, bracing his forearms atop his thighs as he stroked his thumb across her wrist.

The skin there was so soft. Different from the calluses lining her palm and fingertips. He felt drawn to both aspects. Her more delicate side elicited his protective instincts and made him feel needed, while her calluses spoke of fortitude and strength, attractive qualities to a man seeking a true partner in life.

And her face? Still achingly beautiful. Her delicate features perfectly proportioned. Yet the spark of vitality he so loved had departed, leaving a pale imitation behind. No quick smile or compassionate gaze. No blushes ready to color her cheeks at a moment's notice. Her true beauty arose from her spirit, and that part of her had retreated so far that it scared him.

"I, uh, have a reputation in my Ranger battalion." The words emerged on a rasp. Titus cleared his throat and tried again. "They all think I'm impervious to beautiful women. I thought so, too. Took pride in it, in fact." He chuckled softly and shook his head. "Then I met you."

Visions of the first time he saw her flooded his mind. She'd appeared as if from nothing. Suddenly just . . . there. Arms spread wide as she danced in circles. Joy beaming from a face tipped back to drink in the sunlight. Up until that moment, his life had been consumed with duty. Responsibility. He'd been content. Satisfied with his place in the world. Then *she* crossed his path.

"You were the most beautiful thing I'd ever seen. Covered in dirt and leaves and wearing one of the ugliest dresses known to man, but your smile captivated me. So genuine. So cheerful. It almost hurt to look at you. I hadn't experienced that kind of joy in years.

"I couldn't get you out of my head after that. Then when Rowdy found you in the woods . . ." Titus swallowed, and his thumb momentarily stilled its stroking. "It felt like Providence had reunited us. Like we were supposed to be together." His throat constricted over the words. Moisture gathered in his eyes. His vision blurred.

Don't take her from me, Lord. Please. I know I should pray not my will but yours be done, but I'm scared of what your will might be.

Titus slid from the chair and nudged the seat aside. Kneeling by the bed, he clasped Penelope's hand between his and bowed his head as he pressed a kiss against her knuckles.

"I need you, Pen." He couldn't stop the tears this time. Not with his chest cracking open. "These last couple years, I've only been half-alive, but you breathed new life into my soul. You warmed places inside me that I didn't even realize were cold. Please . . . don't leave me."

His forehead dropped to the mattress as his neck bent in supplication. To God. To her. Never had he felt so powerless.

If he could open a vein and take the poison into himself, he'd do it in a heartbeat. But he couldn't. All he could do was sit in a quiet room, listen to her breathe, and pray each time that the next breath would come.

Out of words and lacking the energy or desire to move, he stayed in that position, holding her hand and watching her sleep until his knees throbbed and his feet started to go numb. He released her hand then, laid it out upon the sheet, and caressed the length of each finger before ratcheting himself off the floor.

His gaze never left her as he stood and stretched his aching muscles. He was afraid to let his attention lapse. Afraid she might slip away if he wasn't there to anchor her. It was irrational, but he cleaved to the idea, wanting to believe that he could help her heal. That he could breathe with her. Expand her lungs by expanding his. Yet deep inside he knew it was an illusion, his faulty attempt to control things beyond his control.

He dropped into the chair and buried his head in his hands. "I surrender." The murmured words punched a hole in his chest as the truth bore into his heart. He couldn't save Penelope. Just as he couldn't save Tate. Only one Being held sway over life and death.

His hands tightened in his hair until the tugging on his scalp grew painful. "I forgive you." The words scraped at his throat like swallowed glass, but he forced himself to say them again. "I forgive you for taking Tate." A hot tear seared his cheek.

All this time, he thought he had moved past his brother's death, but standing on the precipice of losing Penelope made the truth raw and clear. Resentment had rooted in the dark corners of his soul. Resentment toward the God who hadn't saved his brother.

He loosened his grip on his hair and lifted his face just enough to see Penelope. Her spirit so gentle and sweet. She wouldn't want him to carry that weight anymore. She certainly wouldn't want him to add to it. He closed his eyes and pictured her dancing with butterflies. He heard her laughter. Saw her beaming smile. Joy radiated from every pore. Until he'd stomped it out. He wouldn't make the same mistake twice.

He bowed his head in submission. "Forgive me," he pleaded, his voice broken. "For holding on to anger. For trying to control things better left to you. You knew what was best for Tate, and you know what is best for Penelope."

Titus had been consumed with his own definition of what was best. For himself. Avoiding the heartache of another loss. Establishing a future with the woman who had climbed into his heart. Feeding the fledgling fire of love that had just started to catch.

But love meant putting the needs of another before his own.

Do what's best for her, Lord. I bend to your will.

For a long time, he sat in the bedside chair, doing his best to surrender instead of fight. The practice didn't sit naturally on his shoulders, but he didn't shy away from the challenge. The Lord knew the desires of his heart. Time to leave the battle in the Commander's hands.

Titus shifted closer to the bed, wanting to be near Penelope. Every moment was precious because no moment was promised. He reached for her hand and held it to his cheek.

"What's best for you, Penelope?" he whispered. "This world has treated you poorly. Beaten you down. Tried to kill you. Are you weary of the struggle and ready for rest? As much as I want to promise that life will be better if you stay, I can't."

If she was his, he'd do his best to protect and provide for her, but even that wouldn't be guaranteed. An outlaw's bullet could easily strike him down and leave her abandoned again.

He pressed a kiss to her knuckles. "You don't have to stay for us, Penelope. Not if you want to go. We want you to be happy. At peace. Doc and the others . . . me . . . we'll be all right."

Titus moved to the mattress beside her. Needing to be close. To peer into her face. Memorize her features. How was he going to let her go? Taking a volley of bullets would hurt less. But he had to find a way. For her sake. She deserved a noble hero, not a man who thought only of his own—

A barely perceptible pressure compressed his fingers.

Titus jerked, his gaze targeting the small hand clasped inside both of his where he cradled it on his lap. Had she just . . . ?

"Penelope?" His heart pounded in his chest as he tried to find enough moisture in his suddenly dry mouth to speak. "Squeeze my hand, sweetheart."

Please. It couldn't have been just a reflex. It had to mean something. It had to.

The pressure came again. Stronger this time.

"Doc!" Titus shouted loud enough to bring the house down, but he didn't care whom he disturbed. "Doc!"

He clutched her hand to his chest, directly over his heart, then leaned forward and brushed a kiss onto her forehead.

"That's it, Pen. Come back to me."

She was fighting. He could feel it. Her breathing was no longer as languid. Her skin not quite as pale.

"Open your eyes, darlin'." Holding tightly to her hand with his left, he cupped her face with his right. The pad of his thumb stroked her eyebrow, then her cheekbone, as if he could help her focus her energy.

Her lashes fluttered.

Please, God. Please.

Tears welled in his eyes and spilled down his face. He did nothing to stop them.

"I'm here, Pen. And I'm not going anywhere. I just need you to wake up for me, all right? You can do it. I know you can."

His voice clogged on emotion. "You're the strongest person I've ever met."

Shuffling sounds accompanied by thumps and grunts echoed around him as the men of the Diamond D flooded into the room. They circled the bed, not saying a word. They just watched. Waited.

Doc shuffled in last, fitting his stethoscope to his ears as he came. Sorrow deepened the creases on his face. "Has she—"

"She squeezed my hand," Titus blurted. "Twice. And her lashes fluttered."

Doc's brows shot upward. He scurried to the bed and pushed against Titus's shoulder. "Move, boy. Let me examine her."

Titus rose, taking care to keep his hold on Penelope's hand. She squeezed it again, as if she'd felt the shift and worried he was letting her go.

Not a chance.

"I'm here, Pen." He made room for Doc, moving closer to the head of the bed. "Right here." He brushed his hand over her hair as Doc positioned the stethoscope over her heart. "We're all here. Open your eyes, and see for yourself."

Her lashes fluttered again. Titus held his breath. Her lids twitched, then slowly . . . torturously . . . lifted to reveal the most beautiful gray eyes the Lord had ever created.

"Titus?" she whispered, her voice hoarse and barely audible as she twisted her face toward him.

"Yes, sweetheart?" Euphoria swept through him with such force, it made him light-headed. She anchored him, though. Her hand in his. Her eyes locked on his face.

A tiny smile touched her lips, and his heart turned a somersault in his chest.

"I'm not ready to go yet."

Thank God.

33

Titus didn't leave Penelope's side the rest of the night. Not that there was much left of it. He'd barely drifted off, slouching in the hard, wooden chair by her bed, when sunlight crept around the curtain edges to wake him.

His eyelids scraped like sandpaper as he pried them open, but he pushed through the grit, determined to check on Penelope. Her slumber seemed more natural now. Deep breaths. A touch of color in her cheeks. She'd even rolled over onto her side sometime since he'd started dozing. Her arm lay stretched across the pillow as if she'd reached for him during the night.

Titus grinned. He rather liked the idea of her reaching for him. Heaven knew he wanted to reach for her nearly every time he saw her now. Only fair for the impulse to work both ways.

Careful not to wake her, he bent forward and bussed a kiss onto the top of her head. She didn't stir, but her lips curved slightly, sending of a twinge of tenderness through his chest.

He stood the rest of the way and stretched the crick out of his neck. Before the men had dispersed to their own beds a couple of hours ago, Doc had assured them that Penelope was out of danger. It might take her a few days to regain her strength, but she no longer teetered on the rim of death's canyon. God had brought her back from the brink.

Needing to work out a few more kinks, Titus sauntered over to the washstand and poured a few inches of water from the ewer into the basin. He splashed the cool liquid over his face, hoping to dispel the weariness and worry that clung to him like the sweat-laced, days-old clothes he wore. Eyes closed, he grabbed for the towel hanging on the washstand bar, then patted his face dry. The water might have refreshed him a little, but he really needed a full bath and a change of clothes. He eyed his haggard reflection in the small mirror above the basin and rubbed at the bristles darkening his jaw. Could use a shave, too. A man should look his best when his lady awoke from a near-fatal nap.

Hearing a soft clatter coming from the other side of the bedroom wall, Titus deduced that Coy or one of the other Diamond D men was up and puttering around in the kitchen. Maybe the fellow could be persuaded to sit with Penelope while Titus slipped out to the barn for a change of clothes. Even though she was out of danger, he didn't want her to wake up alone. She might be confused or frightened.

He padded back over to the bed, sat down in the chair, and shoved his stockinged feet back into his boots.

"I'm gonna step out for a few minutes to get cleaned up," he whispered as he brushed an errant strand of dark hair from her face. "Don't go waking up until I get back, all right?" His lips met her forehead for a pair of heartbeats before he pulled away and headed for the door.

Instead of Coy, Titus found Jeb in the kitchen.

Jeb glanced up from cranking the coffee grinder, his perpetual scowl in its usual place as he met Titus's gaze. "How's our girl?"

"Still sleeping." Titus crossed to the table and leaned his hip against the rounded edge. "Kinda what I expected you to be doin' after the rough couple days you had."

Jeb quit cranking the grinder. "I slept too much already." He wagged his head and let out a grunt of disgust. "Can't believe I let that woman get the drop on me. I told her to leave. Said we didn't want none of her cider. But Angus and Ike insisted on bein' neighborly. And Miss Penny and her soft heart were no help. Still, I shoulda known somethin' weren't right. Should never have drunk that stupid brew." He lifted his chin, his eyes glistening with regret. "Doc trusted me, and I let him down. Let that sweet girl down, too. That kind of failure don't let a man rest easy, you know?"

Titus braced his hands on the table on either side of his hips. "We all feel responsible. Me for leavin'. Rowdy for hidin' the jewels. Doc for not getting back sooner after hearin' your warning shot. But the only one truly to blame is the woman who laced that cider with poison. You did the best you could with the knowledge available to you in that moment. That's all any of us can do. Floggin' yourself ain't gonna do Penelope or Doc any favors."

Jeb shrugged. "Maybe. Still makes me spittin' mad that Penny nearly died on my watch."

"I understand the feeling."

Thoughts of Narcissa LaBelle and Cecil Hunt churned his stomach and poked him in all the sore spots left from the near sleepless night he'd just spent. The need to see them brought to justice burned in his gut, but he tamped down the flaring embers. This wasn't the time to plot their demise. It was time to focus on Penelope and making sure she was all right.

"I'm gonna wash up in the barn and grab some clean clothes," he said as he pushed away from the table. "Will you sit with Penelope for me after you get the coffee on? I don't want her to be alone."

Jeb hung his head. "Doubt she'd want me there."

Titus leaned close to the old drover. "Didn't you know? You're her favorite."

Jeb's eyebrows arched. Skepticism dominated the man's gaze, but a touch of longing rimmed the edges. He wanted to believe it was true.

For all Titus knew, it was. Penelope doted on Jeb. Probably took it as a personal challenge to sweeten his sour disposition.

Titus strode to the back door and fit his hand to the latch. "It won't be for long," he urged. "I'll be back in fifteen minutes."

Jeb shook his head, his nose crinkling. "Boy, it's gonna take longer'n fifteen minutes to scrub that stink outa yer hide." He waved him on, though. "Do whatcha gotta do. I'll sit with her."

"Thank you."

"Uh-huh." Jeb emptied the coffee from the grinder, then dumped the grounds into the pot, dismissing Titus with the turn of his back.

The old grump proved to be right. It took closer to thirty minutes to wash up at the pump, shave in the barn, and don fresh clothes. Titus spared himself two minutes to check on Rex and turn him out to pasture, then hoofed it back to the house, eager to check on Penelope.

She hadn't awoken, but a change had come over her. A frown marred her brow as she tossed about, and small moans rumbled in her throat.

Jeb turned in his chair the moment Titus entered the room, a slightly panicked look on his face. "She started mumblin' and flailing a few minutes ago. I'm thinkin' a nightmare's got hold of her. Wasn't sure if I should try to wake her or not." His attention returned to Penelope. "I tried pattin' her back, but she nearly took my head off with a swing of her arm."

Titus hurried to her side, Jeb eagerly retreating to make room.

"Pen? It's all right, sweetheart. You're safe." Titus cupped her shoulder, but instead of soothing her, his touch sparked greater agitation.

The furrow in her brow deepened, and her head tossed back and forth. Her moaning grew louder and became words. Titus managed to pick out a few.

"Leave . . . alone . . . killing him . . ."

Jeb was right. She was trapped in a nightmare. Only Titus very much feared it was more memory than dream.

He couldn't abandon her to her terrors. He had to help her. Her body might need sleep, but her mind needed comfort, and he only knew one way to give it.

Titus sat on the edge of the mattress and scooped her up against his chest. It didn't matter that she nearly blackened his eye with a wild elbow, or that her skull slammed into his jaw hard enough to knock his head backward. A few bruises wouldn't deter him. She wasn't going to battle this demon alone.

"I'm here, Pen. I'm here." She fought his hold, but he didn't let go. He clutched her to his chest, supporting her head with one hand. "Wake up, darlin', and we can face it together."

She whimpered.

Not knowing what else to try, Titus leaned his mouth close to her ear and infused all the authority of the Texas Rangers into his voice. "Wake up, Penelope."

Her struggles ceased. She leaned back slightly as he loosened his hold. Her eyes fluttered open. "Titus?"

His mouth curved into a smile. Man, but he loved hearing his name on her lips and seeing her pretty gray eyes seek his the moment she awoke. "I'm here, sweetheart. Everything's all right. You're safe."

The fog dissipated from her gaze, but she didn't relax. In fact, she stiffened and latched on to his arms as if he were the last piece of driftwood in a storm-tossed sea.

"Ike! She tried to kill Ike."

Titus rubbed circles into her back in an effort to calm her. "Ike's fine. I saw him myself last night. You don't have to worry."

"Jeb? Angus? I saw them fall. Are they . . . ?"

Jeb shuffled up to the bed. "We're fine, Penny. You're the one that gave us all a scare."

"Thank God." She reached out a hand to Jeb, and the old man took it. "I'm so glad you're all right." The V between her eyebrows deepened. "I should have recognized her. Should have seen the danger. You only drank that cider because I asked you to. Mercy. I could have *killed* you."

"You listen to me, Miss Penny." Jeb wagged a finger near her face. "None of this was your doin', and I won't have you thinkin' it was. That she-wolf done caused all this mess, not you. Besides, it takes more'n a cup of bad cider to take down a Diamond D man."

Jeb cast a sideways look at Titus and gave him a small nod, letting him know he wasn't just parroting the sentiments Titus had tried to impart in the kitchen. He'd accepted their truth.

Titus nodded back. He was all too familiar with the destructive power of self-blame. He'd tortured himself with all the things he could have done differently with Tate until he almost couldn't sleep at night. It had taken him months to realize that even if God had turned back the clock and provided him the opportunity to change things, he still couldn't have guaranteed a favorable outcome. Not with Tate having free will and Nora and George Middleton bent on wickedness. A rather humbling epiphany for a man who liked to believe he carried some influence in the world. That must've been when he'd switched the blame to God, so quietly and without fanfare that he hadn't even realize it had happened.

"A man has no future if he can't let go of the past." Titus could still feel his father's grip on his shoulder as he'd passed along that bit of wisdom one of the few times Titus had come home during his hunt for Middleton. He'd been slow to learn the lesson, but it eventually sank in, leading him to forgive himself, Tate, and even George and Nora to some extent. And now through God's grace, he'd dug up the last hidden piece of bitterness and laid it to rest. Titus wagged his head slightly. God had apparently healed two people last night, not just one.

"I'll go fetch Ike and Angus down here to pay their respects," Jeb said, his scowl brightening to an almost pleasant expression as he patted Penelope's hand. "Might do you good to see them for yourself."

Penelope offered him a wobbly smile. "I'd like that. Thank you."

Jeb barely cleared the threshold before Penelope turned her luminous eyes back on Titus.

"It was Narcissa, Titus. She wore a veil and disguised her voice, but after the others collapsed, she revealed herself to me. She threatened to suffocate Ike if I didn't tell her where the jewels were. Then she actually stuffed her shawl in his mouth and started smothering him." A tiny sob caught in her throat, slicing straight through Titus's heart. "I had to tell her about the ruby. I'm sorry."

He brushed her tangled hair away from her face, then stroked her cheek with his thumb. "You did the right thing."

Her gaze dropped to the sheets twisted between them. "She was so angry. So . . . cruel. She wanted me to *die*."

The smallness of Penelope's voice twisted Titus's gut. He wanted to tear Narcissa's cold, unfeeling heart from her chest, but more than that, he wanted to heal the invisible wounds she'd inflicted on the woman he loved.

"*I* wanted you to live, Penelope. More than I ever wanted anything in my life. We all did." He curled a finger under her chin and gently tipped her face upward until her eyes met his. "Every man on the Diamond D begged the Lord to spare your life. You are a treasure. Loved. Wanted. Never doubt that, even for a second."

A single tear rolled down her cheek. "I love all of you so much." Her words included everyone at the ranch, but her eyes seemed to communicate a silent message that went straight to his heart and set it to beating at twice its normal pace.

Footsteps echoed from the stairs, making it clear this wasn't the time to try to put burgeoning feelings into words. Instead, Titus brushed her tear away with his thumb and offered her a smile brimming with reciprocated affection.

"Here." He reached for the knitted throw draped across the foot of the bed, then wrapped it around her shoulders. "I think you're about to entertain some visitors."

She closed the blanket in front of her and straightened the bedcovers over her lap while Titus organized the pillows into a backrest. Ike entered first, a smile beaming across his face. Angus followed, rubbing his eyes and yawning with a mouth so wide a train could have tunneled through.

Titus stepped back, letting the others have their moment with her. Leaning against the wall, he was surprised when Jeb came to join him instead of returning to Penelope's side.

"We got a problem, Titus."

Titus straightened away from the wall. "Doc?"

Jeb shook his head. "Doc's fine. He's going through his things upstairs."

"Why is he going through his things?"

"Dusty's lucky yellow handkerchief is missing."

What did that have to do with anything?

"And that ain't all," Jeb continued, his voice low and urgent. "All our money's gone. Every last cent. We was all so worried about Penny, none of us gave thought to much else. But that actress must've searched the house for valuables while we were sleeping off her apple-cider potion. She found all our secret stashes. Under Coy's mattress. Inside Angus's sock. Even found my hidey hole in the floorboard. That devil woman drained the Diamond D dry."

34

An hour later, everyone sat gathered around the table for a late breakfast and a family meeting. Titus had tried to sway Penelope into staying in bed to rest, but the minute he left the room, she'd shooed everyone else out and gotten herself dressed. Her dark hair hung in a fresh plait over her shoulder, falling nearly to her waist. Her face remained a little pale, but the fire had returned to her eyes, warming the cold, worried place inside him that had feared a relapse. Her legs held her upright, though, and her chin jutted forward with a determined tilt, daring him to exclude her. As if he had the strength to deny her anything.

He scooted over on the bench seat near the wall and made room for her next to him. He tucked her close to his side so she could lean on him if she tired. Then he piled her plate high with bacon, eggs, biscuits, and gravy and handed her a fork. After closing her eyes and murmuring a quiet prayer of thanks, she tucked into the food with purpose if not enthusiasm. Doc had told her she'd need nourishment to regain her strength, and she seemed to be taking his advice to heart.

Having finished his breakfast several minutes ago, Titus studied the inventory he'd made of the items the men had identified as missing. The sheer length of the list stirred his ire, but he kept his emotions in check. These good men had just been robbed of nearly everything they owned. They needed a level-headed lawman who would shoot straight with them while still offering hope.

"The cash will be hard to recover," Titus admitted, "but the jewelry and other personal items are more distinctive. If we find those in her possession, we'll have just cause to seize her cash as well." He tapped a line near the bottom of the page. "These watches, though, are going to be what puts her behind bars. A woman might be able to make a judge believe it a coincidence that her silver-backed brush set matches the description of the one taken, or that the gold band in her collection belonged to her grandmother and had been in the family for years. But she won't be able to explain the inscriptions on those watches."

Doc took off his glasses, rubbed the lenses on his handkerchief, then propped them back on his nose. "They were supposed to be a Christmas gift. Then Tate . . ." He cleared his throat and looked up to meet Titus's gaze. "I just didn't have the heart to give you yours and leave Tate's alone in that box. I'm sorry, son. If I hadn't been so focused on what we lost, that watch would be in your pocket now instead of in that wicked woman's stash of ill-gotten gains."

"I'm glad it's in her stash, Grandpa." Titus set his jaw. "I'm going to use it to take her down."

"How? You told me yourself she's likely on a train bound for Colorado right now. Out of your jurisdiction. Out of your reach."

Titus quirked a sly grin. "But not out of the reach of a US Marshal. I happen to know one stationed in east Texas. John McHenry. I'll wire him on my way out of Glen Rose. He can meet me at Ranger headquarters, then the two of us can head up to Denver. I'll need to turn in the jewels, let

Captain Bill know to add a count of attempted murder to Narcissa LaBelle's charges, and ask him to get a warrant for her arrest." He turned to Penelope and took her hand. "Now that we have a witness who can tie Madame LaBelle directly to her crimes, we can wire the law in Denver to be on alert. They will likely have her in custody before McHenry and I even step off the train."

Penelope squeezed his fingers. "What if she doesn't go to Denver? What then?"

If she didn't go to Denver, finding her would be nearly impossible. But he couldn't blurt that out and extinguish the few coals of hope still smoldering among the men sitting around the table.

"We'll track her down one way or another." Titus laced his voice with all the bravado he could muster. "But I don't think she'll deviate from her original plan. She lost the gems she'd been collecting, and the items she took from here won't make up the difference. She needs her salary and the freedom of movement her acting gig provides. Plus, she doesn't think she's in danger."

He rubbed the soft skin on the back of Penelope's hand with his thumb. "You're the only one who can positively identify her as the one who distributed the poisoned cider, and she believes you're dead. In her mind, Hunt is too infatuated to turn on her, but even if he does, she's taken precautions to tarnish any testimony he might provide by painting him as the thief. She's clever, and she knows it. But arrogance leads to overconfidence. Let her think she's won. Let her assume I can't touch her once she crosses the state line. Let her vigilance relax. That's all the opening I'll need."

Penelope twisted on the bench to face him, the worry in her eyes making him want to fold her in his arms and promise her that everything would be all right. But there were no guarantees in this life, and he wouldn't make her a promise he might not be able to keep.

"Be careful." Her broken whisper cut straight through his chest. "Narcissa's not afraid to kill to get what she wants." She nibbled on her lower lip.

Titus wrapped an arm around her waist and tugged her close. He pressed a kiss onto her forehead, then murmured low in her ear. "I'll have McHenry there to watch my back, and I'll have you here praying for my safe return. A man couldn't ask for better protection."

She leaned her head on his chest and let him hold her for a minute while the rest of the Diamond D occupants cleared throats, scraped chairs against floorboards, and found reasons to disperse.

He closed his eyes and absorbed the feel of her snuggled against him. Man, but he could get used to this. Titus ignored the nagging urgency in the back of his brain for several long minutes, enjoying the way her hand pressed against his chest, the quiet sound of her breathing, the softness of her hair. But duty couldn't be postponed indefinitely. He had a job to do.

"I have to go."

"I know." She pulled away slightly, and he immediately missed her warmth. Then she cupped his jaw in her hand. Heat immediately flared in his veins. "Come home to me, Titus."

His chest squeezed, making it hard to breathe. *Home.* He'd been away from home for so long he'd forgotten the pull that word could place on a man. Yet hearing it from her lips stirred a longing in him—a longing to redefine the term so it no longer described the place where he grew up but described the place where he would grow old in the company of the woman who held his heart.

He gazed into her soft, gray eyes as he made his vow. "I will."

He dipped his head and brushed her mouth with his. A gentle meeting, featherlight in its newness, yet heavy with promise. Her breath caught, and the sound heated his blood. She lifted her chin, leaning into his kiss and tempting him to pull her closer and deepen the connection they both craved. But he eased away from her instead. Now was not the time. Although the thought of exploring her kiss more thoroughly when he returned made speeding his departure easier to bear. The sooner he disposed of the threat to Penelope the sooner he could find his way home.

Titus had to clench his jaw to keep from looking over his shoulder as he rode away from the ranch fifteen minutes later. Not that Penelope's image wasn't permanently branded on his brain. He could picture exactly where she stood on the back porch, one arm wrapped around a support post, the other lifted in a wave. Her yellow skirt blowing in the wind. Her smile brave, her eyes locked on his. Never had he felt more reluctant to head out on a Ranger job. When he'd mounted Rex, his boots had felt as if they were filled with lead.

Rowdy seemed to have the same lead-filled boot problem. Poor fellow had been horse-shy ever since his accident. Dusty tried to let him off the hook, assuring him that he remembered the way to the cavern Rowdy had shown them. Rowdy ignored the suggestion, his expression making it clear he didn't want anyone poking around in his secret place without him. So when Titus, Dusty, and Coy headed to the barn to collect their mounts, Rowdy came, too. Dusty took one look at the sweat gathering at his friend's temples, though, and informed Rowdy they'd be riding double to save him from having to saddle a fourth horse. No one commented on the lopsided logic, not when it meant salvaging a cowboy's pride.

The ride to the caves took mere minutes on horseback.

Winding through the dark caverns took longer, but they made it to Rowdy's secret vault without incident. Well, unless one counted Coy getting momentarily wedged in one of the narrower passageways. A tug from Titus in the front accompanied by a push from Dusty in the back remedied the situation in short order, but Titus swore he could feel the air in the cavern warm from the heat of Coy's flush even if the darkness hid it from view.

A single lantern guided them through the passageways, but the light multiplied once they reached the main cavern. Rowdy had three more lanterns fueled and waiting inside. He scrambled in and started lighting them while Titus and the others contorted their larger frames through the excavated entrance that had obviously been carved for a man of smaller stature. Once inside, however, Titus caught his breath.

The entire room sparkled. Like a wall made of diamonds. No, not diamonds. Crystals. Titus moved closer to the formations and ran a finger along one jutting formation. Quartz? Scratches marred a section of crystal to his left. Too soft to be quartz, then. Maybe calcite. Titus bent down a bit to examine the scratches more closely. Marks from Rowdy's pickax? No, it was his name. Probably carved with a pocket knife. Titus bit back a chuckle as he ran his finger over the letters. The man had staked his claim.

"H-Here." Rowdy's call had Titus pivoting counterclockwise to face the next wall. The jagged limestone contained numerous indentations and shelves interspersed with occasional crystal formations.

Coy's low whistle echoed through the chamber.

Treasures of all sorts sat on the shelves and inside those crevices. Lantern light glittered as it spilled over shiny coins, bits of bottle glass, nickel-plated fishing lures, tangles of copper wire, a silver spoon, and several cut gems that had no doubt recently been hidden within the seams of Madame LaBelle's corset.

Suddenly, Rowdy's words from a few days ago made perfect sense. He hadn't been claiming the missing stones belonged to him. He'd been trying to tell Titus where to find them. In the Diamond D mine.

Titus rested a hand on the smaller man's shoulder. "I'm sorry, Rowdy," he said. "I didn't understand."

Rowdy shrugged, then handed Titus his lantern and motioned for him to hold it aloft. Titus complied while Rowdy moved along the wall collecting rubies, sapphires, emeralds, and diamonds, some from pockets Titus would have easily missed.

"Is that the rowel from one of my spurs?" Dusty hunkered down near the base of the wall and pulled out a small, nickel-plated wheel. "I thought I lost it out on the prairie somewhere."

"Jeb'll be happy to get his fishin' lures back," Coy said as he fingered one of the feathery hooks dangling from a limestone shelf. "Maybe he'll finally stop gripin' every time he wants to go anglin'."

"Doubt it." Dusty sniffed, then gave in to a full-blown sneeze. "This is Jeb we're talkin' about." Dusty wiggled his nose against his sleeve as if to dislodge any leftover tickle. "We give him back his missin' lures and he'll start griping that they don't all fit in his tackle box."

Coy chuckled. "True."

Rowdy cracked a smile as he collected the last of the pilfered jewels, then sobered as he moseyed back to Titus, his fingers closed over an overflowing handful of what had to be thousands of dollars' worth of precious stones. Titus passed the lantern off to Coy, then cupped his palms.

Rowdy dribbled the gems into his hands in a thin yet steady

stream. "Take." His face twisted as he struggled to say more. "Save . . . Pen . . . nee."

Titus tipped the jewels into one hand and formed a protective fist around them. He tightened his grip until the pointed edges of the stones jabbed into his skin, matching the determination jabbing into his chest.

He met Rowdy's gaze and voiced the vow his heart had already pledged to complete. "I will."

35

Narcissa ran her hands down her burgundy bodice as she posed in front of the full-length mirror the staff at the Brainard Hotel had been kind enough to bring up to her room. Perfection. No other lady in town would be dressed in such style tonight. The elegant design of deep red silk wrapped around her like a boudoir robe, fastening at the waist with a single fleurette. Lace filled in the plunging neckline for modesty's sake, but the lace she'd selected was sheer enough to entice instead of deter a man's imagination. The matching skirt was cut high over each leg to reveal a lacy ivory underskirt, creating the illusion that if she were to unfasten the fleurette and unwrap the dress, she'd be clad in nothing but lace. Of course, no one with proper morality would envision such a thing. They would see only a fashionable dress with Parisian flair. But put her in the company of the right dinner companion, give her a chance to employ a sultry pout and a suggestive whisper or two, and he wouldn't be able to envision anything else.

She hoped her dinner companion tonight would prove to be just such a man. She'd grown weary of hiding behind drab disguises. She'd been in town for a week, keeping to her room to avoid scrutiny and going out only when necessity demanded.

As day after day passed with no mention of her exploits in Texas appearing in the paper, however, boredom began to override caution. Two days ago, she'd ventured out without her wig. Yesterday, she'd left off the hideous calico dress she'd picked up at some no-name general store at one of the train stops between Texas and Colorado and donned one of her fitted walking gowns. How glorious to be back in her own skin. To let her true self shine. She'd even started using her real name and experienced the gratification of seeing recognition and appreciation spark in the eyes of the public again.

This is who she was meant to be—Madame LaBelle, actress extraordinaire—not some ordinary calico Jane with nothing to distinguish her from any of the other hundred women in town.

Tonight would mark the beginning of her grand return. And she'd selected the perfect gentleman to witness her unveiling. He'd been in the lobby an hour ago when she'd passed through after visiting the local milliner. She'd immediately spotted his expensive suit, manicured beard, and the gold signet ring on the little finger of his left hand. He oozed wealth and sophistication, exactly what she craved after hiding away for so long.

He'd been reading a copy of the *Rocky Mountain News* until she'd walked by and given him something more interesting to study. How satisfying to note him bending the page inward, eschewing yesterday's news in favor of watching her saunter up to the desk. She'd made sure to twist in such a way to aid his view while the clerk assisted her with arranging the delivery of warm water to her suite so she could clean up after her jaunt through town. Pretending to be unaware of his attention, she innocently mentioned to the clerk that she'd not need dinner delivered to her room tonight as she planned to dine in the hotel restaurant. When she expressed concern about eating alone in a public room, the gallant man with the newspaper hurried to her rescue. Thirty seconds later, he had introduced himself and offered to escort her to dinner.

Nice to know she hadn't lost her touch.

He'd be waiting for her downstairs now. They'd been scheduled to meet five minutes ago, but it did a man good to wait on a lady. Balanced the scales of power and whetted the appetite.

Stepping closer to the looking glass, Narcissa scrutinized her face. Had the tiny lines around her eyes deepened? She tried to smooth them away with her fingers, but they refused to be erased. She frowned, then immediately relaxed her mouth when lines appeared at the edges of her lips and above her brows.

Tapping the back of her hand against the underside of her chin, she lifted her face and focused somewhere less prone to flaws. Her throat stretched long and lovely. No creases. No sagging skin. What were a few infinitesimal lines around her eyes? The dim gaslight would obscure them. Her beauty shone too brightly to be marred by such insignificance. If she played her cards right—and she always did when it came to men—Mr. Victor Chapman would be too busy admiring her other attributes to notice.

After blowing a kiss to her reflection, Narcissa collected her purse and headed downstairs. She paused at the final landing to allow an elderly couple to precede her. She'd not weaken the impact of her entrance by sharing it with a pair of nobodies. All eyes would be on *her* when she made her descent.

She counted to twenty, giving the interlopers plenty of time to exit her stage, then she rounded the corner. Slow, seductive hip sway. Expression confident with a hint of eagerness. Eyelids slumbering just enough to be provocative. A hint of a smile accentuating her beauty mark.

Not catching any movement in her peripheral vision of a man approaching the stairway, Narcissa paused on the third step from the bottom and swept her gaze over the lobby in annoyance. Good grief. The man was so deep in conversation, he was missing her performance. That would never do. Thankfully, before she could decide whether a turned ankle or an imaginary mouse would serve her purposes better, one of Mr. Chapman's companions glanced her way. His eyes widened.

That's more like it.

He was a little rough around the edges, his dark clothing slightly gray from trail dust. No outer signs of refinement or wealth were in evidence, so she pretended not to see him. Thankfully, his reaction served to signal Mr. Chapman, who finally gave her his full attention and separated himself from his companions. The third man of the group, his back to the staircase, made no effort to turn. Had he no curiosity over the stir she was so meticulously creating? Disrespectful fellow, keeping his back turned to a lady. Served him right to miss out on the visual feast she offered. Lifting her chin, Narcissa aimed a brighter-than-necessary smile at her approaching escort.

"Madame LaBelle, how ravishing you look." Victor Chapman dipped his head politely, but his gaze raked her like an experienced connoisseur of women.

He'd soon learn her vintage was finer than any he'd sampled before.

She extended her hand to him, dipping her chin demurely as if embarrassed by his compliment. "You're too kind, sir."

He took her hand and bowed over it. "Not at all, ma'am. I'll be the envy of every gentleman in the dining room. It's not every day one gets to dine with a world-class thespian."

"You've heard of me?" She infused her voice with enough surprise to sound modest, a tricky feat when superiority sluiced through her veins. But, of course, she *was* a world-renowned actress.

He offered her his arm and led her toward the dining room.

"My home is in Denver, and the entire city seems papered with playbills advertising your arrival. Imagine my surprise and delight when I discovered you right here in Boulder."

A maître d' showed them to a table, one Mr. Chapman silently indicated a preference for, in a corner where they could enjoy a somewhat private tête-à-tête. She couldn't have chosen better herself.

Her companion held out her chair, then assisted her into it. She could practically feel his gaze roving over her figure. So easy. A twist here, a delicate hand to her throat there. By the time dessert was served, the man would be ripe for the picking.

Mr. Chapman seated himself in the chair closest to her instead of the more traditional position across the table. He accepted the menu, then waved the headwaiter away. Flashing a smile her way, he set the menu aside. "What brings you to Boulder, Madame? I would think Denver would be more to your taste with its superior shopping and entertainment."

"Sometimes an artist must seek a quiet place to hide from all the attention." And interfering lawmen. "I adore my audience, but every so often I must take time to refill my creative well. Otherwise, the wearying pace of a touring troupe can take an unforgiving toll. My audience deserves to see me at my best, and I refuse to give them anything less."

"I admire your artistic integrity. Speaking as a person who hopes to attend a future Madame LaBelle performance in Denver, I look forward to seeing you at your best." His gaze traced the lines of her dress. "Though, I daresay, it's difficult to imagine you any better than you are right now."

Narcissa patted his arm with a flirtatious flourish as her breathy chuckle warmed the air between them. "Flatterer."

Victor Chapman captured her hand and pressed it into his jacket sleeve. She could feel the corded strength of his forearm beneath the fabric. This was no wealthy dandy who idled away his time. This was a man who kept himself in robust health. A nice change from the older gentlemen she usually courted. More like Cecil—but rich. Could provide a nice distraction while she laid low for a couple more weeks.

"I assure you, my dear, I only say what I mean."

Goodness. That voice. So low and . . . seductive. Her blood suddenly warmed. This wasn't how it was supposed to work. She was the siren, not him. Yet there was something rather freeing about letting go of her control and letting passion instead of calculation dictate her next move.

She rubbed her foot along his calf. "Perhaps you can order us a bottle of wine . . . Victor?"

It was a bold play, initiating physical contact and using his given name. But she wanted to make it clear that they were to be equal partners in this little game. Judging by the smile spreading across his face, he appreciated her daring.

Thirty minutes later, having consumed half a bottle of wine, a bowl of cream of potato soup, roast lamb with vegetables, and a lovely dish of rice pudding, Narcissa had completely relaxed, thoroughly enjoying Victor's humorous anecdotes and suppositions about their fellow diners. The man had a gift for fiction. He made up story after story, each more outlandish than the rest. She hadn't laughed so much in ages.

"You are quite the entertainer, Victor. I can't recall a dinner I've enjoyed more."

He smiled as he refilled her wine glass. "Coming from a professional such as yourself, I take that as high praise."

She reached up to fiddle with his lapel, then smoothed it against his chest with the press of her hand. "As you should."

Her charming companion twisted slightly in his seat to face her more directly. "A friend of mine caught one of your performances down in Texas."

She dropped her hand from his chest and lifted her newly

refilled glass to her lips. "Oh?" A warning bell clanged softly in her head, but the wine dulled its ring.

"Yes, he wrote me a three-page letter extolling your beauty and your superb acting prowess."

See? Nothing to worry about. Just another infatuated fan. Narcissa swallowed her sip of wine and returned the glass to the table.

"Three pages?" She tittered softly. "My, that's quite a lengthy eulogy."

His smile widened, but something sharpened in his gaze. "Apropos that you should use that term." He shifted his gaze from her and nodded to someone.

"Oh? How so?"

Heavens, but she wanted to look. To turn and scan the dining room for whomever was on the other end of the nod. But Narcissa would not concern herself with such paltry matters. Not when, in all likelihood, he was merely signaling a waiter.

Still, her belly tightened uncomfortably.

Victor leaned close to her. "That's where my friend saw your show," he murmured in a low tone—one that should have been seductive, but instead sounded the slightest bit predatory. "In Eulogy, Texas. Perhaps you remember him." He paused, just as an actor would before delivering a climactic line. "Hubert Hathaway."

"I-I don't recall." She fumbled in her lap for her purse, her internal alarm now ringing louder than the bells of St. James back in Chicago. "I meet so many people. . . ."

Had Hubert been one of the men she'd fleeced? His name seemed vaguely familiar, but she couldn't be sure. Either way, she needed to extricate herself from this dinner and get back to her room.

Victor's hand gripped her knee beneath the tablecloth. The pressure firm. Strong. Not painful, but definitely unrelenting.

"You made quite an impression on him," Victor continued, his face a mask of polite indulgence. "He was quite . . . how did he phrase it . . . *incapacitated* by your beauty. In fact, you rattled him so completely he misplaced the ruby stickpin I gave him for his fiftieth birthday."

Narcissa tried to pull away from his hold, but his grip tightened. "Release your hold on me, sir," she demanded in a quiet voice that wouldn't carry past his ears. As much as she adored being in the limelight, this was one scene in which she didn't wish to play the leading lady. Not if he decided to make his accusations more vocal.

Victor leaned closer, his lips near her ear like a lover whispering sweet nothings. Only there was nothing sweet in the words dripping from his lips.

"Hubert is like an older brother to me, my dear. When we were boys, he was the one who shielded me from harm. It seems he's still playing the role of protector. He knows of my affinity for beautiful women, you see, and when he heard your theatrical company planned to perform in Denver, he thought it wise to warn me of your felonious tendencies. Didn't want me to fall into the same trap he had."

Heart pounding, Narcissa skewered him with her best withering glare. "Are you accusing me of something, sir?" She raised her voice just enough to draw attention from those seated at the tables closest to them. A calculated risk, but one she had to take. Surely, he didn't want to dirty his own reputation by being caught mistreating a lady.

"He might not be, but I am."

Something heavy dropped onto the table beside her plate, rattling the silver against the china.

Narcissa startled, barely registering that Victor had released his hold on her leg. Her attention jerked to the pocket watch that had just crashed against the edge of her plate. A watch that looked quite familiar. One that had a twin. Slowly her gaze crawled upward to find the scowling face of her least favorite Ranger.

"Mr. Kingsley! What is the meaning of this?"

"I *mean* to see you arrested."

"For what?" She tossed her head defiantly. "I've committed no crime. Besides, you have no jurisdiction in Colorado."

The man she'd seen in the lobby earlier moved into view, stepping out from behind Kingsley. "I do." He tipped his hat. "US Marshal John McHenry, ma'am. Pleased to make your acquaintance."

This could *not* be happening.

Don't panic, Narcissa. They have no proof of anything. Any evidence they have is circumstantial. You can brazen this out.

"This is ridiculous." She turned her attention back to Kingsley. "Didn't you get my note? Cecil Hunt is the likely culprit. As soon as I discovered those suspicious gold pieces in his belongings, I immediately turned them over to you. I've cooperated fully with your investigation. You have no right to chase me down and treat me in such a disrespectful manner." Gripping her purse, she scooted her chair back. "Really, accosting patrons in the dining room is deplorable. I'm going to give the manager a piece of my mind."

"You just gonna pretend you don't see that watch?" Kingsley veered off script, completely ignoring her conversation as if she'd never spoken.

"There's no pretense about it," she said with a sniff of disdain. "I have no interest in a watch I've never seen before."

Kingsley folded his arms across his chest. "Strange, since we retrieved it from your room."

Narcissa reared back. "You entered my room? How dare you. It seems *you're* the true criminal here."

Kingsley tipped back his head, his eyes annoyingly cool.

As if her offensive thrust hadn't so much as pricked his skin. "I assure you everything was on the up-and-up, ma'am. The manager let us into your room once we showed him the warrant we held for your arrest."

"Outrageous! I'm leaving this hotel at once," she sputtered as she lurched to her feet. "This treatment is unacceptable."

Dear heaven. They had a warrant for her arrest? How had they convinced a judge of her guilt when they had no concrete evidence against her? She had to get out of here. Abandon the troupe. Hide herself away somewhere. Reinvent her identity. Perhaps San Francisco. There were plenty of wealthy men there. Nob Hill overflowed with them. England might be beyond her grasp now, but she could still snare a wealthy husband. Give herself the life of ease she deserved.

"Get out of my way," she demanded as she tried to push through the wall of men blocking her path. They didn't budge.

She needed ammunition. Something she could use to turn the tables. She grabbed the watch thinking to throw it at Kingsley's head, but the flash of an inscription caught her eye.

"Why, this is *your* watch! That's your name—Titus—isn't it?" She turned to the marshal. "This man's trying to frame me. He must have planted this watch in my room. It's because of that girl. Penelope Snow. He wants retribution." She stopped herself just before admitting she knew of the girl's death. "I . . . kicked her out of my troupe, and now that he's gone soft for her, he's trying to get payback on her behalf."

"I'm the one who found the watch, ma'am," the marshal drawled. "Along with a duplicate time piece wrapped in a distinctive yellow handkerchief. Found some other goodies, too, all matching the descriptions of items taken from the Diamond D Ranch last week. All in the bottom of your trunk. Found a ruby, too." He glanced past her and twitched his chin toward Victor. "One that likely resided in a stickpin not too long ago."

McHenry turned his attention back to Narcissa. "I had me a nice chat with Mr. Hunt, too. He admits to assisting you in your thievery. Painted quite the vivid picture of your aftershow performances."

"Lies!" Narcissa screeched, Hunt's betrayal flaring her rage. She slammed the pocket watch onto the table with a loud bang. "I'm going to sue you for defamation of character. I've never stolen a thing in my life." She'd only taken what was owed her. Nothing more. "Hunt is your thief. I told you that. I had no part in any of it. He and that little tramp Penelope are the ones responsible."

A thundercloud instantly darkened Kingsley's face. He stepped forward, and Narcissa instinctively took a step back. "Watch what you say about my future wife."

Future wife? Penelope was *alive*? How? She'd barely been breathing when Narcissa had left. If the girl had survived, that meant she could testify. She had to be silenced.

"You're a besotted fool, Titus Kingsley. Tell me. Who had more of a motive to steal? A world-renowned actress with a lucrative career or a penniless orphan with a reputation for impropriety?" She leaned toward Kingsley, desperate to keep his attention focused on her face instead of her hands. "I'll see you destroyed for this, Ranger. You and your false accusations, setting up an innocent woman for a crime she didn't commit."

She fumbled with the purse clasp. Slid her hand inside. Wrapped her fingers around her derringer.

"Enough of the theatrics," the marshal grumbled as he reached for her arm.

Narcissa jerked away and pulled her derringer free of her purse.

"Gun!" Victor shouted the warning from behind her. Not giving anyone a chance to react, she fired in the same moment.

Kingsley lurched sideways. Restaurant patrons screamed.

Narcissa shoved past the stumbling Ranger and ran. Only to have a hand latch around her ankle.

Her foot yanked backward. She tumbled. A shriek tore from her throat.

No! She had to get away. This was not how her final act was supposed to play out.

She kicked and wriggled, but the grip on her ankle remained ironclad. Then someone straddled her, twisting her arms behind her back and forcing her face into the tile floor.

"Get off me, you fiend." She writhed to no avail.

"I got her, Kingsley," McHenry said. "You can let go now."

The hand around her ankle finally loosened.

The Ranger had been the one to take her down? Impossible! She'd shot him. She was sure of it. At that close range, not even an imbecile could miss.

"Better summon a doctor," Victor responded, voice tight. "He's bleeding pretty bad." His tone changed, becoming cajoling. "Hang in there, Ranger."

Dark satisfaction curled around Narcissa's heart as the marshal knotted a cord around her wrists. *Bleed, Ranger. It's only fair. If I don't get my happy ending, neither should you.*

36

Ten days. She hadn't seen Titus in *ten days*. Penelope peered past the porch overhang toward the road, wishing she could make him appear. The broom in her hand slowed, but it didn't really matter. She'd swept the front porch so many times this past week no speck of dirt would dare land in such inhospitable territory. It was a miracle the floorboards hadn't splintered from the constant brushing.

Lucky lifted his head from where he'd been dozing in a sunny spot near the railing and yawned.

"Sure, it's easy for *you* to relax. You don't need him like I do." Penelope leaned her broom against the house wall and hunkered down to rub the coonhound's ears. "He carries my heart with him, Lucky. I won't feel whole until he returns."

A small, round wren fluttered down to alight on the railing near Penelope's head. As if it had recognized her aching heart and paid a call to try to cheer her, it sang a peppy song of sweet trilling notes while its head bobbed and its feet shuffled.

A smile twitched Penelope's lips as she watched the little encourager. "How can I possibly be glum with you around?"

The gray-brown bird trilled again, and the words of Christ seemed to slip into her soul. *"Fear ye not therefore, ye are of more value than many sparrows."*

Lucky scrambled to his feet, eager to get a closer look. Startling, the wren took flight.

"Godspeed, little one," Penelope whispered.

She pushed back up to her feet and wrapped her hand around one of the porch posts. *Whatever comes, we'll face it together, Lord. Help me to be strong and courageous.*

God would never forsake her or abandon her. She believed that with all her heart. Yet that didn't mean he would spare her from sorrow and hardship. She'd faced plenty of both during her lifetime. As had Edith, yet her adoptive mother had never let the world sour her disposition.

A childhood memory seeped into Penelope's mind. Edith cradling the large brown bowl she always used for mixing cake batter. Her spoon whipping in a frenzied motion. "*Your life ain't gonna be easy, Penny-girl,*" she had said, "*but it can be good if you remember our Lord's promise. 'In the world ye shall have tribulation: but be of good cheer; I have overcome the world.' There ain't nothin' you can face that he can't overcome.*"

A pang of homesickness stirred in Penelope's breast. She missed Edith. She missed Titus. She even missed Dusty and Doc, and they'd only been gone for half a day, running to town for supplies. Mercy, but she was a mess.

"You still mopin' around, waitin' on that Ranger to show up?"

Penelope sniffed discreetly, then turned to see Jeb moseying up to the side of the house from the direction of the corral. She lifted a hand in greeting and painted on a smile as she reached for her discarded broom, trying to manufacture a legitimate reason to be on the porch that didn't entail moping.

"Leave it," he grumbled as her hand clasped the handle. "There ain't gonna be any bristles left on that thing the way you been going after it lately. No reason to pretend, anyhow.

You ain't foolin' anyone. We might be old, but most of us can recall pining over a gal or two in our younger days."

"Even you?" she teased as he limped around to the steps and hobbled up to the porch.

One bushy gray brow arched while the other slashed down across one eye. "What? You don't think me the courtin' kind?"

The tiniest twitch at the edge of his mouth let her know he was more amused than offended. "I'll have you know," he asserted, "I was considered quite the catch in my younger years. Ain't my fault none of the girls used the right bait to reel me in." A faraway look softened his expression for just a moment. "One got right close," he murmured, "had me hooked and on the line till her daddy made her switch bait and fish in another pond. After that, I headed for open water."

He cleared his throat, his expression hardening back into its normal, surly lines. "You ain't gotta worry 'bout Titus." Jeb patted her shoulder, then shuffled past to seat himself in one of the rockers. A satisfied groan exhaled from his chest as he took the weight off his legs. "That boy's so hooked, he couldn't wriggle off the line iffen he wanted to."

A little thrill coursed through her at Jeb's words. She wanted so badly to believe they were true. She loved Titus. Utterly and completely. She knew he cared for her. He wouldn't have kissed her otherwise. And, oh, how she dreamed about that kiss! So tender and exquisitely sweet. She clung to its memory and built fantasies upon it of courtship and wedding vows and little baby Rangers.

Yet Titus had never spoken of his feelings or the future. There hadn't been time before he left. And after so many days of silence since then, she worried they might never get the chance.

Penelope swiveled and leaned her back against the post, releasing a quiet sigh. "What if he doesn't make it back?"

"Bite your tongue, girl," Jeb reprimanded. "Titus knows his business. He wouldn't be up for a promotion if he didn't, now would he?"

"I guess—"

"He wouldn't." Jeb shook a finger at her. "If you're gonna tie yourself to a lawman, you can't go around worryin' every time he comes home a little later than expected. You'll wear yourself down to a miserable little nubbin. It ain't healthy. Trust your man and trust the Lord. If bad comes, it comes. You can deal with it then. No sense borrowin' trouble when each day's got enough of its own. Besides," he said as he propped his bad leg up on the railing, "I'm the resident pessimist around here. Can't have you stealin' my job."

Penelope chuckled as her head wagged. "I love you, Jeb."

"Love you, too, girl." He lowered his hat over his eyes, leaving only his scowl uncovered. "Now go take a walk or somethin'. Let this old cowpoke get some shut-eye."

Who would have thought that the grumpiest of her new grandfathers would be the one to lighten her mood?

"Come on, Lucky." She thumped the side of her leg to grab the dog's attention. "You heard the man. Let's take a walk."

Tongue lolling, Lucky bounded down the stairs, turned a circle, then looked back at Penelope, a mix of anticipation and impatience in his stance.

A laugh bubbled from her throat. "I'm coming."

Feeling more cheerful than she had in days, she traipsed down the stairs and danced around Lucky, making him jump and bark as the two of them played together. A song filled her soul, emerging in a quiet hum that grew in strength as she headed down the drive. By the time she reached the road, she was singing in full voice while Lucky bounded forward and back, no doubt searching for a rabbit or squirrel to offer a bit of sport.

Tipping her head back, Penelope admired the blue sky, soaking in the beauty she'd been too distracted to notice earlier. Pillowy white clouds. Glorious sunshine. Birds floating on the breeze. Hope shone all around her.

Spotting a cluster of small sunflowers at the side of the road, Penelope wandered over to investigate. Their bright yellow hue made her smile. Perhaps she'd pick a few to take home. Add a little sunshine to the kitchen. Bending down, she reached for a stem, but Lucky suddenly lifted his head and perked his ears.

Penelope straightened. "What is it, boy?"

Lucky answered with a sharp bark, then took off running down the road. Almost as if he were hieing off to meet an old friend.

Penelope's belly squeezed. *Titus*?

Forgetting the flowers, she hurried down the road in Lucky's wake. She held herself to an energetic walk at first, not wanting to make a fool of herself if whoever approached wasn't Titus. But the more steps she took, the less she cared about looking foolish. She *had* to know if it was him. She began to jog, her breathing growing ragged.

A form took shape in the distance, cresting the rise in the road. A man in a dark hat. Atop a trotting black horse. A coonhound jumping around at the horse's feet, drawing the rider's attention. Titus! It had to be!

She began to lengthen her stride until she caught sight of a white stripe crossing his chest. She slowed. A sling? He'd been injured!

Her heart thumping in concern, Penelope picked up her skirt and ran, calling his name. "Titus!"

His head came up. His eyes fastened on her. He was off his horse in an instant and running to meet her, the sling awkward but not inhibiting him at all. Titus was alive. Healthy. Strong. And *here*, thank the Lord. God had brought him home.

As they came together, she slowed her step, not wanting to cause him any further injury, but he wrapped his good arm around her and dragged her against his chest.

"Your arm . . ."

"Is fine," he growled as he lifted her off her feet.

She laughed, her joy too powerful to contain.

Titus loosened his hold just enough for her to slide down and find the ground with her feet. Then his hand came up to her face. He stroked her cheek. Brushed back stray tendrils of hair. Cupped her jaw. He couldn't seem to stop touching her, and she didn't want him to. She'd longed for his touch every day since he'd left. Her eyes slid closed as she tried to absorb the perfection of the moment.

"It's over, Pen," he murmured in a rough voice.

Her eyes fluttered open and met his heated gaze.

"Madame LaBelle is in custody. The US Marshals are overseeing her trial and incarceration since her thieving crossed several state lines, so the Rangers are no longer involved. They put me in charge of returning the items taken from the Diamond D, though. Some of the cash had been spent, but most of what she took from Doc and the others is in my saddlebag ready to be returned."

"Oh, I'm so glad." Those dear men had been through enough on her account.

"You might be called to testify about her visit to the Diamond D and the poisoning," Titus cautioned, "but you don't have to worry. I'll be by your side through it all. I promise."

Penelope fit her hand to his jaw, the smooth skin attesting to a recent shave. "We'll deal with that when it comes," she said, echoing Jeb's recent admonition. "Right now, I just want to welcome home the man I love."

His gaze darkened, giving her only a heartbeat to comprehend his intent before his mouth captured hers.

She grabbed his arm for purchase as the power of his kiss washed over her. This was no gentle meeting of lips. Hunger radiated from him. Hunger and desire. Yet when his thumb caressed her cheek, she felt a tender adoration in his touch that brought tears to her eyes.

Raising up on her toes, she met his ardency with her own, tangling her fingers in the thick hair at his nape. This was where she belonged. With this man. Forever.

After a long moment, Titus softened his kiss, then finally pulled his lips from hers. As if unwilling to sever their connection completely, he rested his forehead against hers.

"I love you, Pen." The quiet words soaked into her heart like a gentle rain upon a sun-scorched garden. They soothed and replenished and brought forth an abundance of joy she'd never imagined possible.

She might have started life alone and abandoned on the steps of a girls' school in Chicago, but God had written this man into her story at just the right moment, and no matter what hardships their future might hold, their ever after would be happy indeed.

Epilogue

Spring 1893

Titus stood in front of the mantle of his new parlor, shifting from foot to foot, unable to settle.

"Easy, Sergeant," Captain Bill McDonald murmured in a low voice from his position at his side. "Your mama sees you fidgeting like that and she's liable to bolt the door to keep you from makin' a run for the hills."

As if anything could move him from this spot. The last few months had been sweet torture. Courting Penelope, learning everything he could about her—her past, her dreams for the future, her taste in furniture.

A grin twitched his lips as Titus shifted his gaze to his mother, sitting in the front row, dabbing a lacy handkerchief to her eye. She'd despaired of him ever taking a bride, and now that the day she'd longed for had arrived, she couldn't seem to stop crying. Happy tears, she'd assured him when he'd caught her wiping streaks from her face that morning in the kitchen. Apparently, cakes held peculiar emotional sway over those possessing strong maternal instincts. Mother had been cooking with Edith Johnson all morning, but icing that cake had sent both ladies rummaging in apron pockets for handkerchiefs.

He'd sent Edith a train ticket, secretly arranging for her to arrive two weeks prior to the wedding to assist with all the preparations. Pen's delight in reuniting with the woman who raised her had been worth every cent. Not to mention that with both of them in the kitchen, the men of the Diamond D had been eating better than ever. It was a miracle he still fit into his dress trousers.

Titus turned his gaze across the aisle to wink at the white-haired woman adorned in a plain gray dress. She flushed pink to match the tiny nosegay of flowers pinned to her bodice, a nosegay given to her from the man seated at her side, a grump of a fellow who seemed to have taken quite a shine to Miss Johnson.

Who knew where love might strike next?

Exhaling an amused breath, Titus scanned the rest of the crowd packed into his parlor. Kitchen chairs, desk chairs, and benches had been brought in from the Diamond D's main house as well as being pilfered from the store of new goods filling the house he and Penelope would occupy together for the first time tonight.

Nope. Don't go thinking about the wedding night just yet, partner. Gotta get through the ceremony first.

Stretching his neck away from his shrinking collar, Titus turned his attention to counting guests. The geezer gang from the Diamond D had all been spit-shined and polished, dressed in their Sunday best. A half-dozen of his Ranger buddies stood at the back, jawing with each other and casting him the occasional knowing look, which didn't help his nerves in the slightest.

John McHenry had made the trip, bringing a gift from Victor Chapman, who had sent his regrets. Titus still marveled at the way Providence had crossed their paths with Chapman at just the right moment. Meeting the man at the Elitch Theatre in Denver had provided resources that Titus and McHenry could not have accessed on their own. Chapman's railroad connections had placed Narcissa in Boulder, and his skillful distraction of the actress while they searched her room had provided the evidence they'd needed to convict her.

Mildred had taken a couple of days off from her new job at a dress shop in Denver to attend. She'd brought Penelope an entire trousseau of hand-stitched linens along with a set of underthings that Titus probably should know nothing about, but after solving a mystery involving a jewel-stuffed corset, there were very few topics he and Penelope didn't feel comfortable discussing.

Titus finally shifted his gaze to the one man in the room who meant more to him than any other. His dad met his eye and nodded approval, making Titus's chest swell with pride. Neither of them could have guessed he'd find a real Penelope when they'd discussed the *Odyssey* all those years ago. How the Lord must've smiled at the irony, knowing what Titus's future held.

Dad had made regular visits to the Diamond D over the last three months. He and Doc had bantered just like old times, arguing over which house plans would be best for their "boy." Seeing the fences mended between those two had warmed Titus's heart, and when he'd turned down both of their suggestions and opted for the plans Penelope liked best, all three of them had bonded over their desire to make the newest Kingsley woman happy.

Titus and his dad had built the house from the ground up, situating it a few hundred yards from the main house with the barn in between. They'd worked side by side, the hands from the Diamond D chipping in their time and expertise along the way. It had been slow going since his promotion had him working more often than not, but the fact that they had done it together made it feel as if love already dwelled within these walls.

And Tate.

Titus dipped his finger into the pocket of his vest and traced the curve of his brother's watch. Wanting his brother close today, he'd asked Doc if he could borrow the watch inscribed with Tate's name.

I wish you were here, Tate. You'd roast me good for falling for a beautiful woman. You might have been right about a thing or two, brother.

A whisper of movement caught Titus's eye from the stairway in the hall. He stiffened, his hand falling away from his pocket as all his attention locked on the flash of blue calico passing by the railing. A hush fell over the crowd, and heads turned in anticipation of the bride's entrance.

Time slowed to a painful degree, but finally, his bride stood at the end of the aisle, her smile shy, her eyes looking only at him.

Titus forgot how to breathe. Penelope. His bride.

He'd seen her in her Sunday dress before, the one she'd made from the fabric Doc had bought her all those months ago when she'd first stepped out of the woods and into their lives. It looked different on her today, though. Perhaps it was the touch of lace that had been added to the neckline. Or the snow-white morning glories she held in a bouquet at her waist. Or the tiny sprigs of yellow flowers that had climbed up from the dress fabric to dance upon her ebony hair.

Never had God created a more beautiful woman—in face, in form, and in spirit. Truly the fairest in the land. Especially when it came to her heart. A heart readily on display as she walked down the aisle, holding tightly to Doc's arm. That glorious smile beaming with love, her eyes sparkling with infectious joy, the slightest blush of humility dusting her cheeks. He wasn't worthy of such a gift, yet when her hand finally slid into his, he thanked God for giving her to him despite his imperfections.

The Lord had blessed him with a treasure rarer than the finest gold or most precious gem, and he'd protect and cherish her for the rest of his days.

Author's Note

I love adding historical tidbits and local lore to my stories, and when I decided to feature a theatrical troupe in this novel, I knew my characters would need to play the Granbury Opera House. I had the privilege of attending a play in the historic Granbury Opera House in 2018 as part of a writers' retreat. This theatre on the square is beautifully preserved and still in use. But my favorite thing about this nineteenth-century opera house is the historical lore surrounding it.

Originally known as Kerr's Hall, the opera house first opened in 1886. The space was most likely used for civic events and local dances in its early years, since it didn't start booking theatrical acts until 1891. Built above a saloon and saddle shop, its stage was relatively small, but it was decorated in a style grand enough to rival the larger theaters of Fort Worth. This grandeur included a set of four drop curtains of artistically painted scenery, of which Henry Kerr was reportedly very proud.

John St. Helen was a bit actor at the theater who also worked as a bartender at the saloon between acting gigs. St. Helen performed scenes from *Hamlet,* and on the rare instances when in his cups, he offered long recitations of other Shakespearean works. Locals noted that St. Helen never drank except on April 14. On that day, he drank to great excess.

Such odd behavior sparked a curiosity that only grew when it was uncovered that he had a cousin living in the vicinity—one whose maiden name happened to be Fannie Booth.

When St. Helen came down with a severe illness and believed himself to be dying, he called in a priest and a few close friends, including saloon owner F. J. Gordon. To them he confessed that he was indeed John Wilkes Booth. He claimed the weapon that had murdered President Abraham Lincoln could be found wrapped in a newspaper and hidden in a certain house behind a certain board. A few days later, St. Helen recovered and, with his secret revealed, immediately fled town. When the house he mentioned was razed in 1938, the gun was found in the very place St. Helen had described. The weapon was wrapped in a yellowed newspaper bearing a headline that proclaimed Lincoln's assassination.

History asserts that Booth was run to ground and killed on a farm outside Port Royal, Virginia, twelve days after the events at Ford's Theatre. Yet rumors and conspiracies surrounding his survival have persisted for more than one hundred fifty years. Whether the man in Granbury known as John St. Helen was actually John Wilkes Booth or not, he was certainly a character of note, and I enjoyed working him into my story.

Winner of the Christy Award, ACFW Carol Award, HOLT Medallion, and Inspirational Reader's Choice Award, bestselling author **Karen Witemeyer** writes historical romances because she believes the world needs more happily-ever-afters. She is an avid cross-stitcher, tea drinker, and gospel hymn singer who makes her home in Abilene, Texas, with her heroic husband who vanquishes laundry dragons and dirty dish villains whenever she's on deadline. To learn more about Karen and her books and to sign up for her free newsletter featuring special giveaways and behind-the-scenes information, please visit karenwitemeyer.com.

Sign Up for Karen's Newsletter

Keep up to date with Karen's latest news on book releases and events by signing up for her email list at the link below.

FOLLOW KAREN ON SOCIAL MEDIA!

Karen Witemeyer's Author Page

KarenWitemeyer.com

Check out the HANGER'S HORSEMEN series from Karen Witemeyer

Ex-cavalry officer Matthew Hanger leads a band of mercenaries who defend the innocent, but when a rustler's bullet leaves one of them at death's door, they seek out help from Dr. Josephine Burkett. When Josephine's brother is abducted and she is caught in the crossfire, Matthew may have to sacrifice everything—even his team—to save her.

At Love's Command

On a mission to deliver a baby to a nearby foundling home, Mark Wallace and Jonah Brooks encounter two women who capture their attention. When a handful of children from the area go missing, a pair of Horsemen are exactly what the women need. As they work together to find the children, will these two couples find love as well?

The Heart's Charge

When her brother dies suddenly, Damaris Baxter moves to Texas to take custody of her nephew. Luke Davenport winds up gravely injured when he rescues Damaris's nephew from a group of rustlers. As suspicions grow regarding the death of her brother, more danger appears, threatening the family Luke may be unable to live without.

In Honor's Defense

BETHANYHOUSE

Bethany House Fiction

@bethanyhousefiction

@bethany_house

@bethanyhousefiction

Free exclusive resources for your book group at bethanyhouseopenbook.com

Sign up for our fiction newsletter today at bethanyhouse.com